Praise for the novels of

PAUL GARRISON

"**A** master storyteller."
Clive Cussler

"**T**he thrills come fast . . . Paul Garrison is in
the vanguard of adventure authors rediscovering what
Jules Verne and other eighteenth century writers knew:
the oceans hold plenty of suspenseful potential."
Denver Rocky Mountain News

"**O**ne of the great ones . . .
Brilliant suspense and clever plotting."
Providence Sunday Journal

"**P**aul Garrison has vaulted into the august company
of spellbinding storytellers like Nevil Shute,
C.S. Forester, Kipling, Conrad, and Stevenson."
Buffalo News

"**T**his is writing that takes you places you haven't been."
Huntsville Times

"**G**arrison out-Clancy's the competition . . .
Unsuspecting readers are guaranteed sleepless nights."
Publishers Weekly

Also by Paul Garrison

BURIED AT SEA
RED SKY AT MORNING
FIRE AND ICE

PAUL GARRISON

SEA HUNTER

A NOVEL OF SUSPENSE

HarperTorch
An Imprint of HarperCollinsPublishers

This is a work of fiction. Names, characters, places, and incidents are products of the author's imagination or are used fictitiously and are not to be construed as real. Any resemblance to actual events, locales, organizations, or persons, living or dead, is entirely coincidental.

HARPERTORCH
An Imprint of HarperCollins*Publishers*
10 East 53rd Street
New York, New York 10022-5299

First HarperTorch paperback printing: December 2003
First William Morrow hardcover printing: January 2003

HarperCollins®, HarperTorch™, and ❦ ™ are trademarks of HarperCollins Publishers Inc.

Printed in the United States of America

Visit HarperTorch on the World Wide Web at www.harpercollins.com

10 9 8 7 6 5 4 3 2 1

For Commodore F. Joseph Thomas

SEA HUNTER

DAVID HOPE KNELT TO EMPTY the urn that the crematorium had FedEx-ed to Tortola. He had sailed south all night and through the morning, racing down the backside of the Leeward Islands, fleeing a ghost that stuck closer than the wind. When he stopped his boat, at last, deep inside the Caribbean, St. Croix lay sixty miles in his wake, South America five hundred ahead, and the vast blue sea spanned barren horizons.

Famous ashes-scattering disasters leapt to mind, gruesome, comic, twisted. The deceased who stuck to the airplane's fresh paint. Weeping mourners fleeing a change in the breeze. Before he'd quit the newspaper business, he'd written about a man who had arranged to have his ashes poured into his ex-wife's central air conditioning.

Hope had found a letter taped to the urn. "Barbara's dying wish," her parents claimed. She wanted her ashes spread on the ocean.

That was a lie.

She had loved the sea, all right. Loved it as fiercely as only an ignorant romantic could love. Loved it enough to die for it. But to express a dying wish, you had to be able to think. And Hope, who had persisted in telephoning the doctor monitoring her coma, knew the truth. Barbara Carey had not voiced a waking thought in the long year since she smashed her beautiful head on a semisubmersible offshore oil rig that she had vowed to stop from "raping"—her furious word—the Gulf of Mexico.

A brave and magnificent woman. One in a million.

Her parents could have hired one of the professional services that scattered ashes for a fee. But it appeared that they were still looking for someone to blame. Hard to blame *them*. For they knew one immutable fact. Barbara's merry band of eco-crusaders would never have set foot on the floating oil rig without the help of a blue-water sailor who had the sense to know they were truly risking their lives.

Who better to bury her?

So Hope had sailed her ashes far from any shore and confirmed with binoculars and radar that they were alone. They sat for a while in the shade of the bimini top. Finally he asked, "Ready?" and carried her down the dive steps in the back of the starboard hull and knelt on the grate.

Mindful of the wind, he submerged the urn in the clear water and slowly unscrewed the top. The powdery ash was sprinkled with larger bits that sank like pebbles. But the dust that remained spread like a ghostly fog. He was wondering whether he was supposed to keep the urn when her ashes enveloped his wrist.

He jerked his hand out of the water and dropped the urn, which commenced a two-mile voyage to the bottom. The low waves dispersed the fog. Heart pounding, stomach churning, he rinsed off, repeatedly, until it occurred to him, So what? They'd shared a hundred intimacies. Why not this?

Mission accomplished, he wiped his eyes on the long-sleeved shirt he wore to protect his arms from the relentless sun. He hadn't known her long, but she had grabbed hold of him all out of proportion to time. A compelling and charismatic soul. And needy? asked a small dark voice. Though a wiser one whispered the oldest adage of letting go, "Don't speak ill of the dead."

When he calmed down, he was struck anew by the immensity of the ocean and how Barbara was quite suddenly and completely gone. Not a bad way to go. Though when his own time came, if he had a choice, he thought he would prefer an eternal version of the celebrated seasickness cure—a quiet spot under a tree.

He cranked out the roller-reefed main and jib, opening his sails to the northeast trade wind, and set the catamaran flying home to Tortola. A pair of scuba-diving couples arriving from New Jersey would be his last paying charter job before he sailed north for the summer. He had to clean up the boat and provision for a week of live-aboard reef exploring.

He was late, having procrastinated the burial—sailing much farther south of the British Virgin Islands than he had to, then sitting around the cockpit for hours talking to her urn. So he pushed the cat hard, constantly tweaking the sails to extract the most power from the wind, adjusting and readjusting the depth of the daggerboard that projected below the starboard hull to keep the swift, surface-skimming, twin-hull boat from sliding sideways.

Racing had the additional benefit of keeping him too busy for memory and guilt and regret. It worked for a while. So well, at first, that he found himself thinking thoughts he had not allowed himself since the accident. I'm ready to meet somebody. Why not? He'd paid his dues. He had been alone—absolutely, celibately alone—with the possible exception of a drunken night with a New York lawyer at the end of Antigua Race Week. Now, at last, it felt all right to admit that he was lonely. It would be terrific to meet somebody who was looking, too. Maybe he would get lucky. He should put out the word to his friends: Hope was prepared to hope. He was savoring that thought, encouraged by a pretty sunset, when the helm jammed.

He reacted swiftly to stop the suddenly rudderless boat, winching in the main and jib sheets to steer her bows into the wind. Then he jumped belowdecks and found what he expected: a loose rudder cable he had neglected to tighten had jumped its quadrant. Crouching in a stifling hot steering gear compartment, he worked the steering cable back into its quadrant groove and repeated an oft-promised pledge to replace the entire steering system with hydraulics as soon as he had the cash.

He was quickly under way again. But if David Hope had entertained the belief that scattering Barbara Carey's ashes would close a black chapter, he was mistaken. The darkness that descended with the sun brought him the worst night since the accident. Every time he closed his eyes to catch five minutes of sleep in the cockpit, the nightmares struck, familiar as a brutal jailer.

Again and again he started awake, already on his feet, gripping the helm, shaking head to toe, and astonished to discover *Oona* coursing over the open sea instead of weaving through pools of blood and burning oil.

By dawn he felt half dead, his blue eyes red and stinging, his heavy swimmer's shoulders knotted with tension, his long, weathered face haggard. It was scored by two weary lines that cut from his nose to his jaw. As if he'd been branded with a number eleven, he thought when he glimpsed his reflection in the mirror in the head. A sneak preview of how he would look when he was old. Or in the grave. People who usually assumed he was ten years younger than his forty-eight would jump this morning to offer their seat on a bus.

He brewed some strong black coffee. It didn't help. He riffled through his CDs. Cyrus Chestnut playing hymns on the piano. He bumped through the tracks. "Onward Christian Soldiers" made him feel better. But not much. "The Old

Rugged Cross" helped, too. But not enough. Somehow, he had to sleep. So he took a careful look around to make sure that he and *Oona* were sailing alone. He set his internal alarm for ten minutes, and the radar to sound if any vessel came within three miles, then prayed—begged—for a peaceful ten minutes, and closed his eyes.

Six minutes later, he saw an enormous dolphin leap from the ocean. The animal rose straight up on its tail, stood taller than seemed possible, and began to spin, burnished gold and red by the morning sun.

Hope suspected another dream. He felt fast asleep and he was experiencing a dreamer's double perspective of a close-up and a long shot. Or was he dreaming a memory of waking for a moment and seeing the creature while he checked that the sea was clear of ships?

It had to be a dream. The dolphin was enormous—supernaturally large—as colossal as a killer whale.

But whatever the reality, at least the big, beautiful dolphin wasn't a nightmare and for that gift he was grateful. Then something outside dream or memory made a noise. It banged against the starboard hull with a sharp, hollow *donk*. Not at all the sound he'd expect of a collision with a large mammal, and Hope snapped awake to see what his boat had hit.

2

AT FIRST GLANCE, THE FIERCE blue expanse of Caribbean Sea still spread flat and empty to every horizon. Nor had he slept through his internal alarm clock. It was still very early morning, the white-hot sun lancing under the bimini. What in hell had he hit?

He scrambled around the boat, looking for damage. They might have sideswiped a half-sunken container that had fallen off a ship. He jiggled the helm. Both rudders were intact. Had she struck the daggerboard it would have spun her around like a top, not to mention bang the hell out of its truck, but that too, thankfully, had not happened. Then, as he started below to make sure that seawater was not gushing through a hole, something winked in his wake.

He grabbed his binoculars from their rack at the helm and focused on a cylindrical buoy painted fluorescent International Orange. It had a flasher, blinking twice a second, which at night would be seen for miles.

He turned *Oona* into the wind to stop her, sheeted in the flapping sails, and started her diesel engines. Inshore an orange buoy might mark a lobster pot, but not thirty miles south of Tortola, not in water a mile deep. It could have broken loose from a drift net, one of the commercial fishing "death curtains" decimating sea life. If it marked a dope runner's drop, he was outta here as fast as the wind could take him.

The gigantic dolphin was still leaping in his mind, still spinning gold and red in the morning sun. His memory was afire with the powerful image. But now he didn't know whether he'd dreamed it or had actually seen it earlier when day first broke. Make it a dream, he thought as he motored *Oona* back to the orange buoy. It sure beat the nightmares; he actually felt rested.

Maneuvering the catamaran alongside the floating cylinder took some doing. *Oona* was fast as lightning off the wind when lightly laden, a real screamer on a broad reach, and a remarkably steady platform even in heavy seas. But at close quarters—his mono-hull friends were quick to laugh—a twin-hull boat forty-five feet long and twenty-three feet wide possessed sailing qualities similar to a garbage truck. Even with her twin screws, she felt like a bicycle rolling too slowly to control.

He saw that the buoy had a whip aerial and, as he worked closer, that the flasher was ringed with cat's-eye reflectors. When he finally could eyeball print through the binoculars, he read the word AFT. It turned in the water, revealing USS *Vermont* (SSN-919).

"Jesus H."

It was a sub-sunk buoy, sent to the surface to broadcast a distress call and mark the scene of the emergency. Somewhere under him a hundred sailors were trapped on a stricken American nuclear submarine.

Hope ran to his radio. *The Sailing Directions* warned against breaking a sub-sunk buoy's tether. No chance of a tether in these depths. This one had broken loose and was riding the current, clearly adrift. But for how long? Were they still alive? Did anyone know?

Three steps led down into *Oona*'s saloon, a wide, light and airy cabin that bridged the hulls. He sat at his navigation station and switched on the long-range Single Sideband.

"Mayday," he broadcast on the emergency channel. "Mayday, Mayday, Mayday." He read his position from the Global Positioning System, repeated it three times, and gave his vessel's name and radio call sign.

Somewhere under him terror ruled. Decks pitched vertically and young men clung to their stations, fighting to regain control of their ship before deepening water pressure caused the sea to rush in. Fighting to keep her from dragging them all the way to the bottom, accelerating with every foot she fell, until their struggle ended in an atom-shattering crash into the ocean floor.

Hope switched on the depth finder he used ordinarily for navigating scuba divers to remote reefs. If the men on the sub heard the sonar "pinging" the depths, they would know that help was on the way.

"Mayday, Mayday, Mayday. Sailing Vessel *Oona,* Victor-Victor-Hotel-Oscar, reporting USS *Vermont* number SSN-919 sub-sunk buoy at 64 degrees, 2 minutes, 13 seconds west, 18 degrees, 1 minute, 4 seconds north."

SSN stood for "Submersible Ship Nuclear." And the ultramodern *Vermont* was the newest of the new Virginia class.

Fascinated by ships in general, submarines in particular—and feeling special affection for the state of Vermont, where his parents had taught him to ski—Hope had followed accounts of its launch avidly. The *Vermont* observed the surface through fiber-optic cameras and sensors instead of periscopes, utilized commercial off-the-shelf electronics to stay cutting-edge on the cheap, and could fight both inshore and on blue water.

A lean and hungry sub for lean and hungry times.

Hope repeated his position and radio call sign, reported the buoy adrift, and asked anyone who picked up his signal to relay it to the United States Navy. By now, if the buoy was working, every satellite the Navy had in the sky would have picked up the distress call. But if it wasn't working, he and only he was on the scene, and so far no one had responded.

He stepped up to the cockpit, and locked the helm so the boat would steer a circle. He could see the depth finder's backlit LCD monitor from the helm as well as the nav station. Under a boat icon, which represented *Oona*'s position, echoing returns were pictured in the form of black squares. He'd used it often enough to be able to distinguish coral and rocks from sunken wrecks, the wakes of passing boats, even a sand or mud bottom.

A single black square materialized at a depth of two hundred feet, directly below the *Oona* icon. It was much too small to be a submarine. He waited, scarcely breathing, for the image to grow into a bigger target. Instead, the single square moved to the edge of the screen. A large fish, probably a shark, it changed course and swam out of range.

Loath to accept that he was sailing over a graveyard, Hope stared at the blank screen. His second graveyard in twenty-four hours. This one about to swallow a hundred vital men, who seconds ago had probably no idea they were about to die. Feeling helpless and useless, Hope studied the sea. Sunny blue and utterly empty, there was nothing to see but some trade wind clouds marching tall and bright.

Could he *hear* the sub? He had a hydrophone he had bought secondhand for his whale-watching clients to listen to the clicks and whistles and creaking-door groans of whales and dolphins. Plugging its long cable into the stereo, he dropped the slim microphone, which was encased in waterproof polyurethane, over the back of the boat.

He heard a faint whistle. It faded, like a distant train, leaving nothing behind but an audio hiss. He turned up the sound. Only speaker hum broke the silence. In a way it was a good sign, he told himself. The last sound he wanted to hear was the thunder of the huge ship imploding in the depths.

Suddenly, a hundred feet ahead, another buoy shot from the sea as if a seed had been squeezed from an orange. Then, behind him, an emergency flare rocketed out of the water, whooshed skyward, and exploded red. A smoke flare followed, gushing orange. They were letting loose everything they had.

Hope turned from the chaos that was erupting around the boat to the depth finder. Black squares massed under the boat icon, representing a big, stationary target 250 feet below. The squares formed up in a long, thick shape that the monitor indicated was nearly four hundred feet long.

When it began rising at a steep angle, David Hope leapt to *Oona*'s helm.

3

THE IMPULSE TO SIMPLY FLEE was almost overwhelming. If the seven-thousand-ton *Vermont* surfaced under him, it would throw little *Oona* clear out of the water in a fine mist of splinters. Hope forced himself to wait for the depth finder to reveal the safest direction.

Of the next moments, it would be the fearful silence that he remembered most. The wind seemed to die. The grinding sound of *Oona*'s engines faded, and she stood stock-still on the water, flat as a table, her creaking sheets and blocks muffled.

Then the squares that represented the ascending ship appeared to slew left. Hope turned right and an instant later the submarine erupted beside him—a huge black cylinder that rocketed skyward at a severe angle. Climbing bow first at a great rate of speed, the sub rose higher and higher, attained an impossible-looking height, and climbed even higher.

Emergency main ballast tank blows were likened to the dramatic breaching of a sperm whale. But David Hope—close enough to observe every detail of a ship the size of a freighter leaping from the ocean as if to eat the sun—could only compare it to a Titan rocket thundering roughshod over the laws of gravity.

And still it climbed. When Hope thought that it had surpassed every physical limit, the submarine exposed its bow planes, and thrust even higher to reveal a sturdy sail, which bristled with photonic masts and radio antennas. Hope thought it odd that they would crash surface with the fragile masts exposed, and indeed two appeared to have bent backward like saplings in an ice storm.

If the submarine climbed any higher, it would dance like his dream dolphin had danced on its tail. At last, still racing forward, it began to topple back down to the sea. Swiftly gathering momentum, falling faster and faster, the huge hull crashed into the water with tremendous force.

The thunder of the impact bellied his sails and the white wave that the sub displaced tumbled at him like an avalanche. Hope threw both engines into gear and skittered away from it, his boat tossed violently.

The *Vermont* sped west, churning an immense wake. Suddenly she bore hard right, and then hard left, and repeated the violent crash turns, zigzagging with astonishing agility. Hope had never heard of them performing such wild maneuvers on the surface.

After a mile or so, the *Vermont* executed a stately turn to starboard. Hope watched the big ship race low in the water, which creamed off its sail like a thick bow wave. Turning, still turning, she swung a full 180 degrees. Seen head on, her sail was short and rounded. It had some sort of square hatch in the center, like the eyehole in a bucket helmet on a Teutonic knight. The dangling masts looked like a plume.

She was growing large.

Hope engaged his propellers, again.

The submarine moved like a mechanized iceberg, 90 percent of her below the water. A very fast iceberg. White water stormed behind her, a boiling propeller wash flanked by a wide wake plowed by her sail. Ahead of her sail, above her submerged foredeck, the vast underbody of the ship pushed an oily swell.

Hope turned *Oona* to starboard. The submarine altered

course and continued to hurtle at him. He reversed his helm. The submarine tracked him. Hope shivered in the tropical heat. Had it locked onto him with radar? It made absolutely no sense that an American nuclear submarine intended to run him down. But whatever the cause, at the speed it was traveling he had less than a minute to do something.

There would be no outrunning a twenty-knot sub with the motors. Under sail, *Oona* might make twenty knots sailing downwind in a stiff breeze with the board up. But sailing downwind would keep the two vessels on their collision course.

No choice but to play chicken to try to fox its radar. He steered straight at the charging sub and let out his sails. They bellied full and *Oona,* lightly laden, jumped. Up and planing in seconds, the catamaran flew at the submarine. In thirty seconds, Hope was so close that the sub's sail towered dark against the sky. He could hear it ripping the water.

The oily swell that preceded the sail was so high it cast a shadow. *Oona* started to bury her bows. He felt her slow and she began to lean forward. Bury them too deep and the speeding cat would pitchpole, end over end like a drunk attempting cartwheels.

They were going under, both bows spearing the leading edge of the swell. Hope wrenched his helm to starboard. She heeled hard and plucked the port bow free. But the starboard bow dug deeper, and the force of forward momentum wracked the boat into an even tighter turn. Hope felt the port hull lift. He looked over in disbelief; in all the years he'd sailed her he had never seen the entire forty-five-foot hull spring from the water. She was capsizing, falling onto her right side. He twisted the helm hard left. The port rudder was in the air, rendering it useless. Then the deep probing starboard rudder bit. She straightened up, slammed her port hull back into the water, and slid along the side of the swell, which was thinning as it neared the black sail.

Hope had the sensation of running onto an unexpected reef. He could see steel under the shallowing water. One of his hulls scraped. He steered right again. *Oona* skittered past the submarine's sail and into its thunderous wake.

A deep hole in the water—a cavitation effect that had been invisible from in front of the submarine—suddenly yawned beside the speeding hull, and into that pit *Oona* started to slide. He tried to steer away, but it was speed—the two vessels' combined forty knots in passing—that saved him. In a flash, *Oona* was past the hole and tossing on the tumultuous wake that enveloped the *Vermont*'s submerged afterdeck.

Home free, Hope thought. But dead ahead he saw a steel object cut the white water—a stern skeg that rose above the back end of the speeding submarine. It would cleave *Oona* like a giant ax.

He tried to turn away. The helm locked. He knew instantly that the loose rudder cable had jumped its quadrant again. *Oona*'s only course was dead ahead, straight at the skeg, and Hope could only pray that the bridge deck that connected his catamaran's two hulls would clear it. It looked two feet high. The underside of *Oona*'s bridge deck was two feet three inches over the water.

Hope felt a light *tick* at his feet. The next instant he was behind the submarine, inside its wake. Two walls of water—the outer edges of the wake—split and angled apart. The cat bobbed on the flats between them, wallowing in white water whipped to an airy froth by the submarine's propeller.

Hope looked back, humbled; the steering failure had been a blessing in disguise. Obeying blind instinct, he would have turned broadside, and the skeg would have cut his boat in half.

Hope played the sheets that controlled the jib and main-sail to steer a quarter mile onto firm blue water before he looked back again. The submarine had stopped. It lay dead in the water, rock steady, like a dark, unpleasant island.

In case the monster started moving again, Hope jumped below and worked the steering cable back into its groove. Back in the cockpit, he quickly reeled the hydrophone cable out of the water. The sub's crewmen were climbing like ants on top of the sail and swarming over the lock-out module, a Thermos-bottle–shaped bulge along the waterline, aft of the sail, which, Hope knew, formed a pressurized commando-launch chamber. He sailed closer, thinking to hail them.

Before he could, clam-shell doors opened in back of the lock-out module. A rigid inflatable boat roared from them, propelled by powerful outboard engines, and came bouncing across the low seas. Hope counted three men in black wet suits and life jackets who were brandishing compact assault rifles, and an officer in blue patrol coveralls with rank badges reflecting sunlight from his collars and a sidearm on his hip. They didn't look like they were coming to apologize.

Hope reached inside a long, narrow cockpit locker. Buried under the British Union Jack courtesy flag that he flew from the starboard spreader when in BVI waters, and *Oona*'s private flag, which depicted the flukes of a sounding whale, and his yellow quarantine flag for signaling Customs upon entering foreign ports, was a five-foot jack staff. He unrolled his United States Ensign and fitted the staff into *Oona*'s stern socket.

The sight of Old Glory's fifty stars and thirteen stripes rippling in the trade wind had no discernible effect on the navy officer, who shouted on a loud-hailer, "Stop your vessel and place your hands on your head."

Hope couldn't believe his ears, though he got the picture when they leveled weapons at him. But instead of raising his hands, he switched on *Oona*'s megaphone and bellowed back, "I can stop her or I can put my hands on my head. But if I put my hands on my head and she continues wheeling ahead of the wind, she's going to take off like a rocket. Your call, mister."

Twin 115-horse outboards screamed. And quite suddenly—in a display of seamanship Hope would recall for many days—the RIB was secured to *Oona*'s starboard hull, an armed diver was standing at the mast covering the hatches with a stubby assault rifle, another was perched on the top of the dive stairs, and the officer was in the cockpit, roaring at Hope to put his hands on his head before he was shot.

Seething, Hope started to raise his arms. Then he thought, This is ridiculous. They're not going to shoot an American citizen. "Screw you. My name is David Hope, master of this vessel, and voter registered in the State of Maine. Who are you?"

"Tell your crew to come up on deck."

"I'm alone."

The wet-suited frogman who had stayed in the inflatable leapt aboard and stormed down the main hatch with his weapon ready. Hope heard him banging doors as he charged from the bridge saloon into the cabins and lockers in the hulls.

"All clear, sir."

"All right, Mr. Hope. What are you doing here?"

Living alone aboard *Oona*, answerable only to the occasional paying customers who usually deferred to him as captain of the charter, David Hope rarely cultivated habits of diplomacy. Still shaking with excess adrenaline from his near escape, he was neither diplomatic nor especially observant.

"What am I doing here? What the hell are you doing here? You nearly killed me, for chrissake!"

"Sit there!" the officer said to Hope. To the frogman on the stern, he said, "Shoot him in the leg if he moves." With that he went below, trailed by one of his men. The second moved forward of the mast. The frogman on the stern motioned with his weapon that Hope should sit.

Hope sank to the cockpit bench, baffled, and more than a little cowed: the specific threat to his leg was eminently believable. He listened to them rummage through his navigation station. Across the sunlit water the huge submarine sat still as a pier. He studied the frogman, twenty feet away at the mast, weapon at port arms, warily scanning the water. When he turned around to look again at his guard six feet behind him on the starboard stern, tears were streaming down the sailor's face.

Hope spoke softly. The armed man at the mast couldn't hear. "Hey, buddy, you okay?"

The wet-suited sailor shook his head. Hope saw that he was much younger than he had thought, probably nineteen or twenty. A couple of years out of high school and scared.

"What happened to your ship?"

The submariner shook his head. Hope waited. Suddenly the kid whispered, "I thought we were going to die. Fuckin' boat was totally out of control. Man, we going down like a fuckin' rock. We was fucked, every one of us."

"What made her sink?"

"Fuck knows." He looked away, stared at the submarine, and glanced forward. The man at the mast was still watching the water.

Hope spoke conversationally. "With all due respect to your boss, I'm just a guy sailing by."

"Ship went wack," the kid whispered. "Like we were all going to die."

"Why?"

"Computers went wack. The machinist's mate was screaming the reactor was going to cook off." He stared at the deck, tears dripping. ". . . Man, we almost launched the tomachickens."

"What are tomachickens?" Hope could guess, but he wanted to keep the kid talking.

"Tomahawk cruise missiles. Woulda started fuckin' World War Three." The sailor wiped his face. "One good thing, we're going home for refit after this shit. No mo' war games in the fuckin' Denmark Strait—shit, man, that's classified."

Hope's shrug promised that he was monumentally uninterested, a trick he learned as a reporter pumping sources: Don't mind me, I'm just drinking this cup of coffee while you spill your guts. Denmark Strait? Four thousand miles up the North Atlantic? The choke point between Greenland and Iceland for submarines heading to or from Russia? A logical site for submarine war games? Never heard of it.

"No problem," he said. "I forgot it already. Main thing is everybody's okay now. Tell me something—"

The angry officer came back to the cockpit. He stood over Hope, his arms crossed. "All right, Mr. Hope, where are you going?"

Hope was about to remind him that he had just read his log when he thought, Why me? Why blame a guy on a sailboat? The boarding party appeared as baffled as he was. Their warship had suffered a devastating and mysterious breakdown. But why do they think I have anything to do with it? It made no sense. . . . Unless they thought that the cause of the breakdown—whatever had zapped their computers—had zapped them from *outside* the submarine.

Their fear and panic were obvious: the sailor breaking down, even briefly; and the officer still wearing his lieutenant commander's gold oak leaf insignia and his name embroidered on his blue coveralls, as if he hadn't had time to change into his boarding-party wet suit. So if they assumed they had been attacked by an outside force, Hope decided, he was probably lucky they hadn't shot him just to be on the safe side. Time to cut Lt. Commander R. D. Royce some slack.

"I'm heading for Tortola," he said. "I'm picking up clients. I have a charter business. I take rec divers out to the reefs, which you already know from reading my log."

"Where are you coming from?"

"A funeral."

"Where?"

"I scattered an old friend's ashes."

"I didn't read that in your log."

"Yeah, well, I haven't gotten around to entering it. I was a little upset. Mind telling me what's going on?"

Lt. Commander R. D. Royce stared at Hope as if the cata-maran skipper had asked for a peek at his nuclear reactor.

Hope said, "Think this through: I found your sub-sunk buoy. I relayed a distress call on two-one-eight-two. You can check that out. Somebody must have heard me. I tried to locate you with my sonar. You probably heard it pinging your hull. I even dipped my hydrophone trying to get a bead on you."

He pointed at the waterproof mike nested in the coiled cable. But the submariner stared at it as if listening for the submarine was proof positive that Hope was up to no good.

"Jesus H., Commander, when I finally did locate your ship, you executed an emergency blow and nearly ran me down."

"What course were you making?"

"Let me make a simple suggestion that you radio Naval Intelligence to check me out. I'm based in Tortola in the winter and sometimes I get to Camden, Maine, in the summer, where I take tourists whale watching. That's why I have a hydrophone, by the way."

He paused. The officer was still staring.

"You can look me up on my broker's website: www. CoxMarine . . . I don't know what problem you're having with your ship, I was just sailing by. But let me suggest that it's lousy PR for the U.S. Navy—which hasn't always con-ducted itself like a publicist's dream—to abuse an innocent American businessman on the high seas. You've already tried to kill me and now you've searched—"

"No one has tried to kill you, sir."

"You chased me with a fucking submarine," Hope roared. "If this were a mono-hull sailboat instead of a fast cat, I'd be dead."

"No one tried to kill you," Royce thundered back. "You were in the way."

"If you didn't want me in the way, why'd you send up dis-tress buoys, flares, and smoke?"

"They were auto-launched unintentionally. No one tried to kill you."

"That's not how it looked from my perspective."

Royce looked Hope straight in the eye. "Radar locked onto your vessel coincident with a short-term shift to malfunction mode."

"Malfunction mode? Why the fuck didn't you shut it down?"

The officer glanced away for a millisecond. "We tried, sir. Believe me, we tried."

In that instant, Hope realized, the guy was practically pleading with him. "All right," he said, "I believe you. But then you searched my boat—without my permission. You *know* that I'm carrying no weapons, no contraband, nothing illegal, threatening, or dangerous. You've seen my passport and my vessel's documents. Give me a break, Commander. I've got places to go. I'm late. Let me go. Fix your computer and—"

"What computer?"

Hope flicked a glance at the sailor on the stern. The kid was back in control of himself, as expressionless as a steel bulkhead.

"The computer," he replied evenly, "that I'm assuming auto-launched your distress buoys, not to mention locking your radar onto my sailboat like I was a Russian missile boat. . . . Obviously something is badly wrong with your ship. I only assumed it was a computer problem. That's what screws up everything these days, right? . . . I'll tell you what. I'll make you a deal. I promise not to say a word about whatever's going on here if you will let me sail away right this minute. I cannot miss this charter. My clients paid half up front. Two young couples—serious divers, nice people— saving expenses by doing their own cooking. They've been saving all year for this vacation and they have a right to expect me waiting there when they get off the plane, provisioned and ready to go. And, frankly, I need the second half. I need the money."

A sudden ripping thunder split the sky.

A Navy jet fighter swooped low over the submarine, screamed to the horizon, and thundered back. He made two more passes, then vanished to the north. A radio crackled on the officer's belt. He walked forward, engaged in a terse exchange, and walked back to the cockpit and ordered the sailor in the wet suit, "Check out the bottom."

The diver pulled on a face mask and went over the port side. He stayed under the boat an astonishingly long time on one breath of air, surfaced next to the starboard hull, and slipped under again, smooth as an otter. When he came up the second time it was at the foot of the dive steps and he hauled himself back on board, breathing normally.

"Nothing, sir. But his starboard keel's chewed up something awful, like he ran over something."

"What did you hit?" Royce asked Hope, watching him closely, as if Hope's entire story would fall apart on this one answer.

"Bottom," Hope lied.

"When?"

"Last spring. It's not a 'keel.' It's a low-drag foil."

The officer glanced at the diver. The diver said, "There's algae growing over the marks."

"Isn't that something you should get fixed?"

"There's always something to fix. It's high on my list. Right after I install hydraulic steering. Can I go now?"

The submariner cast a spit-and-polish officer's eye on a patch in the mainsail where a hapless client had pierced it with a boat hook, the scuffed decks that awaited a thorough cleaning, and the gouges in the teak trim that customers had banged with air tanks and weight belts.

Hope's two-day beard, salt-tangled hair, and Cape Horn ring in his right ear apparently complemented his vessel's offenses against order, and Lt. Commander Royce shook his head with palpable disgust.

"My sister," he said, "is married to one of you."

"One of me, what?"

"A boat guy. You probably don't even have insurance on this scow."

"This 'scow' just saved this 'boat guy' from the worst-run submarine since the Russians sank the *Kurst*. Come on, Commander. You want me to sign something? I'll crank up my laptop, write you a letter: 'I, David Hope, master of the sailing yacht *Oona,* promise not to reveal anything I saw this morning in the Caribbean Sea, thirty miles south of Tortola. I suffered no injury, my vessel no damage. I won't sue, I won't go public. I just want out of here.' Want me to print it up?"

But by then the sub—and Naval Intelligence—had logged onto Cox Marine's website. Back and forth on the radios, they finally did the right thing and conceded that it was pure coincidence that David Hope was sailing overhead when something had gone haywire on the *Vermont*.

Royce extended his hand.

Hope took it. "Interesting morning. Good luck with your computer."

"And you get that bottom fixed."

Hope put *Oona* back on course. Four hours later he was piloting a shopping cart through the narrow aisles of Road Town's Gourmet Gallery.

4

THERE WAS A BAR ON a floating dock in the middle of the Road Harbour Marina where you could sit and watch the boats heading in and out of the Sir Francis Drake Channel. Or you could watch the bartender operate his blender. Or you could stare into the glass from which you'd been drinking numerous rum daiquiris. Which was what the good-looking woman Hope noticed the second he walked in was doing, drinking like someone who was drinking because it seemed, unexpectedly, like the thing to do.

He saw right off she wasn't a tourist. Too solid a tan for that. Nor was she a kid working the boats. A little too self-assured for paid crew, a little older than most. But not so self-contained that she didn't have to prove something. She looked very much like she thought she had to prove something. Guess, he thought to himself. What's her problem?

He sat at the corner of the bar, four seats away, with a view of her profile. Strong nose, high forehead, admirable lips, stubborn jaw. Between swallows, she was staring across the harbor at an Italian mega-yacht that had pulled into Road Harbour the night before Barbara's ashes arrived. *Il Bacione,* adorned with satellite dish domes, black glass, and a serious-looking helicopter on its roof.

The bartender finally put down his book. (Everyone on the island was suffering end-of-season torpor.) He greeted Hope with a lazy wave and a friendly "Welcome aboard, Captain Insomnia."

He splashed a liberal portion of Mount Gay over ice, squeezed in some lime, and brought it to Hope with a glass of water back. "Your troubles are over, pal. This would put a crackhead to sleep—hey, wait a sec! What are you doing here? Don't you have a charter?"

"I got stood up. They didn't show."

"Maybe they missed their flight. They'll make the next one. Plenty of seats this late in the season."

Hope said, "They were on the plane. The plane gave them food poisoning. They're currently in a San Juan hospital having their stomachs pumped. They won't feel much like diving until their vacation is over. May I have another, please?"

"Well, you can keep your half up-front money."

"Most of which I just spent on a boatload of fresh food in the tropics." He looked across the water where *Oona* was riding low at her mooring, weighted down by a week's provisions for five. "May I have another?"

A front was shambling tentatively out of the west, butting heads with the trade wind, streaking the sky with mare's tails. All morning he had kept a weather eye on those thin clouds, thinking he was about to set sail. Maybe rain, which the island could use. Maybe squalls, which he could do without. Now it didn't matter. He wasn't going anywhere.

"Would you please stop staring at me," said the woman drinking rum daiquiris. She had a musical voice that carried, and a nice, different sort of face that would grow on you until you woke up one morning convinced that she was gorgeous. If he had to guess he would say that most days she was cheerful, though this was clearly not one of those days.

Hope said, "I couldn't help notice you were drinking rum with a wine elbow and I was just thinking how when I was young, which today feels a very long time ago, I mistakenly feared that vodka would be my nemesis, if I let it. It never occurred to me it would be rum. And speaking of rum, I had a charter client last year who scoped out the entire Caribbean Basin in a flash. You know what she said? 'Until a container of milk costs less than a bottle of rum, island kids will grow up poor.' She was a smart woman. With a big heart. Noticed things most people didn't. She was alert to need. Aware of injustice. I didn't mean to stare. But you are very nice-looking and apparently alone. My name is Hope. David Hope."

"May I have my check, please," she asked the bartender.

She staggered off under the weight of two big camera bags. Legs like a swimmer, Hope observed over his glass, very strong. Thick in the thighs and calves, rippling with muscle, and it didn't take much rum or even a libido just emerging from a year under wraps to recognize potentially great machinery in the sack.

"An impressive strikeout," said the bartender, a Manhattan dropout who had adjusted remarkably well to the do-little requirements of a tourist mecca.

"She's smarter than she looks," Hope agreed. These two days just kept getting worse.

"From where I sat," said the bartender as he went back to his book, "it sounded like a pitch meant to fail. Like an intentional walk."

Hope told the bartender that he was reversing his metaphors and roused himself from his gloom with the upbeat thought that if you were almost pounded into the sea by a berserk submarine, the operative word was *almost*. It was a thought worth drinking to.

A Mount Gay and a half hour later, when he had still not constructed a scenario that led plausibly to him burying his face in her thighs, the woman came back. She walked up to him and said, "They told me at the office you're available for a live-aboard dive charter."

Hope looked at her. Nothing had changed. A good-looking woman with short, sun-streaked hair, a musical voice, and a face full of troubles. Her lip was trembling, like she was either very nervous or on the verge of tears.

She said, "I understand you were paid half already. Food for five people for a week could last the two of us three weeks."

"Food that will spoil unless I find new clients on very short notice. Sounds like you've got me all figured out."

"No. I mean . . ." She ducked her head. "I'm not trying to take advantage of you. It's just I'm in a jam and you're in a jam and maybe we can work it out."

"What kind of jam are you in?"

"I'm starting a film project with very little preproduction time. And very little money. My, uh, my cinematographer split in the middle of another project and I'm starting a new one from scratch."

"Why'd he split?"

"I don't know."

Hope hadn't written news in ten years, but the questioning habit stuck, though less from curiosity than from an assumption that everything had a simple explanation. Besides, questions up front kept him out of trouble in the charter business.

"Had you worked with this particular cinematographer before?"

"We made six underwater nature films together." Her eyes seemed to be scrunching up behind her sunglasses and her mouth was twitching harder and it didn't take a genius at human relations to guess that the cinematographer had been her husband, or a long-term boyfriend.

"How little money?" he asked gently.

She seemed to take strength in the certainty of numbers, banging them out with the pleasure of something she could believe in. "Your rate for those four divers would have been twelve hundred dollars per person, of which you've already received and spent two thousand four hundred."

She had hit the dollars on the nose. Partner problems aside, she sounded like a professional.

"By the way," she asked, "what's your C card?"

"Rescue." One scuba diving certification level above Advanced Open Water—still no Jacques Cousteau, but not likely to accidently drown the customers while coming to their aid.

"Specialties?"

"Wreck and Cavern. And Search and Recovery, of course."

"Why 'of course'?"

"It's good for business to come back with the same number of divers I take out."

No laugh, no smile, only a dubious "Don't you have Underwater Videographer?"

"I was going to take the course, thinking I could shoot diver weddings, but then this couple wanted me to underwater-video their premarital hooking up, and I thought, maybe this isn't my field."

Again, neither a laugh nor a smile; not even the courtesy of an is-that-true. (Most of it.) She chewed her lip a moment, then blurted, "I can offer you three thousand dollars for three weeks."

Hope considered the turn of affairs. The season was over, he had nothing else in the hopper, and her offer was fair. It was a little bit like not getting sunk by the *Vermont*. A paying customer with a dream.

"Where do you want to sail?"

"I'm hoping to document the breeding habits of oceanic dolphins. I'm looking for *Stenella clymene*—short-snouted spinner dolphins."

"They're pretty far offshore, aren't they?"

"Could you take me to thirty north, fifty-five west?"

Latitude thirty degrees north, longitude fifty-five west was an empty stretch of the North Atlantic a long ways east-southeast of Bermuda where weather, sea conditions, and the impossibility of running to the shop for equipment and repairs promised to turn simple problems into disasters. Making a movie alone that far offshore sounded like a project for Don Quixote.

"You won't get much time for filming. It's the better part of a thousand miles, which could take us a week. Another week back."

Again, she chewed her lip. "What if you dropped me in Bermuda? We could stay out longer."

"Except I'm based here."

"Except everybody here sails north for the summer, right?"

"I hadn't made my mind up about that yet." With the dicey rudder quadrant and her damaged bottom, *Oona* wasn't in the best of shape for a long voyage.

"Three weeks total. Okay?"

Hope thought some more. Not only quixotic, but vague. Breeding habits. What the hell were breeding habits? His editor on his first newspaper job taught him to ask, What, exactly, is this story about? A nature documentary couldn't be that much different. She would need to concentrate on something if she was going to shoot a film anybody wanted to look at.

She misinterpreted his hesitation and said, "I can't pay more. Three thousand will max my Visa."

"No, don't worry about it. The money's fair. Have you done much sailing?"

"No. We always charter powerboats."

Hope nodded. "So you've been on fair-sized vessels that can carry ten or twenty divers?"

"Usually."

Hope nodded again. Made sense for a film crew and all its gear. And rec divers, too, if you didn't mind sharing a boat with a crowd, which many divers, singles in particular, preferred on a vacation.

There was another problem. Decompression illness. The

bends. He said, "Obviously I don't have a hyperbaric chamber on a sailboat. What happens if you get bent? I've got emergency oxygen, of course, but I can't rush you to a shore-based chamber from the middle of nowhere."

"I don't foresee any deep dives. I can't film deeper than thirty feet anyway without lights and I won't have a crew for lights. If I somehow screw up my dive tables and surface too quickly I would go back in the water to decompress."

Hope nodded dubiously. Dunking a DCI victim back in the water as a rough-and-ready way to recompress was definitely not recommended if there was a hyperbaric chamber nearby, though it beat doing nothing. "Okay. Then let me ask you one more big question."

"What?"

"Why," he asked, "if you couldn't stand to sit in the same bar with me—an open-air bar, at that—would you consider being cooped up on a forty-five-foot boat with me for three weeks?"

She looked him in the eye. "I don't have anything against you personally. It was just that you started gassing on like my ex-husband and I didn't really want to hear it."

Hope laughed. "It's been a hairy couple of days. I'm not usually such a gasser-on."

"Yes he is," called the bartender, who had stopped even pretending to read his book. "You should hear him when he gets really wound up."

"Thanks, pal." Hope turned back to the woman. "Seriously, what if other characteristics of mine—not apparent sitting in this bar drinking rum—remind you of your ex-husband? It's still three weeks on a small boat. Too far away to jump off, much less call the cops."

"Your boat is a catamaran; the guest cabins are in the opposite hull from your cabin and the equipment lockers."

"How do you know that?"

"I checked out your broker's website."

Should have guessed. That's where she'd gotten her numbers. In other words, she had stumbled into the marina office to ask if any charter dive boats were available, learned that by no small coincidence the captain mouthing off in the bar was desperately available. So she plugged in her laptop and logged onto the website to check him out. Ill advised her project might be, and an unhappy woman wouldn't be his first choice for a shipmate, but at least she wasn't a fool. So accepting her offer would not be stealing from a baby, Hope told himself. And like the song said, I really need this job.

"I'll tell you what. I'll sail you to thirty north, fifty-five west. I'll push like hell to do it in five days. That'll give you a week and three days filming the dolphins you find there, and then six days north to Maine."

"Maine?"

"I'll drop you in Camden. You can get a plane out of there."

Her face lit up in a big smile, like he had handed her a Christmas present. "You can really give me three extra days shooting?"

"I can try. *Oona* is quick. But just remember that we are at the mercy of the wind. Motor power is not an option. She's much faster under sail and she doesn't carry enough fuel to motor very far anyhow. Any days we make up in passage you can add to filming. Conversely, if we get held up by weather, or the Variable Zone slows us down, we'll lose days. Total time out, three weeks. If we really get creamed by the weather, I'll try to stay a little longer, but we'll be living on rice and water. With any luck, ten full days shooting for you. Deal?"

He stuck out his hand.

She said, "Except there's just one thing."

5

HOPE REACHED FOR HIS GLASS. It sounded like a big thing.

Ms. Heretofore-Forthright murmured, "Uhmm." Then she said, "Are you hungry? I am starving. I'm not used to drinking. Could we get a burger or something? I'll fill you in on what's going on."

Food sounded like a very good idea. Hope said, "You know, I don't know your name."

"Sally. Sally Moffitt."

"Follow me, Sally Moffitt." Hope paid his tab and started walking, away from the boats, onto land, and along a heavily trafficked road to an expensive hotel with an even more expensive open-air dining room built around a swimming pool.

Sally said, "I really can't afford a place like this."

"Don't worry about it. It's on the house. They comp the charter captains so we'll send our clients. You want a lobster?"

"Just a burger is fine."

"Consider this your last major meal for three weeks. I'm having a lobster, maybe two. I'll enjoy them more if you have one, too."

This joint, too, was suffering Tortolan Torpor. The pool, which would be brimful of hard-body drunks during high season, held one overweight man who lounged forlornly at the water bar in the middle. The only people at the tables were in a group of twelve that sat in the awed silence peculiar to deeply discounted tour parties. Their waiter was plodding like a man who expected a measly tip. He greeted Hope warmly, as the charter captain was known to share the wealth when the meal was free, and offered them any table in the house. Sally chose one overlooking the harbor and sat where she could see the mega-yacht she'd been staring at from the marina bar.

Hope took a wild guess that she was mooning over a wealthy Italian, which turned out wrong by at least 180 degrees.

Sally agreed to eat a lobster. Hope ordered two for himself, and iced tea. Sally wanted black coffee. She was rubbing her temples. Hope said, "Looks like neither of us is good at drinking in the afternoon."

"It seemed like a good idea at the time." She took a roll from the bread basket, broke it, buttered a piece, and chewed hungrily.

Hope asked, "So what's this 'just one thing'?"

She looked at him, then looked away at the distant yacht. Nice-looking woman, Hope thought again. Very nice, as a matter of fact. About thirty-five. He liked her short, no-nonsense hair. Barbara had worn hers similarly. Made an active life simple. Pretty blue eyes, a little fragile, maybe, though fragility seemed a temporary state. She was suffering, but she didn't wear the permanently aggrieved expression of a habitual sufferer.

"You know what a rebreather is," she said, still gazing at the harbor. "A CCR."

"Mixed-gas, closed-circuit rebreather." A carbon-dioxide-absorbent canister coupled with an onboard computer that blended air and oxygen, the CCR allowed divers to stay down much longer than regular scuba gear.

"It's like magic. It doesn't make bubbles. The fish don't mind that we're there." Suddenly, her eyes were sparkling; she wasn't nervous anymore, and didn't seem heartbroken. She went on excitedly, "They swim about their business and we can enter their space—so close it's like we can look over their shoulders and see what they're seeing."

"Of course, with no bubbles, what's to tell a big fish you're not dinner?"

Sally gestured impatiently. "You hit your BCD dump value to blow bubbles in his face."

A buoyancy compensator device *could* be used for scaring fish instead of maintaining neutral buoyancy. Hope forbore commenting that the average rec diver who pulled that stunt would sink like an anvil, and said, in the diver shorthand she employed, "CCRs are hot now. The rec divers are really into it. I had to gear up to boost the bottles."

"So your website said."

"Frankly, they made me nervous. They're too unforgiving. Screw up and you're dead before you know it."

"They require extra vigilance," Sally agreed emphatically. "But for an underwater cinematographer the rebreather is the best thing that's come along since scuba."

"Is that what you dive with?"

"We could only afford one of them. Right now my husband has it. Ex-husband." She turned from the window and looked him full in the face. "I need your help getting it back."

"That sounds like a job for your lawyer."

"I don't have a lawyer. Besides, lawyers would take forever. It's mine by right of years of hard work. Years, supporting him in everything he did." She stared hard at David Hope, dry-eyed, angry.

"Sweat equity," Hope nodded sympathetically. "But I'm confused. You said 'ex-husband.' Are you actually divorced?"

"Separated."

"May I ask how long?"

"Four days."

"Ummm . . . Sally—"

"He dumped me!"

Hoped glanced at his iced tea and wished it were rum. Thank God he wasn't paying for this meal. His charter had just flown out the window.

Sally said, "He can keep the condo and the van; all I want is the gear that I need to shoot my film."

"But it's been only four days. Maybe you'll work something out."

"No way."

"How long have you been married?"

"Six years. Together three before that. I started out as his camera assistant, when he still had a big outfit, and became his still photographer. I worked my way up to line producer. He shot film. I recorded sound, wrote the grant applications, arranged transport, kept the books, and did the shopping. . . ."

"What did he do four days ago? Run off with a younger woman?"

"Not younger. Richer." Her face set and some of the music went out of her voice. "The minute I saw her goddammed *Il Bacione* I knew it was over."

"That *Il Bacione*?" Hope asked, nodding at the harbor.

"Her yacht," Sally answered bitterly. She stared across the water. "Phony 'countess.' She was in Cancun and before that in Belize and all of a sudden—big coincidence— she's in Tortola. She's no more a countess than you are. But she's got tons of money. She can underwrite his films with her pocket change. I want that rebreather. I need it. It's mine by right."

"I understand," said Hope. "And think you're absolutely right. But I don't understand how I of all people can persuade him to give it back."

"He won't give it back," she said scornfully. "I have to *take* it back."

"Take?" echoed Hope, fearing exactly where this was going.

"Liberate."

"Steal."

"Retrieve. It's mine."

"Would it be possible just to buy a new one?"

"For fifteen thousand dollars? I don't have fifteen thousand dollars. And even if I did, it's mine."

"So why not sell the condo and the van?"

"The condo is in Fort Myers and mortgaged. The van is ten years old." She reached across the table and closed a very strong hand on his arm.

Hope felt a sexual jolt—how wonderful to be touched. But he knew full well that she was not coming on to him. This wasn't a hint of I'll sleep with you if you do this for me. But she was still seductive—compellingly so—in the basic sense of persuasive, squeezing his arm, one human to another, drawing him into her sphere, demanding that he do the right thing.

"David, will you help me get back what I rightly own?"

"I'm not a burglar. You need a second-story man."

"No, I don't. I need a sailor."

"Why a sailor?"

"He moved it aboard his girlfriend's yacht. I found out where it's kept."

"How?"

"I made friends with one of *Il Bacione*'s stewardesses."

I'll bet you did, thought Hope. You've got a gift for convincing. Still, he asked, "Why did she tell you?"

"She hates her boss. She told me the whole layout, everything I need to find it. She's leaving the pilot hatch open for me—she even promised to help me load the stuff." Sally treated Hope's arm to another thank-God-to-be-touched jolt. "David, I've planned the whole thing. *I'll* go aboard and get the rebreather, and a few pieces of gear. I just need you to drive the boat."

"No."

They sat in silence waiting for the lobsters. Along with his charter, out the window had flown whatever fantasy Hope had floated that Sally Moffitt was the woman he was going to meet, now that he was ready. The one who was as eager to hook up as he was.

When the lobsters finally arrived, drifting to their table on island time, Hope made a halfhearted stab at conversation. "All the years I've been in the Caribbean, I still can't get used to lobsters with no claws. I'll be glad to get back to Maine."

Sally stared at her plate.

Hope feared she would start crying. He said, "I don't usually eat these guys anymore. They're getting fished out, smaller and smaller. On the other hand, the people catching them are trying to make a living."

Sally said, "Greg was my mentor and my film partner. But it was always a Greg Moffitt film. I have to prove that I can make my own career as a nature documentarian. The only way I can do that is by shooting a really difficult open-ocean film instead of a standard tropical reef project. It can't just be another 'jaws and claws.' "

"Haven't the spinner dolphins been filmed? The jumpers?"

"You're thinking of *Stenella longirostris*, the long-snouted spinner—the acrobat. Very little is known about short-snouted spinners. I've got to shoot these animals like no one ever has."

Hope nodded. She was hoping in one fell swoop to obliterate past mistakes, make up for lost time, and show the bastard.

He said, "I wish I could help you. I mean, you can't just board a rich person's yacht. They have security guards. They have alarms, they have live-aboard crew. They'll call the cops. I happen to live here half the year. Somebody'll get arrested. Worse, somebody'll get hurt."

"I can't charter your boat without the rebreather."

"I'm aware of that. Maybe if I were younger and dumber I'd help you. But I'm through taking crazy chances."

"He has used me and betrayed me. I have a right."

"I don't deny that. But I have also sworn off 'good causes,' especially when good causes involve 'risky business.' "

"Have you always been a charter captain, David?"

"No."

"What did you do before?"

Unimpressed by the clumsy change of subject, and doubting that Sally would even hear his answer, much less care, he gave her the standard version he reserved for paying customers. The answer that he delivered with a self-deprecating smile to make it seem personal.

"Before this I was a real estate mogul—fixing up old houses to rent—and before I was a mogul I was a crusading journalist unearthing betrayals of the public trust."

"So you've had success more than once? I'm still working on my first."

There was no budging her from the subject, so he answered soberly, "I've made my living."

"But I'll bet you also made your name."

Hope shrugged. "I can't say it changed my life."

"Well, it would change mine. For the better. That's all I'm trying to do. Make my own name—I don't *fucking* believe it!"

"What?"

"They just walked in."

Pretending to signal the waiter, Hope turned around for a look at the proof, not that he needed it, that Road Town, Tortola, was a mighty small town. A mob of Italians was flowing into the dining area, elegantly casual, smoking like chimneys. Hope counted four or five couples, some silver-haired oldsters, and a scattering of beautiful children. He turned back to Sally. "Which is your husband?"

"Guess."

Towering over the sleek Italians, his chest bulging in a faded cotton polo shirt, the underwater cinematographer looked for all the world like a tired old bull who'd somehow fallen in with the thoroughbreds at Churchill Downs. "Tall, handsome older American with white hair. Looks like he's about sixty."

"Fifty-five. He had a heart attack last year. Almost killed him."

"Would you like to go?"

"I can stand it if you can."

Hope pretended to signal the waiter again. The woman for whom Greg Moffitt had left his wife was in her forties, slim and stylish, and looked very happy with her catch.

"Spumante!" the Italians chorused, and the waiter galloped to the bar. *"Spumante per tutti!"*

Sally's husband spotted Hope and Sally at their table in the window. In the instant before Moffitt's broad, bluff face flushed red with embarrassment, Hope was sure he saw a flash of undisguised affection for the wife he had dumped.

She was head-down over her lobster, snapping legs with her fingers. Hope said, "I'll tell you one thing, Sally. The man still likes you."

She looked up, popped a leg between her lips, and sucked out the meat. "Of course he likes me," she replied, adding in a glance an unspoken, *You idiot.* "We were friends. We were partners. We had great times. We made six films together. But in the end, he did what he wanted and he didn't care how much I was hurt. It's over." She placed the now-hollow lobster leg parallel with the others on her plate, scrubbed her lips with her napkin, wiped her fingers, and stood up. "Excuse me. I've got things to do."

Hope watched her go. She walked briskly past the Italians, ignored a furtive glance from her husband, and hurried out the door. He glimpsed her moments later on the road, legs churning purposefully, shoulders pitched forward, head high, focused like sonar on what lay ahead.

Hope strolled back to the marina, decided he could not afford to spend any more money in the bar, rowed out to his mooring, and sat in *Oona*'s cockpit to watch the sun go down behind Fort Burt. He still wanted a drink. There was plenty of rum on board, but when he stepped down to the saloon he changed his mind and brewed coffee instead.

While he was waiting for the coffee he pulled *The Illustrated Encyclopedia of Whales and Dolphins* from the shelf and looked up Sally's short-snouted dolphin. Little was known about *Stenella clymene*, which lived only in the Atlantic. Sketchy evidence from groups of the creatures found stranded on the beach suggested their schools were segregated by sex. Which also suggested, Hope supposed, that Sally Moffitt would have a heck of a time filming their breeding habits.

The dark came down fast and before he had finished his second cup of coffee the Italian yacht—moored a quarter mile away—glowed like a Saks Fifth Avenue Christmas window. Even its name was lit in neon, like a cruise liner's. A new low for show-off consumption, Hope thought. Except that *Il Bacione*, "the big kiss," was kind of a nice name for a woman's yacht. He shrugged amiably, willing to concede that the thought canceled out the deed.

Il Bacione was riding a harbor mooring, just off the empty cruise ship docks. In winter there'd be dozens of such vessels, clustered like a fleet of East Indiamen that had gathered to convoy through the pirates. Tonight it floated alone, but for the much smaller, darkened hulls of the few sailboats still waiting for delivery crews to take them north to New England or east to the Med. And speaking of north, that's where he should go, the sooner the better, to set up for the summer tourist season. Although he was not looking forward to arriving in Maine broke and with the boat in need of bottom work he could have done less expensively here in the BVI if he had the cash.

Around eleven, a seventy-thousand-dollar inflatable tender slid from the yacht's stern launch hatch and sped to the hotel pier. Laughing and whooping, the Italians scrambled aboard. Hope picked up his binoculars. He could only trust in a kind God that Sally Moffitt wasn't watching, too.

Greg Moffitt was feeling no pain. The big diver slung his girlfriend over his shoulder and climbed into the bow of the boat, where he stood swatting her rump and bellowing in a voice likely heard across the Drake Channel, "Home, James! Home before the old geezer falls asleep."

The heavily laden tender roared back to *Il Bacione*. The passengers disembarked without anyone falling overboard—a small miracle, in Hope's opinion, as dinghy drownings were the number one cause of death in the yachting world. The crew stowed the launch. Stateroom lights began winking out and the mega-yacht grew dark. While remnants of the party continued whooping it up on the afterdeck, Hope fell asleep on his cockpit cushions.

When he woke up and saw the star-studded sky he was shocked and delighted to discover that he had slept a full two hours without a nightmare. He lay still, savoring peace. Flitting through his mind was a vague memory of dreaming of the big dolphin again. And another memory of the *Vermont*. But a benign image, this time—*Oona* riding the submarine's hull wave like a gull on the wind.

The harbor was quiet. The party across the water was over, *Il Bacione* dark except for her neon name board and her anchor lights. He scanned the water around the yacht with a pair of mil-spec night-vision binoculars that Barbara's merry band had left behind in the confusion.

No boats; no motion disturbed the crisp green image. He raised the glasses and inspected the yacht's decks. Suddenly, he locked onto motion. Up on the helicopter deck that overhung the afterdeck where the party had been he saw a silhouette moving rhythmically against the stars.

It was too dark and too far to distinguish faces, much less sexes. But it was clear that two lucky people were employing the safety railing to maintain their respective positions while getting eagerly and inventively laid.

He lowered the binoculars. Motion below drew his eyes to the water.

"Christ on a crutch! I knew it. I knew it. I knew it."

Here she came, rowing a large fiberglass dinghy with a determined if not precisely accurate stroke. He couldn't distinguish Sally's face, but her rowing stance was the seated version of her busy walk. It bespoke a woman who convinced herself that she could go it alone—board the yacht, load her diving gear onto her boat, and make her getaway—without any help from a wimp charter captain. What she didn't know was that two people—who were very likely the anchor watch—were having sex on B deck, on a railing that afforded a fine view of any rowboats that attempted to approach empty and leave full.

Any second there'd be shouts and searchlights. It was amazing they didn't hear the oars. Then he saw a towel or some cloth hanging from the side of the boat and he realized with sudden admiration that she had muffled her oarlocks like a smuggler.

Sally rowed right under their noses. And when Hope focused on B deck again, he learned that Sally Moffitt dwelled under a very lucky star tonight. The couple had reversed positions and were now locked mouth to mouth, sliding off the railing and sinking toward the supine in the shadow of the helicopter.

Sally disappeared around the other side of the hull. Five minutes passed. Ten.

Hope stood up, inserted a winch handle, and began cranking. Just in case, he told himself, she falls overboard and starts drowning. As the jib unfurled, the wind caught it and swung *Oona*'s stern. When the sail was out and shivering, Hope scoped out the yacht again. Nothing. No sex. No Sally. He moved to the mast and raised his mainsail. Then he took his binoculars farther forward and loosened his mooring line until a single turn around the cleat held *Oona*'s widespread double nose to the wind.

He scoped out *Il Bacione* again. Down at the waterline, Sally's dinghy slipped around its stern. She dipped her oars and began pulling across the harbor. Up on the yacht, the lovers rose from the deck like sinuous ghosts and returned to position one on the rail.

Sally got twenty yards and was almost home free when they spotted her. Hope heard shouts. A flashlight beam darted about, ineffectually. Then another, a big handheld thousand-candle-power halogen light jumping wildly, stabbing the dark and suddenly pinning Sally's dinghy like a spear. The rowboat was heaped with diving gear, camera cases, underwater lights, and a slew of canvas bags.

A siren shrilled. The big motor yacht was suddenly ablaze in electricity: deck lights, side lights, work lights, painted *Il Bacione* stark white. From her upswept bow to her elegant stern, naked and near-naked people were running out on deck, yelling. Sally Moffitt ducked her head and rowed harder.

Road Harbour was a mile wide and a mile long, surrounded by land north, west, and east. Its shores were indented by marina piers and shipping docks, which were dimly lit so late at night. The hills surrounding were dark with only an occasional house lamp burning. Its waters, too, were shrouded in darkness, speckled here and there with anchor lights, a rapid red blinker at the end of the marina dock, a quick flashing white on the cruise ship mooring dolphin near *Il Bacione*, and a pair of channel markers flashing red and green half a mile away at the entrance.

There were a thousand places to hide, but none for very long. Come daylight it would be like trying to disappear on a New England town green, where everybody knew everybody and the cops knew the strangers. The only guaranteed escape was to the southeast, through those red and green flashers, where the harbor opened into the Sir Francis Drake Channel between cliffs fringed with reefs.

Hope said, "No, no, no." His sails were out and the wind was stiff. *Oona* was straining to go. But even though he had anticipated the farce across the water, the last thing in the world he wanted to do was throw off his mooring line.

A fast catamaran like *Oona* would cover the half mile between the anchored *Il Bacione* and the harbor mouth in two or three minutes if the landbound wind cooperated. But a fast catamaran was still a sailboat, while a powerful motorboat like *Il Bacione*'s mile-a-minute, high-speed tender could make the half mile to the harbor mouth in thirty seconds.

He couldn't help her. He could only watch with a kind of sick fascination, as if he were witness to a highway accident beginning in slow motion: a big rig smashing through the guardrail, drifting across the grassy median, tumbling into oncoming traffic.

Then Sally's husband started yelling into a megaphone. *"You cunt! You controlling bitch!"*

The loud-hailer echoed his big voice off the surrounding hills. Hope, forced to reassess his earlier conclusion that Moffitt still loved Sally, doubted there was a man or woman asleep in Road Town who did not wake to the man's opinion of the woman he'd been married to for six years.

"Bring back my outfit. What the hell do you need it for?

You think you can shoot without me? Just 'cause you're a hotshot diver doesn't make you a shooter. There's some things even you can't control, you bitch. Somebody get a boat."

Laughter trilled across the water. "Catch her, Greg! Tallyho! Boat! Boat! Tallyhooooo!"

Hope muttered, "Oh, for Christ's sake!" Angry at himself before he even started—but powerless to ignore the fact that one miserably hurt woman was being hunted by a pack of rich people who didn't really need what she had in the boat anyhow—David Hope slipped his mooring and ran to his helm.

6

OONA DIDN'T DO HIM ANY favors. Instead of falling off the wind to fill her sails, the catamaran drifted clumsily backward, with her jib and main flapping like damp laundry. He eased their sheets and played the rudders, coaxing them to bite the water. At last, the sails bellied. He sheeted both in hard.

But heavily laden with food, water, beer and wine, and fuel, she was not the light-footed ballerina she'd been yesterday when she saved him from the berserk *Vermont*. Nor was she in her element in the landlocked harbor.

The cliffs and nearby hills played hell with the wind. Here it blew a stiff breeze from the southeast; there a lull; then a hard gust from the north. In the dark there was no reading the water surface to see where it was coming from next. The catamaran picked up speed. Buffeted by a wind shift, she fell back.

When her course from Hope's mooring to the anchored yacht carried her onto more open water, he felt the wind freshen and veer from the northeast. Praying it would hold and not suddenly back-blast him with a huge gust in his face, Hope steered for a dark spot that would place him between *Il Bacione* and Sally's rowboat.

"You cunt! Bring that back, you controlling bitch!" thundered against the hills. Hope ducked down to look under the sails. The yacht was close. They still hadn't launched a boat. Sally was rowing hard, stroking a fairly straight course to nowhere, heading like a frightened animal for the dark.

Oona was accelerating at last. Hope felt a familiar tightening of his stomach. At speed in close quarters she had a grim habit of getting even more unwieldy. He would have his hands full slowing down before he overshot the frantically rowing Sally. To make matters worse, the distance between them was difficult to gauge in the dark. Where the water was streaked by shore lights and the brightly lit *Il Bacione* it was even harder to tell what was going on. All he knew for sure was that the distance between them was diminishing rapidly.

"Controlling bitch!" boomed suddenly in his ear. He ducked to look under the sails again. God, he was right on top of her. He threw his helm hard to port, headed up. *Oona* skidded sideways, almost crushing Sally's dinghy.

"Grab this!"

Hope threw the first free line he found. He missed her boat, but Sally lunged and plucked it out of the water.

"Wrap it around something!"

Oona was starting to move again as her sails filled. She began sliding past the dinghy. Tangled in the heaped gear, Sally couldn't find anything to tie onto. The rope started burning through her hands. She dropped it, lunged to the bow, found the painter tied there, and threw that mooring line to Hope. He caught it on the fly and secured it to *Oona*'s port hull's stern cleat.

Forging ahead, the catamaran dragged the dinghy farther from the brightly lit yacht.

"Where the hell did he come from? You bitch, you got a boyfriend already? Where's that fucking tender, you dragass wops!"

"Quick!" yelled Hope. "Get the stuff aboard."

He set *Oona* for the harbor mouth, a half-mile away, locked the helm, and jumped down the dive steps. "Pass it to me."

First aboard was the precious rebreather. And now he was partaking of a felony. While the "few pieces of gear" he humped aboard next could outfit a remake of *Sea Hunt*: three heavy camera boxes, several padded bags, an aluminum case of clanking metal, two heavy sea bags, and finally six compressed air and gas tanks and a portable generator.

Hope looked over his shoulder to see where they were headed. Lark Bank's green flasher still on the right, Scotch Bank's red to the left. But *Oona* was veering to starboard, straying out of the channel.

"That it? Get on. Get on." He grabbed her hand and pulled her aboard and shoved her up the steps. When she was safe in the cockpit he inhaled what felt like his first breath of air in five minutes.

He let the dinghy's painter out so that it rode between *Oona* and his own inflatable, which was trailing on a longer line. Praying their lines didn't foul, he climbed up after Sally, grabbed the helm, and nudged the cat toward the middle of the channel. The Lark Bank green was coming up fast. Two more minutes and they would be out of the harbor.

Sally was laughing wildly. "That was fantastic. You looked like this huge white bird flying to my rescue. I got it all. I got it all. Thank you, thank you, thank you."

In thirty seconds, the speeding catamaran pulled between the flashing red cone and green can that buoyed Lark and Scotch banks. Ahead, a huge black night sky filled with stars loomed over dark, empty deep water. Almost there. Then behind them Hope heard the high-pitched roar of powerful outboard engines.

The pursuit was clearly visible, four or five people on *Il Bacione*'s high-speed tender waving halogen spotlights.

"They don't see us yet," said Sally and indeed the twin-

engine inflatable was veering toward the Scotch Bank side
of the channel.

"They will," said Hope. The halogen spots were slashing
all over the channel and his prediction came true with a
vengeance. One moment the triangles of *Oona*'s sails were
cutting dark swaths from the brilliant stars; the next they reflected snow-white the first beam that struck them.

"There's the cunt!" Sally's husband's voice roared across
the water.

"Jesus H.!" said Hope. "He brought the megaphone." It
would be almost funny, if people weren't racing around
dark, reef-studded waters at sixty miles an hour.

"I told you he gasses on. You should hear him at a Wild-
screen film festival with a drink in one hand and a mike in
the other. What are we going to do?"

"Do? We're not going to *do* anything, we're caught."

"No!"

"Sally, they can go four times as fast as me on my best
day."

"No. No. There must be a way."

"Silly bitch. I'll put you in jail."

Hope looked toward the shoal water beyond the Lark
Bank buoy and thought, I do not want to be a fucking knight
in shining armor.

There were five or six fathoms immediately outside the
channel, plenty to float *Oona*. But farther into shore, closer
to Burt Point, reefs lurked just below the surface. At night,
he could see no clues indicating where they lay.

"Can you steer for a second?" Hope asked.

"I never steered a sailboat."

"Just pretend it's a motorboat and head right there." Sally
clapped both hands on the helm and stood behind it, stiff as
Captain Ahab awaiting a hail from the masthead. "There!
Left of that green flasher."

Hope switched on his forward-looking depth finder and
the Global Positioning System and ran forward to raise the

daggerboard into its trunk in the starboard hull. With *Oona*'s draft reduced from eight feet to three and a half, he scrambled back to the cockpit and took the helm.

Il Bacione's inflatable was catching up fast.

"Open that hatch," Hope told Sally. "Put on a life jacket."

"What are you going to do?"

"I'm going to pray that tender driver is making his first visit to the BVI."

Hope turned the boat downwind and let out the sails. Then he steered straight at the loom of the land. The cliffs rose like a dark brow against the stars. Eyeing the rapidly changing images on his depth monitor and the numbers spooling on the GPS, he drove the big cat into the shoal water so close to the beach that he could see waves breaking in white foam.

"Run him aground!" Sally's husband bellowed in his megaphone. *"We'll nail him on the beach. Hey, controlling bitch, your boyfriend's gonna wreck his boat on account of you. You picked yourself a doozy, fella. Hope you have insurance."*

The tender roared closer. When less than ten yards separated the two craft, it slowed to match *Oona*'s eight knots and in doing so, sank down from its surface-skimming plane until its powerful engines were digging deep in the water.

Half blinded by their lights, Hope veered closer to the beach, where the darting spots illuminated the breakers smashing the shore. Sally asked, "Do you know where you're going?"

One eye on the GPS, the other glued to the depth finder, Hope muttered, "My cook did a little dope-running in her youth."

"What cook?"

"The cook some charterers pay extra for."

The inflatable growled nearer.

"Look out!" cried Sally. "Here they come!"

The inflatable was suddenly bearing down on them, angling swiftly alongside. Two burly crewmen were scrambling onto the rubber sides, braced to jump, and Hope could only conclude that they were drunk as skunks to take such a chance.

"Don't!" he yelled. "You'll break your fucking necks."

"We're coming aboard," Sally's husband roared into his megaphone. *"Back your jib!"*

Hope's depth finder finally showed him the reef he'd been praying for. "Your husband," he told Sally, "has been reading too much Patrick O'Brian." He wrenched the helm hard right and steered inshore of the reef, trying to squeeze *Oona*'s wide hull through a narrow channel between the coral and the rocks.

Right next to them, the inflatable struck. Shallow of draft, its strong, rigid bottom slid over the coral with a loud crunch that did little damage. But with her stern squatting deeply, she smashed both propellers on the reef. The outboards screamed—music to Hope's ears. They had sheared their propeller blades. Engines freewheeling, the inflatable bobbed helplessly as a cork as the surge sluiced it toward the beach.

Hope squeezed *Oona* through another reefs-and-rocks slot, then took the wind on a broad reach and put the cat on course for deep water. In less than five minutes, they had crossed the twenty-fathom line. The harbor was behind them, the black night ahead.

Sally was jumping around the boat, high as the moon. "We did it. We did it. Oh my God, we did it." She fell to the cockpit floor and hugged the rebreather. "Thank you, David. Thank you very much. Now I can do anything."

He couldn't see her face in the dark, but all of a sudden he thought he heard over the rush of water and wind clipping past his ears that she was crying.

"What's the matter? You okay?"

"I don't know," she sobbed. "I don't know. It's just

that . . . I guess this is it. It's final. I'm gone. He's back there—is he okay? They won't drown, will they?"

"They're on the beach by now. The best you can hope for are coral cuts and sea urchin spines in their feet."

Beyond the land, the wind was blowing pretty hard out of the east and *Oona* was drifting to leeward. Hope lowered the daggerboard to stop that sideways slippage and set her reaching south-southeast across the Sir Francis Drake Channel. Sally noticed the lights of Road Town behind them and the distant glow of Spanish Town on Virgin Gorda to their left. She looked at the compass.

"Why are you going south? Shouldn't we head up the channel to cut north?"

"Just in case your husband tries to make this a bigger deal than it is and finds another chase boat, we'll take Salt Island Passage directly out to sea."

He could shape his course north after he rounded Virgin Gorda. By sunrise they would be an anonymous speck of sail bashing up the Anegada Passage.

"Won't it take more time?"

"We will sail more miles," Hope explained. "But on better points of sail, so we'll go faster. You won't lose much and, like I said, we won't have to worry about your husband suddenly showing up with a rocket launcher."

Sally fell silent for a moment. She was standing beside and behind him in the dark and when she did speak again, it was softly, as if to herself. "Now I really have to make my film. No excuses."

"Let me just get us past Peter Island and I'll show you your cabin. You can get some sleep."

"My head's spinning too much to sleep."

"Big day," Hope agreed. He was looking forward to spending the rest of the night alone on deck. It had turned into a "big day" for him, too, rather suddenly and unexpectedly sailing north to Maine where, thanks to Sally, he would arrive a few bucks ahead of the game. The sleep he'd caught earlier in the harbor had set him up nicely. It was a beautiful night, the warm wind was honking, and even with all the extra weight *Oona* felt lively.

"I have to tell you something."

"What!" He jumped. Concentrating on his GPS and sonar, while straining to distinguish which low shadows ahead belonged to Salt and Cooper and Peter islands—and which might represent an unlighted slow-moving island freighter or a coked-up drug smuggler debating whether *Oona* was a disguised Customs boat that he should open fire on just to be on the safe side—Hope had forgotten that Sally was still standing right behind him.

"I am not a controlling bitch."

"I never thought you were."

"But you heard what he said. My husband—ex-husband."

Hope thought, keep it light: "Everyone in the British Virgin Islands heard what he said. I'd imagine most of them figured there were two sides to the story."

"You've got to believe me."

"I believe you."

"Listen to me. No matter what he said, I am *not* a controlling bitch."

"He also called you a 'silly bitch.' Obviously you can't be both. So nobody, especially me, is taking anything he yelled seriously."

" 'Silly bitch' is belittling, 'controlling bitch' makes me sound like a monster."

"Excuse me, Sally. I've really got to concentrate to get us out the pass." Hope snapped his harness tether onto a jackline and sprang forward to make an unnecessary adjustment at the mast. When he came back, Sally was staring at their starlit wake. He stepped past her to inspect whether the dinghy and his inflatable were riding comfortably astern.

"Hey, wait a minute. Where did you get the dinghy?"

"I found it at the Customs dock."

"What?"

"When I prepped to do this—before I met you—I told you, I scouted around and found the stewardess who knew where Greg had stashed the rebreather. So I had to find a boat."

"You stole the British Customs Officer's boat?"

"No. It's not his. Somebody told me it was impounded—what are you doing?"

"Setting it adrift. Somebody'll find it and tow it in."

"No! I need it to dive from."

"That dinghy tied to my boat ties me to this whole stupid mess. At least if I'm not towing a vessel Customs impounded, there's less physical proof I helped you get away." He cast off the painter and it fell astern in the dark.

"But I need it."

"Let's get something straight right now. The rescue of a paying customer aside, I am not a reckless captain. I am concerned first and foremost with the safety of my passengers and my boat. This is my home and my business. It's all I have. And your safety is my responsibility. I will deliver you to your dolphins and then I'll deliver you safe to Maine. But I'm not taking any more chances."

"Things worth doing are worth taking chances for."

"Not reckless chances with anybody's life."

"But, David, what you just did, sailing to my rescue and saving us from Greg, that was incredible."

"I didn't say I'm not a competent seaman. I said I'm not reckless."

"No, no, no. You were too good at that. You've been reckless."

Sally was imbuing him with heroic powers he did not possess. Maybe having been dumped by a powerful husband, she was living a life short of heroes. But this was no night to tell her that, and he sure as hell did not feel up to the conversation such an observation would provoke. So he said,

"Show me a guy in his forties who's never been stupid, and I'll show you a liar."

"You were good at it and I bet you liked it."

"It was a neat trick," he admitted. "But I came close to losing the boat. I wouldn't do it again. If those guys had jumped, Jesus. . . . In the heat of the moment people don't realize how easily they can get hurt or killed."

"David, it would be really helpful if you went back and got that dive boat."

"You can use my inflatable—it's a fine dive boat, and you can also dive right off the stern steps—excuse me, I'd like to concentrate on getting us through this pass."

"I don't see any lights."

"There aren't any. That's why I'm trying to concentrate. Before they invented GPS nobody but smugglers sailed these waters at night, and even they cracked up."

There were no lighted buoys marking the channel, and no handy radar reflectors warning of reefs. He showed Sally how his GPS kept him safely in deep water, aided by the depth finder, which gave him a picture of what lay ahead.

She pointed to the left. "What's that shadow?"

"Salt Island."

"How can you tell?"

"Familiar territory. The *Rhone* is off Salt. The old sunken mail steamer from the 1860s? I take a lot of divers out here."

Sally said, "It's the money."

"What money?"

"He left me for the money."

This is, Hope thought to himself, a lot like a blind date from hell.

The boat gave a barely perceptible wiggle, which told him he was passing through the current riled by the twin pinnacles of Blonde Rock. With fifteen fathoms of water ahead— and in another three miles, hundreds of fathoms—Hope found a bright star to steer by and settled in for a comfortable run. He could engage the auto-helm—a wind-directed self-steering device—but he feared that if he looked like he had time on his hands Sally would never shut up.

"Everything else was fine," she was saying. "Greg was happy. I know I still turned him on. Most of the time. It's just that it was getting harder and harder to raise money for the kinds of films he wanted to make. And then she came along in Belize—at least I think that was the first time—and she could write a check. . . . Do you have any idea what film stock costs?"

"No."

"Try a hundred dollars for ten minutes. And don't ask what it costs to get it developed. Then add in the cost of crew and transportation. . . . I think Greg just got tired of struggling."

The difference, Hope thought, between this and a blind date from hell was a very huge difference: Here every sea mile that passed under *Oona*'s hulls took him farther away from a good-night peck on the cheek and a promise to telephone.

"If she were younger than me, then I'd be really upset, thinking he left me for young sex with some little hard body. But she's older. At least ten years older than me. Wouldn't you say?"

"At least," said Hope. "I didn't get that close a look, but she had to be forty-five."

"At *least* forty-five."

"At least."

"Of course Greg is older. A lot older. Maybe age doesn't matter as much to an older guy. Do you think it does?"

"I guess it depends on the guy."

"Do you run around with little girls or do you date women your own age?"

Hope answered with letter and verse from the PC operating manual: "I tend to find women my own age interesting. But I don't make rules."

"Meaning," Sally shot back, "that whoever you're with

now is lot younger, probably—Greg was the same way. Look how much I was younger than him. And his first wife was younger, too. Not as much as me, but a lot—so how old is your girlfriend? Twenty-five?" She was angry, hammering at him. It seemed that "liberating" her husband's rebreather had not erased as much hurt as she had hoped. Hope knew he wasn't the target. He was just convenient. But that didn't mean he wasn't pinned in her crosshairs. Nor was she a woman who could be ignored. And as she had earlier, she took his silence as agreement.

"*Younger* than twenty-five? What do you talk about?"

"I don't have a girlfriend."

"Am I supposed to believe you're gay? Because I don't."

"No. Just unlucky."

"Well, how old was your last girlfriend?"

"About your age, I'd guess. Maybe a little younger."

"Were you together long?"

"No."

"Why'd it end?"

"Sally, please, it's late—"

"I happen to be in the midst of an ending myself, so I'm curious what happens to people. I'm sorry to push, but somehow, right now, this all seems very important to me."

"She's dead."

"What?"

"She died last week."

"Oh. Oh my god. Oh, David. I am so sorry."

"It's okay. I'd been expecting it for a long time. She was in a coma for a year. But I buried her ashes yesterday."

"I had no idea, I'm rattling on like an idiot. It's been such an insane day—I'm so sorry."

"It's okay. You had no way of knowing. And like I said, she actually 'died' a year ago."

"Oh, god, that's what you meant when you said, 'It's been a hairy couple of days.' "

Hope seized the opportunity to lighten up. "Also, I almost

got run down by a submarine. Damned near killed—anyway, what I would like to do now is get you settled in your cabin so you can get some sleep. If we're going to make good time to fifty-five west thirty north, we'll need you to stand watch to relieve me. So get some sleep and I'll show you around the boat in the daylight."

"I apologize. Please forgive me."

"No sweat." He saw her peering anxiously at him in the starlight, so he extended his hand. "I forgive you. I really do. Here, shake on it."

They shook hands. Sally said, "That's very nice of you. I appreciate it."

"Okay, what I'm doing now is I'm turning on the radar and setting the alarm, which should warn us if any ships get close and give me a few moments to take you below—here, I'll take one of these bags, you take the other."

Over his several years of ferrying paying customers about the Caribbean, he had refined *Oona*'s interior for the comfort of strangers. He showed Sally light switches to illuminate the steps below, and the cabin lights, though he asked her to leave them dark while they were under way in tight waters so as not to impair his night vision. She was impressed by the spacious saloon, as were most people expecting a cramped sailboat.

"Sorry for the motel-modern decor, but it wears well and most of the customers don't seem to notice." If Sally noticed, she looked suddenly too tired to comment.

He took her down into the starboard hull.

"This is your side. The aft sleeping cabin is the nicest—I did some teak work in it—and you can use the forward cabin for your camera gear. I'll stow the diving stuff in the dive room, which is aft of my cabin. In the other hull. Here's a light switch for your sleeping cabin. It's a two-way, you can turn it off from in bed. Okay? Please shut off lights when you're not using them, to save the batteries. There's the head. Electric flushing, just push the button. Try to go easy on shower water. I usually hose down on deck and reserve the fresh water for a final rinse. Are you hungry, by the way?"

She wasn't hungry.

"Well, if you change your mind, there's all sorts of stuff in the food cooler—just don't hold the door open. And there's coffee and tea. You'll find soda and juice and all that in the drinks coolers. There's one in the galley and another in the dive room. Plenty of fresh fruit and juice in those coolers, too. Okay?"

She had been taking in the details like a computer, focusing on each thing he pointed out, and he had the strong impression that tired as she was, she could still remember every detail. She looked longingly toward the bed.

"I'll catch you in the morning," Hope said. "Give a holler if you need anything."

She said, "Thank you. Thank you. You're being very nice to me."

"You're my only passenger. Welcome aboard." He backed out of her cabin and headed up on deck, shaken by a vision of aching loneliness.

The Anegada passage—the way out of the Caribbean into the North Atlantic—was never pleasant. By midmorning, it had whipped itself into a saltwater roller coaster composed of steep seas closely bunched. *Oona* was too heavily laden for such extreme conditions, and big waves were getting trapped under the tunnel between the hulls and slamming the bridge wing. Hope covered her vulnerable cabin lights with Lexan storm windows, a precaution he would have taken before heading offshore if they hadn't left port like pirates fleeing the hangman.

Sally came on deck looking green. She moved to the side as if considering throwing up, and her shorts and long-sleeved shirt were immediately drenched by the water flying over the cabin.

"Better stay behind the dodger," Hope called, beckoning her to join him where the canvas and clear plastic screen protected the center of the cockpit.

"The website said catamarans are smooth."

"On the Internet nobody knows you're lying through your teeth."

"It also said catamarans don't throw spray."

"It's not spray. It's called 'sneezing.' Only happens on a cat. Air compresses the water under the front of the tunnel and creates a cushion. Water can't escape out the back of the tunnel. So it goes the only way it can, forward, and 'sneezes' over the cabin."

"It feels exactly like spray. Is it going to be like this all the time?"

"No, no, no. Consider this your brief baptism by fire. We're bouncing along the top of a thermohaline squeeze play—warm water from the Southern Hemisphere is rushing out to the Atlantic and cold Atlantic water is heading south, making for the equator."

She shot him a look that accused him of falling into gassing-on mode.

"We'll be out of this by tonight," he promised. "She's a bit overloaded for these short, steep seas."

As he spoke, another slab-faced wave banged into the bridge deck between the two hulls and *Oona* ground to a near halt. "She usually clears the seas."

"But she's making an exception for me?"

"It's not her fault. She'd be fine cruising the Caribbean, but she's overloaded for out here. Take a shot at steering. That usually helps you feel better. Here. Take the helm." He pointed at the compass. "Just keep her a bit left of north."

"Three hundred and forty degrees?"

"That's fine."

"But that's not due north. Aren't we supposed to be headed north?"

"Tangentially," Hope said. "The wind's backed a little; we'll make more speed on this course."

He stretched out on a cushion and closed his eyes, opening them occasionally to watch Sally concentrate on the helm. Quite suddenly sleep closed in around him, dark as an underwater cave. And just as suddenly it was lit by fire and he was back in the burning oil rigs, the water blood red, obstacles everywhere, the sea running hard, and the rudder useless.

Part of him wanted to yell, It's over. I buried her. But who would listen? Another part asked, Why did the nightmare come back? What did I do? But no one cared about that, either. The important thing was that the boat would not respond to the helm and dead ahead a burning rig was toppling.

"You're right," Sally announced. "I feel better."

Startled awake, he sat up, grateful for the interruption. "Hungry?"

"Not yet—oh, did I wake you?"

"That's okay." His stomach was a hollow pit; he lay back again, and clasped his hands behind his head to stop them shaking. "Give me a yell when you're hungry. I'll whip up some breakfast."

"Did you sleep last night?"

"I'm doing fine."

"Did you steer the whole night?"

"The auto-helm did the work. All I had to do was look around now and then. It's amazing how close you can get to another vessel and not see it. Especially at night. But even during the day. The sails block a lot of your view and you can make the mistake of thinking there's nothing behind them."

Sally took the cue to look around, ducked her head to look under the sails. Suddenly her whole body went rigid. She stared past Hope, over his shoulder, and her eyes grew enormous.

"Oh my god," she breathed, and Hope jumped to his feet, fully expecting to see either a slab-sided container ship lumbering down on them, or, more likely and almost as bad, a Virgin Islands Search and Rescue Atlantic 21 lifeboat bearing an angry husband flanked by Royal Virgin Islands Police.

A hundred feet behind the catamaran, close enough to hit with a baseball, a huge dolphin was dancing on its tail.

"Don't lose sight of it. I have to get my camera."

7

SPOOKY, THOUGHT HOPE. IT LOOKED like the immense creature he had seen—or dreamed—before the submarine almost killed him. Except that in the midday light it didn't gleam red as it had at dawn.

The giant soared again, closer to the boat, pushing off on its tail, driving out of the water. As it spun, it seemed to drill through the air itself, carving its ascent the way a bird achieved lift with its wings. It splashed down on its side and vanished.

Sally raced back with a camera bag. It leapt again, sleek, shiny gray, and immensely powerful. She took out a stubby digital video camera, attached a long lens with practiced ease, and trained it on the creature as it flew from the broken seas.

"Unbelievable. David, slow the boat. We've got to get closer."

Hope eased the sheets. He noticed that Sally was shooting with both eyes open—right eye glued to the eyepiece, her left scoping the view beyond the camera. "What kind is it?"

"I don't know."

"You don't know? I thought you said you were a dolphin expert."

"I've never seen anything like that in my life."

"I have," said Hope.

"Please be quiet, I've got to focus." Her voice had changed, grown soft yet intense, like a big game hunter murmuring to her gun bearer, and he knew she meant her mind, not the camera, which probably focused automatically.

Marking the number of turns by its dorsal fin, Hope counted six complete revolutions for each vertical jump. When gravity tightened its grip, the creature fell slowly as if it floated. And as it spiraled downward, it tilted left until it landed horizontally, flat on its side with a huge splash. When the splash had settled, it was gone. And then—*boom*—with no warning, up it came again from a different sector of the sea, driving out of the water to drill another hole in the sky.

"Steer closer," said Sally.

Hope did what he could, but as the boat headed upwind, she lost way and began to settle on her hulls.

"Faster! It's moving away."

"Not without the engines."

"Don't start the engines. They're very sensitive to sound."

Oona got cranky and began hobby-horsing, pitching up and down on the chop. Hope coaxed her into falling off the wind, and she filled her sails and circled around on the opposite tack until she was again moving steadily toward the creature.

"Do you see any others?" called Sally.

"I think it's the same one."

It certainly jumped like the same creature each jump. And they had yet to see two at the same time. "Don't they usually hang out in groups?"

"Steady!" called Sally.

Hope played the helm. "Darned thing is toying with us." It was circling the boat, as if inspecting them while they inspected it. At a range of a hundred yards it rose halfway out of the water and took a long look.

"It's spy-hopping," Sally said. "Trying to figure out who we are."

"Looks to me like it's trying to figure out what's for dinner."

"Can you get me closer?"

He had halved the distance already, and as he nursed *Oona* even nearer, Hope was struck forcibly by the sheer size of the creature. It was leaping like a spinner dolphin, but it was twice as big. Also, the spinners he had seen jump at sea appeared almost clownlike in their exuberance. This thing was no clown. It was all business. And it looked darned near twice the length of the dinghy, which would make it twenty feet long.

"It's huge," he murmured.

"Almost as big as a killer whale," Sally agreed in a voice tight with excitement.

But it was no killer whale. Hope had seen pods of the black and white orcas while whale watching. While orcas were a kind of dolphin, the bulky hunters with their towering dorsal fins weren't "dolphinlike" in appearance. What they looked like were killer whales and only killer whales.

This had a certain bulk to it, but it looked primarily like a dolphin. And it played like a dolphin. A very big dolphin. Except that "play" just wasn't the right word to describe its purposeful thrusts from the water to get a better look at them. He shivered. Killer whales were known to smash into boats to knock people into the water, as if they were knocking penguins off ice floes.

"Where'd he go?"

"I don't know."

A minute had passed since it spy-hopped. Sally had her camera aimed at the next spot in the pattern she had deduced from its jumps, but nothing broke the rough water. After a while, Hope said, "He needs air, right?"

"He can stay down for quite a few minutes if he feels like it."

"But he's got to come up again."

"But if he's just breaking surface to breathe, we'll never see him in these waves. They don't spout like a whale."

"Want to hang around?"

They circled the area for fifteen minutes, but saw nothing. Hope asked again, "What do you want to do?"

Sally thought long and hard. "No," she said reluctantly. "There's no guarantee it will stay here. Let's get moving. I wish I had him on film. I wasn't set up for film. I should have had my camera loaded. Dammit!"

"You got video."

"Video's fine for the record. And you can hardly tell the difference with this digital camera. But there's still a stigma to video. You're not taken seriously. Serious nature documentarians don't 'shoot video,' they 'make films.' "

While Hope got the boat banging and smashing into the steep seas again, Sally braced herself in a corner of the cockpit and played her tape back in her viewfinder.

"Good stuff?" Hope called to her.

"Stunning. What an amazing creature. . . . What did you mean, you had seen one like it?"

"I saw him the other day. Or one like him."

"Are you sure?"

"Damn sure. If you saw that again, you'd know."

"Tell me. What? What did you see?"

Hope didn't feel like going into the whole was-it-a-dream-or-was-it-real thing. He assumed now that it was real, that he had awakened, as he often did, for an automatic safety look, had seen it jump and had fallen back to sleep with the memory burned on his retinas.

He said, "I was about thirty miles south of Tortola. The morning of the day I met you—just yesterday. Right before the sub almost creamed me."

"What did it do?"

"It jumped. Like this one. Great big jump, danced on its tail and spun like a top. It was dawn, so the light was very beautiful. He looked all shiny red and gold. I thought he seemed big at the time, but it's hard to tell sometimes how far you are from something."

"So it could have been smaller and farther away?"

"Could have been."

"Except," she pressed. "This reminded you."

"Like I told you."

"Could it be the same creature?"

"Sure. I suppose. What are we talking, two sightings one hundred fifty or two hundred miles apart? Dolphins migrate, right?"

"They're great voyagers," said Sally. "They go where they want. . . . I can't tell you how strange it is for me to see something that I've never seen before, but should know. I mean, if there's such a thing as a dolphin like that, I should have seen one or read about it or heard stories . . ." Still holding her video camera, she peered back at their wake. "I feel blessed to have seen it."

"It's what I like about going offshore. You'll see stuff that you just can't tell anybody about." He laughed. "Sailor friend of mine—ship sailor—seaman on a freighter—once told me, every true sea story starts with the exact same words: 'No shit. This really happened . . .' "

Sally played her tape again. Then she brought it to Hope at the helm and ran it for him. Even on the camera's tiny viewfinder, the creature seemed to radiate unusual presence.

"A charismatic beast," said Hope.

"Greg would *kill* to have shot this."

"Sure you don't want to stick around?"

"I'd love to. But it could be ten miles from here already. Two hundred miles tomorrow."

"My gut says no," said Hope. "My gut says it's nearby."

"How often is your gut right?"

"About half the time."

Sally laughed. "I'm going to take it as a gift—a what-did-you-call-it story, 'No shit. This really happened?' and move on."

A sea jumped up and banged the catamaran bridge deck. "Jeez, when is this boat going to settle down?"

"By dark," Hope promised her. "Feeling sick? Try chewing saltines."

"No, I'm much better. That thing sort of knocked it out of me."

A side sea whopped *Oona* on the starboard hull and shoved the cat into a yawning trough. She hit bottom with a wet bang. Sally went flying to the deck with her camera shielded in her arms.

"You okay?"

Sally inspected her camera. "Fine."

Oona clawed her way back to the top of the next wave, from where she commenced another gut-wrenching lurch. Sally wedged herself into the corner of the cockpit and said, "I wish Greg were here."

Astonished, Hope asked, "Want to go back and get him?"

She hugged the camera tighter. "No way."

"Then why do you wish he was here?"

"He gets really, really seasick the first couple of days on a boat. He'd be in agony."

The sea calmed the farther north they sailed. By the middle of the night, *Oona* was coursing over Atlantic swells at a smooth fourteen knots. Hope set her on track with the autohelm and slept in the cockpit, one step from the helm, while Sally stood watch. He slept well again, no nightmares, no dreams at all that he could remember. Some of the thanks had to go to his client.

He had no doubts about Sally Moffitt as a watch stander. She was alert and observant. And while his sleep-deprived mind might wander on occasion, the hard-driving Sally would prefer to be boiled in oil rather than doze off when duty called. Which made her a superlative shipmate for sailing shorthanded offshore; if she would only shut up about her husband.

He relieved her at three in the morning.

She came up from her cabin at dawn, talking a mile a

minute, though at least she handed him a mug of coffee first. "Good morning, how are you, I feel so much better. It really is a smooth boat. I slept like a log. I thought it was going to be tough sleeping alone after all these years, but I gotta tell you, I'm enjoying it. Greg was so damned big. He took up the whole bed. And I won't miss the snoring, either. God, the water's a beautiful color—like robin eggs. This is the Atlantic Ocean, now? So we're making good time—hey!" Peering past the sails, she finally realized that the sun rising through yellow clouds was dead ahead. She checked the compass. "Why are you headed east?"

"The wind backed north. Soon as it veers east again, we'll head north."

"Are we losing much time?"

"Not yet."

"God, I hope not."

"The trades tend to blow more easterly in April. It'll veer pretty soon." He was not looking forward to the Variables, the belt of dicey winds above the trade wind belt. Sally would go bananas with every shift.

"I'll be right back," said Sally.

She jumped below and returned with a camera bag. When she opened it, she held the camera up for Hope to see. "Film," she said, "sixteen-millimeter." She screwed on an enormous lens and patted the outfit lovingly. "This one's been through the wars. Greg had it when we met."

"He's going to miss that," said Hope, recalling that her original idea was to steal only the rebreather.

"Now he can afford a new one. You know, Greg always had offers. As long as I knew I could see the women coming a mile away. Why this time?"

"What's the old saying, just as easy to ditch your wife for a rich girl as a poor girl?"

"Am I supposed to be flattered?"

"Dolphin!" cried Hope, thinking, Thank you, Lord. "To starboard. To the right. See him?"

The crescent shape was slicing in and out of the water in long, horizontal jumps, and drawing near. "He's going to pace the boat."

"That's not him. It's much smaller."

"There's another."

Sally identified them as ordinary bottlenoses.

There were three powerful creatures, ten feet long with smooth dark bodies, pointed snouts, melon heads, and the perpetual grins that had gained the species their worldwide *Flipper* fame. They surged alongside and close to the bow.

"They're going to ride the bow wave."

"Lotsa luck," said Hope. "A cat doesn't throw much of a bow wave." And indeed the dolphins quickly surmised that the boat lightly skimming the surface did not cast a dolphin-lifting wave like a ship. They dropped back and tried to play instead off the stern, which did peel a curly wake.

"They must see your camera," said Hope. "I've never had them this close."

"Sorry, guys!" Sally called. "I'm not wasting expensive film on bottlenoses. Wait a second, I'll do your close-up in video." In a smooth, quick action, she slipped the sixteen-millimeter back in its padded bag and picked up her digital video camera. An instant after she pressed the record button she gasped, *"Ohmigod, what's that?"*

A long steel-gray column was rising swiftly from the blue-green depths. It was overtaking the boat as if *Oona* were standing still, and Hope's first panicky thought was another submarine. A cooler logical voice argued, It's not as big as a submarine. But it was still catching up and a frightened voice cried an equally absurd, *Torpedo*.

Shifting course at the last second, it smashed into the bottlenose nearest the boat with a force that flung the ten-foot animal completely out of the water.

8

THE OTHER BOTTLENOSES WHEELED WITH the effortless grace that had been smashed out of their companion and went to its rescue, one coursing alongside the victim flopping on the surface, the other in swift pursuit of their attacker.

"It's the big one," said Sally. She had her eye glued to the camera and Hope was amazed to realize that she had videoed the entire encounter.

He let loose the sheets and *Oona* slowed. The wounded dolphin was still on its side, flopping fifty yards behind the boat. The dolphin circling it dived suddenly. Hope followed the trajectory of Sally's long lens toward a roiled stretch of water. He grabbed his binoculars and focused on two crescent shapes leaping from the ocean.

A heavy body soared up under them at double their speed. Twice as long as the bottlenoses and ten times their weight, it struck like a hawk scything sparrows. A second bottlenose went tumbling.

Hope looked at Sally in shocked disbelief. She was still rolling, eyes open, steady as a tripod, tracking the silvery flash of the two bottlenoses streaking toward the boat.

But if they were fleeing for the shelter of *Oona*'s broad

shadow, nothing could protect them from their pursuer's sudden burst of speed. The instant they reached the starboard stern, the steel-gray column soared under them again, driving them to the surface. Hope grabbed the helm instinctively, bracing for impact. He saw a flash of teeth. Blood showered, sparkling like rubies in the sun.

The weight of the attack smashed both bottlenose dolphins into *Oona*'s starboard stern. All three creatures hit with loud thumps that shook the boat. The bloodied animal slid halfway up the dive steps before it splashed over the side. Seconds later, Hope saw the two bottlenoses racing south. Closer astern the wounded animal was swimming slowly on the surface, struggling to catch up with its mates.

The big attacker had disappeared.

Hope took a deep breath and looked at Sally. She was filming the retreat. Her face was dead white, drained of blood, and when she finally lowered the camera he saw that her hands were shaking. He steadied his own hands on the helm.

"That was more like a shark."

"No," she said shakily. "I don't think so."

"Have you ever seen anything like that?"

"Not with dolphins."

"I mean that was a mugging. That was totally unprovoked. It just tried to kill them."

Sally swallowed hard. "I've seen films of killer whales attacking seals, like that. I've heard that dolphins batter sharks. It is so rare to capture predation on film " She lowered her camera and stared hard at it. "Damn, I was shooting tape."

"Was it the one from yesterday?"

"I think so. Damn, damn, damn, I can't believe I did that."

"I hope there aren't two of them."

"Damn! Greg always says, it's the moments you miss that make you better. At this rate I'm going to be brilliant." She rewound the tape and as she watched it in the camera's viewfinder she began to cheer up. "Wow. Unbelievable . . . David, what is that thing? Where are you going?"

Hope had sprung to his feet and was descending the bloody dive steps, holding fast to the rails. On the bottom step he stooped to pick up something that gleamed. He brought it to Sally. It was a heavy peg-shaped tooth, round and thick as the through-the-deck bolts that anchored *Oona*'s winches.

Sally was thrilled. "It's a dolphin tooth."

"Not a shark?"

"No way. Look how smooth it is. This is fantastic. We can get a DNA test on it."

Hope got a bucket and sluiced the blood off the steps. Then he sheeted in the mainsail and jib and put *Oona* back on course.

"There he is!"

It was ahead of the boat, jumping on its tail and spinning with that now-familiar drill-a-hole-in-the-sky action.

Sally jumped onto the cabin roof and ran forward with her camera, over the foredeck and onto the beam that connected the bows.

"Safety harness!" Hope yelled. He buckled into his own, clipped onto the jackline, and ran forward with a harness for Sally, who was leaning over the bows with her legs wrapped around the head stay.

"Always, always, always hank on. Here, I'll help you into this."

"Don't shake my camera."

It led them north-northeast, occasionally spin-jumping, but mostly swimming fast, barely breaking the surface to blow a low, puffy, often invisible vapor and inhale fresh air. Suddenly, it vanished.

They circled for an hour. Finally, reluctantly, Sally said they couldn't waste any more time. Whatever it was had disappeared; if they got lucky it might come back. Hope altered course to the east for more speed and put *Oona* in the control of the auto-helm. While he made a sandwich lunch—glancing repeatedly out the windows for the strange creature—Sally pored through the marine life library that he kept current for his clients. She brought the whales and dolphins encyclopedia to the table and while they ate discussed what they had seen.

"It's enormous."

"Bigger than any dolphin I've ever seen," said Sally.

"And it bites," said Hope.

"It's alone, which is really strange."

"And it bites," Hope said again. "I thought dolphins were supposed to be nice."

"There isn't anything like it in any of your books," Sally marveled.

"And you—who know quite a bit about dolphins—have never heard of such a thing? Ever?"

"There are seventy-eight known kinds of cetaceans—including whales, dolphins, and porpoises. The largest family is the twenty-six oceangoing dolphins. Delphinidae. They have beaks and dorsal fins like this one. But they don't get that big. I've never seen anything like this. Never. He spyhops like a killer whale. He jumps like a spinner. He's almost as big as a killer whale. But not as bulky. Maybe there's some other clue on the tape."

She brought another padded gear bag up from her cabin and hooked a DV VCR to Hope's thirty-six-inch television. "Great TV, beats my laptop for a monitor. I didn't expect such video on a sailboat."

"When they're not diving, my clients expect a floating rec room."

She played the tape of the dolphin attack. The camera had captured icily clear footage of the huge animal rocketing out of the water and slamming into the smaller dolphins. If video wasn't as good as film, Hope missed the distinction.

"Dammit," Sally railed at herself. "I screwed up."

"What do you mean? It looks great."

"Don't you see where I jumped? I jerked the camera."

"I jumped, too."

"See?" She rewound and played it again. "There. Look at that. I blew the shot. . . ." She gnawed her lip. "Greg would have stayed cool. But I was so surprised."

"Shocked," said Hope.

"I've got to train myself. I'll practice with the video camera. I'm not a great shooter. I never have been. All Greg would let me do was sound. The only thing I ever got to shoot was B-roll."

She turned up the volume and the stereo speakers emitted a muffled roar. "What is that? Oh, shit, the wind is screwing up the mike. I've gotta put a condom on it."

"A condom?"

"A foam sock." Again, she gnawed her lip. "I don't even know if it will help."

"What if you took the microphone off the camera and I held it for you—angled it away from the wind?"

"We can try," she said dubiously. "If it comes back." She played the tape again. "That damned wind rush—you can't hear when they hit the boat. We'll have to foley it in."

Hope, who was getting used to her habit of talking as if they were some sort of professional film partners, even though they clearly were not, didn't bother asking what she meant by "foleying" it in, though it obviously had something to do with sound. Instead, he cleared the table and washed the dishes. He was just finishing wiping down the galley when he saw the animal spy-hopping from the top of a tall Atlantic swell.

"Dolphin! Hundred yards off the port beam."

Sally was up on deck in a flash. "Safety harness," he yelled after her. While the creature churned circles around the catamaran, Sally gave Hope a separate wireless shotgun microphone and he tried to hold it at an angle that both captured the sound from the direction she was shooting and shielded it from the wind.

Sally patted the headset she was wearing and called, "I'm still getting that noise!"

It wasn't working. The wind direction shifted every time he turned the boat to track the big dolphin, while trying to hold the mike, watch the animal, and steer the boat and shift the sails simultaneously. The auto-helm would free up a hand, but the auto-helm—which shaped a course vis-à-vis the wind directing its wind vane—could not follow a dolphin, but only hold the course set to it.

"Hold on," he said. "I've got an idea." He ran below for an alligator spring clamp and used it to fasten the microphone to the wind vane. Now when a course change changed the direction the wind blew across the deck, the finely balanced vane swiveled the microphone to the proper angle.

Sally kept pressing her headset to her ear. "Whatever you did worked beautifully. I'm getting great ambient sound. I can hear the wake, I can hear the sails and the rigging. Thank you."

"Anytime."

By evening, they discovered something even stranger about the creature. It wouldn't go away. It had kept its distance all afternoon, yet had stayed in sight most of the time, jumping and spinning and spy-hopping at regular intervals, occasionally veering from its northeasterly course to circle *Oona* like a wary cat.

"It's following us," said Hope.

"No, it's not," Sally countered in a voice of barely contained excitement as if she wished it were following them, but was afraid to spook it by speaking the observation aloud.

"If it isn't following us, it's certainly hanging around."

Sally had to admit that it seemed attracted to them.

"So much for going swimming," said Hope. "The teeth on that thing will keep me out of the water for a year."

The sun sank behind a cloud line that looked so much like a rugged mountain range that it seemed they might run aground. As darkness gathered around the boat, the animal swam in close and rose in a spy hop.

Hope used the binoculars to study it studying him. "What happens now? Will he follow all night? Don't they sleep?"

"They don't sleep much. The water keeps them afloat, so they don't have to 'get off their feet' to rest from the strain of fighting gravity."

"But they probably have to rest their brains."

"I've always thought that they have to 'reboot' their sonar. I mean, they process millions of click-and-whistle echoes to locate prey and identify friend and foe and communicate with each other. Information must flood their brains."

"Do they sleep like ducks? One eye open?"

"Half a brain at a time. When their left cerebral hemisphere sleeps, their right stays awake. Remember, dolphins have to keep swimming and surfacing to breathe."

"Half-catnaps."

"Deeper than that. When a hemisphere is off-line, they don't click and whistle."

"This one doesn't have any friends to click and whistle with anyway."

Sally stood up and gazed up at the stars, which were quite suddenly bright. Then she surveyed the sea and said, so softly that Hope had to strain to hear, "It's like a gift from God."

"What do you mean?"

"The chance of a lifetime. It's what every naturalist dreams of. It's the ultimate subject for a documentary." She looked at him, expecting agreement.

"What," he asked, "is the ultimate subject for a documentary?"

"If that animal is an entirely new kind of creature that no one has ever seen before, I'm going to make a film about identifying a new species."

9

"DO YOU THINK IT'S REALLY a new species?"

"We couldn't find it in the books."

Hope nodded toward the saloon. "That isn't exactly the Library of Congress down there."

"I *know* there isn't anything like it in any book. A dolphin that big would be at least mentioned in any basic text. And being solitary would be mentioned, too. So would that spinning jump."

"Maybe he's a mutant."

"A freak of nature?"

"Wouldn't that make him an outcast that no other dolphin wants to be around?"

"An Ishmael dolphin?"

"That alone would make it one for the books."

"And an awesome film."

"Hey, you must know plenty of dolphin experts. Why not radio them?"

"I already thought of that," said Sally.

"I've got e-mail on the single sideband radio. It's slow, but—"

"No. I can't risk somebody finding out and moving in on me."

"Who?"

"There are plenty of filmmakers, much better funded, who would jump on this in a flash. Starting with Mr. Greg Moffitt."

Hope figured that Sally had sailed into obsession territory again, and nothing he said would change that. Sure enough, she took his silence as opposition.

"Greg would be all over that dolphin like a dog on a bone. And with that 'countess' bitch paying for it, he could afford multiple cameras, spotter planes, and everything. No, my best hope—my only hope—is to film it from every angle in the water and out. Then get the money somehow to edit a ten-minute demo and then shop the demo to get backing for a full-length feature."

"*In* the water? You're not diving with that thing."

"Of course I am. I've got to get into its space."

"Let me rephrase that," said Hope. "I will not be part of you going in the water with that monster. Shoot all you want from the boat. If you want to go swimming with it, get another captain."

Sally nodded briskly. "When the time comes to look over its shoulder, we'll figure something out. . . . The sooner I've got some film in the can, the sooner I can approach *National Geographic* and *Nova* and HBO."

"What's to stop *National Geographic* from funding their own expedition to come out here?"

"I won't tell them where we shot the film until they fork over the dough." She looked at Hope. "Can I trust you to keep this to yourself?"

"I'm already getting out of this what I need."

"What's that?"

"Hydraulic steering."

"What?"

"The cable-quadrant system is a mess."

A guarded, suspicious expression drove the smile from Sally's face. "Are you trying to put me at ease? What are you saying? I'm supposed to trust you because all you want is a new steering wheel?"

"You can trust me because you can trust my word."

"David, I think you should become my partner in this."

"Nooo, thank you."

"I think we should share. So we both have a stake in the film."

"You're paying me plenty already."

"But I have to be able to trust you."

Hope, whose natural placidity was starting to erode under her badgering, answered coolly. "I told you, you can trust me because you can trust my word."

"That's just words. What if—"

"You want facts? The fact is, *Oona* is a boat. She needs work. She always needs work. My steering's a mess. And everyone's telling me I need the bottom fixed. So maybe if I pick up enough charters this summer I'll do the bottom, too. Maybe not."

Sally was staring at him. "Are you putting me on? Because if you are, this is important to me and—"

"I crunched a foil last spring—the mini-keel under the starboard hull. To work on it, I've got to have the boat hauled and that ain't cheap. There aren't that many yards with ways or cranes wide enough to haul multihulls so I'm not in a great bargaining position. The money you're paying me will be a big help with the steering; whatever else I earn I can put toward the bottom. If I feel like it."

"That's all you want? To get your steering and your bottom fixed?"

"Not my bottom. The boat's bottom."

To Hope's surprise, Sally forgot about beating out her husband long enough to laugh at a lame joke. She sobered quickly, however. "Are you serious? That's all you want in life?"

"That happens to be a lot. This boat is my home and my business. So, right now, that's 'all' I want in life." (Along with meeting someone who wanted to get met, which he kept to himself.) "So don't worry. I won't rat you out to your husband."

"Even if he offered you a new bottom?"

Hope smiled at the good-looking woman who might, or might not, have just given him a little opening, and said, "I'm going to get my own bottom."

She returned a chilly glare. "Are you hitting on me? Because if you are, forget it."

Hope thought that was harsher than his mostly innocent comment deserved—particularly since she had arguably set him up for it—and he said, "I heard good advice in a poker game once. I think the guy was quoting Nelson Algren. 'Never—' "

"I know, I know," Sally interrupted. "Never sleep with a woman who's got more troubles than you. Greg loved that corny line. I think he was warning me not to be difficult."

There were times, thought Hope, when he felt a warm kinship with Greg Moffitt.

"So are you comfortable with that?" Sally asked. "Because I don't have time for it."

"With what?"

"Not coming on to me."

"It was the furthest thing from my mind and will remain so, I promise."

"Good. Because if I don't sleep with another man until the year three thousand it will be too soon. Last week I thought I was a happily married woman. I'm still adjusting."

"I noticed," said Hope.

Her expression changed from briskly armored to hurt.

So wounded, even, that Hope felt compelled to add a gentle "I'm not surprised."

She didn't hear him. "Do you realize," she said, "if I could get ten minutes of tightly edited film of such an intensely acrobatic creature I would have a shot at the great golden goose."

"What golden goose?"

She looked at Hope as if surprised to see him on the boat. "Greg's name for Imax. The great golden goose of nature films. . . . In fact, you know what?"

"What?"

"I'm going to concentrate on shooting video."

"I thought you said film was preferred."

"Yes, but I can edit video right here on the boat. On my laptop. The quality is beautiful, anyhow. And that way I can jump off the boat in Maine with my ten-minute demo all ready to sell. I'll take it to a post-production house to clean it up and hit the ground running."

She nodded briskly and looked out at the sea again, as if willing the creature to rise from the dark. Then she gave a soft, mirthless laugh. "Greg would die if that dolphin got me a contract with Imax."

Sally had captured several of its dances on the wave tops, where it performed as exuberantly as a spinner dolphin. When they played it on *Oona*'s TV they saw that the animal was marked by a long spiral scar that twisted from the blowhole atop its head and halfway to its tail.

"Dolphins scar easily," Sally said. "They have very thin skin, but it heals quickly. Have you ever seen a Risso's? They're covered in white scars."

Hope pictured the animal corkscrewing against some sharp floating garbage some polluter had dumped overboard. "Could have crashed into something. Or maybe somebody tried to harpoon him. Thought he was a great white shark. A lot of sickos like to kill big things."

Adding up all his views of it, Hope decided that it was no exaggeration to say it was twenty feet long—which made it as big as a killer whale, though it seemed subtly leaner in the forward section, with a head tapering to a long bottlenose or spinner snout.

"Maybe it *is* a killer whale. They're dolphins."

"It's not a killer whale. They have a heavier head and a blunter face. It's not a spinner dolphin, either. It just happens to jump like one."

"Wow! Look at that." On the screen it had breached completely out of the water, before falling back again on its side. Immediately it porpoised in a long horizontal leap, low to the water and resubmerging with a knife-clean slice. An instant later it was lobtailing—beating the water with its tail; then it flipped around, stood on its head, and flailed its tail flukes in the air. The sequence ended with another eerie spy hop, where it thrust its head out of the water and eyed Sally and Hope and *Oona* with what Hope could only characterize as the cool, knowing gaze of a cynical cop.

"That is one smart animal," Sally said.

"Or hungry," said Hope, shivering as he had the first time he had seen it rise to look. "Or maybe it's just lonely."

Sally said, "Greg always said, you can really screw your head up assigning animals human emotions."

"What do *you* think?" Hope asked.

"Greg was right."

"Maybe Greg could tell me why it's following us."

At Sally's request, they sailed slowly through the night, holding a northeasterly course at a lazy five knots. Hope doubted that the dolphin would sleep all night long, but Sally was the client, and if she wanted to go slow so they wouldn't outrun the creature, then that's what she was paying for. Though he did remind her that they had a long way to go before they reached their original goal southeast of Bermuda.

"This is more important," said Sally.

Dozing in the cockpit, Hope awakened to a clear dawn. He looked around, concluded it would be another beautiful trade wind day, and tried to remember his dreams. Nothing scary. He glanced into the saloon. Sally was still below in her cabin. Clipping his harness to the dive stairs rail, he descended the back of the port hull and had his shorts half unzipped when he jumped back.

Heart pounding, eyes locked on the water behind the boat, he backed stealthily up the steps, crossed the cockpit, and descended into the main cabin and down the starboard companionway into Sally's hull. Her door was open for air and she was sprawled on her face, hip cocked prettily under a thin sheet, a shapely shoulder bare. He rapped quietly on the door frame and whispered, "Sally?"

"What? What?"

"Shhh!"

She saw him touching a finger to his lips and sat up blinking. The sheet slid down her breasts. Hope put serious effort into politely looking away.

"Bring your camera," he whispered. "Ishmael's back. Ten feet off the port stern."

10

"LET ME GO FIRST."

Hope watched from the main saloon steps as she padded across the cockpit, quiet as a cat, the video camera ready on her shoulder. When she spotted the dolphin she was able to stand stock-still as she commenced rolling tape.

If the sound-damped camera made any noise, Hope could not hear it from a dozen feet behind her. But the dolphin exploded into motion, diving away from the boat with a powerful upswipe of its tail. Enormous flukes flashed and it was gone.

"Damn!" said Sally. But when she finally lowered the camera and turned around, her face was shining. "That is such a great animal. I *love* that animal. Thank you, David. Thank you for spotting him."

"Sorry he ran."

"He'll be back."

Hope ducked below and made coffee and toast, which he brought up to the cockpit along with the overnight weather faxes. He studied them—while Sally scanned the water with the binoculars—and concluded that nothing awful was bearing down on them at the moment, although he would keep a sharp eye on a depression forming over Bermuda. That one could turn very unpleasant very quickly.

Before he had another cup of coffee he walked around the decks checking for wear of lines, blocks, and the shrouds and stays that supported the mast, paying particular attention to the toggles under the furling gear on the headstay. He had learned the hard way that there were varying grades of stainless steel and that *Oona*, like most boats, had not been fitted with the absolute best. He was upgrading, as he could, bit by expensive bit.

When he got to the cockpit, it took him a moment to spot Sally, who was standing on the bottom port dive step, buckling into her rebreather. She had changed into a skin-colored one-piece bathing suit. "What the hell are you doing?"

"I'm going to get in his space when he comes back."

"That's insane."

"I know what I'm doing."

"Not on my boat."

"No way I'm not diving," Sally yelled with sudden ferocity. Hope shook his head in disbelief. Sally said, "Please, David, listen to me. I have to enter the animal's psychological space. I have to give the film the riveting sense of being the animal, looking over its shoulder, seeing what it's seeing."

"Well, it's not going to be seeing me in the water," countered Hope. "And I doubt even you are nuts enough to dive alone."

Divers stayed alive by obeying rules. Starting the first day of his first certification class, Hope's instructors had drummed rules into him until they were second nature: Obey the laws of physics; obey the gear manufacturers' warnings; don't stretch the dive tables; when in trouble, remember there was no situation you couldn't make worse; stop, breathe, and think before you act. But underlying all of them were two absolute iron rules of scuba: never hold your breath and never, never, never dive alone.

"I'm safer diving alone," Sally said, "if I don't have to look out for you."

Hope had heard that before from professionals and to a

limited extent the pros had a point: You could get into a lot of trouble looking out for a screwed-up partner. But he strongly preferred the safety factor of a backup brain, a buddy with a second set of eyes to notice a mistake before it turned fatal.

Sally looked past him. "There he is!"

It was a couple of hundred yards off, lobtailing and spinning.

Sally sat on the second step and started pulling on her fins. "Would you please just suit up? Stand by if I get in trouble?"

"It will kill you, and when it's done killing you, it will kill me if I'm stupid enough to get in the water with you."

"Except for trainers who have provoked them," Sally shouted back, "I have never heard of a dolphin hurting a human being. By all accounts they like people. They've even been known to help swimmers in trouble."

Hope hurried down the dive steps and crouched so they were face-to-face. "That bottlenose it tossed out of the water like a beach ball must have weighed six hundred pounds. You weigh about a hundred and thirty. When it hits you, the last thing you will feel will be every bone in your body breaking."

Sally's strong jaw set. She glared straight into his eyes and Hope saw an expression that combined desperation, determination, and astonishing bravery. The bravery rocked him back on his heels. It meant that she did understand the danger.

She said, "I am willing to take the chance, David! I would rather die than be known as Greg Moffitt's assistant for the rest of my life. That creature will let me earn my own name."

"Here he comes," said Hope.

The big dolphin was porpoising, skimming wave tops, charging the boat like a runaway torpedo. Hope looked at Sally and was relieved to see that even she thought that a twenty-foot mammal swimming at twenty miles an hour was a sobering sight.

"This might not be the moment," Hope said gently. "He seems a little frisky this morning."

"My God, he's big." She lifted her camera to her shoulder, sprawled back on the steps, bracing herself with her legs, and rolled tape. "Later," she murmured. "He'll calm down later. Then I'll go in."

"What do you want the boat to do?" Hope asked.

"Just keep going like this. I'm getting wonderful shots of his tail stock." She was shooting over the creature's head, down the length of its back, as it swam behind *Oona,* effortlessly matching the boat's seven knots with nonchalant upthrusts of its tail.

Sally had three minutes of tape when it stopped dead in the water. *Oona* pulled swiftly away. "Stop!" cried Sally. "Something's wrong."

Hope headed up until the sails were shivering in the wind. The catamaran settled deeper, slowed, and began to pitch on the long, heavy swells. Through the binoculars he could see the creature's dorsal fin circling slowly, a couple of hundred feet astern. In a swift explosion of movement, it sprang from the water, stood for a long moment on its tail, crashed on its side, and dove out of sight.

Within half an hour Sally Moffitt was beside herself.

"It's gone. It's gone. I should have dived. I *knew* I should have dived. Now I've got nothing."

Irrational though he knew it was, Hope felt guilty for delaying her dive until it was too late. He racked his brain for some way to make it up.

"Hey, would a hydrophone help? Listen for his voice. If he clicks or whistles?"

"Where would you get a hydrophone?"

"I bought a used one for the whale watchers. I wired it so they can hear it through the stereo."

He plugged in the cable and lowered the underwater microphone into the water.

"Let me run it through my DAT," said Sally.

As handy with her sound gear as Hope was with *Oona*'s sails—and armed with a seemingly limitless supply of adaptor cables—Sally soon had Hope's hydrophone wired into a digital audiotape recorder that she clipped to her belt and fitted with a headset.

"Okay, now if we get lucky, I'll have time-coded backup audio I can synch into my video."

But the sea gave them no dolphin clicks, no groans or whistles. Sally listened morosely, hunched over in the cockpit, a hand pressing her headset to her ear, listening to it hiss.

Suddenly Hope sprang into action again.

"Where are you going?" she called.

"Up the mast."

He hanked a free halyard to his safety harness, led the bitter end back through the harness and over his shoulders as a belaying line, and climbed the fold-out mast steps to the first spreader. Forty feet up, he unlimbered his binoculars and scanned the sea. The air wasn't as clear as earlier, but from this height he could see twelve or thirteen miles to the horizon.

The dolphin wouldn't have just vanished forever, he told himself. Not after hanging around for three days. It would be back.

A fuzzy spot to the southwest set his pulses moving. A blow? The vapor spout as it exhausted spent air and gulped fresh? He longed to call down to Sally that the dolphin was back. But no, what had drawn his eye was farther off. A ship, probably. Creeping over the horizon. He lowered the binoculars to scan the nearer waters. When he looked southwest again, the fuzzy object had formed up like a tower. Tall and lean, it was a silhouette that suggested an oil rig under tow.

But when Hope shifted the glass around it he could see no tugboats. Soon it became apparent that the tall, narrow object was moving a lot faster than an oil rig tow and heading directly toward *Oona*.

"Do you see him?" Sally called.

He glanced down. She was cupping her mouth to be

heard. "Not yet." The wind whipped the words away and Sally called, "What?"

"NOT YET!"

"What are you looking at?"

"I'm not sure. I think I'm hallucinating." He steadied the binoculars against the mast. Maybe he was hallucinating, but what he thought he saw was a vision from another century—a tall, narrow pyramid that looked like a square-rigged ship bearing down on them under full sail.

Two months from now tall ships would begin converging on New York City for the Fourth of July. But he hadn't heard of any of the old training vessels being in the area. Maybe it was one of the new windships built specially for the ultra-high-end luxury cruise trade. He descended the mast steps and switched on a handheld short-range VHF radio to call to be sure they saw him. They were already hailing him in what sounded like a German accent.

"The sloop-rigged sailing yacht ten miles northeast of me. Do you read me, sloop-rigged sailing yacht?"

"Ten miles?" Hope said to Sally. "He's bigger than he looks."

He switched on the radar, and sure enough a bright target was crossing the ten-mile ranging circle. Hope moved the cursor to it to derive its bearing and speed.

"Wow. He's smokin'. Nineteen knots under sail." Faster than most engine-powered cruise liners. He thumbed TRANS-MIT and returned the hail. "Good morning, sailing ship to the southeast, this is the catamaran *Oona* headed northeast at eight knots. Which side would you like to pass me?"

"Oona. *This is the sailing vessel* Star of Alabama. *We will stop to windward of you. The owner wishes me to ask whether you would join him for lunch."*

Hope looked at Sally. "That thing has an 'owner'?"

"Lunch?" she asked. "Lunch in the middle of the ocean?"

"Probably better than anything I can cook. You want to go? Your charter, your call."

"That's probably what scared the dolphin."

"It's not going to make noise anywhere near as loud as a steamship."

"Don't worry, he could hear it."

"Do I tell him no thanks?"

"Can you find out who the owner is?"

Hope keyed the handheld. "*Star of Alabama*? Who is your owner?"

"The owner is Mr. William Tree. I will be alongside in thirty-seven minutes if you would choose to stop and wait."

Sally's eyes grew huge. "William Tree?"

Hope said, "William Tree as in the oil business?" When Barbara was living aboard, the saloon had been papered with frenzied, if not always verifiable, website printouts cataloging excesses of power. In the pantheon of environmental villains, if he recalled correctly, the Gulf Coast Trees had been among those that Barbara's eco-crusader pals had ranked as more dangerous than corporate farmers, genetically engineered seed producers, the pharmaceutical industry, and the World Bank. Hope had kept a salt grain handy, but had nonetheless been intrigued by how globalization had increased the behind-the-scenes power wielded by a few dynasties like the Trees.

"No," said Sally. "He's on a ship. It must be William Tree as in Tree Marine Institute. And the Tree Marine Park? I don't believe my luck."

"What do you mean?"

"Tell him yes! Tree Marine Institute gives grant money for documentaries. They're wonderful."

"Aren't they the same Tree family as the oil business?"

Sally shrugged impatiently. "What oil business?"

"Offshore exploration, drilling, and pollution."

"Tree is not a name I associate with oil."

"Just because their name isn't Mobil or Exxon or Shell doesn't mean they don't call the shots through holding companies. They have tons of their people in public office—either connected by blood or beholden to them. They've stacked the regulatory agencies and the Pentagon and bought a slew of safe seats in the House and Senate."

Sally was not looking a gift horse in the mouth. She said, "All I know is they're rich beyond belief. Oh my God, this is fantastic. I can't believe we're going to meet him face-to-face."

"I'll stay on the boat."

"No. No, please come with me."

"I don't know anything about grants and marine research. But if they're who I think they are, they're nobody I want to have lunch with."

"What do you mean?"

"It's a good thing they have marine parks because thanks to their offshore drilling there's going to be a lot of dead sea life everywhere else. They got rich on oil and natural gas; they grease their way around environmental regulations backing political hacks and lobbyists."

"I can't hate them for being rich."

"It's not just rich. It's the power. They're like their own private branch of the government."

"All I know is that the Tree Institute pays for tons of valuable research and they're very generous to filmmakers."

"So you've got no reason not to go."

"I would feel better not going alone—look, David." She reached across and touched his arm. "This is troubling me. You are part of this. You should share in whatever we get for filming that animal. Be my partner—let's have a straight business arrangement that makes you my business partner instead of my employee."

"I'm not exactly your employee. Think of me as a contractor."

"The charter deal would stay the same, of course. I'm just saying that I want you to have a stake in whatever we got out of this."

"You say stake, I hear golden handcuffs. I really don't

want to be committed beyond sailing you and helping you film, as originally promised. This is your thing."

The radio squawked. Hope thumbed TRANSMIT. "Please stand by, Captain."

Sally said, "Just so you know how I feel about it. We can talk again, anytime you change your mind."

"My other problem with lunch is a practical one: What about the boat? No way I want her towed."

As if reading his mind the captain of the *Star of Alabama* radioed, "Oona. *If you decide to accept Mr. Tree's invitation, I will supply riding crew for your yacht that we may sail in company.*"

"What's a riding crew?" asked Sally.

"Seamen to sail *Oona* while we eat lunch."

"Perfect," said Sally. "Tell him yes. Please."

Hope looked at the *Star of Alabama,* which was growing large as it neared. It was furling its topsails, but there was not a man in the rigging. Topgallants and royals were disappearing automatically, rolling up into their yards like self-propelled window shades. Politics aside, he was very interested in a close look at the unusual ship.

"Okay," he said. "I'll go with you."

"Thank you, David. I really appreciate it—I have to get some clothes on. Would you take care of my gear?" She dove down the saloon steps. She turned back and looked him up and down. "Do you have something to wear?"

"Wha'd you have in mind?"

"It's probably air conditioned. It might be a little cold for shorts."

Hope thumbed his handheld. "Captain, please tell Mr. Tree thanks for the invitation. How do you want to handle getting us aboard?"

"*With your permission, Captain, we will effect the transfer by inflatable boat once you're in my lee.*"

"Sounds fine," said Hope. The long hull standing to windward would block some of the swell and most of the wind. "They might do best to approach my port stern steps."

The ship's captain repeated Hope's instructions, which would allow the inflatable to maintain control by approaching from downwind.

Hope asked, "What speed do you want to maintain during lunch?"

"Can your boat make eight knots?"

"Eight knots will be fine as long as this wind holds. She's a catamaran. So if you have anyone who sails cats it would be a big help."

"My second officer was an Olympic finalist for Poland. It will be no problem, Captain, she'll be in good hands."

"Thank you, Captain. It sounds like he'll do fine. I'll talk to you again when you get here. Over and out."

The *Star of Alabama* continued to grow larger as Hope put Sally's buoyancy jacket, weight belt, tank, and fins back in the dive room and changed into a clean shirt. But it wasn't until the ship was gliding alongside that her true size was apparent. Considerably longer than the *Vermont*, the last heavy vessel Hope had sailed close to, and standing, of course, much higher over the water, the windship had five masts.

The middle and main masts looked easily twenty stories tall and carried four square sails each in addition to the royal and sky sails Hope had seen furled earlier. The yards—the cross-trees from which the sails hung—looked as wide as *Oona*'s mast was tall. The fore and mizzen masts carried five sails each. And the aft-most mast, the jigger, flew four plus a fore-and-aft-rigged spanker. They were complemented by a wind-grabbing assortment of jagged jibs and staysails, which were automatically furling as the ship slowed.

"I can't believe that one guy owns that ship," Hope called to Sally when he heard her banging around the saloon. "She's got to be six thousand tons."

Sally stepped into the cockpit. She had changed into a

plain white scoop-necked dress with a short black jacket and was wearing large, dangly gold earrings.

"Wow. *You* clean up well."

"Thanks," she said briskly, with a censorious glance at Hope's frayed shorts and battered running shoes. "When you've accompanied your husband to as many grant interviews as I have, you keep the uniform rolled up in your seabag."

"Well, you look very grantable."

"You better hide your log."

"What for?"

"The same reason I took my tape with me—the riding crew. I don't want anyone learning about that animal."

"So maybe these Trees aren't as nice as you say?"

"I'd rather be paranoid than stupid."

Hope stepped below, took the log from the nav station, and encased it in a waterproof plastic Ziploc freezer bag, which he stashed in the oily bilge underneath the port motor. He closed the engine box, washed his hands in the head, and went back up on deck. The *Star of Alabama* was looming like two city blocks of office towers. Easing her sheets, she spilled the wind from what looked to Hope like an acre of sail.

A twin-engine rigid inflatable raced between the two vessels. The RIB was about the size of *Il Bacione*'s big-bucks tender; but its crew of Asian seamen was outfitted in jaunty "sailor" costumes—white ducks, red neckerchiefs, and wide-brimmed straw hats—that reminded Hope of a summer-stock production of H.M.S. *Pinafore*. He figured the broad-faced East European with lieutenant's bars on his epaulets for the Olympic sailor.

In the bow stood a smiling officer who looked as pleasantly competent as the concierge in a Four Seasons Hotel.

"Good morning, sir!" he called in an English accent. "Good morning, madam. Bill is delighted that you'll come to lunch. My name is Philip. I will see you back to the ship while Lieutenant Starskowitz looks after your catamaran."

Starskowitz stepped over the safety lines, saluting Hope as his foot touched the deck. A Filipino seaman followed close on his heels. Starskowitz barked an order. The Filipino knelt to snub the inflatable's painter so Sally and Hope could climb down. The rising and falling swell was only partly blocked by the huge sailing ship, but Sally crossed easily between the two boats. Hope paused to offer his hand to Starskowitz and said, "She's riding pretty heavy."

"*Ja*. I see crossing water. No problem."

"You'll find cold drinks and stuff in the cooler in the main saloon."

"Thank you, sir. She is handsome yacht."

Handsome was not a word that even Hope, who loved her dearly, used to describe his clunky-looking catamaran, but he chalked it up to the language barrier.

As the tender motored toward the huge windship, Philip said, "Bill adores meeting new people, which, as you can imagine, doesn't happen often in the middle of the ocean."

"Where are you headed?" asked Hope.

"Bill will be the one to answer that, I'm afraid. Mine is not to reason why . . ."

"I thought maybe this was a passenger vessel on a delivery."

"Good lord, no. There are no passengers, only Bill's guests and the people who work for him. You'll see. It is quite phenomenal."

"It's magnificent. Did he build it?"

"As I understand it, he oversaw every weld."

"So this entire ship is a pleasure yacht?"

"I would say that the *Star of Alabama* is certainly Bill's pleasure. But at the same time serious business transpires aboard her. She's a floating laboratory, after all. I rather doubt there's a marine research facility to equal her anywhere on land."

"And you?" asked Sally. "Are you a scientist or one of the ship's officers?"

"Oh Lord, no, not in the sense you mean. I mean, I know the *Star* as well as any man, but I'm more a sort of, shall we say, majordomo. We've got scads of people to look after, after all: seamen, engineers, cooks and stewards, guests, not to mention our scientists and IT specialists—oh, may I tell Bill the names of his guests?"

"David," said Hope. "David Hope."

"Sally Moffitt."

"Excellent. It's all first names with Bill, though he likes titles and may occasionally address you, David, as 'Captain Hope.' "

Philip radioed their full names to the ship by repeating them into the handheld VHF clipped to his life vest. The boat pilot took a swell on the rise and drilled right through an open pilot door at the ship's waterline. A seaman hooked onto a cable that hauled the loaded boat safely inside the hull and up an inclined ramp. The pilot door clanged shut and Sally and Hope, exchanging awed glances, stepped into a dry corridor bristling with security cameras.

Philip urged them through a watertight hatch into a carpeted hallway hung with oil paintings and sculptures that sparkled with moving light. "This way, please. Bill is waiting in his quarters."

11

PHILIP PAUSED AT THE DOOR. "I recommend you brace yourself. His rooms are quite a sight. Bill calls them his Captain Nemo Lounge. But I've noticed people flinch the first time they enter."

He knocked and flung the door open. Despite the warning, Hope backed up a step, convinced for a second that the sea was cascading down on them. Sally gasped, then gave a moan of deep appreciation. They had descended to a deck below the waterline and Tree's walls were pocked with underwater portholes. But the truly startling effect was the ceiling, a sixty-foot-long glass-bottomed aquarium that teemed with exotic fish.

Yellow and blue tangs, spotted coneys, striped tiger groupers, speckled angelfish, triggerfish, goatfish, and parrotfish cruised their domain in splendid suspension. The ceiling seemed to ripple, which put the filtered sunlight in constant motion.

Centered beneath the aquarium, commanding the view ports, stood a vast red leather armchair as wide as a couch and as tall as a throne. On the table beside it sat a vase of fresh roses and a combination speakerphone and intercom with many buttons.

"Well, welcome aboard," drawled a soft, sweet voice, and a hugely fat man bounded in from a connecting room. "I'm so glad you could come to lunch."

Hope had never stood near a man so enormous. Draped from neck to sandals in a black velour sweatsuit, Tree was not particularly tall, but Hope guessed that he must weigh close to five hundred pounds. His frame was stacked with rolls of flesh that bulged from his arms and broad shoulders and thighs and combined in a belly so vast it was more square than round.

"David? Sally? I'm Bill."

Tree shook Hope's hand in a strong grip, and bowed his head over Sally's. Then he staggered backward and collapsed onto the red leather chair. The physical struggle to swing his massive legs for those several steps into the room had taken its toll. Sweat glistened on his face. He gestured feebly at a fan sitting on the floor and wheezed to Hope, "Please turn that on. Ah need a breath of air."

Hope, gripped by a sudden fear that the fat man would die before he got the fan switched on and aimed the cooling breeze on him, sprang to do his bidding.

"Thank you, David. That's much better—Philip, now that our guest has graced your employer with life-sustaining air, perhaps you could stir yourself to bring me a glass of water."

Philip brought a crystal goblet from the sideboard, saying, "Sorry, Bill."

Pressing a handkerchief to his brow and sipping water, William Tree inspected Hope and Sally with an interested smile.

Hope overrode the impulse to look away from the grotesque and inspected him back. He looked like a fastidious man who had just stepped out of a barbershop: clean-shaven; an elegant wave combed into his light brown hair; fingernails buffed. And on closer examination, the face perched atop the mountainous body was a handsome one, with a strong jawline, a well-proportioned nose, and wide-set eyes that changed from gray to green in the shifting light.

His smile fixed on Sally. Came the drawl again, clear, soft, and strangely compelling. "I admire your earrings. Left to you by your grandmother, I'd suppose?"

Sally couldn't hide her surprise. "How did you know?"

Tree laughed. "Well, *my* grandmother always said a lady can get away with wearing big jewelry so long as she can say, 'It's a family piece.' "

His laugh was infectious and Hope was suddenly glad they'd come.

"Well, I'm sure people are always telling you that you two make the most attractive couple."

Sally, caught utterly off balance, looked to Hope for rescue, and Hope said, "Actually, we're not a couple. Sally's my client. She chartered my boat."

"Well, you surely fooled me. I thought you were the closest of companions. . . . So where are you sailing your client, Captain Hope?"

"Maine. Sally's filming a nature documentary."

Sally gave him a grateful smile.

"On what subject?" Tree asked her.

"The breeding habits of *Stenella clymene*—short-snouted spinner dolphins. David's going to swing me east of Bermuda on his way to Maine. No one's filmed them breeding."

"Well, I'm not surprised, considering their cloistered habits."

"So you know *Stenella clymene*?"

Tree chuckled. "Whenever I hear the words 'know' and 'dolphin' uttered in the same breath I'm reminded of Mr. Jacques Cousteau admitting late in his long and fruitful life, 'Few branches of knowledge have made smaller strides since ancient times.' "

Sally laughed easily and Hope settled back to enjoy watching a pro in action as she replied, "I remember filming interviews at an invitation-only, cream-of-the-crop cetologist conference in California and I was congratulating myself thinking, Wow, this is it, I'm at the epicenter of the field. Then an old professor piped up in a little voice, 'When you look at the explosion of research since World War Two and the efforts of thousands of scientists, you see that our knowledge about dolphins has progressed from almost nothing to just a little bit.' "

"Well," said William Tree, "we'll keep on trying to do our bit here. In the meantime, I'm so glad you could take time to visit at such short notice. Did Philip take good care of you?" The majordomo was standing by with an attentive smile.

"Perfect," said Sally, who looked disappointed that Tree wasn't more interested in the breeding habits of *Stenella clymene.* Hope wondered if she would trust Tree with information about Ishmael.

"Philip is a man of many talents," Tree drawled on. "If he weren't busy overseeing the preparation of our lunch, I'd ask him to sing for us. He's got the sweetest tenor voice. Except he's shy and it's hard to get him to sing out. He suffers from low self-esteem, isn't that so, Philip?"

"Not this morning, Bill."

Tree laughed. "Keep that Prozac coming. Or are you back on the Zoloft?"

"Celex, today."

"Well, whatever works. Now don't let me keep you from preparing lunch, Philip."

The majordomo exited smiling.

Tree snapped his fingers. "Sally Moffitt! Of course. I'll bet you're married to Greg Moffitt. Now *there's* a film-maker."

"We have separated," Sally answered, with an iciness that Tree didn't appear to notice as he leaned over to press a button on his speakerphone. "Malcolm, would you come down here, please?"

He looked up to see Sally staring at the glass ceiling.

"I see you admire my aquarium. When I was a little boy men who worked for my daddy took me on the bayou in a glass-bottomed boat. I'd lay on my belly all day and watch the fishies. Well, I eventually grew too big to lay on my belly—meaning that if we installed a glass bottom in the *Star of Alabama* they'd need the main-brace winch to stand me up again. But I still wanted to watch the fishies. So I just turned everything upside down."

"It's amazing," said Sally.

"When I found her hull the shipyard was building her to be a passenger vessel—a fancy cruise ship—and *that* was supposed to be the swimming pool. Well, I just knew that I had to have her. You come back at night sometime and you'll see a sight. Bioluminescent fish all aglow? They're my night light."

"How'd you get her away from the cruise line?" asked Hope.

"Captain Hope," Tree replied, "something tells me you would enjoy a look around the ship while Sally and I visit."

Hope glanced at Sally and when she didn't say anything to keep him there, he said, "That would be great. She's a beautiful vessel."

"Well, we try—there you are, Malcolm."

In walked a youngish officer in a starched white uniform. Hope pegged him for another Brit. "Malcolm, this is Captain Hope from that little sailboat. He'd like very much to tour the *Star of Alabama*. Malcolm is our third mate," he explained to Hope, speaking as if Malcolm had abruptly melted into the bulkhead. "He knows the ship like he knows his own wife—probably better, come to think of it. I bet Amanda wouldn't want to hear that, would she, Malcolm? But it's the Lord's honest truth, considering we don't let him get home to Hampshire that often. Malcolm, why don't you take Captain Hope and show him around? I'll bet he's got a million questions." He turned to Sally, chuckling, "Even young sea dogs got plenty to chew over. Have fun, boys. Lunch in thirty minutes."

"See you," Sally called after them.

Hope waited until they were riding up in a walnut-paneled elevator to say to Malcolm, "I've got to ask the crass question. What did the ship cost?"

"Bill *says* he spent eighty million dollars. But everyone knows it had to be closer to a hundred. And that's before you tally up his art collection."

Emerging on the main deck, Hope located *Oona* sailing a safe two hundred yards off the beam of the great ship. It was unusual to see his own boat under way and his eye would have lingered longer, but for the awesome spread of the *Star of Alabama*'s snowy sails, the powerful standing rigging, the miles of running rigging, and the spotless teak decks that looked like they'd been looted from half the rain forests in the world.

"It looks like he got his money's worth."

"Steel hull and masts, aluminum yards, and stainless standing rigging—yes, sir, he surely did. Lloyds rate her 100 A1 plus. Here, let me show you something you'll rather enjoy." He led Hope to one of the control pods scattered about the deck. "Care to reef a topsail?"

Hope followed his gaze up the mainmast higher and higher until his neck hurt. At Malcolm's urging, he toggled a joystick on the control board and a sail the size of a circus tent rolled smoothly up into its hollow yard.

"Wow!" He felt like a little kid set down in the middle of a huge electric train board. "Can you brace the yards from here, too?"

"Certainly."

"Could I?"

"Go right ahead—switch the selector to YARDS . . . Right. Select MAINSAIL . . . Right. Now move the stick."

Hope looked skyward with pleasure. At the touch of his finger, heavy Dacron lines on either side of the ship—the weather and lee braces that angled from the main deck to the ends of the yards—shifted the gigantic mainsail's angle to the wind.

"Not too much or the captain'll see it luff and then we'll have fireworks. German, you know."

Another touch and the yards returned to their previous position and lined up with the others. "What are the red buttons?"

" 'LOCK' is obviously, hold everything steady. 'LET FLY' is Bill's own modification: quick release, preferring in an emergency to write off a few sails than the entire mast, what?"

"*In*-credible. I mean, it was labor costs more than anything that doomed commercial sail."

"It's coming back," said Malcom. "We man her with a smaller crew than a similar-sized freighter. I've seen a mate and four seamen drive her through a Cape Horn gale."

From Hope's point of view as a small boat sailor the young officer's cheerful boast conjured an unsettling image of the five-hundred-foot ship plowing blindly through the sea in the hands of people too busy to watch where they were going. "What happens when something gets in your way?"

"We've excellent forty-two-mile radar. Here, let me show you." Malcolm led him to the pilot house, which was set far forward between the main- and foremasts. The quiet, multi-windowed space offered views fore, aft, port, and starboard of the vessel's decks and the sea beyond. Packed with the latest satellite-assisted electronics, the radar of which Malcolm was very proud, and the engine and thruster controls, it was presided over by a silent officer of the watch and an equally silent helmsman. Looking back through the forest of masts, Hope could see a traditional spoked sailing ship wheel, mounted near the stern. It moved in ghostly repeat to the helmsman's actions in the pilot house.

"We steer by the aft wheel whenever Bill comes on deck.

He's a great admirer of the old ways. Always asks that we send the men aloft to make sail."

"What for? I thought it's all powered."

"He had the upper topgallant sails rigged so he can watch the lads shake them out by hand."

"That must be fun on a dirty night."

Malcolm smiled as if he really did believe that the seamen climbing a two-hundred-foot mast in a howling gale would find it great entertainment. "Yes, I suppose it is, rather."

"Does he come up often?"

"Not that often. He's rather self-sufficient down there and getting around, as you can imagine, is not easy for him."

"What do you suppose he weighs?"

"Five hundred and ninety pounds, last time we weighed him," Malcolm said matter-of-factly.

"What did you weigh him with?"

"A game fish scale. It registers up to a thousand."

"How can he live like that?"

"He's got a very strong heart. Would you like to see the engine room?"

They walked aft on a teak deck that shone almost white in the sun. "Your decks look cleaner than my galley," Hope said. "Is she equipped with automatic holy stones?"

Malcolm returned polite laughter through a thin smile. "Actually, Bill brought some twenty Mexicans with him who do nothing but."

They paused to gaze into the aquarium that formed the ceiling of Tree's lounge belowdecks. Bracketed fore and aft by the main and middle masts, it was as long and wide as a health club swimming pool and twice as deep. Hope tried to see Sally and Tree through the glass bottom, but the water was too busy with darting fish and he could only guess which darkish blob might be Tree sprawled in his giant chair.

"How come that bull shark doesn't eat the yellowtail snappers?" Hope asked.

"I understand it has developed a taste for horsemeat," said Malcolm. "Now *here* is something Bill is mighty proud of."

A massive old anchor rested on the deck behind the aquarium. Its corroded iron flukes and shank and stock wore a thick crust of barnacles. "Looks like his Mexicans are falling down on the job."

With another thin smile, Malcolm pointed out a brass plaque affixed to the anchor, and Hope read, " 'This anchor, weighing two thousand pounds, was retrieved from the wreckage of an unknown Yankee blockade vessel likely sunk by Confederate forces in the Gulf of Mexico.' Unknown?" he asked. "What makes him think it was a blockade ship?"

"Bill's got archaeologists tracing the connection."

An elevator, entered by a companionway behind the traditional helm, took them down four levels. As they stepped out Malcolm handed Hope ear protectors from a rack and took another set for himself. "She's got diesel auxiliary engines to rival a modern tugboat. They're off line when we're under sail, but the electrical generators are plenty loud on their own."

It looked pretty much like other engine rooms Hope had toured, though more brightly lit and impossibly clean. Malcolm waved to four Mexicans who were mopping everything in sight and they waved and smiled back.

In the forward bulkhead, Hope noticed a watertight door, dogged down and marked, NO ADMITTANCE: AUTHORIZED PERSONNEL ONLY.

"What's behind that NO ADMITTANCE hatch?" he asked when they were riding back up in the elevator.

"Support chambers."

"What's a support chamber?"

"For the laboratories," Malcolm explained. "Machine shop, chemical storeroom where the scientists get their glassware, filters, adhesives, batteries, dissecting instruments, dry ice, that sort of thing." He checked his watch. "Lunch—not an event to which one arrives late."

Returning through the painting-lined corridor, Hope could hear the busy noise of many conversations. This had to be the oddest experience he had known at sea, to be so suddenly plucked from the open deck of a small boat that rose and fell at the mercy of the waves and plonked down inside a ship so luxurious he might as well be in a mountaintop hotel. A crowd of people were just taking seats.

In the half hour Hope had toured the ship, the Captain Nemo Lounge had been transformed into a curious blend of college dining hall and private club. Forty scientists in jeans and T-shirts shared a long, narrow refectory table with the ship's uniformed officers. The silverware was actual silver, Hope noted; the water and iced tea glasses, crystal; the china, bone.

William Tree presided at the head with Sally Moffitt on his right. To his left sat the *Star of Alabama*'s captain, resplendent in gold braid. Hope was shown to a chair well below the salt between a taciturn Russian, who wore the elaborate uniform of a *Star of Alabama* engineering officer, and a painfully shy Indian computer scientist who made a visible struggle for the courage to say, "Welcome aboard."

But Hope at least had a chair.

Others, including Wendell—a powerful bodybuilder who had rolled Tree's double-wide throne to the table and cranked the lifting screw to the height of the table—and a dozen or so Mexican servants and Filipino seamen, ate standing at the serving counter, talking quietly among themselves.

Directly across from Hope was a rail-thin American marine biologist with long stringy hair. He was older than he looked, Hope realized, and extremely loquacious, talking a mile a minute as he tore into his fried chicken and okra. The Tree Institute, he told Hope, was a "lifesaver for a guy like me. Academia has gone totally corporate since I was a student; in a big university these days you waste half your time covering your back, another half negotiating layers of bureaucracy, and a third half in meetings. Here, your time is your research time. Period. Bill makes darned sure nobody bothers you. I've gotten more done this year—I'm surveying codfish stocks—than in the past five years at my last job—and I was a tenured full professor. Top of the heap. Well, this is a much higher heap. Plus, Bill pays better. It's all about money. It's just like when the Getty blew away the other art museums. The Tree Institute's investment made it, overnight, the number one place to do top-notch marine science."

Hope admitted that today was the first he had heard of the floating research institute on the *Star of Alabama.*

"Bill's not big on publicity. But those who should know, do know. Bill is paying for his own Manhattan Project for marine research. He started a few years ago and already there's a waiting list a mile long: marine biologists, animal behaviorists, IT guys. If you're the best, Bill will pay you twice—*twice*—what any university offers. What you publish is yours and he shares patents. And if you happen to come from India or Taiwan or one of those places, Bill will get you your green card and set your family on the fast track for American citizenship. He'll get your kids into private schools. He'll get you your mortgage—the man owns his own bank and he just puts it at our disposal. Like the Stones said, he knows what we want, and he knows what we need."

Hope glanced up the long table, where Tree—unable to sit close and thus compelled to balance his plate on the broad shelf of his vast belly—still provided an elegant contrast to the double row of scruffy scientists hunched over their chicken licking their fingers. For William Tree dined with his silverware, wielding knife and fork as fastidiously as a dowager at tea, pausing between small bites to make conversation as he stripped meat from bones. Sally, looking very pretty and thoroughly at home, threw back her head and laughed at something he said.

"Sounds," Hope said to the marine biologist, "like no one ever leaves the Tree Institute."

"Why would they? We've got fish wells, we've got any lab gear we can think of, we've got an IT and computer support staff that would put MIT to shame. They fabricate shark tags that drop off on command to uplink every depth that fish has swum for the last six months. You name it, we've got it. U.S. Navy hydrophones—two-way, unidirectional, omnidirectional—we can record cetacean conversation and play it back at them. We've even got our own deep submersible."

"You have a submarine?"

"Two of them. We've got a four-person deep job good to three thousand feet. Plus Bill bought us a U.S. Navy midget sub—SDV, Swimmer Delivery Vehicle—that was designed for Seal special operations. Excellent for trolling the neuston layer."

"What's the neuston layer?"

"The first layer below the surface. All this equipment allows us to amass real data on fish stocks, pollution effects, climate change, migration patterns. It's an amazing opportunity to do research and really do something to stop the destruction of the seas."

Hope didn't really feel like debating a zealot, but Jesus H., wasn't this former academic old enough to think to ask where the money came from? Or to question the clout Tree's "generosity" gave him over all of these scientists? He could hear Barbara Carey ranting in his head. Then he looked up the table at Sally and he wondered, on the other hand, if the source of the money mattered when good work was being accomplished. Not a thought Barbara would have loved.

"Captain Hope! Captain Hope!" Tree was calling him. "Come up here and visit. Jose, grab his plate."

The windship's German captain rose hurriedly from his chair and left the dining room. A Mexican servant seized Hope's plate and silver, napkin, and water glass and put them at the captain's place, which another servant had cleared.

Hope traded glances with Sally. She looked wired, and Hope had seen enough of Sally Moffitt by now to assume that time out for a leisurely lunch and chitchat, when she wanted to get down to business, was driving her nuts.

"Ah do hope you're enjoying your chicken," Tree drawled. "We don't eat fish aboard the *Star of Alabama*. Somehow when you study the critters and observe their travails, you don't really want to bite into 'em."

"Excellent fried chicken. But I was wondering where you got the delicious salad."

"Jose's brother runs our hydroponic greenhouse, his mother tends our ducks and chickens, and his dad takes care of the milk cow."

"Live food, just like on an old man-o'-war," said Hope, and William Tree beamed. "We try, we surely try."

Hope was struck again by how handsome a man Tree was. And by how rapidly he himself had gotten used to what the numbers in isolation—590 pounds—made sound grotesque. It was not that the hugely bulging figure wasn't grotesque, but that he was so much more—an interesting, charismatic, compelling man.

"Sally's just been telling me about her husband."

"Really?" said Hope, doubting that they would be invited back.

"Have you met him?"

"Only in passing." He looked at Sally, wondering where the hell this was going.

Tree said, "Well, divorce is a terrible thing, but often the best solution. Sally, do you suppose that once the dust has settled you'll still make films together?"

"No," said Sally.

"Too bad. Greg Moffitt's a heck of a filmmaker. I've admired his work for years."

"I've got my own project now, as I was telling—"

"Well, I hope it's unusual. There's a sameness creeping into the underwater nature films lately. I hope you're onto a truly unique approach to your subject. Or a truly unique subject." He added, before Sally could answer, "I've always wondered how he got some of those amazing shots of those turtles' matin' ritual."

"The discomfort factor ran pretty high that time," said Sally.

"Well, I imagine discomfort's how you pay your dues photographing animals."

Sally smiled easily. "The upside is the turtles don't have agents. And we didn't have to get releases signed, either."

Tree laughed. But before Sally could work the conversation back to mating dolphins, he turned to Hope. "I'm curious, Captain, why *Oona*?"

"Beg pardon?"

"They tell me that your sailboat is named *Oona*. I wondered how you settled upon such an unusual name."

Hope felt Tree's undivided attention settle heavily on him, as if the name of his boat was fascinating stuff and Tree couldn't wait to hear more. But Hope sensed something darker. The aimless chatter and the intentionally silly mask evoked a chilling memory of an event far from Tree's splendid dining table.

"I thought that *Oona* was a nice narrow name for a wide boat."

"Well, what do you mean by that, may I ask?"

"Catamarans get a bad rap. Traditional mono-hull sailors think they're ugly."

Tree laughed his rich laugh. The laugh peeled open the old memory and in that context Hope recalled fear. Twenty years ago, a wasteland of knocked-down factories in the gutted heart of what had been a vibrant New England city. New Britain, Connecticut. Or was it Meriden? Couldn't remember, didn't matter. Probably blocked it—an empty field of broken bricks and a black guy his editor had told him to track down. He had tracked him to a meet alone at night in the wasteland, where a mugging felt more likely than information. Dark night, silent but for a nearby interstate. It was

New Britain; he could recall the drive in; and he could still feel the growing apprehension.

Face-to-face, they were talking, like Tree was talking, laughing about nothing, making words to fill the void while they felt each other out.

The black guy wondering if Hope had a gun. He did not: he had a pen and a tape recorder. Or wondering if Hope was wired; he was definitely not wearing a wire. He wasn't a cop, he was a jerk kid on a crappy newspaper that was playing Gotcha! with a politician who deserved better.

Hope recalled wondering, Am I paranoid or racist, but doesn't every sense I have tell me this guy is going to hit me over the head and take my money? Like right this minute on the *Star of Alabama* every sense was telling him that William Tree was bad news and he and Sally could be in big trouble in the middle of nowhere.

Tree was still mining *Oona*. "Oh, I thought it might be your mother's name. Fine old-fashioned name, I believe Geraldine Chaplin's mother was named Oona, was she not?"

"She was," said Hope. He had read a new biography of FDR recently, a charmer, like Tree, who never lost sight of the big picture. Beware of men who know what they want.

"Eugene O'Neill's daughter," said Tree.

"I did have a favorite aunt—great-aunt, actually—named Oona, so I guess that's where I heard it first." He scratched the back of his head where the black guy's friend had hit him with the brick.

"So what is it you like about this catamaran?" William Tree asked, with a smile to include Sally, who was directing an expression at Hope the charter captain interpreted to mean, Will you stop gassing on and let me get back to my film? "If wide is all it is, I'd make a fine catamaran?" he laughed. "But seriously, what would make a sailor court the mockery of his shipmates with an 'ugly' boat?"

"Speed, stability, and space. It's like I'm sailing on a millpond on two very fast sailboats connected by a living room and porch—the bridge deck that connects the two hulls."

"All the comforts of a double-wide house trailer."

Hope shook his head solemnly. "I wouldn't trust a house trailer this far off the beach."

Tree nodded with a rumbling chuckle.

Hope said, "What I didn't fully think through when I bought her was I've got to pay for maintenance for two sailboats, too."

"And a living room and porch."

"At least she's only got one mast to tune."

"You know the old saying about yachts. Have to ask, can't afford it?"

"Fortunately, I never asked—or I'd still be on the beach."

"Well, I'll agree with you there. Too much thinking will stop you from achieving anything."

"Why *Star of Alabama*?" Sally interrupted.

Tree studied Hope's face for a long moment before he turned to answer Sally. "Oh, I was always in love with those wonderful old names from sailing ship days. Don't they just fill the mouth? *Mogul of Bengal. Royal Captain. Star of Bombay.* . . . Maybe I was born too late, but we're from Alabama, so why not sail my very own *Star of Alabama*?"

"It's a wonderful name."

Hope said, "I gathered from the scientist sitting opposite me that you rarely put into port."

"Isn't Dr. Rod a talkative fellow? I thought you'd enjoy it if I set you near someone who could fill you in on what we're doing here. Of course, Rod only joined us recently. He might not see the full picture yet."

Hope said, "What is the big picture? I gather you've created some sort of floating research park. Almost a combination floating Woods Hole marine lab and National Ocean Service."

"Well, that's mighty high praise. I would just say in a nutshell we are cataloging the unusual."

He looked from Hope to Sally.

"The *Star of Alabama is* a windship. We can stay out a very long time, as Dr. Rod noted, because we require so little fuel. In that respect we're very much like a nuclear submarine. And we are also relatively quiet in the water. Compared to a motor vessel. Our endurance and our relative silence allow us to observe phenomena and creatures we might ordinarily never see with engines churning."

"Like what?" asked Hope.

"Whatever's out here—the other morning—I cross my heart and hope to die, this is the God's honest truth—a white whale sidled right up to that port."

"A white whale? Like Moby Dick?"

"Nooo. A little feller, no more than twenty-five feet, thirty feet."

"Probably a minke whale," said Sally. "They're very inquisitive."

"If he was, he was some kind of mutant albino. For a minute he and I were eyeball-to-eyeball. And that, Sally, is the sort of thing you should attempt to film if you ever hope to get the sort of notice your husband got when he was in his prime."

Hope looked at Sally, expecting her to take the bait—for bait it was, unless he was really misreading this. It almost sounded like Tree knew about the dolphin. Sally said, "I know I've got my work cut out for me if I'm ever going to make a name like Greg Moffitt."

Hope felt a sort of affection for her as he watched her stick stubbornly to her guns. He said to Tree, "That scientist I was talking to? Rod. He claimed this has become the leading marine research facility in the world."

"Well, he would like to think that, I'm sure. Having just joined us, he's a mighty happy camper. And it's very flattering to think that way; something of an exaggeration—though we try. We surely try. And we've got our work cut out for us, because our rivals tend to feed at the public trough, while we support ourselves by ourselves. We don't take government handouts, we don't accept grants. We pay our way. And in that we are in the forefront. Mark my words," he said with sudden vehemence. "We are at the beginning of a new order. It's our years coming up now. Decent folk, folks of means, will take charge of saving the environment. I mean, heck, look at me. I could be sitting pretty behind a big old desk down home making money hand over fist like my granddaddy Tree; or I could sit around doing darn all, like my wealthy friends who were born in the end zone, bragging they made a touchdown; instead, I'm using my God-given advantages to support marine research, helping species thrive."

He laughed and said, "Of course there are certain members of my family who say, 'That's good, William, you just stay out there and play with your fishies and we'll take care of business here at home.' I am not universally missed."

Hope said, "I read an article about a Tree family that Washington insiders call 'the Forest.' Are you in that forest?"

Tree rolled his eyes. "Oh, Lord, that article. What was that other phrase they bandied about? Forest and . . ."

" 'Shadow government'?"

Tree gave a jolly roar. "They set back the good name of noblesse oblige two hundred years."

Hope joined in his laughter. "They certainly were impressed by how many of you go into public service."

Tree sobered. "We serve. But it would be a mistake to think we're a charity. We develop technology and energy for the marketplace and the nation's defense."

"Which did the article exaggerate the most, the forest? Or the shadow government?"

"I'd say the forest," Tree replied affably. "Afghan warlords can't hold a candle to us when it comes to feuding."

"And the shadow government?"

Tree's smile never wavered. "We know when to close ranks."

"Well, it's really interesting to meet you," said Hope. "I thank you for lunch. Sally, we should be getting back to the boat."

As Hope expected, Tree protested, "Oh, don't rush off. We're just getting to know each other. Don't you pay any mind to my political ranting. Just comes over me now and then. Sally, let's just visit. Tell me more about your film."

Hope stood up. "I'm going up on deck, see how my boat's doing."

"Go right ahead."

"Is it okay if I have another wander around?"

"Enjoy yourself," said Tree and he turned to Sally, saying, "I just get wound up sometimes, and before I know it, I'm talking a blue streak."

Sally said, "Don't worry about it. You reminded of my husband—but in a good way. I have to ask you, are you personally involved with the Tree Marine Park in Florida?"

Tree seemed to swell larger with pride. "Involved? I built it."

"No! You're kidding. I love that place."

Hope gave her a look that she was laying it on pretty thick. Who the hell else would have built the Tree Marine Park? But a steely glint in her eye told him to get lost.

He headed up to the open air.

The main deck was bathed in sun and wind, a welcome change from the depths of the Captain Nemo Lounge. He climbed three steps up the ratlines of the aftermast shrouds for a look at *Oona*. The cat was skimming along beautifully in the hands of the Polish sailor, who had jib and main trimmed smooth as the wings of a supersonic jet. But she looked very small.

He descended to the deck immediately below the main deck. Under the multiple eyes of the ever-present surveillance cameras, he walked a long corridor of open doors past computer workstations and laboratories. The men within—he had yet to see a woman—were tapping keypads, staring at screens, peering into microscopes, cooking test tubes, or staring dreamily into space while pressing headsets to their ears.

He spotted Dr. Rod hunched over a monitor and knocked on the door and said hello. The ichthyologist returned a distracted wave that sent him on his way.

On the next deck down he found a lavishly appointed dive room, with compressors for filling tanks with mixtures of exotic deep-dive gases. They had a hyberbaric decompression chamber for divers who got the bends. And he counted at least ten rebreathers like the one Sally had risked arrest for. The ship also carried a fleet of motorized underwater sledges.

Deep in the windship's hold he discovered their four-man submarine and an underwater sally port to launch the sub straight down from the bottom of the hull. Then he noticed a strange odor. The ship aromas of oil, salt, and painted steel mingled with a curious reek of animals. The scent grew stronger down a long corridor at the end of which he found another hatch stenciled, NO ADMITTANCE: AUTHORIZED PERSONNEL ONLY.

There was no lock. No need for one with all the security cameras storing videotape of every entry and no way for an intruder to escape the ship. Hope quickly undogged the top and bottom latches and swung the door open.

It was a second underwater sally port, a fifteen-foot chamber too small for the submarine. Hanging on hooks from the bulkhead were several strange harnesses. When he stepped closer, he found them fitted with what looked like an enormous syringe. It was considerably longer than a turkey baster and nearly as big around, except where it tapered to a needle-sharp point.

"Sir!"

He hadn't heard them coming up behind him. Hope turned, smiling easily. A ship's officer he hadn't seen before and two burly Chinese seamen.

The officer sounded Australian. "What are you doing sneaking about?"

"What sneaking?"

"Can't you read?"

Hope pointed at the ceiling, which was ribbed with pipes and wires. Aimed down, sweeping the hatch, the corridor, and the hold, was a triple-lens security camera. "They're all over the place. So if I go anyplace I shouldn't someone will be along shortly, like you are."

"We'll take you back to Bill."

They didn't exactly grip his arms, but they walked so close that they might as well have, marching from the hold up a deck and back to the Captain Nemo Lounge.

Tree kept the four of them waiting in the doorway while he explained to Sally the superiority of free enterprise over government bureaucracy: "My business–government philosophy could be called 'proactive procurement.' In proactive procurement qualified people in industry develop new technology to present to a government and military that are too bureaucratic to know what they need. Right now, you've got the government making rules against cloning, for instance, as if you could legislate against scientific progress. What a waste of resources. Hell, a man ought to be able to clone what he wants. I always thought it would be kind of wonderful to breed a predatory hummingbird. Watch that little devil spearing robins."

Sally winced.

Tree laughed. "Don't you find it's fun to let your imagination wander. . . . No, point is, things are changing for the good, like I said. Folks appreciate that we deserve inexpensive gasoline because the right force prevails. For fifty years my region sent visionaries to the Congress—even the worst liberals were held in check—now we're in charge—there you are, Captain Hope. Sally and I were about to send out the cavalry."

"I'm afraid I annoyed your security guys. Looking around."

"They'll forgive you," Tree smiled. "Thank you, Richard. I'll take him from here. . . . By the way, Captain Hope, while you were wandering, Captain Grandzau informed me there's a blow coming up. He suggests you might do best to head back to your boat now. I'm terribly sorry. I'd been kind of hoping we could extend this into dinner."

Hope said, "That's a neat little submarine you've got down there."

"I've been fixing for a while to go on a treasure hunt. There's a sixteenth-century Spanish gold ship two miles down I've had my eye on since a pipeline crew spotted it on their remote TV."

"Sunken treasure two miles deep?"

"We've got the dive technology aboard the *Star of Alabama* to recover treasure deeper than that. Did you see my Yankee anchor? We hauled that up from a mile and a half."

"Could you use this same equipment to explore for oil?" Hope asked.

"Not on this ship," William Tree laughed. "That's the sort of thing my granddaddy did. I've got bigger fish to fry."

He shifted his affable smile from Hope to Sally. "Now, Sally, before you go, let me repeat my offer. We will happily fund any underwater wildlife film you want to make that we find interesting. But not, I'm afraid, your breeding habits project. Segregated sexes getting it on could be mighty interesting to some people, but it's just not our style. I hope you understand."

"I do and I really appreciate it," Sally replied, struggling to appear just as affable. "Thank you for lunch. I had a wonderful time."

"So did I," echoed Hope. "Thanks for having us."

"Well, we must visit again," said Tree as if they were from neighboring country clubs instead of floating on the Sargasso Sea three hundred miles south of Bermuda. "Now, Sally, here's my card."

Wendell the bodybuilder leapt closer, pawing a card from his jumpsuit.

"You get in touch anytime, e-mail, whatever. I'm sure

Captain Hope'll let you use his single-sideband radio if you want to say hey."

"Anytime," said Hope. "Where are you headed?"

"Well, Azores, for the moment. Back to 'Bama for my birthday and then, if things work out, into the Caribbean to check out that treasure ship. But you never can tell about us; we change course any time the boys see something they think we should investigate. We're a bit like the Gulf Stream: we come up from the south, we meander, we swirl off, we stop like eddies. Fact is, we go most everywhere and at nineteen-twenty knots, get there pretty quick."

"Almost five hundred miles a day."

"We try."

They crouched under flying spray on the bow seat of the tender that raced them back to *Oona*. Sally stared at the water as if willing the big dolphin to suddenly rise alongside for its close-up. Hope eyed the way *Oona* was riding down at the head. He decided to shift a dozen heavy cases of soda and water and canned food farther aft. The blow that the *Star of Alabama*'s captain had predicted looked to him like a norther and he wanted to get the bows up where they belonged before the storm struck.

Second Mate Starskowitz and the Filipino deckhand were waiting on the dive steps, anxiously watching the sky. They handed Sally and Hope aboard, transferred quickly into the tender, and roared back to the *Star of Alabama*.

The great ship shifted its yards, shaping an acre of sail to the wind, veered east-northeast, and began angling swiftly away from *Oona*. Quite suddenly, David Hope and Sally Moffitt were alone again in a little boat.

12

HOPE SAID, "I'VE GOT TO shift some weight. You can give me a hand if you like."

She was passing him six-packs of Coke when he noticed that her eyes were glistening.

"What's wrong?"

"That bastard."

"Who?"

"Tree. How dare he praise Greg right in my face."

"I think he was just trying to give you advice."

"Well, I don't fucking need that kind of advice."

"Why didn't you tell him about Ishmael?"

She wrestled two more cases out of the locker before she said, "I was going to. It was on the tip of my tongue. But . . ."

"But what?"

"You'll think I'm paranoid."

"Maybe not."

"No, forget it."

Hope said, "Look, I felt like something was wrong, too. The rich guy wants something. And when a rich guy wants something from a poor guy, you've got to ask, what's his problem?"

Sally shook her head. "No. That's not what I'm talking

about. And it's certainly not why I didn't tell him about our dolphin. I'd rather keep filming the animal—if it comes back—on my own as long as my money holds out. I can always go back to Tree in the future, if you'll continue to help me."

"You didn't sense something off about Tree?"

"No. Aside from being the fattest person I've ever seen in my life, he's a typical foundation guy—well aware that he's got the power to write the check."

Hope went on deck for another look at the sky. The big windship was visible to the east, eight or ten miles away, and seemed to be sailing on a course parallel to *Oona*'s. He reefed the jib a few rolls and looked automatically for the big dolphin. Nothing. Although it would be hard to spot in the gray seas making up. It could be a hundred yards off and he wouldn't see it unless it jumped or spy-hopped. With another look at the heavy sky, the darkening sea, and the distant sailing ship, he went below to shift some more weight.

Sally was playing her videotape on the big-screen TV. "What," Hope asked, "was the 'real' reason you didn't tell Tree about Ishmael?"

"I'd have taken a chance and told him if I thought he'd back me. But I was afraid he'd hand it over to Greg."

"Now I do think you are paranoid," said Hope.

"Yeah, well, fuck you. I don't care what you think."

"Well," said William Tree, finishing off a plate of pigs-in-blankets, "of all the times for a couple to give each other the silent treatment—are you sure that microphone is working, Ah Chi?"

"Yes, Bill." The Filipino electronic engineer who had accompanied Second Officer Starskowitz as riding crew on *Oona* had changed out of a borrowed seaman's costume into a black velour jumpsuit some twenty sizes smaller than

Tree's. A lithe, wire-thin, alert man, he stood anxiously in front of the red chair. Tree was drawling orders into a sat phone that connected him with Washington, Mobile, and New York, while covering the mouthpiece, repeatedly, to pepper Ah Chi with questions.

The long-lens masthead-cam monitor showed *Oona* as a white speck on the horizon. The radar repeater screen pinpointed a range of nine miles. Which meant that the two vessels were testing the limits of the five-watt surveillance transmitter that Ah Chi had wired into a dome light in the catamaran's saloon.

"A kick in the behind has a bigger impact than a limo-load of lobbyists," Tree finished a conference call with two cousins on Capitol Hill. "Report back tomorrow. Love you both, but don't make me come looking for you."

He placed a quick call to assure a cousin by marriage who managed the Tree Marine Park that the EPA had been persuaded to drop an annoying environmental investigation. Then he rested the sat phone on his belly and donned a headset to better hear the fading surveillance signal.

"Ah Chi. Where did you say you found their log?"

"In the bilge, under an engine."

"Now that's about as paranoid as a person could be unless they had a lot to hide. And what had they written?"

"I told you, Bill—"

William Tree cast a wintry eye on the engineer. As a child in the southern Philippine jungle, Ah Chi had wired radio bombs for Islamic separatists. But a scholarship to Rensselaer Polytech and the largesse of Tree employment were turning him lazy. "Tell me again," he ordered in tones that promised savage retribution, "what did their log say?"

Ah Chi noted from the corner of his eye that Wendell the weight lifter was stirring. He apologized, "Sorry, Bill. All it said was that they had seen a very large dolphin and the woman is filming it."

"You didn't by any chance think to read back several days in their log, did you?"

"No, Bill. I just looked for the dolphin, like you said. Since they left the BVI."

"Well, that's a shame."

Pentagon people on his payroll had informed him that David Hope's sailboat was present when the USS *Vermont* went haywire. And now here David Hope was again. Once was coincidence. Twice, enemy action? Except that, so far, Tree had been unable to draw a connection.

Nothing in Hope's background suggested that he was any more complicated or dangerous than the Navy had concluded when they boarded him—an aimless drifter who happened to live on a sailboat. While reports from Florida and the BVI indicated that Miss Sally was also pretty much what she appeared to be: a bright, lively woman done wrong by an aging fool.

Thoroughly disgusted with the paucity of conversation aboard *Oona,* and annoyed with himself for not more closely micromanaging Ah Chi, Tree started to remove the headset. A sudden clatter stopped him. He raised a heavy hand.

"Wait! I hear something."

A half hour had passed since the cassette recorder had taken down a vehement Sally shouting, "Yeah, well, fuck you. I don't care what you think." Now David Hope broke the silence. It sounded like he was calling to her from another part of the boat.

"You know what I think?"

Tree grunted with as much amusement as he could muster at the moment. Master of his little vessel Captain Hope might be, but the poor devil sounded like some miserable husband in a dreary tract house trying to appease a disappointed wife. Times like these, Tree thought, he was glad to be alone. He heard some more banging around before Sally finally called back, *"No."*

"I think that whole Tree Marine Institute is a front."

"For what?"

"Under the guise of saving the environment they can sail that ship into protected waters where no one's allowed to explore for oil."

William Tree howled with laughter. "Oh my Lord, what an imagination."

"What did they say, Bill?"

"Shhh!" The signal was fading. Tree punched a button on his phone. "Captain! Steer two points west. Stay within nine miles of that boat."

Suddenly, Sally Moffitt was standing right under the microphone booming, *"Where did you get that idea?"*

"A few things." Hope's voice, too, came in closer, as if they were standing face-to-face in the middle of the cabin. *"The deep-sea submersible. All the satellite positioning gear. I saw some very sophisticated sonar."*

"That's all fish stuff."

"Which they could be using to sonar-map the bottom. . . . What if I told you that I think they have dolphins aboard?"

"They'd eat everything in the aquarium."

William Tree pressed the headset firmly to his ear. Hope had put his unchaperoned wanderings to good use.

"Not in the aquarium. They've got a well belowdecks."

"What's a well?"

"An opening in the bottom of the ship. It's enclosed within bulkheads that rise above the waterline to keep the sea out. Same principle as Oona's *daggerboard truck."*

"It would be used to launch divers instead of dropping them over the side."

"Or dolphins."

"Did you see dolphins?"

"No. They were probably swimming away from the ship."

"Did you see slings for lifting them out of the well?"

"No."

"So you're just guessing."

"No. I smelled them. I smelled animal, belowdecks. Not fish. Mammal. Like in a zoo."

"Really?" Sally Moffitt sounded suddenly very interested, Tree thought. *"They use their echolocation to penetrate the sea bottom to root food in the mud. But I don't see them sonar-mapping for oil."*

"You tell him, sister," Tree chuckled.

Whatever Hope's lame answer, the signal drifted, faded, and was lost, and when Tree heard Hope's voice again he was saying, "I'm going to take in sail."

Tree removed his headset, but left the recorder running. About time Hope reduced sail. He could feel the *Star of Alabama* respond to a changing sea, pitching majestically on deepening swells and taking on a stately roll. He motioned Wendell to help him out of his chair, thinking he'd enjoy going up on deck to watch the sailors furl the topgallants.

Wendell extended a mighty arm, but not before he had planted his feet firmly on the deck. When the *Star of Alabama* rolled, Tree's nearly six hundred pounds presented a mass that once moving was hard to stop.

"Why'd you let them go, Bill? What if they find out what's going on and tell someone?"

"In that unlikely event . . ." He grunted to his feet, and clung to Wendell's hand. ". . . Ah Chi has made it possible for us to give them radio trouble. Haven't you, Ah Chi?"

"Yes, Bill."

"How'd he do that?" asked Wendell.

Ah Chi looked at Tree. Tree said, "Tell Wendell how you did it."

"When Bill radioed them for lunch, we also transmitted a front-door coupling virus. First when they answered on the SSB and another when we called back on the VHF."

"Like a computer virus?" Wendell asked.

Ah Chi yawned. *"You* could think of it that way."

"Are we boring you?" Tree asked dangerously.

"No, Bill. I'm just trying to explain to Wendell that it's

not exactly cutting-edge technology. Compared to what we're working on, it's just last-century military electronic warfare stuff. But for Hope's off-the-shelf civilian gear, it's bye-bye radios when you give the order to activate the virus."

Wendell followed the exchange with his eyes. Like a cat, Tree thought, watching birds through a dirty window.

"Well heck, Bill, why not sink their boat and be done with them?"

Tree answered his handsome and not overly bright body-builder with mock exasperation. "Wendell, Wendell, Wendell. Knowing that you spent your recent youth in various forms of well-deserved detention, I find it unfathomable that you can commingle such cynicism and such naivete in the same body."

"Come on, Bill, I'm just asking why not sink them now, to be on the safe side?"

Tree laughed. "Because," he explained, "I don't know yet whether they're a coincidence or an enemy. Or an asset."

Oona's barometer fell sharply in the hour after they returned to the boat. The high, thin cirrus cloud cover of the early afternoon thickened into dark gray rolling slabs. The sea was making up, turning a pewter color as the wind backed north and blew harder. A sudden gust clocked twenty-five knots. *Oona* buried her port bow.

David Hope cranked his mainsail down into the boom and hanked on in its place a short, heavy storm trysail that he hadn't had out of the locker since he'd left the Gulf of Maine the November before last. Twice already he had furled the jib until it was rolled to storm jib size. But when a harder gust banged the thin sliver that remained, he furled the jib completely. Then he came about, onto a starboard tack, altering course a hundred degrees from the north to west-southwest.

Sally started up from the cabin, then stopped at the washboards that Hope had installed to keep seawater from cascading below, and frowned at the almost total absence of sail, though the boat was still making seven knots. Then she cast a suspicious eye at the compass.

Hope explained before she could open her mouth. "This gale will be moving on a southeast track. I'm hoping to get behind it. But if it gets really hairy we'll have to turn around and run with it."

"Back?"

"The good news is northers don't usually last too long."

"What's the bad news?"

"It would be a good idea to put your foul weather gear and your safety harness on now. There's trousers and jackets in a locker in the dive room. I think you'll find your size in yellow."

Sally nodded dubiously, obviously not pleased with the change in course. But after looking around for a while at the gray seas, she said, "I know we just had lunch, but maybe I should make some peanut butter sandwiches and coffee. In case we want fuel. Would you like some?"

Hope took the gesture as a peace offering and said, "Excellent."

When she brought the coffee she was wearing her safety harness.

Hope said, "You asked if I saw slings for lifting the dolphins? I'll tell you what I did see. Harnesses."

"What kind of harnesses?"

"Heavy nylon and Velcro straps that could fit around their heads."

"To strap on telemetry gear maybe, to track them by radio signal."

"No, these things were attached to a huge needle—a hollow needle like a hypodermic."

Sally's eyes widened. "You saw that?"

"Several of them—I read something somewhere about

training dolphins to be weapons. You know what I'm talking about?"

Sally nodded. "Greg told me that many years ago, way back in the Cold War, both the United States and the Soviet Union were investigating the possibility of using dolphins as weapons—exploiting their intelligence and willingness to learn tricks. Greg claimed that the U.S. Navy actually used them in Vietnam. Apparently both sides had projects called 'swimmer-nullification programs' where they would train dolphins to attack commando scuba divers. It was really weird, but the idea was the animal would wear a giant hypodermic needle attached to an air tank. When the animal stabbed a diver with the hypo, a trigger would inject the diver with a blast of compressed air that would kill the man with an embolism."

"Why would Tree do that kind of research?"

"I'm sure he's not. Greg said the entire program was pretty much a bust. There have got to be better, cheaper ways to fight commandos. . . . The navy first got into it when they taught trained dolphins to carry messages from the surface down to a scuba diver to save decompression time. But now with modern underwater radios, who needs it?"

"And as strong and smart as the animal is, it can't carry heavy weapons that would do real damage like a bomb."

"It was a twisted idea from the start and I can't imagine anybody bothering anymore."

William Tree sprawled on his back on a specially reinforced deck chair, sipping bouillon and staring up at the sails where six seamen struggled to furl the main upper topgallant. "Bravo!" he cheered as they manhandled the wildly flapping Dacron. "Malcolm, what's it blowing up there?"

Malcolm, who was manning one of the hydraulic sail-control pods, checked the topgallant wind-speed counter. "Nearly a full gale, sir."

Tree flicked on his handheld VHF radio. "Nice going, boys. You'd have done John Paul Jones proud."

Wendell climbed up on the ratlines to see over the rail, and squinted west where the sunset would be painting the sky if gloom hadn't settled so heavily. Even when the *Star of Alabama* rose on a swell, David Hope's forty-five-foot catamaran was barely distinguishable from the whitecaps. When the ship sank in a trough, the sailboat vanished from sight.

"Hey, Bill?"

William Tree barely heard Wendell. Distressful thoughts were closing in on him: He was rich, he was powerful, and he was well practiced at getting his way; no man he knew could manipulate people better than he could; he should fear nothing. But he was dreading attempting to explain this current mess to the matriarch of the Tree clan. And his finely honed survival instincts told him that he should not dodge Martha Tree much longer.

"Hey, Bill?"

"What is it, Wendell?"

"Do you suppose maybe it's following them?"

Tree was galvanized into a seated position by the sheer brilliance of Wendell's insight. He stared at the bodybuilder in astonished admiration. With fifty scientists aboard, it was the weight lifter who had figured out the problem. Out of the mouths of babes.

"That is a very interesting thought, Wendell. Well done— why don't you and I go warm up and get ourselves a bite to eat." He extended a hand, requesting he be helped to his feet. Signaling the several Mexicans loitering to provide backup, Wendell jumped down from the ratlines, gripped Tree's hand, and timing the ship's roll with exquisite precision, hauled his boss upright.

Tree hailed Malcolm, who was gazing up anxiously from a hydraulic control pod, hurriedly furling more sails. "Tell the boys for me they did the ship proud," he called as the group shuffled slowly toward an elevator.

"Hey, Bill?"

"What is it, Wendell?"

"*Why* do you suppose it's following them?"

"I don't know. But I do know that I've got a shipload of marine biology geniuses in my employ and one of them had darned well better find out."

13

AS WILLIAM TREE'S SERVANTS HELPED him belowdecks where a warm Jacuzzi bubbled, David Hope and Sally Moffitt were bracing for a long, cold night. Even with the catamaran's bows riding properly, thanks to the weight they had shifted toward the back of the boat, *Oona* was starting to sneeze. The wind caught the fine spray forced up from the tunnel and flung it over the cabin like hail. Hope took a stinging faceful when he ventured from behind the dodger for a better look at the stormsail. He turned away and ice water poured over the collar of his foul weather jacket and down his back.

Off to the darkening east, the *Star of Alabama* had disappeared.

He turned forward again to inspect the seas and debate strategy. This didn't look so bad, yet, that he would be forced to run before it. As long as the catamaran didn't take too much of a pounding running across the seas, and as long as the wave crests weren't so big that they'd threaten her stability, he could stick to this west-southwesterly course around the back side of the depression.

Oona's self-steering was holding its own thus far. It would be a smart move to go below and rest while he could in case the gale made sea conditions too heavy for the self-steering and he had to pull a marathon session at the helm. He checked his decks one last time in the fading light: no loose lines; none chafing; the deflated dinghy lashed bow, stern, and athwartships to six strong through-deck bolted pad eyes; the stormsail sheet wrapped cleanly around its winch; the sail itself bellying smooth and hard, but not straining.

He worked his way around the outside of the cabin, tightening the dogs that clamped down the Lexan storm shutters that protected the cabin windows. Suddenly, he felt an icy shiver creeping down his spine that had nothing to do with the dousing of salt water. A strange feeling compelled him to look off the port beam. He thought he saw something dark moving alongside. He jumped down to the cockpit and switched on the work lights, which illuminated the decks and sea around them. At the edge where the light met the dark, thirty feet from the boat, the big dolphin's head thrust from a foaming white crest.

For a while outside of time, the feeling would not let him go that the animal's eye was seeking his through the gloom. As if a curtain were swept aside, the wind, spray, breaking seas, and lowering dark seemed to disappear, leaving only a pool of work lights, with him in the cockpit and the dolphin in the water. His gaze locked on its empty eye and, almost as if it had caught someone staring at it, the creature slid beneath the surface.

Hope shoved open the hatch and yelled, "Grab your harness. He's right next to the boat!"

Sally, who had taken to stashing the video camera next to the companionway, scrambled over the washboards, with her camera in one hand and the harness in the other. "Thirty feet off the port side a second ago," Hope said, helping her into the harness and reaching around to buckle it.

She shrugged him away. "Is the mike ready?"

"Yes, ma'am. Rigged on the wind vane."

He snapped her onto a jackline he had rigged down the center of the cockpit.

"Starboard side!"

There on the right, emerging from the water, only to dive again, straight at the boat. It went under the widespread hulls and emerged again in the bright light. "You sweetheart," Sally called. "Come to Mama. Come to Mama."

Dark and shiny, it porpoised alongside *Oona* in quick, low jumps and then surged ahead of the boat and cut sharply across the bow.

Sally whipped the camera from left to right, cursing the dodger when it blocked her view. One eye in the viewfinder, one staring across the top of the camera, she focused on the water, waiting.

"He's going under," said Hope, who had jumped onto the cockpit seat. "Coming up port side . . . here he comes."

Sally was ready and hit the RECORD button as the creature rocketed up from a crest. "Beautiful," she whispered. "I love your lights."

Down it went with a big splash. The wind drove the spray into the dark. The creature broke surface, porpoised alongside the boat, and cut across the bow again and again in what soon revealed a pattern of diving under, surging ahead, and slicing across the bow from port to starboard.

"It's like he's trying to herd us," said Hope.

"They hunt like that in groups," Sally said. "They drive fish in a circle, or crowd them up on the beach."

"Let's hope he doesn't have bigger friends who'll eat the boat."

"He's trying to make us turn," said Sally. "He's trying to steer us."

"Where?"

"He wants us to turn to the right."

"Sorry, Ishmael. We're not turning to the right. Not 'til this gale blows past."

Sally lowered her camera. "Don't think I'm crazy, but . . ."

"But what?"

"There are many instances of dolphins guiding people away from danger."

"Legends."

"Stories, some definitely true, about—don't look at me like I'm a space cadet. This is real."

"I've heard those stories. But tonight, the danger is there, in the north." He pointed right toward their former course north. "Safety is where we're going in the southwest."

"Dolphins are incredibly sensitive to their surroundings."

"I don't dispute that. But he hasn't seen the weather fax and I have."

"You're making a joke. The weather fax could be wrong."

Hope shook his head. "The barometer is reading just what it predicted and the wind is blowing like it said it would and the seas are moving exactly like I'd expect from the report. Do you feel that swell? That's from there." He pointed north again. "They've been building all day. Which tells me that the gale is coming from the northwest, just like predicted, and it's heading southeast, just like predicted. Watch—I'll show you."

He stood up and faced the wind. Then he pointed with his right arm, straight out from his side. "I'm facing the wind, which is blowing counterclockwise around the depression that is causing this gale. I point at a right angle. There. There's the center of the depression. North. It's headed southeast. If I go north I get pummeled. Which is why we are heading west-southwest. No matter how much Ishmael wants us to go north."

"For three thousand years people have reported instances of dolphins saving humans."

"I'm not questioning his motives, I'm questioning his judgment."

"You could be wrong. What if its amazingly refined aural

and electromagnetic receptors tell it that the storm is shifting? Since your last weather fax. What if it senses that the worst danger has shifted to the west? Shouldn't we accept its help?"

Hope looked at her earnest face. Then he looked at the seas frothing in the pool of the work lights. Full darkness had fallen, the night so black they could have already been swallowed unknowingly by an oversized killer whale.

"And even if he is not communicating with us," Sally insisted, "wouldn't he himself swim the less stormy course? He's got to surface four times a minute for air. Won't he avoid the heaviest seas?"

Hope believed in the weather fax. He believed in the barometer. He believed in the information underfoot—the subtle signals from the swells that *Oona* was transmitting through her decks. He believed in his own finely tuned senses. And he believed that his years of experience sent him messages through his gut that were usually true. But the problem was that those same years of experience reminded him that forty or fifty miles could make the difference between an unpleasant night or drowning. The sea had a long history of making wrong out of right, and brutal ways to punish arrogance.

"Okay. We'll give it a try. We'll turn north."

"Thank you," said Sally. "And you won't regret it, I promise. I just know that he's really trying to help."

"Would he care to give me that in writing?"

Sally laughed. "I'll ask him."

"Okay, we're going to come about. Shouldn't be too bad with the one little stormsail. You're going to release that sheet when I tell you and I'll haul in this one. But I'll start the engines first. We don't have a lot of way on us, so we'll want the props running in case we have to push her around."

He did as he said and was glad of it. As he steered to starboard, into the teeth of the wind, some gusts shifted suddenly from the east and the sail refused to fill. The boat began falling backward. The wind shoved it back, while the swells, which were driving out of the north, lifted the bows as if doing their damnedest to stand her on her stern.

Muttering a quiet, if not entirely calm, "Son of a bitch," Hope engaged his port engine and gunned it forward. Still, she hung in irons—locked dead to the wind—and quite suddenly began falling backward.

He reversed the starboard propeller and hit the diesel for all it was worth. The propellers churned, the port prop cavitating wildly as she lurched into a trough and raised her port hull. Then, slowly, they began to bite, hauling her across the wind until the sail filled and she staggered ahead on a port tack. He left the engines idling in neutral, a precaution that later might save their lives.

"I think I see him ahead of us," said Sally. "Ohmigod!" She shouldered the digital camera and stepped boldly into the spray, rolling tape. From the helm through the streaming dodger windows, Hope saw the dolphin jump. Twenty feet ahead of the bows, so suddenly close that if he were driving a car he'd have stomped on the brakes. It cleared a crest and danced on its tail like the first time he'd seen it on a calm Caribbean dawn.

"He's happy we're on the right course," Sally called.

It looked to Hope more like a victory dance. The animal had gotten its way. He engaged the self-steering, made sure it would hold, and went below to the comparative quiet of the cabin for a look at the barometer. It had fallen two-tenths of an inch the last half hour. The depression was getting deep and his gut worried that they were sailing deeper into it, too. The wind speed was about the same twenty-five knots. Although while he watched the indicator, a gust clocked forty. He glanced at the weather fax receiver. Nothing new had come in. No major alarms. Or were they bouncing around too much to catch the radio transmission?

With the engines idling he had plenty of juice to power

the SSB. He switched on the radio, hoping for an update on the weather. The Bermuda weather guy was just signing off. He tried to bring in a shore-based American station but the atmospherics were not cooperating. The closest he got was St. Thomas, six hundred miles astern. Just as the announcer finished describing a balmy, trade wind evening, *Oona* took a nasty hit on the port side that practically threw him out of his chair. He hurried up to the cockpit before another big one overrode the self-steering.

The seas had grown larger in his brief absence. No big deal, yet. But the wind was starting to blow the tops off the crests. Time to ship the dodger before the wind shredded the fabric.

Sally was still peering into the gloom ahead of the work light, raising and lowering her camera when she thought she saw the dolphin.

"What are you doing?"

"Securing the dodger," he said, folding it to the cabin top. "Before it blows away." He held it down with his body as he wrapped the canvas with sail ties and secured the frame to the pad eyes he had installed for that purpose. Now every time *Oona* dipped a bow, the cockpit was doused with cold spray.

Sally said, "I can't really see him anymore. But every now and then I think I get a glimpse. So I know he's there."

"Can we assume," Hope asked, "that he'll have the courtesy to inform us of a change in course?"

She flashed him a smile and it occurred to the charter captain that of all the many clients and guests he'd had aboard, Sally Moffitt took the least notice of heavy seas, breaking waves, and blowing spray. After her initial bout of seasickness in the Anegada Passage, now she might as well be coated in Gore-Tex for all she seemed to mind cold and wet.

For an hour or so it appeared that Ishmael was right. Hope stayed at the helm, steering for twenty minutes, then letting the wind vane give him a rest for five. The wind didn't decrease speed, but it didn't go up much, either. In that time, of course, the seas kept growing, but it would take the wind many hours—all night, in fact—to build them to maximum heights. Nor did the wind shift direction, so they remained relatively orderly.

The fourth or fifth time he tried to hand control the boat to the auto-helm for a rest, an enormous gust shrieked through the rigging and swatted her off course. The boat skidded downwind onto a beam reach, which caused her to accelerate lethally. Hope lunged for the helm, headed up to spill the wind, and got her under control.

"Fair warning," he told Sally, who was standing beside him. "No more auto-helm."

"Do you want me to take a shot at a steering?"

"I'm okay." A dark night was no time to teach her the niceties of dodging crests and steering out of troughs.

She ducked below and returned with hot coffee.

"I checked the barometer."

"Falling?"

"Three-tenths."

"Ouch." He'd been eyeing the windspeed indicator. Now it was topping thirty knots. A Beaufort scale Force 7. Quaintly called a "near gale." If it were daylight they would see breaking crests and white foam streaking the surface. "Any sign of that damned fish?"

"Mammal." Sally raked the water ahead through the long lens of her camera. "A flicker. Could be him. . . . Do you want to change course?"

"A little late for that. I'm afraid we're committed."

14

THE WIND WAS ROARING MORE loudly by the second and Sally had to yell to be heard. "But why can't you still sail around the back?"

"I'm not sure where the back is anymore. Besides, if I fall off the wind she'll be sailing a lot faster than is safe and taking these seas smack on the beam, which is definitely not safe."

"You said you could turn away and run with it."

"Not my first choice. I'll have the same speed problem if I try to run. It's not like we've got a five-man blue-water racing crew aboard. At least butting into it like this I can control our speed and pray the seas don't get too crazy."

Sally stowed the camera, took his binoculars, and searched for the dolphin. Probing the light margins ahead of the bow, she said something that Hope couldn't hear over the wind.

"What did you say?"

She raised her voice. "I hope I didn't talk you into something stupid."

"I'm an adult. I'm old enough to make my own stupid decisions."

An hour later the seas were growing steep and *Oona*

started pounding. Hope steered closer to the wind to slow her down. She lost too much way to steer. But when he headed downwind to let her speed up, the pounding started again. The starboard hull was taking the punishment, slamming into the faces of waves, then dropping into their troughs. With each drop, she pitched forward, tilting onto her nose.

By midnight Hope felt his strength draining from his limbs. He needed rest and he longed for the relative warmth and quiet of the cabin, but he couldn't risk leaving the helm for even a moment. Sally, whom he had ordered below, kept popping up asking if he needed anything, and the next time her anxious face appeared at the hatch he asked her to bring him an amphetamine from the medicine locker. "It's got a combination lock," he called. "Thirty-seven, thirty-seven, fourteen."

She looked worried when she brought him the pill and a fresh water bottle, but all she said was "Why the lock?"

Hope steered around a vertical sea, drove the boat through a soft crest, and swigged down the speed. "I had a druggie client once," he explained. "Don't worry, I'm not a junkie, I just need a boost."

It had been over a year since he'd taken one and it kicked in nicely and brought with it the preternatural sense of clarity, tinged with a lunatic impression of wisdom which he tried to ignore.

"Are you hungry?" she asked.

"Yeah, more chocolate, more peanut butter."

When she came up with a giant Reese's, she said, "You actually look like you're enjoying yourself. Or are you stoned?"

"Both." He dodged another steep sea just in time and nearly lost it when the boat headed so far downwind that it leapt ahead like it had been kicked. The starboard hull started feeling light. The port bow buried. He wrenched her upwind.

"Good to be alive," he told her. "I'm hoping to stay this way."

When dawn broke yellow, he felt closer to dead than alive. But he began to hope that they had come through the worst of it. Sally announced that the barometer was rising—which probably meant more wind before things settled down, but at least the process of settling down had begun. And while the seas were big, there was real space in the troughs between them, and they were taking on gentler contours.

"I'm just going to set the auto-helm and put my head down here on the bench. Stay with me, please, and yell if you see trouble." He watched the auto-helm behave itself over several seas and lay back and closed his eyes.

"What did you say?" asked Sally.

"I feel like I'm a hundred years old."

"I don't see Ishmael."

"Maybe we got lucky and ran over the son of a bitch."

He slept for a full half hour. Then he checked the weather fax.

"See this? He took us right through the worst of it. We'd have been better off west-southwest. He did his damnedest to sink us."

"It's a bit much attributing malice to an animal."

"I'm not saying he's malicious. I'm saying that the dolphin took us where he wanted to go. He has a mind of his own." Hope cast a weary eye on the still-rolling sea. Streaked with foam and spindrift, it looked sullen, as if disappointed it hadn't swallowed *Oona,* though willing to wait for another try.

"I think the more interesting question is why did he want us to come with him in the first place."

Sally looked at him.

Hope said, "Any ideas?"

"No. But it's a good question. If he wasn't trying to save us."

"One more saving like that and I'll trade my boat for a house in the desert."

Hope slept a while and woke finding the sea much calmer except for a mountainous swell that posed no threats compared to the short, breaking sea they had encountered earlier. He ate some and then sat blearily at his nav station.

Assuming the creature did have a mind of its own and wanted something, what did it want? That was very likely unknowable. But there was a better question, more to the point and possibly more knowable: Where was it going?

He opened Chart 108, *North Atlantic Ocean, Southeast Coast of North America*. A yellow left parenthesis shape marked the land that rimmed the western side of the ocean from the Virgin Islands, up the U.S. coast, to Newfoundland. To the right the chart was entirely white, the open North Atlantic, in the middle of which sat Bermuda.

He penciled in *Oona*'s current position three hundred miles to the southeast. Then he marked the approximate spot south of Tortola where he had first seen Ishmael, and made another mark in the Anegada Passage where he had next seen the animal with Sally. He connected the three marks with a pencil line and found them nearly parallel. Then he placed his parallel rulers on the line between the Anegada Passage and their current position and walked the rulers to a compass rose. Fifteen degrees. The dolphin had been swimming a steady north-northeast course since he had first sighted it. If it continued on that course it would swim off the chart before they passed Bermuda.

He unrolled a faded Number 11 Chart that he had picked up for a buck in a junk shop: the larger-scale *North Atlantic Ocean, Northern Part*. The vast area it depicted was bounded on the west by Cape Canaveral, Florida, to Baffin Island and by Morocco to Norway on the east. The giant island masses of Greenland and Iceland plunged down from the north like a pair of mismatched teeth.

He penciled in *Oona*'s position southeast of Bermuda. On this larger-scale chart Bermuda looked like a fly speck near the lower left-hand corner. Then he walked fifteen degrees from a compass rose and drew a line that angled up and up and up the North Atlantic until it soared off the chart at a point between Iceland and Greenland.

The Denmark Strait was where the *Vermont* had been headed for war games, before her breakdown. Interesting, except that a course variation of a single degree west or east would veer the dolphin into a Greenland fjord instead, or one of the volcanic islands off Iceland. A two-point change, into the Norwegian Sea. Three, west to Newfoundland or east to Ireland.

He called Sally and showed her the chart. "Here's where we met him. Here's where we followed him. Here's approximately where he's going if he stays on the course he's been making since we met him. Though he could end up anywhere between Greenland and Iceland."

She traced the line to the top of the chart. "How far is this?"

"Four thousand miles, if he keeps going. It's cold up there. Does he mind the cold?"

"That depends on what breed he's most like, but probably not. Most of them have plenty of blubber and it's really a matter of what they eat. Killer whales go everywhere. But we have no reason to believe he'll stay on this course."

"Except that he has so far, including straight through that gale. He's sticking to it like a ferryboat."

Sally said, "It will make it easy to follow him if we know that this is his course."

"What do you mean?"

"Well, we can stick to the same fifteen degrees and even when we can't see him, we'll know he's near."

David Hope stood up and stretched. His head spun. He was still feeling a powerful afterbuzz from the speed he had dropped last night. He was stiff and sore and not entirely inclined to trust his senses at the moment.

"But," he said, "if that animal doesn't change course he is headed into the high latitudes of the North Atlantic. It means sailing into iceberg waters around Greenland. It's cold, it's blowing up a gale, and depressions rampage through there like clockwork. So I'm sorry, but the North Atlantic in early spring is no place for an overloaded forty-five-foot catamaran manned by one professional sailor and one filmmaker."

"Wait, wait, wait. One step at a time," said Sally. "How far are we safe? I mean, we're fine now, aren't we?"

"No thanks to our navigational consultant."

Sally bent over the chart. She found the Maine coast and touched it with her finger. "Where's Camden?"

"Above Portsmouth."

"Oh, right here. What is this, about forty-four degrees?"

"Right."

She traced a line due east until it intersected with the north-northeast projection Hope had drawn. "Forty-five degrees west. Let's round it off to an even forty-five north, forty-five west."

"Round what off?"

"Let's follow Ishmael as high as Camden, Maine, and agree at that point to turn west to home."

"Follow him another two thousand miles?"

"Not quite."

"That's all the way to the Flemish Cap."

Sally clutched her heart and cried in a frightened little-girl voice, "Oh, no. Not the Flemish Cap."

"What?"

"The movie?"

"What are you talking about?"

"Didn't you see *The Perfect Storm*? No, no, Captain. Not the Flemish Cap."

"Oh . . . right." Hope looked at her, shocked. "You made a joke. I never heard you make a joke."

"I used to make lots of jokes. I was a mimic in school. Do you want to hear Madonna?"

"The movie made the good point that the Flemish Cap is very far from Maine and our friend seems to be swimming even farther east of it. Are you asking me to follow him another two thousand miles?"

"Not quite two thousand."

"And then kiss him good-bye and sail fifteen hundred miles west against the wind?"

"She's a catamaran. She's fast."

"Not against the wind."

"You'll tack. What do you call it, you'll reach, right? You'll go fast one way, then fast another, and we'll be home before we know it."

"Across the Grand Banks full of fishing boats and fog."

"Can't we loop around them, down here?"

"Through shipping lanes? That should be fun. Undermanned express container ships. Not to mention stray icebergs. Ah"—he tapped the chart—"and here's an opportunity to butt heads with the Gulf Stream."

"Is all of this sarcasm a way of telling me that it is not safe for *Oona* to sail those waters?"

Hope hesitated. "Well, I certainly wouldn't want to go any farther than forty-five north."

"We won't. I promise."

"Whether or not you get enough tape by then?"

"There's no point to shooting tape if we drown in the process."

"Sensible." Hope smiled. "I'm surprised."

"David, all I want to do is shoot enough for my demo tape." She grabbed his hand. "Be partners! Join me. I'll pay what I promised, but share this with me."

"No. No thanks. One of us needs a clear head."

"We both have clear heads. We're clearheaded people."

Hope shook his. "I mean the sort of clear head that comes with detachment."

"This is too big for one person. I need support so I can put my main effort into shooting."

"I'm not a film producer."

"You're a can-do guy. You've got what it takes: you're observant, you're alert, you're organized. Sure, the boat seems a little run-down—I'm not criticizing; it's a lot to handle for one person, alone. You keep your tools and dive gear in tip-top shape."

"I told you," said Hope, "I'm deeply committed to bringing the majority of my clients back alive."

She didn't hear a word. "Now I know you're not ambitious, but I can teach you what—"

"I promised I'll take you to forty-five north," Hope interrupted in grimmer tones, thinking he would sail her to the Arctic if it would get her off this business stuff. He didn't want a business partner. He wanted a woman to wake up with each morning.

"What if it's more than three weeks? I can't pay you any more. I don't have it."

"I'll take an IOU. When you raise the money to make the film you can pay me back at the same weekly rate."

"That's too generous."

"No, it's not. It's good business. I can use the money and I certainly trust you to pay me when you get it."

"I may never get it."

"You'll get it. I know you. You're an all-or-nothing person. You'll get the job done. And when you become a famous filmmaker, you'll hire me for your next project. You'll pay me and someday you'll return the favor."

"Why do you trust me?"

"My gut tells me that hijacking a boatload of diving and film gear was an aberration."

Sally laughed. "Of course it was. And it was my stuff anyhow."

"But no farther than the Flemish Cap. And not even that far if the weather gets crazy."

Sally said, "I looked at the weather fax. There aren't any depressions coming this way."

"Today," said Hope. "You'd be surprised how fast they move."

"But we're okay for now."

"As long as you understand that I'm the final judge of when it's time to cut away."

"Speaking of cutting away, I've got to shoot B roll, establishing shots and wild sound."

"Of what?"

"I need boat scenes to cut away to and to establish where we are and what we're doing and how big we and the boat are compared to Ishmael. So if we agree we're going on to the Flemish Cap, I've got to get to work."

"What do you want me to do?"

"Watch for Ishmael."

"Okay."

"And run the boat."

"That's what I'm here for."

"And make lunch."

"Half-hour nap, first."

He awakened in ten minutes, drenched in sweat. Another nightmare, totally undefinable, and he lay on his back with hands behind his head trying to figure out what set it off. The boat was skimming along on a nice, smooth, even keel, rising and falling on rhythmic swells. Cloud-washed sunlight was streaming softly through the companionway. All he could recall of the dream was dark and red.

Then he heard Sally banging something heavy in the cockpit. He swung his feet to the deck, splashed cold water on his face at the galley sink, dabbed it dry with a paper towel. Whatever it was banged again and he went up to investigate.

"What the hell—"

"Oh, did I wake you?"

She was standing on the side deck, sans safety harness, wearing a wireless headset. Arms raised over her head, breasts straining her long-sleeved cotton work shirt, she was about to throw the dinghy's mushroom anchor overboard.

"Don't do that," said Hope.

"It's tied on," she answered, indicating with brisk explanatory nods the tangled coils of anchor line at her feet, the camera on a cockpit cushion with its RECORD light winking red, and the wireless microphone clamped to the autohelm wind vane to point down at the water beside the boat.

"Don't throw that anchor."

"I need a splash. For wild sound? Remember I told you I need to edit in sound? I'm trying to record the splash."

"There's a loop of line around your foot. The boat's making twelve knots. If you drop the anchor overboard that loop will take you with it like Captain Ahab when he harpooned Moby Dick. You'll hit your head on the hull and drown before I can save you because you're not wearing your safety harness. Don't throw that anchor."

Sally looked down and stepped hastily out of the errant loop. "Damn. I'm sorry. I didn't notice that—would you?"

"Would I what?"

"Drop it while I record?"

Hope pulled a safety harness from the cockpit locker, buckled into it, pulled out another for Sally, and traded it for the anchor. While she hanked on, he shook out the tangled line, flaked it so it would uncoil freely, secured the bitter end to a cleat, and passed the anchor under the lifelines. "Say when."

Sally unclamped the mike from the wind vane, knelt on the deck, and aimed the mike at the water rushing past.

". . . Three . . . two . . . one . . . When!"

Hope tossed the anchor and it plunged into the water with a satisfying *plunk*.

"Excellent," cried Sally. "Let's do another."

Hope hauled in the dripping line.

"That was really great," said Sally. "This time let's try to get it a little closer to the hull."

Hope dropped it closer, but not so close that it would mar the paintwork. "Wonderful," said Sally. "Let's do another."

Hope threw the anchor six times before she thanked him warmly. As he stowed it, he said, "I have the funniest feeling we're being watched."

"Ishmael?" Sally grabbed the video camera and replaced the tape with a fresh blank. She looked down from the sea only long enough to scribble "Splash sound" on the cassette box.

"I don't see him," said Hope, who had grabbed the binoculars. "But he's out there, I can—there! Ummm, maybe."

Hope felt sure the animal was near, but if he was, then he was flaunting his capacity to snatch air while barely breaking the surface. They caught many glimpses through the afternoon as they held their north-northeast course, but no confirmed sightings and nothing to shoot, as supposed blows dissolved in whitecaps, collapsing crests, or shifting sunlight.

"He's playing with us."

"Let him. We're busy."

What Sally dubbed the "SS *Oona* Foley Studio" had scored an easy success with the anchor splash. But recording a credible re-creation of the heavy thump that shook the decks when the fleeing dolphins and their pursuer crashed onto the dive steps was proving a lot harder.

They started by dropping cockpit cushions on the deck. The sound was too light. They tried pounding the bench's seats with pillows. Too hollow. They pounded the cushions with pillows. Better. Sally played it back through the stereo and they listened carefully.

"Dull," said Hope.

"Too dull," Sally agreed.

Hope whacked the cushions with an oar, to no avail. Whacking pillows didn't work, either. He swatted the hard belly of the mainsail with the flat of the oar.

"Too sharp."

He tied up a bundle of *SkinDiver* and *Alert Diver* magazines and dropped it on the deck.

"Close."

"But a little 'whackish.' "

"Definitely whackish."

They broke for coffee and oatmeal cookies. "Isn't this kind of fake?" asked Hope.

"What's fake?"

"Making up noises. You're supposed to be shooting a documentary, which is like nonfiction, right? Like a newspaper instead of a novel. But we're faking the noise."

"We're representing what we heard."

"We're making it up."

"We are *re-creating* the sound that the dolphins made when they crashed into the boat. I'm not a journalist. It's not like a news crew wiring a truck to blow up and shooting the explosion to prove that the gas tanks are dangerous."

"The audience is trusting you to tell the truth."

"Have you seen or heard me try to make a sound that's different than what you heard?"

She had him there. "Not yet," he said. "But it seems . . . dishonest. I don't know, dishonest."

Sally said, "When I was first out of school—"

"What did you study?"

"I minored in marine biology."

"You're a scientist?"

"No, no, no. I just got my bachelor's; then I found a job doing research for an underwater nature documentarian."

"Greg."

"Before Greg."

"Wait a minute. If marine biology was only your minor, what did you major in?"

"Stop interrupting. I'm trying to make you understand that re-creating sound is not faking."

"Sorry, but when you ask a person what she studied in college and she tells you her minor, you sort of wonder why she's hiding her major."

"Psych."

"You're kidding."

"My mother was a very unhappy person. I thought I might become a shrink."

"What brought you to your senses?"

"I was having too much fun diving—and they invented Prozac and she got a lot happier—which might help you sleep, by the way."

"Thank you, Doctor."

"Getting back to the moment? . . . The documentarian sent me to London to the BBC. They have the world's greatest sound library. If it's a noise, they've recorded it, compiled it, stored it, and can locate it. They probably have twenty kinds of explosions, thirty doors closing, flowerpots falling, waterfalls, rain, subways—they've even got every imaginable kind of fart, if you can believe it, all cataloged and labeled. Anyway, one day I was snooping around and I wandered into a studio where they were foleying in the nat sound for a nature film about a meerkat."

"Don't they record the sound when they shoot the film?"

"No. They've got their hands full just capturing the image. And you might be a hundred feet away with a telephoto lens."

"What's a meerkat?"

"A sort of mongoose in South Africa. It has stripes. It's really cute. Anyway, the sound guy watching the film on a monitor was hunched over a tin baking pan filled with sand and every time this meerkat moved he would scratch his fingernails through the sand. I was shocked. I was young and dumb and absolutely blown away by the BBC and their amazing library and here's this guy wearing a vest and a bow tie scratching sand with his fingernails. So I asked, 'How do you know what a meerkat sounds like?'

"He looked at me like I was a cockroach. Then he kind of straightened up and huffed in his belly and puffed out his chest. He had an accent right out of Monty Python: 'Young woman, I happen to be the world's leading expert on the sounds made by meerkats.' "

Hope laughed.

Sally said, "I slunk away. Even though I wanted to ask—and would have if I'd been older—if you're the leading expert, are there lesser meerkat sound experts who can't quite cut it in the big leagues? But I promise you, David, that I will never, ever put in a sound in this film that's any different than what we heard. Do you believe me?"

"Absolutely."

"Do you have any more ideas how to make that thump?"

The cockpit cushions were covered with vinyl. They tried pounding the saloon couch cushions, which were covered in a tight tweed. "Sounds like somebody beating a carpet."

They tried beating a scrap of carpet Hope kept around for people to wipe their feet on when the boat was at dockside. "It doesn't have the depth."

Finally, thoroughly fed up with the lack of results—and with the effects of the long, hard night beginning to wear them down—Hope went below to make some dinner and Sally retired to the cockpit with her camera in hopes of Ishmael surfacing. He had thawed steaks earlier and now, with a cool nip to the evening wind, they seemed like a particularly good idea. He washed and trimmed and seasoned the meat with salt and pepper. When he went up to rig the charcoal grill in a hanger over the leeward side, Sally, who earlier was sure that she had seen Ishmael lurking close by, worried that the animal had disappeared again.

Hope started the engines for hot water and for the electricity to power the microwave to bake the potatoes. He washed the last of the greens he had bought in Road Town, separating the surviving leaves for a small salad. Then he opened his best bottle of wine, a fine Côtes-du-Rhône some kindly soul had left behind.

The fire would be hot by now and he started up the companionway with the steaks. *Oona* chose that precise moment to challenge a slab-sided wave that dropped her sharply into a trough. Hope and the steaks went flying back into the cabin.

When he picked himself up and made his way to the cockpit he saw Sally standing on the afterdeck, tentatively aiming the camera behind the boat. Hope said, "Don't turn around. Can you just point the mike down behind you at the floor of the cockpit? Don't turn around."

"I won't turn around." Sally removed the microphone from the camera and pointed it back down behind her.

"Rolling?" asked Hope.

"The camera is on." She pressed one hand to her headset. ". . . three . . . two . . . one."

Thuuump!

She whirled around. "That's it! You did it—what's that?"

"It was dinner."

"Do it again." He was still holding the other steak.

"That was yours. This one's mine."

"We'll wash them!"

". . . Three . . . two . . . one."

The steak landed beside the first one with another satisfying *thuuump!* And later, after they had hosed down the deck and rinsed, reseasoned, and grilled the steaks, Sally Moffitt raised her glass to David Hope.

"I want to make a toast."

Hope put down his knife and fork and picked up his glass. "Toast on."

Sally looked him in the eye. "This is a strange time for me. And sometimes a wonderful time." She smiled down at the table that Hope had set with candles and cloth napkins, then glanced left and right out at the sea. The night was black in the east, though the dying day still rimmed the west horizon silvery yellow.

She cocked her glass at Hope like a fighter pilot's thumbs-up and grinned. "I would like to propose a toast to the world's leading dolphins-crashing-into-a-catamaran-sound expert."

*   *   *

"Well," said William Tree. "It appears they've made up."

He picked shrewdly through a bowl of mixed nuts, then touched his intercom to speak to the bridge. "Nicely done, Captain," he said affably, though he was feeling anything but affable, which was hardly surprising considering the disaster taking shape. "We'll stay within nine miles for the night—no lights."

15

"WHAT IF THEY SEE US on radar?" asked Wendell.

"They'll think we're just a big, nasty ship. But they won't know what ship. Nor will they know how nasty—pipe down, now, they're talking."

He switched the transmitter that Ah Chi had secreted in *Oona*'s dome light to speakerphone just in time for them to hear David Hope say, "If you want to catch some sleep, I'll wake you at midnight if you want to relieve me on watch."

Sally Moffitt said, "Good night. Excellent dinner, thank you."

William Tree said, "Well, that's that, unless he's in the habit of talking to himself, darn it all—Wendell, you go about your business, now, I've got to make a call."

"Aunt Martha?" asked Wendell.

"Good night, Wendell."

Wendell hung his head and lumbered out. Tree watched with some affection. The bodybuilder, who usually floated so lightly on his feet, was slumping off like a child who'd been ordered to bed before dark.

He picked up a secure satellite phone. But he just couldn't work up the courage to dial yet, so he put it down on the broad shelf of his belly and touched, instead, his intercom.

"Dr. Rod, would now be a convenient time for you to drop down here for a visit?"

It was a question that allowed only one answer and Rod appeared in the Captain Nemo Lounge in sixty seconds. He looked awful in rumpled sweats and had the red, slitty eyes of a man who'd been staring at a computer screen all day and all night. Tree could see the effort that went into Rod's attempt at a cheerful "How's it going, Bill?"

"Perhaps you can tell me. Where is my killphin?"

Rod looked too weary to fence. "In a nutshell?"

"In a nutshell."

"We can't find it."

"That's an empty nutshell, Rod."

"We'll keep looking," Rod said.

"At lunch, yesterday, you played the naive scientist convincingly. Captain Hope actually quoted you to me. You came across as something of an idiot savant, if not a plain darned fool, and I'm beginning to fear that it didn't take a lot of acting skill on your part."

"I resent that, Bill."

"Rod. The Tree Institute for Marine Research has created a powerful new naval weapon that can stop a nuclear submarine in its tracks."

"*I* designed it," Rod shot back.

"From my concept of a unique and extremely valuable living weapon."

"Please, Bill, I'm too tired for games."

"You allowed my unique and extremely valuable weapon to escape."

"I had plenty of help," Rod shot back. "It was not entirely my fault the animal escaped."

"You cannot simultaneously blame the help and hog the credit. With my money and the full backing of my research institute you helped implement my concept for a weapon that not even Jules Verne could have imagined."

Rod yawned. "We could debate our individual roles all

night if you like, Bill, but my time would be better spent rallying the troops to get the goddamned animal back."

Rod's elaborate yawn sealed his fate. The chief scientist had gotten mighty big for his boots and Tree had been fixing for some time to cut him down to size. He shifted in his giant chair to open the drawer in the side table that held his intercom, saying as he strained to reach inside, "You have lost a seminal weapon."

Rod watched him fish around inside the drawer. In a sudden rush, Tree's hand emerged gripping a long-barreled antique revolver.

"What?"

"My killphin feeds itself, defends itself, and attacks so stealthily that the first the enemy knows he's been attacked, his systems are going down faster than a cheerleader on the team bus."

"Bill, what is that?" The muzzle drifting his way looked wider than a garden hose.

"This is a six-shooter—a seminal weapon, too," Tree answered. "An earlier great leap forward. While the inventor still loaded it in a manner similar to the muzzle-loading weapons of his day—tamping cap, black powder, and ball into these chambers—he gave us six shots before we have to load it again. The idea launched a thousand improved means to deliver deadly force, culminating in the multiple-ICBM warhead. It probably seems a piffling achievement to a computer jockey like you, but it was cutting edge in its time, and when you meet its inventor in Heaven you will find you have much to talk about."

Rod was listening with half an ear, acutely aware that the shockingly wide barrel was swinging toward his forehead. This was not the sort of thing he had signed on for. His fast-track career had attracted many patrons among the very rich, and menacing attendants were a common accoutrement of those who could afford excessive self-regard. So William Tree was not the first man Rod had encountered who maintained bodyguards like the knuckle-dragger Wendell and the ship's piratical seamen. But in the ten long years they had worked breeding the killphin, William Tree had never before made even veiled threats to life and limb.

Tree said, "I see you thinking, 'He can't shoot me. That old firearm would wake the entire ship.' I see you thinking, 'Even Bill can't get away with murder.' "

"You need me, Bill."

"I need you to find the killphin. If you can't, then I don't need you. And in fact your role in its creation makes a damned nuisance of a connection to me if the worst happens."

"We can find it."

"I've lost faith, Rod."

"Bill, for Christ's sake. You're talking nonsense. I can find it. We're bringing its telemetry back up to speed even as we sit here. But, frankly, even if I couldn't, you *can't* get away with murder. There are ninety people on the ship who'll know you shot me. They're not all Third World peons. You have to go ashore sometime, and when you do, they'll turn you in. So can the cheap threats and let me get back to work." The scientist started to stand. Tree's gun moved with him and the resolution in the fat man's eyes made him sink fearfully back into his chair.

Tree said, "Everything you said would be true in a rational world. But you are forgetting the one thing you've never understood about my ship."

"What's that, Bill?"

"Every man on this ship is beholden to me for something he considers the most valuable thing in his life, whether it be his child at boarding school, or his mansion on the hill, or something as mundane as his brothers' and sisters' green cards, or as extraordinary as continued access to the databases that hold his life work. In other words, what landlubbers safe in their beds might call absurd is normal here."

"Meaning what?" Rod blustered.

"Your body will be out the garbage chute in five minutes."

Rod felt his hands trembling uncontrollably. The garbage chute was as green as Greenpeace. The windship's plastic, glass, and metal trash was compacted for recycling at the next landfall. Only biodegradable organic waste spewed from the back of the windship, and only after machines had sliced it into readily digested fragments.

"Now perhaps you'd like to leave behind a sealed envelope with your guess as to which one of those men might report to someone or other that they suspect that your disappearance was untimely."

Shaken to the core, fear spiraling out of control, Rod raised pleading eyes, only to have his gaze lock on the gun barrel pointed at his face. He spoke in a desperate rush. "Look at the facts, Bill. First, the killphin was programmed to swim north-northeast to the Denmark Strait. It's doing that, headed straight for Submarine Romper Room. Second, it carries a submarine sound-signature library that your people copied from the Pentagon—which identifies Russian, British, and American nuclear submarines by the noises they make underwater, which means it should have steered clear of an American submarine. Third, you —"

Tree's eyes glinted dangerously.

"I mean we. We arranged a surprise real-world 'sales demonstration'—a controlled, limited disruption of a British nuclear sub. Your idea, right?"

"A kick in the behind," Tree said, "far exceeds the impact of a limo-load of lobbyists."

He had developed the weapon at the family's own expense, knowing that the Pentagon would be forced to buy it to prevent some foreign navy from obtaining the power to render nuclear submarines helpless.

But the "sales demo" had gone catastrophically haywire. The killphin had stopped obeying command signals. It broke company with the ship and vanished until it attacked an American submarine in the Caribbean.

Rod resumed babbling. "Despite the fact that it went nuts, Bill, something is keeping it on course. Conclusion: inertial guidance is still operating. That's our big advantage. It won't let us near it. But it will let them. Ergo, we follow the sailboat."

Tree said, "I'm giving you a deadline."

Rod's entire body sagged with relief. A deadline, even an impossible deadline, meant that he wouldn't die tonight.

"When?" he asked.

Tree gazed up at the lighted aquarium. "The sailboat could peel off for Maine at any minute."

"We have to stop them, Bill. If she's shot video of it, she could blow the whole thing."

"If they turn away, we'll invite them for a last supper. . . . As for you, Rod. You get my killphin under control before he crosses fifty north."

The numbers raced through Rod's mind. Seventeen degrees of latitude. A thousand miles. The killphin had been averaging 150 miles a day. "That's only one week."

"Unless he ramps up to full speed."

Rod raced back to his laboratory.

Tree had Philip deliver a plate of boned ribs. When he was done, he felt as empty, but there was no avoiding his satellite phone. Fear could drive a man like Dr. Rod a long way. But fear couldn't surmount the impossible if the task were truly impossible. So it was with a mildly trembling finger that William Tree touched number one on the speed dial.

She answered with a thin, reedy "Hello."

"Hello, Aint Martha," he drawled in warm, sweet, buttery tones.

"William! I haven't heard from you in ages. Where are you—in the jailhouse?"

Tree laughed long and loud at her ritual greeting. "No, ma'am."

"Well, what are you up to?"

"Oh, I just wanted to hear your voice, Aint Martha."

"Oh, go on."

"Well, I've been kind of busy here, working hard."

"Enjoying success?" she asked, an edge creeping into her voice.

"We're catching up."

"When, William?"

Martha Tree's sons and nephews and grandsons included a United States senator, two governors, a long-serving deputy secretary of defense, numerous intelligence officers, a general, an admiral, and an even dozen oil executives and Washington lobbyists. That William Tree was her personal favorite did not exempt him from what the men of the family called the Martha Question: Does your action advance or retard the Trees' interests?

"Well, it's hard—"

"William, have you at least figured out exactly where you went wrong?"

"Yes, ma'am. Sort of . . . Near as we can make out, it picked a fight with another loner."

"There's another? You told me you'd made only one."

"No, no, no. No, ma'am. Only one." (A smallish lie, easily defended if she ever caught it: additional hybrids were nearing maturity—she couldn't expect him to put all their eggs in one basket in a decade-long project—but none had been "enhanced," yet.) "No, ma'am. I just meant some other big angry bull of a thing. Probably some mean old tiger shark, and those two went at it like a pair of tomcats."

The infectious chuckle that rumbled from William Tree's cavernous chest was contrived to invite his listener to remark upon a titanic clash of six-thousand-pound, twenty-foot sea creatures battling to rip each other's guts out. Aunt Martha remained silent, forcing Tree to run with the ball.

"Clearly, the tiger shark lost, Aint Martha. But it seems that our killphin suffered some damage during the fight."

"What sort of damage?"

"Oh, he's fine, near as we can make out."

"Well, I've been wondering, William, isn't it possible it would contract some sort of infection and die and bleed to death, or something?"

"He's got such an immune system he could cruise gay bars, pardon my French."

"What sort of damage?"

Crux, thy name is Martha. "Well, he does seem to have lost some of his telemetry support."

"Telemetry support?" she echoed, and he realized he had blundered into patronizing her, which was a bad mistake. "Telemetry support sounds like a fancy word for antenna. So you can't radio your Frankenstein anymore, is that what you're telling me?"

"His transmitter's working fine. We're getting a whole cartload of data from the electrodes in his brain. On the other hand, it would be fair to say that he no longer responds to our commands."

"What do you see it looking at?"

"Nothing yet, ma'am. We are not receiving thalamus data yet."

"So it swam off again?"

"Well, yes, except that perhaps it's acting a little more purposefully than 'swam off' might imply."

"Purposefully?" Her tone, William Tree worried, could have chilled enough beer to fill the Cramton Bowl for the Hornets playoffs.

"Well, all the work on it we did aside, there's no denying we must have given it some elements of a mind of its own."

Aunt Martha cut him off sharply. "In other words, with a mind of its own, it escaped. It wasn't let loose. It let itself loose?"

"As would any caged creature."

"Well, at least it's still just a dumb animal. Perhaps, with a little luck, it will just swim away and vanish in the sea. Is that likely?"

"Well, it's still an animal, Aunt Martha. But I don't know

whether it's accurate to call it dumb. It knows what it wants, and it's fixing to get it."

"Dammit, William, stop pussyfooting around! What does it want?"

"It seems to want another submarine, Aunt Martha."

There was such a long silence that Tree, again feeling forced to say something, blurted out the obvious, "Which is pretty much what it was designed to do."

That elicited deeper silence until Tree asked, "Are you still there, Aunt Martha?"

Aunt Martha said, "I am flabbergasted. When other caged creatures turn themselves loose they don't hunt submarines. Good Lord, William. You have really done it this time . . ."

"Now don't you worry."

"You are talking about agents of the Tree Institute who report directly to you being responsible for accidentally sabotaging a nuclear submarine manned by a hundred American sailors."

"It could be British this time. There'll be UK boats at the war games, too."

"American or British makes no difference. We are discussing nuclear submarines that could be bearing enough missiles to destroy many cities. My God, you'll slaughter more people than—" The old woman stumbled, unable to come up with a suitable comparison on the scales of mass murder.

"We're fixing to stop him," William Tree promised. "I've got every scientist on the ship working on it and I've a pretty fair connection on my own. I think it's our big break. He's been following this little sailboat for some darn reason and—"

"William, I will tell you right now, I may love you, but I will do whatever it takes to protect the family from the fallout of your scheme."

"Now wait one minute, Aunt Martha, you encouraged me to pursue this thing from the beginning. You saw its potential and you gave your full support, for which I am mighty, mighty grateful. In fact, it would not be fulsome to acknowledge that this project would never had taken off without your support and approval."

"You'll find neither in writing."

Tree felt as if the sea had crashed through the viewports. For a while the only sound he could hear was the startled breath wheezing through his overburdened lungs. No letters. No e-mail. Not even, he realized with a frightening skip of his heart, a single word recorded on the telephone. Over the course of ten years, all their discussions had taken place outdoors at Mandalay, Aunt Martha's Gulf Coast estate. Over tea. Alone in her gazebo. Just the two of them. The white-haired Southern matriarch and the favorite fat nephew chattering as happily as jaybirds in a cherry tree.

"Aunt Martha, that statement smacks of betrayal. But I will regard it as no more than hot words in the heat of the moment."

"If your killphin attacks another submarine, you are on your own."

"This is a hell of a time to pull the rug out from under—"

She cut him off. "Good-bye, William. If we speak again it will be when you report that you have solved this problem."

"We will speak again within a week. I promise."

Her voice softened slightly. "I'm aware of the gravity of the situation. The family resources are still at your disposal."

Tree hung up smiling.

He flung his huge arms wide, pounded the deck with his slippered feet, and yelled to the fish swimming above his head, "Thank you, Aunt Martha!"

He had talked the old woman out of his worst fear. She had left open his lines of communication to his Tree cousins in the Pentagon, the NSA, and the CIA who could access data streams from satellites and Atlantic sonar. He still had his eyes and ears.

16

PRACTICING DISUSED SKILLS WITH THE sextant, David Hope took several sun shots to fix *Oona*'s position three hundred miles northeast of Bermuda, which put them a thousand miles east of Cape Hatteras, where the Gulf Stream turned its powerful drift east across the ocean.

Oona, too, was veering eastward. Assuming that Ishmael stuck to his course—and nothing the creature had done in the past suggested it wouldn't—when they crossed the latitude of Camden, Maine, they would be fifteen hundred miles downwind of their ultimate destination.

"Might as well spend the summer in Ireland," Hope muttered at the chart table.

"What was that?"

Hope jumped. Lost in the chart, he had forgotten that Sally was just across the cabin, editing on her laptop, which was plugged into the TV through her DV VCR player.

"I said it would be easier to sail to Ireland if that damned animal doesn't change course."

"Ireland is beautiful in the summer."

"Too many tourists. I'm going to catch some sleep. Do you want lunch first?"

"David, look at this."

He crossed the cabin, braced himself against the deepening swell on a ceiling hold, and peered over her shoulder. Raw Ishmael tape was playing in a window; the rest of the screen looked impossibly busy with time lines that represented video and audio. "Why's the picture so grainy?"

"I'm zoomed in for a close-up. Do you see that?" She fingered her trackpoint so that her cursor arrow pointed to the big dolphin's back. "What do you see just behind its dorsal fin?"

"It looks like a scar. Like tooth marks."

"I'm not talking about that. He's got a few scars. Scars are common. They get bit by sharks. They heal quickly. Look at this." She moved the cursor in a tight circle.

"What's that black thing?"

"That's what I'm asking you."

"I don't know. It's probably just something on the tape."

"It's not. Look at this shot." She clicked another point on the time line and a different picture formed up. She zoomed in. Again, despite the grainy fuzziness of the picture, he saw the same black line jutting from Ishmael's back, just behind his dorsal fin.

"What is that?"

Hope studied it. "Weird . . ." He moved around, and looked from several angles. "I once saw a huge swordfish that had a harpoon sticking out of its back. It had somehow escaped a fisherman."

"Could that be a harpoon?"

"What's left of one. It's not long. Unless it's very deep inside him. Except, if it's that deep it would have killed him."

"You'd think its body would reject it."

"It could have been hit recently. Or maybe the head has barbs, which hold in the flesh."

"That poor animal."

". . . I'm not sure it is a harpoon. The shaft—if that is a shaft—looks awfully thin. Wouldn't we have seen a harpoon when it came in close?"

"Everything happened so fast."

"Or he was harpooned after he attacked the dolphins."

"Who out here would have thrown a harpoon at him?"

"What if he was riding a ship's bow wave and some bored sailor took a shot at him?"

"I'll play back the tapes."

"I still think it looks too skinny for a harpoon—hey, maybe it's a crossbow arrow."

"What do you mean?"

"A biopsy dart—you know, like scientists shoot for taking a flesh sample."

"But biopsy darts are pulled out for a sample."

"Maybe it got stuck in him. Maybe it went in too deep and it got stuck and the retrieval line broke."

Sally played back every raw tape from the first she had shot in the Anegada Passage. Each time she blew up the picture by zooming in, they saw the slim black object sticking several inches out of the animal's back.

"It's been there all along."

Remembering something he had read, Hope thumbed through his dolphin book. "See? Look at this. They've strapped antennas to dolphins."

"For tracking," said Sally, leaning close to peer over his shoulder. "But ours doesn't have any straps."

Hope's book had an artist's illustration of a small torpedo-shaped transmitter with a miniature whip antenna.

"So let's say the technology has improved and they could implant the radio under his skin. Then all you'd have visible would be this little antenna."

Sally didn't like it. She argued that Hope's suggestion made no sense at all: even if a biopsy dart had lodged in the animal it would have fallen out by now, while no transmitter small enough to implant under the skin could have enough batteries for electrical power to last more than a few days. A harpoon with a barbed head was by far the more likely object protruding from the big dolphin's back.

"I see your problem," said Hope. "And I sympathize."

"What? What problem?"

"If that is an antenna or a flesh-sample dart, then your new species already belongs to somebody else."

"No! No one has ever seen a dolphin like that before." She brushed past him and went up to the cockpit, where she began scanning the sea with the binoculars.

Hope lay back on the saloon couch and closed his eyes. Sally was a smart woman. She didn't need him to belabor the likely. Maybe it was a harpoon. But if it was either a biopsy dart or a data link antenna, was there a more likely source than William Tree's shipload of marine scientists?

Except, why hadn't Tree just come out and asked, " 'Hast seen the white whale?' "

Lt. Commander R. D. Royce was surprised to be under way. Like everyone else aboard the USS *Vermont*, with the exception of the captain, he had assumed the submarine would be recalled to New London, Connecticut, following the breakdown. Of those disappointed and those delighted, Royce fell somewhere between the two camps, proud that her crew's reputation gave the bosses confidence that they could sort her out while far at sea, yet a little apprehensive considering the magnitude of the computer failure that had almost sunk them.

But the Navy had come to understand that given sufficient bandwidth via satellite, the computers could be thoroughly and completely scrubbed and scanned without dragging her home and disrupting missions in every corner of the globe. The same software vendors' long-haired virus hunters who would be stumbling around the ship at dockside were troubleshooting by satellite link.

It was, the captain explained to the crew, very much like logging onto the Internet to download a ScanDisk crash fix from Microsoft. To Royce and the officers, he said the same, only with a tilt to one eyebrow that a dedicated captain-observer might interpret as mildly skeptical.

So far the Big V was passing every test with flying colors. In fact, it was almost as if the near catastrophe hadn't happened. The shore-based troubleshooters had isolated the problem and tracked it down to a smallish software code error in, of all innocent places, the GPS navigation program. It was something of a letdown—such a screw-up could have happened to a ferryboat. Royce, who revered the captain, was concerned that "the Old Man" was not entirely convinced.

But the brass were. So the *Vermont* was still at sea, steaming three hundred feet under at cruising speed—taking her time on a lazy loop across the Atlantic around the Azores, after which, if the computers kept coming up clean, they would head north to mix it up with the Brits.

17

THE CORRIDORS AND ELEVATORS ON the *Star of Alabama* were broad enough to allow Wendell to steer William Tree's double-wide electric wheelchair from laboratory to laboratory when Tree deemed it necessary to instill a little terror. First stop was the Marine Mammal Training Department, where the institute's behaviorists tended the ship's guard dolphins.

The well—the ship's underwater trap door—was open when Tree arrived. A lanky trainer with a gray-flecked ponytail was peering into the gurgling mouth of the sea.

"Expecting someone?" Tree asked.

Hughie Mick was a good ol' boy from the bayous, whom Tree had known since childhood. Spare of form and wary of eye, Hughie had the mournful, guarded demeanor of a car thief bumping into the sheriff. But the man had always had a way with animals. He could teach dogs to mind a property line, cats to fetch, and bottlenose dolphins to carry long-legged girls in bikinis around the Tree Marine Park on their backs.

When pressed hard for his secret Hughie would duck his head and allow in a quiet voice that it helped to be smarter than the dolphin. Outsiders, Tree had cautioned, would favor such modesty over technical accounts of operant conditioning or Hughie's unvarnished " 'Fore you reward him with food, you gotta make him hungry."

It had been Hughie Mick's job to train the killphin to swim directly to the submarine's sonar nose cone. Once there, the animal had to fight the underwater wake to hover beside the moving ship. He had done his job well and was convinced that whatever went wrong with the hybrid was not his fault. So he answered Tree's "Expecting someone" jibe with an uncharacteristically bold, "Davy Jones. Hey, there, Wendell. How you doin', Bill?"

"Just fine," Tree snapped. "They out?"

Hughie said, "I'll tell 'em you're here." He toggled a switch on his control panel. Overhead speakers emitted a string of metallic clicks and a sharp whistle.

Tree peered into the well, tapping his fingers on the bulkhead. "No sign at all of our friend?"

"Sorry, Bill." He nodded at the water that led under the ship and out to the sea. "I was kind of hoping these boys would click up with him, but it hasn't happened yet."

"A body would think," Tree groused, "that with all the expensive hardware we installed in him he'd stick a mite closer."

Hughie shook his head and hitched up the jeans forever sliding down his skinny hips. "It don't matter what your science boys installed in him, he's still an animal. Animals do what the heck they please. Least 'til someone convinces them it's in their better interest to do as they're told."

Whistles and clicks emitted from the speakers. The water surged and a bottlenose dolphin popped to the surface.

A long, deadly stainless steel needle gleamed from the swimmer-nullification harness that embraced the dolphin's forebody from its grinning face to its pectoral fin. Tree usually remarked that it looked like a unicorn with a taste for bondage and Hughie always agreed. But Tree was in no mood for bantering with the help this morning.

"Has it occurred to you that if our friend were to suddenly decide to come home this fellow could kill him with that rig?"

"It has," said Hughie, reaching into the water to scratch the dolphin's chin. "Which is why it ain't loaded." He indicated the compressed air bottle still on the harness rack. "He's just practicing—how you doin' there, fella?"

"Well, heck, even poking that needle in the killphin wouldn't do wonders for his health. Why don't we dispense with the harness 'till this is over?"

It was not a question. Hughie replied, "You're the boss, Bill," and turned his attention to the dolphin. "Yes, yes, yes, you're a fine dolphin. You're the finest dolphin in the whole big ocean. You come here, let me get this off you. . . . Okay. Go on now! Git! Git out there and catch a fish—and, hey!"

Wendell's jaw dropped as the big bottlenose reversed its dive and spy-hopped half out of the well, as if to listen to Hughie Mick warn, "If you run into that big guy, you stay out of his way. And tell your buddy the same. Lead him on home, but don't rile him. He'll make ce-ta-cean gumbo outta both of you 'fore you can count to three."

In the corridor, Wendell whispered, "Hey, Bill. Do you think they understand what Hughie's saying to 'em?"

Tree, wise to Hughie's ways, had seen him palm his ultrasonic signal generator. He told Wendell, "I have no doubt they do, Wendell. Just because they can't say, 'Yes sir, no sir,' doesn't mean they've got no sense."

Next stop was the hospital, which was centered around a 60,000-gallon acute care medical tank nearly as wide as the ship. Equipped with X ray, endoscopy, and ultrasound to treat stranded or wounded dolphins, it served primarily as a postoperative intensive care facility.

Wendell rolled him past the tank into the operating theater. The surgeons were staring at a big-screen TV, studying video replays of the killphin's telemetry implant. Everyone got hastily to their feet. None could meet the bleak gaze of the huge man in the wheelchair. If anyone aboard ship was responsible for the loss of communication with the hybrid it was the surgical team that had implanted the antenna.

"Correct me if I'm wrong," said Tree. "But it looks to me like we've got a slew of high-priced vets killing time."

The chief veterinarian said, "We're just trying to put it to good use, Bill. Who knows what shape it will be in when we get it back."

"*If* we get it back," Tree corrected. "I suppose you're fixing to install a new unit?"

"It is our consensus that changing out the unit would be preferable to attempting to reseat whatever's come loose."

"I look at you vets and I feel a certain empathy with what that creature is enduring. I recall when *my* doctors performed a stomach staple procedure on me to help control my weight. Their staples popped loose in a week. They wanted to cut me open again and do it over. I said, no way. For all I know, next screwup you'll staple my spine to the operating table."

The surgeons exchanged quick glances and decided as a group that the remark did not invite a laugh. Tree said, "How long will it take?"

"Well, dolphins heal quickly, Bill."

"And what about the generator?"

"It should be fine, Bill."

"That's what they told me about my staples—let's go, Wendell. Let's go see if the neurosurgeon has any bright ideas." The bodybuilder started to maneuver him out the door. Tree stopped him and swiveled around to address the veterinarians again. "Now's your chance, boys. Phone ahead the boss is coming and he's on the warpath."

He found the neurosurgeon and his bright young interns holed up in the quiet, dimly lit cabin that served as their conference room. Like the vets, the interns were grouped around a video monitor. The surgeon, himself, was staring morosely out a port at the Atlantic. If there was anyone aboard the *Star of Alabama* madder than Tree that they'd lost communication with the killphin, it was, Tree knew, Dr. Daniel Stern.

Somewhere in that blue-gray wasteland swam the pinnacle of Dr. Dan's career. His work on the killphin's eyes had implications for artificial brain extension as enormous as they were controversial. In theory, what Dan had done to the killphin could be done in spades to humans, whether it meant wiring artificial limbs directly to the brain, or hooking their brains to central data storage, or even fixing them up to control machines with their thoughts.

Like all of Tree's scientists, Dan Stern believed they were working under a top-secret U.S. Navy contract. Slathering to publish his amazing achievements, he knew he would have a long wait to see his work published in the *Journal of Neuroscience*—the downside of accepting unlimited funds from the Tree Institute. But until the animal got loose, at least he could hope and look forward to the distant day when he could publish.

Stern did not look over when his interns leaped up at Tree's approach, chorusing, "Good morning, Bill."

"Good morning, protégés." Tree turned from the monitor to the porthole. "Good morning, Dr. Dan."

Stern growled a barely civil reply in his Brooklyn accent, which grated on Tree's ear.

Tree admired talent, and in the hierarchy that talent conferred, Dan Stern was an aristocrat. He spoke gently, with concern. "You look like a man who regrets his chosen career path this morning, Dr. Dan."

"Take a look at the fucking monitor," Dr. Dan replied. "Rod's gang comes running in here last night. 'It's energized,' they go. 'We're getting a picture.' "

"Well, good."

"Look at the picture, Bill."

The interns backed away so Tree could see it. Tree rolled closer in hopeful anticipation. Of all the projects by all the oddball geniuses he had ever supported, Dan Stern's visual neuroscience experiments never failed to send chills down his spine.

The monitor flickered. Black-and-white images took shape. A school of fish, seen from a distance, drew near, then suddenly close. The fish began to circle, massing tightly. Then, as if a camera had been dropped into the bunched fish, the writhing, panicking mass suddenly filled the screen. What looked like gray smoke pouring from the center of the image was their blood.

"He's feeding," said Tree. "He's herding fish and tearing into lunch."

Dr. Dan had linked multi-electrode arrays to hundreds of cells in the thalamus area of the killphin's brain, the region that received information from the killphin's eyes via the optic nerve. When the data were transmitted to the *Star of Alabama*, the ship's linear decoding computers reconstructed images. They were in essence eavesdropping on the information passing from the killphin's eyes to its brain. Before Dr. Dan accepted the Tree Institute's millions, such experiments had been limited to cats in a laboratory.

"It still amazes me," said Tree. "We are seeing the ocean through the animal's eyes."

"That's videotape," Dan said bleakly. "You've seen it before."

"I *know* that," said Tree. "And I would admire it equally on the thousandth viewing. What are you getting now?"

"Show our beneficent benefactor the new stuff," Dan muttered.

An intern changed tapes and keyed the player.

"Well, speaking as a layman," Tree drawled, "it looks like someone forgot to pay his cable bill. Maybe the computer can enhance it."

"It's already enhanced. The raw stuff looked black as the bottom of the Puerto Rico Trench. We ran it through twenty million bucks of supercomputer. Presto: a snowstorm."

Tree's natural optimism drove him to ask, "What's that in the upper right corner?"

"Fuck knows, Bill. Maybe he's eyeing a tuna for breakfast. Maybe it's a submarine's towed array. Maybe it's a sailboat. But it's probably a software ghost. Unless they upgrade that signal, the animal might as well be blind for all the good it does us."

"Dr. Dan, I've never heard you so low." Which was a lie. In truth, the brilliant Dan Stern had displayed serious depressive symptoms during his years working for Tree.

"Bill, I've got my whole life invested in this damned experiment. If that animal just disappears, I am fucked."

"Let's look at the bright side."

"It took me three years to implant two hundred and ninety-seven electrodes in its thalamus."

"Well, you've learned a lot and we can move ahead."

"You know what I learned? I learned it will take me three years to do it again."

"Well, what do you suggest?"

"If they can't restore one hundred percent signal? I think I'll just kill myself."

Tree nodded gravely. Then he said the only thing he could say when Dan got in one of these moods. "Jane and the kids would be devastated."

"It's in my contract you take care of them forever. Remember?"

"I remember you were adamant on that subject."

"Just so we understand each other."

"I just don't understand why you can't celebrate your great talent and look on the bright side."

Dr. Dan looked at Tree with an expression as distant and unreadable as an Uzbek on a donkey observing a Lexus convertible.

Tree said, "I am totally aware that none of this is worth a bucket of spit if we can't communicate. Don't worry, Dan. I'm fixing to lean harder on Rod."

"Lotsa luck."

"Telemetry, Wendell."

The bodybuilder wheeled the fat man into an elevator. They descended two decks and started down a long companionway. Deep in the working spaces of the ship, they had left behind the mahogany-clad bulkheads, the paintings, and the carpets. The ceiling was ribbed with plumbing and the thick electrical cables that powered the telemetry room.

"I imagine Rod misses his posh upper-deck laboratory. But right now it's in the telemetry boys' laps."

"You know what, Bill?"

"What is it, Wendell?"

"I'm having a tough time thinking about that poor dolphin swimming around the ocean with antennas sticking out of its back."

"Killphin, Wendell. Killphin. He's a hybrid, half spinner dolphin, half killer whale."

"It jars me."

"It jars me, too, Wendell, to think that intelligent, willful, highly adapted ocean mammals are in the clutches of human beings. But he's not the only one. Don't forget, there are scads of regular dolphins swimming around the ocean with antennas sticking out of their backs."

"There are?"

"Installed, supposedly, by kindly researchers committed to helping dolphins."

"But we're not helping the killphin."

"The heck we're not. We gave him life."

"It still jars me."

"It's no different than riding a horse or milking a cow, Wendell. Or training that dog you keep pestering me to buy for you. The Lord gave man dominion over the beasts."

"But the Lord never said you should wire it up like a swimming Circuit City."

"I differ with you there, Wendell. For one thing, I'm sure the Lord would approve any weapon guaranteed to stop war."

If, Tree reminded himself, it worked as planned. In theory,

thalamus electrodes, GPS guidance instruments, and a satellite radio transceiver would permit its masters to launch attacks in any ocean in the world. In practice, the killphin had no master.

"For another thing, it is not even remotely a swimming Circuit City. If it were, it would do what I told it to do. Hughie Mick is right. It has a mind of its own. Heck, Wendell, wired or not, it's picking fights and following sailboats and doing what it wants, when it wants. Aint Martha's right to call him 'Frankenstein.' "

"I heard the people on the sailboat call him Ishmael. Like in the Bible."

Tree sobered abruptly. He looked down at his belly and flicked a crumb from his sweatshirt. "Ishmael was an outcast."

"That's why I say 'poor killphin.' He doesn't know who his friends are—he ain't got no friends, no family, nothing he can count on like other animals. Dolphins are friendly animals, Bill. Hughie Mick told me that they like each other. Heck, when I watch 'em in the marine park they're screwing half the time—boy, girl, they don't care. If they was people you'd say they was tramps or queer as a three-dollar bill—"

" 'Promiscuous,' " Tree said stiffly, "is the proper word for their, um, activities, that you're attempting to describe."

"All I'm saying is dolphins shouldn't have to live alone."

"The killphin's a hybrid. Killer whales are clannish, it's true, living in pods usually run by the females. Sort of like us Tree men, in some ways. If you could imagine Aint Martha as a mama killer whale."

"It's not funny, Bill. He's got no pod."

"But he's half spinner and spinner dolphins couldn't care less who their folks are. So he's not quite the family man you're making him out to be."

"All I'm saying is how'd you like to be swimming around all by yourself forever?"

"I do, Wendell. Fat men have no friends."

"I'm your friend."

"You work for me. If I didn't pay you, you'd skedaddle."

"No I wouldn't, Bill, and don't you ever say that."

Tree steered his electric wheelchair into the telemetry lab. He was trailed closely by a troubled-looking Wendell. "Good morning, Dr. Rod."

"Good morning, Bill."

"Well?"

"The killphin is holding his course north-northeast. The sailboat is right behind him."

"Can you turn him?"

"Not yet."

"Dan wasn't very impressed with the quality of the signal you sent him."

"We're still trying to enhance it. The guys are trying it from a new angle."

"From what I saw it better be a heck of an angle."

"At least the signal is strong enough to track now. We're thirty miles behind him and receiving enough to triangulate him pretty consistently."

"Knowing where my killphin is at is worth darn all if he won't let us get close enough to control him. . . . I've been wracking my brain why he likes that sailboat and hates my ship. I've been talking to Wendell. Neither of us has a clue."

"I'm not sure," Rod said carefully, "that it makes decisions quite like we do."

"It has a brain," said Tree.

"Yes, but 'likes' and 'hates' aren't necessarily part of its agenda. Nor, strictly speaking, would the animal have an 'agenda.' "

"Maybe not, but Wendell's gotten me thinking that it can't be one hundred percent happy with everything that's been done to it. And since it doesn't meet other creatures like it, its social instinct is thwarted and frustrated. That battle the killphin won with the shark probably stemmed from its anger or confusion."

Tree pretended to ignore the two technicians in the corner, who were rolling their eyes. Instead, he glowered at Rod, waiting for an answer.

"It's just an animal, Bill. Brighter than some, probably. Unusual. But 'animal' is still the operative word."

Tree continued as if he hadn't heard. "Frankly, I think we're dealing with a mighty testy animal. But while it's darned dangerous in that mood, it's also 'ambivalent.' For some reason it seems to like that boat of theirs as much as it hates my ship. For some reason, they make him feel good, but we made him feel bad."

Rod glanced at Wendell and got back an empty-headed smile. An expression, Rod realized, that Wendell would probably wear while punching someone in the face or throwing him in the garbage chute on Tree's orders.

Tree said, "Of course he associates a lot of misery with us. But what did they ever do for him?"

"You're anthropomorphizing again, Bill."

"I am trying to figure him out," Tree replied. "Which is more than you're doing."

"You're making it more complicated than it is," Rod shot back, making a pleasant discovery that imminent death had made him brave. If Bill was going to order him thrown down the garbage chute in six more days, what did he have to lose?"

"Sometimes," Tree murmured, "I can feel what he's going through."

From the corridor came cheers and joyous whoops. A bald engineer rushed in, wild-eyed.

"Rod! We got another data stream."

"Which one?"

"Thalamus!"

"Yes!" Rod ran into the corridor, long hair streaming, with assistants stampeding after him. When they were alone, Wendell asked, "Don't you want to go with 'em, Bill?"

"They are celebrating smaller things than you and I can see."

"But it sounds like they're closing in on him."

"Step by little step. . . . Well, that's what they're paid to do. But you and I are going to go find Hughie Mick and bring him to the scientists."

"They don't like Hughie," said Wendell.

"How could anyone not like Hughie?" Tree asked. He knew—and used the fact to advantage—that people often made the mistake of talking out loud around well-muscled Wendell as if he were a stone-deaf statue.

"They call him the circus trainer."

"Well, we're going to sit the 'circus trainer' down with the P-H-D behaviorists and find out why my killphin's got a thing for that sailboat."

18

A HIGH-PRESSURE SYSTEM SETTLED around *Oona* like a gigantic bell jar. The wind weakened. The sea settled. The boat slowed to a poky four knots. Ishmael, who'd been forging ahead at ten knots, kept going.

They had just crossed latitude thirty-seven north at longitude fifty-two west—an intersection of round numbers on the chart when Bermuda was seven hundred miles astern, Chesapeake Bay a thousand miles west, the Flemish Cap nine hundred miles ahead. Nearly three thousand miles of open ocean stretched between the stalled boat and the Denmark Strait.

"An Atlantic High," David Hope said to an impatient Sally Moffitt, "reminds us how warmly sailors greeted the invention of the steamer."

"Are you sure we can't use *your* engines?"

"We don't have the fuel and we'd scare our friend."

"Our 'friend' has disappeared."

"Don't worry, this will pass. Weather fax says it's moving east."

"When?"

Oona ghosted slowly in the light breeze. Hours crept past. Occasionally they thought they spotted Ishmael coming back for them, but weren't sure. The wind died. *Oona* drifted. Her sails slatted, banging back and forth as the swell underlaying the calm surface lifted her up and put her down in a never-ending and increasingly annoying rhythm. Ishmael seemed to have disappeared completely.

Hope was inclined to wait such miseries out. He managed to distract Sally for a while, by getting her to set up her editing system so they could zoom in on the videotape of whatever was sticking out of the big dolphin's back. But as soon as it was apparent that there was no new information to be garnered from the tape, Sally resumed pacing around the boat like a lion in a bankrupt circus. Finally, at three in the afternoon, Hope said, "I'll give the high a shove."

He rolled in the useless jib and furled the mainsail. A puzzled Sally followed him down to the dive room, where he put on a tool belt. Then he opened the steering compartment, clipped on work lights, and crawled in. "The best way to make the wind blow is to take advantage of the calm to repair my steering. I can guarantee it will start honking as soon as I've got it in pieces."

Sally opened the hatch that led to the dive steps and peered at the flat sea. "I hate this."

"The other thing to do is you could start cooking something complicated. The wind will blow the second you're whipping up a meringue."

"I don't cook like that."

"Can you do cookies?"

"Sure."

"So do cookies."

"I'd rather watch for Ishmael."

Hope discovered that he had undertaken the repair just in time. The strands of the steering cable were separating, having jumped partway out of the quadrant grove at some point, weakening the cable dangerously.

He bit the bullet, got a hacksaw, and cut out the entire section of cable. As soon as he had chucked the stranded length overboard, the wind puffed. Working quickly, he replaced that whole section of wire, crimping in a new length. In the middle of the operation the wind returned as he had predicted and *Oona* started drifting uncomfortably before he got it all back together.

At the helm, as the boat got moving, he said, "It's like getting a brake job on your van. You're back where you started, but at least we don't have to worry about it."

"There he is!"

The creature erupted from the ocean, a hundred yards ahead of the boat, spun six complete revolutions, and splashed on its side like a kid cannonballing off a diving board.

Sally leapt up on the cabin roof. She had the camera rolling when it jumped again. "Wow. He's wild today."

"He's celebrating," said Hope.

"What?"

"Us."

Sally lowered her camera and looked at Hope. "That's a funny thought. He is, isn't he?"

"He seems to like when we're moving fast. Have you noticed? He only really jumps when we're kiting along. In fact, from the first time I saw it, his only big tail dances are when the boat is flying—let's see what happens if we stop."

He steered into the wind. *Oona* sank off her plane and came to a bobbing stop on the swell.

"See him?"

"David, get the hydrophone. He's nearby. Maybe he'll talk."

Hope paid out cable and waterproof microphone. Sally plugged it into her DAT recorder. As soon as the hydrophone hit the water her eyes opened wide with delight.

"Listen!" She pulled Hope to her and pressed one of the headset earphones to his ear. Hope heard loud creaking noises and a series of sharp, frantic-sounding whistles.

Sally clutched Hope in her excitement. "Ohmigod, he's talking to us."

"What's he saying?"

"Go faster or something. I don't know. But we've got his voice. Ohmigod. David, I love you for your hydrophone. You are a genius. Listen to him! He's there. He's alive. He's talking to us."

Ishmael continued clicking, groaning, and whistling for a full five minutes, then abruptly went quiet.

"He's leaving," said Sally. "He's giving up on us. . . . Let's go, let's go. Let's catch up."

Hope coaxed *Oona* into backing away from the wind. Jib and main filled. She staggered into motion and leaped into a twelve-knot plane. "Where is he? Where is he?"

"There!"

A quarter-mile ahead, Ishmael was spin-dancing against the sharp, blue sky.

"Why is he doing that?" asked Hope. "Why do they 'spin-dance'?"

She tugged off her headset as she answered, and let it rest around her neck like a black collar. It was a sexy look, thought Hope, a high-tech frame for the eager, self-assured intelligence that lit her face. "One possibility is that they signal their friends that they found food. The splash landing is percussive. The sound will carry a long, long way underwater."

"The rhythm section for the clicks and whistles? But this guy doesn't have friends."

"Another hypothesis has pelagic dolphins jumping to herd their prey. In which case, what we're seeing is the top side of a maneuver aimed at driving fish to the surface."

"Which raises an interesting question," Hope mused. "How *does* Ishmael eat? Dolphins feed in groups, right? But if dolphins hunt together, how does Ishmael hunt by himself?"

"They eat in groups when they're in groups. Sometimes they're alone." Sally gnawed her lip. "The puzzling thing is, dolphins that have to contend with deepwater sharks far from shore tend to live in large groups. But not Ishmael."

"He's huge. If I were a shark I'd think twice about tangling with him."

"Regardless, he's perfectly capable of catching food alone."

"But what I mean is, who taught him how to hunt, if he's alone?"

"What do you mean?"

"Someone had to show him how. The old teach the young."

Sally looked at him sharply. "What do you mean, 'someone'?"

"His mother or father, I guess. I mean, dolphins have mothers and fathers. Even weirdly different strange dolphins. Even if he's a twisted mutant there's a dolphin mother somewhere who'll tell you, 'Ishmael was always a good boy.' "

She did not smile back.

Hope asked, "What's wrong?"

"I hate the way you said somebody already owns him."

"All I meant was if that is an antenna sticking out of his back, then at some point somebody got close enough to install it."

"I think it's a harpoon."

"Or close enough to pop him with a biopsy dart."

A line squall glint in her eye told Hope that she didn't want to hear his biopsy dart hypothesis again, either. Not to mention his opinion that the most likely dispensers of antennas and biopsy darts on the North Atlantic this week happened to be William Tree's marine biologists on the *Star of Alabama*.

Hope shrugged the thought away. An adult charter client was entitled to her fantasies as long as she could defend them to herself. Besides, what did he know? He had no proof of a Tree connection. It was just a gut feeling. He wondered if they would see the big ship again. Able to cross five hundred miles of ocean in a day, it could show up quite unexpectedly. He looked around. He saw the cable straining over the back of the cockpit.

"Son of a gun, I forgot the hydrophone."

He hauled the cable out of the water, fearing the mike had been yanked off by the boat speed, but it was intact.

"Well, if we ever need a boat recording . . ."

Sally appeared lost in gloomy thought, so he switched off her DAT himself, and unplugged and stowed the hydrophone below.

Returning to the cockpit, he made his customary inspection of the sky—still bluer than blue without a hint of better wind. He said, "Look at it this way: We've been following Ishmael for fifteen hundred miles; if anyone 'owns' him, we do."

Sally brightened. "Besides, we own the videotape. And now we've got audio. And don't forget, we have his tooth."

"*You* own the videotape, the audio, and his tooth. I'm just driving."

He was driving late that night when the wind firmed up, veered west, and blew a crisp, steady fifteen knots across the boat's beam. The broad reach was *Oona*'s happiest point of sail and she soared, skimming the dark sea like a bat. The sky was ablaze with stars as bright as Hope had ever seen them, their light so intense that two hours into his midnight-to four watch he thought he could see a ship in the far, far distance.

But if it was not a ghost of his imagination, it burned no running lamps. Nor did it come closer or answer him when he hailed it on the VHF. It was so unusual to actually see another vessel out here. On most of his voyages between Maine and the Caribbean, he would encounter none from harbor to harbor. It wasn't worth taxing the batteries to run the radar all the time. But he switched it on now, just to be on the safe side.

"Good eyes," he congratulated himself.

A big target glowed on the otherwise empty screen. He clicked onto it with the cursor. The radar calculated that it was a full nine miles away on a course almost parallel to *Oona*'s. Hope radioed it again. "Vessel to my east on course zero-one-five? Do you see me?"

No reply. But as he watched, their courses began to diverge, the radar indicating that it had begun to veer farther east. As it was making twenty-one knots, Hope assumed it was an express container vessel bound for Europe from an East Coast port like Wilmington or Jacksonville. When he checked the radar again, the distance between them had increased to fifteen miles and it was still angling away. By dawn it would be many miles below the horizon.

The night was so perfect, the boat so lively, that he hand-steered for an hour just for the sheer pleasure of matching skills with the auto-helm to drive faster than it could. At the end of the hour he switched on the radar again. For twenty-four miles ahead, twenty-four miles astern, and twenty-four miles to either side, the sea was his and his alone. He cast his head back and looked up at the stars: the area of a circle equaled pi times the radius squared. Over eighteen hundred square miles. A wonderful stretch of empty space.

Sally came up at three-thirty, and a perfect night suddenly felt even better. Gone were the days when he preferred the night watch alone. By the stars, Hope could see the shape of her face and the gleam of her eyes and the tiny diamond studs she wore in her ears and the flash of her smile.

"You're early," he said. "You've got another half hour of sleep."

"Couldn't sleep. . . . God, it's beautiful."

She sat on the bench opposite in the cockpit and stretched her legs and hooked her toes on Hope's bench. "Any sign of Ishmael?"

"Not a fin."

By now they knew that if the big dolphin slowed down to sleep, he would catch up in the morning. "I did see a ship. Radar shows him long gone, but you might want to keep an eye peeled east."

"It's so empty. We could be the only people in the world . . . you, me, and Ishmael. What is that animal going to do when we leave him at forty-five, forty-five?"

"I'm still wondering why he jumps like that."

"I have another theory. Dolphins are great mimics. They imitate other animals, their jumps, their behavior, even their noises. You know what I think? I think he saw spinner dolphins jumping and taught himself to imitate them."

"Could be. Or is it social? Is he trying to communicate with us?"

"They say that young dolphins frolic around as a way to learn to leave their mothers," said Sally. "With most animals play is a learning activity."

"Speaking of mothers, how the heck old is he?"

Sally shrugged. "Who knows? His tooth looked brand new. Orcas don't reach full size until they're twenty. I think they start sex earlier. Maybe he's still young. Maybe he misses his mother."

Hope cast his head back and looked up at the stars. Vega stood bright overhead. The Big Dipper was wheeling on its handle in the northwest. The usually pale Pole Star seemed close enough to caress. "I think he's looking for a girlfriend."

"I think you're anthropomorphizing."

"Seriously, couldn't the jumps be like dancing? Two beings communicating up close?"

"Now you're romanticizing him. Dolphins are actually extremely promiscuous animals. They'll screw anyone they meet. Just to say hello."

"Fun way to communicate."

"They don't even differentiate between sexes."

"Boyfriend, girlfriend, who cares?" said Hope. "For all we know, Ishmael's a she."

"Ishmaela?"

"The need is the same. The desire's the same. The point is, he or she is looking. Any way you cut it, it gets lonely out here."

Sally Moffitt poked him with her toe. "David, are you hitting on me?"

Hope cupped her heel and held it lightly. "Yes."

"Well, don't."

"I won't apologize."

"It's only two weeks since my husband dumped me."

"And only ten days since you returned the favor by stealing his rebreather, three cameras, film stock, videotape, a tripod, a DV VCR, underwater lights, a portable generator and most of his tools and all of his battery packs. Not to mention that fat little disc drive you back up on. . . ." He cast her a smile he knew she could see in the starlight and asked, "What's that backup called?"

Sally poked him with her other foot. "You know what it's called. It's written on the box. And you know darned well I can't fit all my material on my laptop hard drive."

"But what's it called? Video something?"

"VideoRaid."

"Emphasis on the 'raid.' " Hope laughed.

"That's not funny. I had a right. And I need separate media storage. I can plug it into any editing system." She poked him again. "Stop laughing at me."

"I'm not laughing at you. I'm laughing at the situation."

Sally grew quiet.

Hope said, "Come on, I know something of what you're going through. It's only eleven days since I buried my friend."

"I don't think it's the same," she said. "From what you said. . . . Or is it?"

"Only because I knew it was coming," he replied soberly.

"Well," said Sally. "Maybe I did, too."

"Since Belize?"

"That's when her 'countess-ship' showed. But, oh, Jesus, things were getting bad a year ago. I knew. Ever since the heart attack, I ended up being Nurse Nancy. 'Don't eat that steak. Don't drink that bourbon'. . . . What kind of love affair can you have with a self-destructive patient? . . . But that doesn't mean that I'm ready to hop in the sack with some guy I just met."

Hope said, "I guess I should let go of your foot."

"Not that the guy would stay long. I'd drive him away just like Greg."

"I'm healthy as a horse," said Hope.

"Oh, I'd find a way. Before I was Nurse Nancy I was Ms. Producer, taking charge of everything. I mean, somebody'd got to sweat the details. But there's an invisible line between producer/wife and bossy mother, and one day I crossed it." To Hope's surprise, she sang softly, " 'Gonna produce that man right out of my bed. . . . Gonna produce that man right out of my bed . . .' "

"So I guess I should let go of your foot."

Sally said nothing for what seemed to Hope a long enough time not to let go. Then she said, "I guess you should. I mean, no offense, David, I think you're very nice—"

"Excuse me while I step overboard."

"What?"

" 'Very nice' is the kiss of death. When I was a kid, girls' mothers used to tell their daughters, 'Why don't you go out with David. He's very nice.' Needless to say, I didn't get out much."

"More than nice," Sally amended. "You're very sweet."

"Be still my heart."

"Very gentle, very supportive . . ." She smiled in the starlight. Then she reached out and touched his face. "You're a man who likes women. Give me a man who likes women, every time. Greg, jerk that he could be, liked women."

"There's an endorsement."

Sally laughed. "You know what I mean. Men who like women are fun to be with. They make good partners. They're great in bed—and I'm sure you are. . . . Wise hands. . . . Probably a great kisser, too."

"No need to take that on faith," Hope interrupted.

"And I like you. You deliver what you promise. You were a big help with the sound. It was ingenious, the way you rigged the wireless mike. But what I really loved was how you kept gnawing away at the *thump* problem. We could be—what am I saying?"

"Good question," said Hope. "What are you saying?"

"I'm married and dumped and busy and I've got to stay focused—do you understand? I'm a mess."

He placed her foot gently back on the bench and stood. Sally jumped up beside him, asking watch-change questions: "Same course? North-northeast? Should I reef the main?"

"Steady as she goes. . . ." This was ridiculous. There had to be more to say. He said, "The helm feels good. A little less play in it. But the self-steering's doing fine. . . . Well, good night. I'm going to catch some sleep. I'll be on the couch in the saloon, if you need anything. Keep an eye out for that ship. Switch on the radar if you're in doubt. . . ."

Sally looked across the starlit water where Hope indicated the ship had been. "Anything else?"

"Yeah. You're not married. And you're not a mess."

At that instant an oversized sea hissed against the port hull and *Oona* did him the biggest favor of his life by stumbling on the breaking crest. He fell backward, but, wise to the catamaran's ways, easily kept his feet by pressing against the bench. Sally, not as accustomed to a stable platform tilting suddenly, crashed into him.

He felt a searing impact of breasts and thighs. When he closed his arms around her he thought what a strong and shapely woman she was. She felt so much more solid than the tall, leggy Barbara. His hands felt like they were on fire.

"Oh, for Christ's sake," Sally said. "This is ridiculous. I'm not ready for this, even if you are." But by then she was already kissing his mouth. Hope had a sensible thought: Don't blow this; I'm starving, but she's only hungry. Such a strong body. But her lips were so soft. It occurred to him that he was having trouble breathing. Then they were breathing together, sinking to the hard deck, and Sally was whispering urgently, "Could we just start with holding?"

"Holding?"

"Just . . . holding, kissing, you know?"

Hope had another sensible thought: Sally might not be as hungry as he was. But she was very lonely. As lonely as he was. So he asked, through her lips, "You mean sort of like a first date?" and while disappointed, was not surprised when she stopped kissing his mouth long enough to whisper, "Thank you."

"Am I so noble it makes you want to throw up?"

Sally, reverting to type, unable to reply with a short answer, said, "My first thought was that you made me hope you'll ask me out again. Then I think maybe he doesn't want to be with me. Like he's still too hung up on the woman who died. Or maybe he's ready, but I'm not his type. Like he's secretly relieved to get out of this."

Hope took her hand and pressed it to his groin. "Do I feel secretly relieved?"

Sally took a deep breath and Hope braced for a very long answer. That there was, instead, a god in heaven became apparent when she whispered, "Could we talk about this later?"

19

HOPE WOKE WITH THE SUN in his eyes and Sally's hand on his brow. "I hate to wake you," she said softly. "But that looks pretty serious."

He had slept heavily for over an hour. His entire body from the top of his head to the soles of his feet felt suffused with well-being, and with his head pillowed by her thighs it was difficult to imagine anything at all serious.

Sally pointed. Hope sat up to look. A black cloud with white teeth was chewing up the ocean two miles ahead of the boat.

"Son of a bitch. We must be near a Gulf Stream eddy. It's a line squall."

Sally said, "A splash woke me. I think Ishmael was warning us. Is that as bad as it looks?"

"Worse," said Hope, springing to his feet. "It'll tear the mast off like a toothpick if we don't take in sail. Good morning." He kissed her mouth, and while he started both engines he ordered, "Get the foul weather jackets and the harnesses! Close the hatch and put in the washboards when you come up. And grab a couple of diving masks."

Engaging the engines at quarter-speed to keep the catamaran moving forward, he rolled up the jib.

Then he started to reef the main.

He felt so light and so happy that even while automatically organizing the boat for the onslaught, he found it hard to actually fear the squall bearing down on them.

Reality arrived on a breath of cold air. The icy puff was followed immediately by a bitter wind that headed the boat and stopped her dead in her tracks. The squall was racing at them. The closer it got the higher the black cloud towered until it blocked the rising sun. The white beneath looked like surf pounding a beach.

A second gust screamed through the rigging. The reefed mainsail thundered. The first drops of cold rain flew by horizontally.

He had left his stormsail hanked onto the baby stay, in its bag, which was secured to pad eyes in the abbreviated foredeck. He made a snap decision to raise the minuscule stormsail and furl the main completely.

Back at the helm, he shoved the throttles wide open. The little engines ground loud and hard and *Oona* shuddered. Lightning flicked ahead.

Sally finished sliding the washboards into their grooves and shut the hatch. Hope braced the wheel with his body while she helped him into his foul weather jacket and the harness, and stretched the diving mask over his head.

"I'm not sure why," he told her. "But I think we'll do better to meet this particular misery head-on and hunker down until it passes."

"Playing it safe?"

"Better safe than sorry."

Thunder rumbled. The first sounds were distant, like deep vibrations. But suddenly, with a blinding flash, it was exploding all around them as if they had sailed into a steel drum beaten by giants.

Rain fell hard, pounding the decks, frothing the sea, flattening waves. Another thunderclap felt like it would blow them off the boat. Wind shrieked. Lightning flashed continuously, firing the black cloud with eerie purple hues. Then the bone-white surf was all over them, rearing above the bows, burying the cabin roof, and cascading into the cockpit.

Oona staggered. To David Hope and Sally Moffitt, chest deep in raging white water, it felt like skiing in an avalanche, with the same awful feeling that it wouldn't end until it ended badly. Hope was dragged from the helm. His safety harness jerked him up short. Then the catamaran's natural buoyancy wrenched her up to the wildly blowing surface.

A second wall-like wave bore down on them. The boat slid sideways, presenting her vulnerable beam to the tumbling sea. Lightning lit the sky. Thunder shook the deck. Hailstones pelted the sail, drummed on the cabin roof, and slashed the figures struggling with the helm.

Hope throttled back the starboard engine and waited what felt like eons for it to slow enough to jam it into reverse, then gunned it. The counterrotating propellers swung her head to starboard. The charging sea buried the starboard bow, and smashed with such force into the front of the bridge deck that Hope feared for *Oona*'s structure.

Playing it safe, he realized, was getting them killed. "We're outta here," he yelled to Sally. "We've got to run with it."

Sally, observing the seas churning at them, asked, "How can you turn now?"

Hope, laying out a plan to wait for a trough and scoot around in it, saw a momentary flat spot open between crests and took a big chance. Still reversing starboard, he turned the helm hard over, revved both engines, and spun her like a top.

A slow top, he realized with a sinking heart. Wobbling, staggering, buffeted by seawater that ripped cavernous holes in her path, she turned in a stately, almost glacial pace until, at long last, the wind was at their backs. Straightening up the wheel, he moved the starboard engine to ahead, placed

Sally's hands on the wheel, and used both hands to let the stormsail sheet fly.

Oona stormed forward, running like a frightened cow. Raked by hail, drenched by spray, Hope pulled the diving mask over his eyes so he could see and steered for their lives.

"The only good thing about line squalls," said Hope, massaging the elbow he had bashed on the jib winch when a cross-sea nearly toppled the boat, "is they don't last long. But they'll kill you if you're not battened down. Next time you see Ishmael, tell him thanks for the warning—oooh, you got really whacked on your thigh." Thrown across the cockpit by the same cross-sea, Sally had tangled her legs in her tether. Hope knelt. "Let me kiss that, make it better."

They were inside the Gulf Stream. The water was a deep indigo blue, compared to dull green in their wake. Squalls still roamed the horizon. Weeds floated beside the boat. The air felt warmer, too, a wonderful change from the icy squall, and the sun was hot on her skin.

Suddenly Sally jumped away from him. "Ishmael! *There* you are!"

The huge dolphin corkscrewed skyward, and fell back with a splash that sparkled in the sun.

"Wonderful," Hope muttered, climbing to his feet.

"Well," said Sally. "No time like the present."

"For what?"

"Ishmael's close-up."

"Underwater?"

"Yes."

"No."

"Hey! Don't pull rank on me just because we had fun last night."

"I'd like to have some more fun tonight—maybe get to third base—so I've got a stake in you not getting eaten by Ishmael."

"This is what I do," she said. "This is my work."

"It's too dangerous."

She took both his hands and stared into his eyes. "David. When I get in-its-face shots of an enormous, never-before-seen-or-filmed new species of dolphin, it will launch my career into the stratosphere." She kissed him hard, then made a telephone out of her right hand and pressed it to her mouth. " 'Please hold, National Geographic, I've got Imax on the other line and HBO knocking on my door.' I'm going in, David. I've got gear to check and a dive plan to make up and I don't want to talk about it anymore."

"Could I say just one thing?"

"No."

She went below and reappeared, shortly, at the dive platform in the back of the port hull. She had put on a white one-piece Lycra dive skin. The thin fabric was sufficient protection for the warm waters of the Gulf Stream, Hope supposed, the color intended to make her fairly invisible to creatures swimming under her. It was also a powerful reminder of her sexy roundness.

"Did you apply that with a spray or a brush?"

She gave him a distracted smile, without taking her eyes from her gear, focused like a helmsman in a hurricane. When she was satisfied that everything was in order, she said, "Could you please stop the boat?"

Hope headed into the wind, sheeted in the sails, and let *Oona* drift. Sally put on her buoyancy compensator and stepped into her weight belt and checked the quick-release buckle. She inspected the rebreather again, and fitted the unit to her backpack. Hope picked it up and held it while she strapped in.

She jumped up and down to test that it fit snugly. She checked the gauges console that held the rebreather's instrument display. She took test breaths from her regulator. She clipped her light meter onto her vest and handed Hope the video camera encased in its polycarbonate underwater housing.

He stepped on her right fin to hold it down while she kicked into it. She leaned against him for balance to tug it around her heel. Hope steadied her with an arm around the boxy rebreather and they repeated the procedure for her left fin.

He scanned the sea anxiously for the big dolphin. If the animal behaved according to its usual pattern it would not venture near the boat when they were stopped. Which was fine with him. Then all they would have to worry about were sharks, equipment breakdowns, and getting lost on a startlingly vast and empty sea.

"How am I going find you when you come up?"

She patted the side of her air supply. "Day-Glo yellow folding flag. You can see it over a mile away."

Hope handed her a glass signal mirror with a sighting hole drilled in the middle. "If you surface up- or downwind of me there'll be no cross-breeze to flap your flag."

"Thank you." She tucked the mirror in her vest.

"Got a dive plan?"

"Yes."

"Care to share it with the guy on the boat?"

"I'll submerge to thirty feet, swim straight out a mile and back."

"A mile? This isn't a reef. It's open ocean."

"Bye-bye."

Encumbered by the heavy backpack, weight belt, face mask, air hoses, snorkel, and long, stiff fins, Sally shuffled sideways to the edge of the dive platform.

"You look," Hope told her, "half sexy mermaid, half industrial robot."

She reached to put her regulator in her mouth, saying, "Thanks for last night. I hope you had a good time, too."

"Excellent time," said Hope. "Try and make it back in one piece. We'll do it again."

Sally Moffitt stepped into the swell with a bold stride, scissored her fins together, and came to a rest beside the platform. Hope handed her the camera. She adjusted her BCD for negative buoyancy, tucked into a ball, kicked her legs high in the air, and disappeared under the boat.

He thought he glimpsed a flickering white glow of her skin suit. The moving waves magnified the roundness of her legs and bottom and he flashed on a stirring vision of a long, slow, orgasmic voyage home to Maine.

Then the sea reflected the sun, blinding him to what moved below. The closed-circuit aqualung released no bubbles and Hope had the eeriest sensation that he was sailing alone and that he had only imagined he had taken a passenger—more than a passenger. An excellent shipmate, alert, observant, helpful, neat habits. Sexy as all hell. Terrific to hold on to. Great to look at. A woman a lucky guy could spend happy times with—if she didn't dump him good-bye at the dock.

He sprang to the cockpit, seized a handheld GPS and noted his exact position. The satellite readout was precise to a yard. He looked at his watch and sat down to wait, calculating and recalculating how long it would take a woman to swim underwater a mile out and a mile back. She hadn't told him which direction. But it had to be north-northeast, where, if Ishmael had stopped when the boat stopped, the animal would be waiting.

20

THE RICH BLUE WATER CLOSED over Sally Moffitt, warm as her own skin. Sunlight dissolved, shaping a rippled stairway to the indigo depths. It was so quiet that she could hear her heartbeat.

She cleared her ears. She equalized pressure, exhaling through her nose into her mask and releasing more air from her BCD.

Strands of living weed drifted by, testifying to the Gulf Stream's long voyage out the Straits of Florida, up the Eastern Seaboard, and across the ocean. Transparent salpas, marble-size strangers to the cold Atlantic, had hitched a ride from somewhere. A waterlogged seed pod may have joined the current in Belize.

A sharp *click* broke the silence. She looked back. A shadow loomed in the astonishingly clear water. But it was only *Oona* perched on her twin hulls like an equals sign. Nor was the clicking noise dolphin talk; just the closed-circuit rebreather's solenoid dispensing oxygen.

She descended below the wave surge until pressure embraced her chest. She turned her back on the boat, settled the camera as comfortably as she could, and extended her body in a streamlined, horizontal attitude. She checked her air

gauge, her depth gauge, her compass, and her watch as re-
flexively as a speeding commuter monitored mirrors, radar
detector, and the road ahead. Then she began a steady, re-
laxed flutter kick and swam away from David Hope's catamaran, on Ishmael's north-northeast track.

She moved as stealthily as a fish, though not as easily. The
squarish shape of the rebreather was a drag in the water, and
distance swimming in the bulky outfit was slow compared to
the streamlined cylinder of a scuba tank.

The solenoid clicked reassuringly. The rebreather would
dispense air all day and night. The limits would be the
diver's energy. At some point, her strength would drain, her
legs would tire, she would dehydrate and succumb to cold
and hunger.

She checked her gauges every few minutes: depth, decompression computer, oxygen pressure, rebreather primary
display, and oxygen sensor secondary display all read normal. Her compass confirmed her course.

Just to be sure, she surfaced after fifteen minutes and
searched for the boat. It was a mile away, but not directly behind her. She had veered way off course, shoved east by the
current. She dove to thirty feet again, altered course to the
west, and when she had swum five minutes, turned north
again.

Sound entered the killphin's consciousness through its lower
jaw. Oily, acoustic-sensitive tissue carried the vibrations to a
deeply isolated inner ear, muffled from the sea by pockets of
air.

Sally Moffitt registered on several levels. The huge animal heard—long before it could see her—the rhythmic beat
of her fins pounding the water, the occasional sharp tick of
her rebreather, and the steady thud of her heart.

Combative, vigilant, and hungry, it transmitted ex-
ploratory bursts of ultrasonic clicks that were focused by the

lenslike fatty melon on its head. The sound waves bounced off Sally Moffitt and echoed back to its dish-shaped upper jawbone. The time it took for the clicks to return established how far away she was. The patterns of their echoes revealed where and how fast she was swimming.

It moved closer, its senses goaded to high alert, and scanned her with an array of wavelengths that would provoke hopeless envy in the sonar technicians on the USS *Vermont*. The multiple frequencies' echoes revealed distinctive layers of hard metals and plastics and soft flesh and denser bone.

The killphin closed rapidly, circling well beyond the human range of vision underwater, and inspecting her with repeated microbursts of high-frequency sounds so brief as to be detectable by no other creature. Its sonar detected the threatening hard-soft-hard pattern of a diver with an air tank on its back and a weapon in its hands.

Sally Moffitt stopped swimming and turned 360 degrees to look around. She checked her gauges: on course; twenty-five minutes out; all readings normal.

An enormous shadow rose from the indigo blue.

She raised the camera and hit the ROLL switch.

The killphin's tapered nose permitted it to see ahead with stereoscopic vision. At a distance of one hundred feet, and thirty above, the human holding a weapon appeared to be a light-colored slash in a field of blue-green, like the underbelly of a fish. The killphin halved the distance with a powerful upsweep of its massive tail. Close in, its aural and visual senses paired up to guide the attack.

21

THE WARM SEAWATER CARRIED SOUND nearly four times as fast as the air, and a thousand times farther.

Sailing a box pattern below the horizon, waiting for David Hope's catamaran to move again, William Tree's windship strayed closer. The killphin felt a frightening vibration in its jaw. The ship's rumble activated primitive fight-or-flight responses so intense that they muffled the echo returns that put the big predator in sync with its surroundings, its enemies, and its prey. Clicks and whistles it had transmitted disappeared like bubbles.

Sally Moffitt was buffeted by the pressure wave of the killphin's swift passing. She whirled the rolling camera toward the source but saw only a flash of motion that could have been a fish, a dolphin, or the play of sunlight on the surface, and then it was gone.

She waited half an hour, moving only to hold her own against the current. Then she swam south for thirty minutes, surfaced, searched the empty sea, and finally spotted the catamaran perched atop another wave, three hundred yards to her right. She took a bearing with her compass, and swam until she saw the twin hulls directly overhead.

She hovered at fifteen feet for several minutes to decompress. Just as she was about to break for the dive ladder in the back of the port hull, she stopped dead in the water. The sailboat's starboard hull was a moonscape of deep dents and gouges. She swam under and ran her glove over the surface. Lightly coated with soft green algae, it still felt rough and cracked.

She came up behind the boat and called, "I'm back!"

Hope bounded down to the dive ladder and took the camera from her. "I was about to send the cavalry."

"Sea horses?"

He grinned back and helped her up. "Any luck?"

"I think he came close, but I didn't get any tape."

Hope handed her a bottle of water. She chugged it, her mouth dry as dust, even though rebreather air was supposedly wetter than scuba. He helped her take the backpack off. Sally pulled off a fin, exposing a raw blister on her big toe.

"Do you know that the bottom of the starboard hull is all dented and cracked?"

"Yeah."

"It looks pretty bad."

"It's been that way for a year."

"I think you should look at it."

"I've seen it."

She looked at him. Captain Cautious was stepping way out of character. "When?"

"When what?" His face was closing up, bleak as a mountain fortress.

"When," she pressed, "did you last see it?"

"March." He carried the rebreather pack through the aft hatch into the dive room. "I'll top up your cylinders."

Sally followed him into the cramped, gear-cluttered space. Hope turned away from her to hook up the booster pump. "This last March?" she asked. "Last month?"

"March a year ago."

"It's possible," she said "that it's gotten worse since then."

"It's not the kind of damage that gets worse."

"Would you do me a favor and take a look? It scares me."

"I told you I was going to get it fixed when I got to Maine. And you pay me. I can't do anything about it out here."

"I think you should take a look. We should be prepared to do something if the hull is going to break up. Before we sink."

Hope said, "Okay. I'll look." He stepped into his cabin and closed the door. Sally pulled a second bottle of water from the dive room cooler and drank it. She waited for him, puzzled, until he emerged in a bathing suit. He grabbed a pair of long skin-diving fins from their rack and a small face mask and snorkle.

"Would you like to try my tank?"

"Snorkel's fine."

He sat on the dive steps, tugged on his fins, pulled his mask over his face. Then he pushed off, floated in a sitting position for a second to clear his mask, bent at his waist, and reached down with his hands. Leading with his fingertips, he kicked under in a streamlined surface dive.

Sally looked around for Ishmael. Some puffy clouds rode overhead. A hazy dark spot that might be a far distant squall coming their way lay in the west. But no spinning dolphin broke the deep blue moving plain. Only some whitecaps— the wind was picking up—and a fuzzy lightness in the east that might be a cloud below the horizon or even a light-colored ship.

She looked at her watch. Forty-five seconds since David went down. She thought of the rush she had felt—the pow-erful surge of something big speeding past. What if Ishmael was right under the boat, waiting to defend its territory again? What if the animal was charging David right now, right below her feet?

David popped up next to the dive steps and hauled him-self aboard, kicking with the fins and pulling himself up with his strong arms. He removed his mask. "Looks like it will hold a while longer," he said casually.

"How much longer?"

"A long time. Don't worry. She's very strong."

"David, what's going on?"

"What do you mean?"

"I mean that Captain Cautious is suddenly devil-may-care. Why are you so casual about that damage? What is going on? I don't understand."

He pulled off his gear, got a towel, dried off.

"Shall we go, boss?"

"David."

"Ishmael's waiting. The longer we sit here, the longer he's got to give up on us and head north-northeast. The wind's honkin'. We should fly."

"Aye, Captain."

But, Hope discovered, Sally wouldn't let it go. As soon as he had the main and jib out and pulling hard and the auto-helm adjusted to keep *Oona* on a fast reach and Sally had showered off and changed into dry clothes, she said, "Stop me if it's not any of my business, but I really want to know why you are so casual about that damage."

"It's not any of your business."

"I just pulled the floorboards up in my cabin. There are *bulges* in the fiberglass."

"Been there for a year."

"They look like they leak."

"Not a lot."

"I'm baffled."

"But not silenced."

"David, you must know by now that I'm not the kind of person who just sits quietly. Like I told you, I don't know a lot about boats, but I get the awful feeling that this one could sink suddenly, without any warning."

"Okay," said David.

"Okay, what? Would it be safer to sleep on deck? I'm afraid of getting trapped in the cabin if the hull suddenly breaks open."

Hope said quietly, "She won't go down fast. She's not a mono-hull with eight thousand pounds of lead in her keel. Plus, she's got crash boxes—foam-filled watertight bulkheads. Even with her decks awash, it'll take her a long time to break up." He looked at Sally, who was sitting silent, with her mouth open in a stunned O. "There've been times I've wished she *would* sink," he said. "Or half wished. I feel a little guilty, putting you at risk, but it's not going to happen. She's strong. She'll make it to forty-five-forty-five and home to Maine. I promise. If she doesn't, we've got a dinghy, we've got a canopy life raft, we've got EPIRB to send a mayday. We'll get picked up eventually. But none of that is going to happen because we're not going to sink."

She looked like she believed him. Or at least wanted to. And her next question was in a soft voice, and deeply personal. "Why did you hope your boat would sink?"

Hope, who a moment before had shifted into talking mode, was suddenly unable to speak. Sally eyed him speculatively and asked in the same quiet voice, "Is this about the woman who died?"

He nodded. "Her name was Barbara. Barbara Carey."

"About how she died?"

"Yes."

"Was she injured when you ran aground?"

"We didn't run aground. . . .The water was half a mile deep."

Sally waited a long time. Finally she said, "I'd feel better about your state of mind if you were crying."

"I'm done crying."

Again, she waited. Hope, silent, finally stood up and took the helm and overrode the wind vane. *Oona* picked up half a knot on the speedometer.

"David. Would I be way off to suggest that you're stuck in some kind of posttraumatic stress?"

"Way off."

"You hardly sleep at all."

"I'm running the boat. I've never needed much sleep. Especially at sea. I catch up now and then on the beach."

"When you do sleep you have nightmares."

"I don't have nightmares all the time."

"Do you have any idea what sets them off?"

"Yeah, I'm beginning to see a pattern." He stared straight ahead as he spoke. "In fact, I think I finally see a way out of them."

"Good."

"Just in the last week. If I take a crazy chance—like pirating out of Tortola—I get nightmares. When I don't take chances, I don't. Just in the last week. Before I was getting them all the time."

"Stop taking chances? You're Captain Cautious already."

"Could you come up with a new nickname?"

"On top of not sleeping and nightmares," she replied, as primly self-contained as a schoolgirl reporting the day's lessons, "you exhibit classic symptoms of a condition called exaggerated startle response. Do you know what that is?"

"Yeah, loud noises make me jump."

"Not just loud. I'll interrupt your thoughts and you jump like I poked you with a hot needle. Posttraumatic—"

"Enough, Nurse Nancy. I'll see a shrink as soon as I get the bottom repaired."

Sally stiffened. "Considering what I've shared with you, that was a hateful thing to say."

"I'm sorry. Like you said, I'm stressed."

"You can hang on to that forever. It's a great excuse for almost anything."

Hope rounded on her angrily. "Let's just drop it."

22

WHAT HOPE HAD ASSUMED WAS a breakaway eddy of the Gulf Stream turned out to be a broad northeasterly meander of the ever-shifting bed of the transoceanic river. Both *Oona* and Ishmael flew along, picking up an extra three knots from the powerful current, the big mammal swimming over two hundred miles a day, with the catamaran easily keeping pace.

Knowing that storms tended to follow the Gulf Stream's track, gorging on its warmth, Hope paid closer than ever attention to the weather faxes, radio reports, and his barometer. But a huge, intense high-pressure system nearly two thousand miles wide was making a slow, stately passage across the North Atlantic. Like a broad-shouldered cop who swaggered a sidewalk clear of muggers, the high forced storm-brewing depressions to pass harmlessly to their north and south. The swells generated by those distant disturbances formed orderly ranks, while the wind, holding steady from the west and northwest, blew more with than against the eastward-flowing current. They sailed, in consequence, on a magically peaceful sea.

Warm, gentle days and night skies ablaze with stars. All the ingredients of an idyllic, romantic passage, Hope confided ruefully to Sally, if only the captain could sleep without waking up yelling.

Sally cut him no slack. Polite but distant, she concentrated on Ishmael, who continued on his north-northeast track as if on rails. While Hope refused during his increasingly long waking hours to talk about Barbara's death, Sally was haunted by her husband's betrayal—and increasingly vexed by the threat that the object they had observed behind the big dolphin's dorsal fin really was a data link antenna implanted there by scientists who not only knew of the animal's existence but had a role in its behavior.

Thus neither she nor Hope were immediate candidates to extend a pleasant night of mutually satisfying groping in the cockpit to the next natural phase on one of their comfortable berths. But as annoyed as she was with Hope's reluctance to let her help him and as threatened as he felt by her efforts, affection and sexual interest flared powerfully between the man and woman whom William Tree had pronounced at lunch "a most attractive couple."

They had a screaming argument over her diving again. Hope tried to make it clear that he admired Sally's bravery and determination. But she was uncomfortable with the compliment, because she knew that way down inside she felt unsure and believed that admitting that would blunt her edge. The big animal ended their battle by disappearing for a long, anxious day.

Laying awake in the cockpit, waiting for another nightmare to tear his head apart, Hope wondered whether this dolphin chase wasn't just repeating his old pattern of going along with a woman's enthusiasm as he had with Barbara. The bigger picture was even worse: Was he really ready to surrender the isolation in which he had taken refuge since Barbara? How was this current isolation different from the retreat to the boat from larger life many years ago? What the hell was he afraid of? What was he hiding from?

The fine weather held as the Gulf Stream slipped them

painlessly, almost seamlessly into the slower-flowing but still warm and clear North Atlantic Current. By then Hope was tapping the barometer when he read it, hardly believing how long the beneficent high held on. The storms inside him, however, raged on.

Midmorning, the fifth day after Sally's dive, despair flooded his heart. He engaged the auto-helm and went forward to where Sally was sitting with her camera in front of the cabin on the abbreviated foredeck, watching for Ishmael. Her patience amazed him. As impatient as she was toward her goal of proving herself a natural history filmmaker, when it came to the actual work of capturing images, she would wait and watch in hot sun or cold spray as quiet and uncomplaining as a statue. Hope slumped down beside her, bleary-eyed, trembling.

"What am I supposed to do?"

She grabbed both his hands.

"The oldest advice in the book is now the newest," she said earnestly. "Talk. Tell me what happened to Barbara. But just talking isn't enough. You must keep telling me what you felt while it was happening."

"It's the oldest cliché, too."

"It's the hot subject in the journals again. Listen, if you don't get some sleep you're going to die. Do you have any better ideas?"

"Not living room therapy."

"Talk works."

"Oh God, I'm in the hands of a psych major. Are you sure you're not trying to fix your mom by proxy?"

"I told you, she's very happy on Prozac. Which might help you, too."

"Alcohol is my drug of choice, thank you very much."

"I haven't seen you take a drink since that Côtes-du-Rhône with the steaks."

"You should see me on the beach."

"But you're rarely on the beach, you're on the boat." She

nudged him with her shoulder. "Come on. Go with me on this. Talk to me."

Hope looked at her. He could feel his whole being struggling between shutting down and jumping overboard. He stood up suddenly, braced himself on the boom, and said, "I'd rather talk to Ishmael."

"Oh, for god's sake."

"No, I mean it. All this 'talk' stuff has given me an idea."

Sally looked thoroughly fed up. "What?"

"We got him on the hydrophone, right? We have the recording."

"On which he was more forthcoming than you."

"Let's play him back to himself."

"What?"

"We'll see what he thinks of himself."

"How?"

"We'll somehow waterproof one of the mini-speakers from a sleeping cabin, drop it over the side, and crank the volume."

Sally stood up, intrigued. "Okay, why?"

"Draw him near when the boat's not moving. We'll get him close enough to film and video. We'll get a look at that harpoon or whatever. Pat his back and scratch his chin. Feed him something. Make friends. Maybe even talk him into following us home to Maine."

The mini-speaker was about the size of a baseball. It had been advertised as marine quality, guaranteed moisture-resistant. Though you weren't supposed to throw them overboard. If only he could somehow encase it in polyurethane like the hydrophone. There'd been a hobby craze once where you could encase mementos in clear poly like a Jurassic grasshopper preserved in amber. There were probably a million poly kits all over America in a million basements and garages. But none in the middle of the Atlantic Ocean.

He poked around in his tool chests and stared for a while at a can of thick grease. Maybe he could coat the little speaker with Vaseline. Maybe not. He wandered up to the bridge cabin where Sally was juggling adaptors to wire her DAT recorder into the stereo. He looked around. The galley was speaking to him. He pulled open a drawer and whipped out a roll of plastic wrap.

"Yes!"

Robbing speaker wire from various speakers around the boat—which meant a tedious repair job when he got to Maine—he fashioned a cable long enough to lead out of the main saloon and over the side twenty feet underwater.

Then he connected it to the mini-speaker, making damned sure it could carry the weight. Then he started wrapping the speaker and several feet of wire with the plastic wrap, running the clingy stuff around and around and around until the speaker looked like a fruit basket in a cheap hotel.

"What do you think?" he asked Sally.

"Can you hear through all that?"

"Run the tape."

She turned on the DAT full blast. Giant dolphin noise boomed in his hand. "Excellent." Over the side it went, after he stopped the boat, and carefully down into the warm blue water.

Sally loaded her cameras, checked her batteries, and said, "Ready!"

Hope rolled the audiotape they had made of the big dolphin's clicks and groans. Then he dipped the hydrophone into the water and listened to check that the speaker was working. It was. His headset filled with the recorded noises. In the pauses between whistles and clicks, he listened for answers. But the dolphin didn't come.

They played its sounds for an hour. Finally, Sally lowered her film camera and said, "With his hearing, I'm sure he can hear it for twenty miles."

"So what's he waiting for?"

"All I can think is that dolphins have passed the mirror test. They know the difference between reality and a reflection. It's just possible that he knows his voice, recognizes it, and recognizes that something is therefore off."

"Maybe he's too far off."

"Let's keep doing it."

Another hour passed. Hope was disconsolate. Sally said, "Have you ever held a telephone to a cat's ear?"

"No," said Hope. "Not that I can recall."

"Well, I have, and what happens is you say to the cat, 'Listen to Daddy.' Daddy says, 'Hi, cat.' The cat looks up. Recognizes the voice, looks around, and immediately loses interest. If it can't see Daddy and can't smell Daddy, it knows that Daddy isn't here. I'm afraid that Ishmael knows hearing himself makes no sense, so the heck with it."

"Well, I never said he was stupid. I was just hoping we could have a talk."

"Speaking of which," said Sally. "Would you like another shot at telling me what happened to Barbara?"

"Why?"

"The other night you were kinder to me than any man I can remember."

"Oh, come on, it was no big deal, I just went along with what you wanted."

"In kindness, timing is everything. You were kind when I needed kindness. So I owe you. Tell me what happened to Barbara."

"You don't owe me anything."

"Have you told anyone before?"

"No."

"Did you talk to anyone who was there?"

"No. Everybody scattered."

"What do you mean, 'scattered'? Why?"

"Afraid of getting arrested. Or beaten up."

"Did you scatter?"

"No, I couldn't."

"Why not?"

"I had to stay with her."

"Why?"

"She was my passenger. I was her lover."

"Would you tell me what happened?"

Hope shrugged. "I fucked up."

"How? How did you fuck up?" She stepped close and touched his shoulder. With her other hand she extracted a long chrome winch handle from its rubber rack. "And if you call me Nurse Nancy again, I'll brain you with this. . . . Where did it happen?"

"Let me get the boat moving first."

He hauled in the sheets. The empty sails filled and *Oona* skipped lightly to a plane. He took the wheel, preferring to have something to hold on to and a compass to watch while he tried to talk.

23

"WE WERE IN THE GULF of Mexico. They were towing a humongous semi-submersible oil drilling rig into what had been a protected no-drill zone before the government eased up the environmental regs. We caught up with them about two hundred miles south of Mobile, Alabama."

"When? Night? Day?"

"Night."

"What did you feel?"

Hope grinned. "Scared shitless."

"Why?"

"Why? What do you mean, why? It was pitch-black, a heavy sea was running. I couldn't use the radar."

"Why not?"

"They'd have picked up my signal. Known we were there."

"Who?"

"Who knows? They were called Metro Drilling. Just a corporate shell name for a shell game. It could have been any of them."

"What were you doing there?"

Hope said nothing.

"Hmm?"

"Well, it's a good question. We had made a gigantic flag out of a huge spinnaker sail. Picked it up for pennies because it had blown out. So we sewed up the hole and then we painted this gigantic . . . dolphin, actually, of all things, on it. Funny, I hadn't made the connection before. But you know, dolphins are everybody's symbol of free nature and all that. Then we painted an oil rig piercing the dolphin like a giant spear. It was really dramatic. One of the kids was a heck of an artist—he'd worked on stage sets—and I gotta tell you, this thing looked amazing. It must have been eighty feet high. The idea was, we were going to hang it from the top of the derrick in the middle of the night. An old newshound buddy of mine was with CNN and I had him primed to send a news helicopter out from Pensacola to shoot it at dawn."

"He was going to send a helicopter on your word?"

"He wasn't risking anything. The deal was I'd radio him when we'd done the deed. He'd get credit for a very dramatic picture that would make all the morning news shows."

"Whose idea was this?"

"Barbara's. I was just driving."

"It was like a publicity stunt?"

"A lot more than that. You pull off a big PR win and donations come in and the legit groups get invited to the hearings and there are interviews and people write about it and it might help turn public opinion against big oil and their politicians."

"And what was Barbara—other than being your girlfriend?"

"She used to call herself an eco-terrorist. I persuaded her that these days 'eco-crusader' might go down a little better."

"At least among Christians."

Hope smiled. Sally said, "Sorry, I didn't mean to interrupt. Was she in an organized group?"

"She'd bounced around. In and out of the Earth Liberation Front movement. And Greenpeace, of course. But she and her friends were operating alone when I met her."

"So she wasn't going to blow the rig up. She was just going to hang a flag on it?"

"Some of them were blowup inclined," Hope replied. "Barbara saw I'd have no part of that and she hatched the flag scheme instead."

"Did you feel good about that?"

Hope gripped the wheel a little tighter. He said, "What I couldn't make her understand was that the risks—the personal risks—were almost as high. I mean, we were talking about hoisting a hundred-pound sail up a forty-story derrick in the dark."

"Brave woman."

"Damned fool."

"Did you try to talk her out of it?"

"Sure. She said, 'I'm fighting for an ideology I believe in.' What can you say to that? It's like you telling me, 'I've got to dive into the personal space of a three-ton mutant dolphin.' I knew it was nuts. She didn't see it that way. . . . Neither did you."

"Does it bother you that you drove the sailboat anyhow?"

"If I didn't, she'd have found someone else."

"And left you?"

"Someone who wasn't competent."

"It sounds like you got all bases covered."

"What do you mean?"

"It wasn't your fault."

Hope stared at her. "Of course it was my fault, for Christ's sake. I was there. I screwed up."

"But—"

"There's no but. Nobody twisted my arm. I did it."

Sally said, "Okay. That's how you got into the Gulf of Mexico at night. What happened once you were there?"

Hope looked around at the sunlit beauty of the deep blue water. It was as if they were sailing in an isolated bay, surrounded not by land, but by the vast Atlantic. Ahead a day or so waited cold gray water, but for the moment *Oona* basked in almost tropical luxury. He engaged the auto-helm and sat on one of the cockpit benches. He stretched his legs. Then he put his hands behind his head like a prisoner of war.

"This I've not told anybody. And if you tell anybody I'll say you're lying."

Sally took the bench opposite. "I think you know me better than that."

"Sorry."

She waved his apology aside as if the words weren't worth the effort. "What happened?"

"There were four tugs and anchor handlers towing the rig. They each had half a mile of cable out—the towlines—most of it underwater. The water acts like a spring to equalize forces so the wire doesn't part. I mean, these are enormous forces. The tugs are probably ten thousand horsepower each. The rig weighs more than a ton. Momentum was carrying it and they were making five knots with a tailwind. It would take them ten miles to stop. So the tugs keep their radar glued ahead.

"We took down my radar reflector—" He pointed up at one of the shrouds where a boxy tangle of aluminum enhanced the target that the sailboat presented to the radar pulses from passing ships. "—and approached from astern, figuring the tugboats would confuse us with the bigger target. They didn't expect anything small coming up behind them, anyway, and the rig showed up on their radar like a hefty island.

"Plus, like I said, the night was so dark it could have been the Spanish Main. No moon. Overcast hiding the stars. Black as hell. My biggest worry about getting seen was the light spilling from the rig itself, and that I didn't have to worry about until we were right alongside.

"I knew there was a sizable riding crew. They can't tow them unmanned, in case a wire parts or it's taking on water or something catches fire . . . I figured there had to be several watch standers and mechanics and engineers busy tend-ing machinery. . . . There again they would be watching foward, watching the tugs—it's human nature.

"I came in as fast as I could—the wind was honking, and we zeroed in on their lights at a good fourteen–fifteen knots. The rig was riding high on two big pontoons; they flood them to steady it when they anchor to drill a well, but they're towed dry. On top was an accommodations section and a helipad off to one side and the drilling derrick. I figured the riding crew would be inside the accommodation unit. So I came up on the opposite side, next to the part that held the derrick.

"You have never seen anything as high as that derrick looked from down on the water. Or for that matter, the pontoons. They looked four stories high and the derrick shot up from there like a stairway to heaven. So here's where it got tricky. I had to hold the boat alongside this rounded pontoon long enough to offload everybody and our spinnaker flag onto these boarding ladders welded to the side."

"Everybody?" Sally interrupted.

"Barbara and her retainers."

"Retainers?"

"I'm joking. I shouldn't be. I used to call them her merry band. She had three strong, young, not awfully bright, deeply committed fellow eco-crusaders who would gladly lay down and die for her if she asked."

"How did you fit in?"

"She knew that they needed adult supervision."

"Are you joking again?"

"No. She was very smart, very dedicated, and she knew she needed adult help."

"Were they in love with her?"

"Of course. Everybody was."

Sally said, "Back to the moment."

"They were three strong backs and I had to drive the boat alongside this thing moving at five knots—which isn't that slow when you're trying to jump onto it in the dark."

He paused to look out at the water again. They might be leaving the North Atlantic Current sooner than he had anticipated. Squalls far ahead possibly marked where the northern edge joined the cold water beyond.

"The platform was rolling a little on the swell. But *Oona* was also bouncing up and down on this damned cross-sea kicked up by the wind and the rig itself.

"I wasn't sure how to handle it. We were towing a high-power inflatable that they'd gotten their paws on somewhere as an emergency escape boat and I considered transferring them into that for the final run. There were both good and bad reasons to do that. But in the end I didn't trust them to handle the inflatable in those seas, so I said, Okay, we're going in. Eddie and Rick first. They were strong—solid jocks—and pretty agile. Then Joseph. Not so agile, but really powerful; Joseph had worked his way through college as a roustabout, so he knew his way around an oil rig. Good kid. I figured that way I'd get the muscle aboard and then Barbara and I would pass lines to haul over the sail. If anything went wrong, I'd have her with me until the last second."

"How did Barbara feel about that?"

"She was focused on the job. She knew what the muscle was there for. The setup made me feel better, but it also made sense."

"Could I ask something?"

"Please. It's easier to answer questions than talk cold."

"At this point—when you were boarding the moving platform—you had taken charge?"

He looked at Sally, blinking his eyes. "If I had taken charge I'd have said, 'Okay, everybody. There's the monster rig that we are *not* going to risk our lives boarding. Wave bye-bye—we're going sailing instead.' "

"That would have been hard to do in a crowd of true believers."

"I would hope—I would pray—that if there was a next time I would do the right thing."

"Why you? Why was it your job?"

"Like I said, I was the 'adult.' I was captain of the boat. I knew what I was doing. As much as anyone could know in a situation like that. . . ."

"You said, you 'hope.' Do you think you would?"

"What do you think?"

"I don't know. I'm not a shrink." She smiled at him and gently kicked his bare foot with hers. "I just do amateur stress management, speaking of which, we're dodging at the moment. What happened? Did you put them aboard?"

"All aboard, painted sail and all. I cast off before the riding crew noticed my mainsail flapping alongside, dropped back a few hundred yards out of the light. My friends were doing the hard part, climbing a long slog to the top. But waiting, I've got to tell you, was the longest two hours I have ever lived. I kept scoping the derrick with the night glasses. You've seen pictures; it's like a layered latticework of steel beams and piers. Finally spotted them about halfway up. They looked like little green ants in the glasses, inching up and up and up. The higher they climbed, the more the height magnified the rig's pitching and rolling on the swell.

"The wind started getting weird, so I cranked the engines. I figured no way the riding crew could hear them over the noise of the rig's own machinery and the wind. I had to be ready to go in fast. We maintained radio silence. Anyone working the tow could have picked up the handhelds. So I couldn't know until the last minute that they were ready to be picked up.

"Then I saw the white glow of the spinnaker. I scoped it through the night glasses. There was our big beautiful dolphin with an oil rig spear in his heart! Reality TV on your morning news. They'd done it. They'd flown the flag. Now all they had to do was climb down the derrick and get off the rig without being spotted. I started slowly catching up."

Hope stopped talking and stared out at the sea. The

squalls he thought he had seen ahead seemed to have vaporized. So had Ishmael.

"I wished I'd gone aboard with them. What a ballsy feat they had pulled off."

"Somebody had to stay with the boat."

"I was the best sailor. And the least committed to the cause. I guess I envied their commitment."

"Bull."

"What?"

"You committed your entire boat—business and home—to their nutty scheme."

Hope looked at the water, up at the sails, cranked the jib winch a couple of clicks, and looked out at the water again. He shook his head and grinned at her. "I thought shrinks were supposed to listen, not talk."

"Didn't you commit?"

"I didn't look at it that way."

"You probably should have— Did Barbara fall from the derrick?"

"She made it down to the main deck before everything went to hell."

"What happened?"

"I screwed up. They radioed me to come in. I headed full throttle to the pickup point, at the bottom of the pontoon ladder. But with the tow moving at five knots and *Oona* making only seven and a half, I was galloping to the rescue like molasses. And the closer I got the crazier the seas kicked off it.

"I saw them come over the side. One. And then two. Three. And, finally—finally—four. Barbara taking up the rear. They started down the ladder they'd gone up, down one of the columns, in the same order. And over the bulge of the pontoon and down its ladder.

"I made my pass. I still don't know what happened, a sea whipped under the boat and stood me on my ear. *Oona* hit something so hard with the starboard hull I thought we'd sink for sure. It might have been a prong sticking out of the pontoon, or the pontoon itself, but somehow that sea picked us up and slammed us sideways against it. That's what did all the damage to the hull. . . ."

"Didn't the riding crew hear you hit their rig?"

"No. The rig was so huge, it was like smashing into a Hudson River pier. Who would notice at the Plaza Hotel? I didn't know how badly I'd been damaged, but there was no time to check below because they were still hanging on to the ladder at the bottom of the pontoon.

"I lined up for another pass. Suddenly I heard someone on the radio say, 'Oh, shit.'

"A searchlight whipped around the platform. Then I heard a lot of shouting. Then work floods switched on, bright as a factory floor. From where I was down on the boat, I couldn't see beyond the rim of the platform. But it was pretty clear the riding crew had tumbled to the fact they'd been boarded and I had about two seconds to get my people off the pontoon before they noticed us over the side.

"*Oona* finally plowed up to the ladder. The first guy, Eddie, tumbled aboard, wrapped a line around a cleat, and raced back to the stern and started pulling their speedboat alongside. Rick came next and ran back to help Eddie and I'm thinking, Jesus H., they're going to blast off in the speedboat, leaving me to escape on a sailboat. I looked to see what Barbara's going to do—split with them or stick with me?"

He stopped talking and stared into the distance.

"What did she do?" asked Sally.

"I underestimated her."

"She stayed with you?"

Hope shook his head. "Joe hit the deck, but there's still no Barbara. I yelled, 'Where's Barbara?'

" 'She's gone back up,' he said.

" 'Up what?'

" 'The rig,' he said. 'The crazy broad'—his words—'is going to chain herself to the derrick.'

"I looked up and there she was, just climbing into view on her way back up the derrick. So I keyed my handheld—way too late for radio silence now—and I raised Barbara, who had hers clipped under her chin. 'What are you doing?'

"I could hear the wind whipping across the rig and then I heard her, with a little scared tremble in voice. She was breathing hard, climbing fast. She was in great shape, but that was her second time up the damned thing in half an hour. 'We're caught,' she said. 'They'll pull down the flag. Radio your news friend. Tell him I'll be up on the top wearing bright yellow. It'll make a great shot.'

"She hadn't told me, earlier, but it was her fallback position all along, in case something went wrong. Under her black jumpsuit she was wearing fluorescent yellow tights. She had a whole slew of handcuffs to chain herself to the rig." Hope shook his head in disgust. "Apparently it never occurred to her that they have plenty of bolt cutters on an oil rig. I started arguing with her, then I noticed the guys in the speedboat were untying their lines.

"I was really freaking out: 'Where the hell are you going?'

" 'We're out on parole. If we get arrested, our asses are grass. Barbara told us to split.' They cast off and roared away like a gang of bank robbers."

Hope sat still shaking his head. "I mean, it was almost comic. All four of them—both committed and committable. Certifiably nuts, but so dedicated—so brave—and coldly practical: run away to fight again another day. I guess that's how you win causes, but my instinct would be never to leave her. . . ."

"Let me guess," said Sally. "You tied the *Oona* to the ladder and boarded the oil rig."

"What was I supposed to do? Leave her there?"

"You're what my mother used to call a male chauvinist pig. Couldn't you respect Barbara's decision?"

"Jesus H. Why can't you respect mine? She was important to me. I couldn't see leaving her alone with a gang of angry roustabouts."

"I'm sorry," said Sally. "But I just think you're awfully hung up on always trying to make things right—go on, I'm sorry I interrupted. You're right, I could never be a shrink, I talk too much. Then what happened?"

"I don't know, exactly. I didn't see her actually slip. But as I cleared the rim of the pontoon, I saw both her arms shoot up. Like she was trying to grab the air."

24

SHE CAME DOWN LIKE A brick. A long, silent, upside-down free fall. She was utterly motionless, as if she knew her fate and would meet it with dignity. . . . Near the bottom, the derrick flared out. She hit a crossbeam. Bounced. Hit another. Bounced. Hit a third. Bounced, arms and legs flying. It was like watching a woman get kicked by giants.

"She finally fell past my line of sight. I climbed the column as fast as I could. When I got onto the main deck, I saw a crowd standing over something. Huge bruisers standing around her. Nobody said a word. They were just staring at this beautiful woman with half her face crushed. It was like everybody present suddenly realized there's been a tragedy and nothing that seemed important a minute ago mattered one bit.

"She went into convulsions. A security guy whipped out a handheld and radioed for a medevac chopper. I've done all the first aid courses for my Rescue C card, of course, and the rig had an EMT guy on board. Between us we tried to clear the blood and bone splinters out of her airway, got oxygen on her, and tried to keep her from swallowing her tongue. Strapped her to a stretcher; buried her in blankets.

"She went into shock, of course. The EMT guy pumped

in fluids. After that there wasn't much more we could do but wait. So we just sat on the deck and watched her. I held her hand. It kept twitching, like jolts of electricity.

"We were a long way offshore; it took the helicopter nearly two hours. Trauma team piled out, trached her to help her breathe, and hustled the stretcher onto the chopper. Last I saw of her was flashing lights in the sky. . . ."

Sally waited a while and then said, "What did you feel? Numb?"

"Not at all numb. In the two hours we waited the numb went away and I felt totally destroyed. My first thought was how much I'd miss her. My second was I knew it was my fault—yes, I know, she would have gotten there somehow one way or another—I've told myself that twenty times— but my sailing her onto the rig delivered her to the exact moment she fell."

"Are you blaming yourself for delivering her to her fate?"

"If I hadn't crashed on that first pass, I'd have gotten them off before the crew blew the whistle and it would have been too late for her to climb back up. . . . I remember thinking, They can charge me with accessory to manslaughter or whatever the lawyers would call it and I'll plead guilty and go to jail."

"Did they charge you?"

"I was standing there with tears running down my face. The security guys huddled. Then back and forth on radios. Finally, then the boss—security captain—comes over, nudges me hard. Big guy about my age. Retired military. Low voice. 'The lady's on the way to the hospital, but the docs don't think she'll make it. Her friends in the speedboat got away. Thanks for stopping to help. We'll give you a hand casting off.' "

"They just let you go?"

"It was more like they kicked me off."

"Why?"

"I wasn't paying attention—I was dying inside, starting to

paralyze—but looking back, my guess is the guys on the ground made a command decision to keep it simple."

"I can't believe they let you go."

"Anyone could see that Barbara was a goner. They knew that there were going to be investigations up the wazoo. Coroners from every port that claimed jurisdiction, cops, Coast Guard, company security. They sure didn't want a big public criminal trial or lawsuits making heroes out of the brave defenders of the environment and devils out of the horrible oilmen.

"Their best bet was to blame the unknown perpetrators on the speedboat that got away. Without me there'd never be a trial. Barbara sure as hell wasn't going to testify. When you think about it, it made perfect sense. It wasn't their fault she got killed. They were just doing their job. They wanted me gone. Two seamen escorted me down the ladder and stood by until I shoved off.

"The rig disappeared east. I went south. Before I knew it, I was sailing in the dark. . . . I kept trying to find out about Barbara. I kept checking in with people on the ham radio net, and eventually heard she was in a coma. I blew out my plastic radio—phoning her doctor. He was a straight shooter, kept telling me that it would be a miracle if she ever woke up and even if she did, there was so much brain damage that there'd be no one home. . . . I holed up in Honduras for the hurricane season. Worked my way up to the BVI in time for the charter season. Put my life back together, sort of, except for the nightmares. Actually, I even worked them out. Got so I could function on never more than an hour. Very helpful on a charter boat. Hello, the captain is awake. . . . I kept calling the doctor, of course. Then all of a sudden, out of the blue— what is it, three weeks ago—her ashes came. The poor thing had hung on a year . . . strong woman. A year is a very long time. . . ."

Sally sat uncharacteristically quietly for a while. Finally, she asked, "When did you start having nightmares?"

"Rounding Cuba, three nights after it happened. Scared the hell out of me because the first time, at least, I had no idea it was a dream. Not that knowing it's a dream makes it less scary, now. It's so weird. It's the same one every time. Rigs are toppling, spouting oil into the sea; the oil catches fire. And as the flames catch up with the boat, the burning water turns to blood. . . ."

". . . And?"

"And, so much for talking, Sally. Not that I don't appreciate your kind ear."

She stood up. "It was worth a try."

Hope said, "But it's like when we played Ishmael's voice back at him. No wonder he wasn't impressed. It's not going to change his life. He's heard it before."

"But he tried to communicate. We played his question back because we just didn't know the answer."

"Knowing he's trying to communicate is not the same as knowing the question."

She cupped his cheek in her hand. "Very funny. . . . But it's still a good question. What is Ishmael saying to us?"

Hope manufactured a weak smile. He felt drained. "He's pleading, 'No more questions.' "

She pulled his head to her chest, hugged him tightly, and kissed his brow. Hope had noted this spontaneous affection lately. They had yet to work their way back down to the floor of the cockpit yet, much less a soft berth, but they were abruptly pressing close and then kissing. Then Sally was sitting on his lap. "Am I too heavy?"

"I'm of the Anthony Quinn school. When a boy finally grows into a man he wants a woman he can grab on to."

"Greg liked me this way, too. I don't know what he's doing with that skinny Italian."

"More to the point, what are you doing with me? At this moment."

"Kissing. Holding. And hoping you've recovered from your cockpit therapy enough to—*ohmigod!*"

Hope felt her stiffen the way she did whenever she spotted the animal.

"Do you see him?"

But she was looking down the companionway, into the saloon. "Will you stay up on watch?" she asked.

"Alone? Weren't we heading for a rematch?"

"You just gave me an amazing idea. I want to try it on the AVID."

"What?"

"I'm going to find out what he's saying to us."

Hope yawned. "We don't even know it was us he was asking. It's a big ocean. He could have been asking anybody."

"I'll check to see if you fall asleep."

"Fat chance."

Sally went below, turned on her laptop and the DV VCR and Hope's television, and booted up her Sound Forge audio editing program. From the Play list she selected the digital audiotape recording they had captured of the big dolphin's voice.

She donned her headset to better hear over the rush of water under *Oona*'s keels. While that never-ending "white noise," which was amplified by the hollow resonance of the boat's hulls, was not as loud in the saloon as in the sleeping cabins, it was plenty loud to distract.

Pressing her left hand to the earpiece and jiggering the mouse with her right, she listened repeatedly to their five-minute hydrophone DAT recording of the animal's clicks and whistles.

The screen displayed the audio waveforms visually on the monitor. These noise prints allowed her to browse the PLAY bar for patterns. Keying Magnify Mode, she zoomed in on specific sections to scrutinize them in minute detail.

Not a clue. Except, she noticed after a while, that what sounded like complex sounds were actually repeating the same short pattern over and over. It might or might not be significant. But whatever Ishmael was "asking," he seemed to be "asking" over and over and over.

Up in the cockpit, as night fell and stars speckled the sky, Hope began to feel sleepy. He slipped below quietly, so as not to disturb Sally, who was deep in thought at her computer, and set the radar ship alarm for six miles. Then he returned to the cockpit, praying that sleep would overtake him. Instead, when he closed his eyes he saw Barbara falling from the derrick. I should open my eyes, he thought, and stop this. Before he could, he fell asleep.

When the nightmare struck and the tallest rig he had ever seen began toppling swiftly onto *Oona*, he steered away from the spearlike derrick, only to see a taller one crashing down on him from a new direction. He reversed the helm. *Oona* skipped away and the derrick splashed harmlessly into the sea. He looked ahead into a wall of fire and woke up, sweat-drenched, trembling. He was on his feet, standing at the wheel, hands poised to wrest control from the auto-helm.

He hadn't expected that any good would come out of Sally's cockpit therapy. But he had harbored secret hopes. And now he stood at the wheel, deeply disappointed, until it gradually dawned on him that he didn't feel wrecked or even tired. Puzzled, yet grateful, he looked up at the stars. Bright Regulus had moved into the west.

His heart soared. He had slept for four full uninterrupted hours. He ran below to tell Sally. But from the companionway step, he saw her hunched over her computer, deep in concentration. He backed quietly up into the cockpit.

He was hungry. He took a swig from a water bottle and thought about trying to sneak down and grab a bite from the galley without disturbing her. Before he could act on the thought, his mind shifted to the night Barbara was killed. Her death was raw in his mind again, but something about it felt different. Telling someone else the entire story had subtly changed it. Memories he had taken for granted seemed slightly less graven in stone than before. Of Sally's many questions, one stuck in his head.

Openly incredulous, she had asked, *"They just let you go?"*

The drilling rig's security detail had thought fast on their feet. Extremely fast. Or unbelievably fast? Eliminating him as a witness, they had granted their bosses the power to reduce their version of Barbara's death to a bland, yet unassailable "A known eco-terrorist boarded us from a speedboat that disappeared when she fell. . . ."

"Son of a bitch," Hope said aloud. What if letting him go—or rather, chasing him off—had not been a low-level command decision? It was too big, too fraught with legal disaster, for the men on the rig. Orders had to have come from the top. It was their bosses who had radioed, Let him go! Get rid of the guy on the sailboat. Eliminate the one witness who would make us go public. And by the way, boys, look for something in your Christmas stockings.

Maybe Barbara's merry band weren't as paranoid about corporate power as he had always thought they were. He owed his freedom to people of such consequence, they weren't afraid to take a chance on a bold action. But why, he wondered, did this seem important to him now, a year later and thousands of miles away at sea? It didn't change the fact that Barbara was dead and gone. If anything, it reminded him of Commander Royce of the *Vermont* allowing him to sail away after satisfying his initial suspicions. Not Royce, of course, who was too far down the food chain to make big decisions, but his captain, or the sub skipper's superiors at the Pentagon.

"Son of a bitch," Hope said again, the connection finally dawning. Blinded by his willingness to go along with Sally's dream of discovering a new species, he had ignored some pretty obvious clues and failed to ask some pretty important questions about the strange, huge dolphin. Sally's protests aside, the odds were that the monster was wearing an an-

tenna. And if it was, Hope was willing to bet that it was re-
laying data to the Tree Marine Institute. So the big question
was, why had William Tree beat around the bush about "unusual" or "interesting" sightings, instead of asking straight
out if they had seen the dolphin?

At first light, he made his deck rounds checking for chafing
and slipped lines, eyed a steeliness in the sky ahead that
looked very much like they would soon be departing the
warm North Atlantic Current, and went down to the bridge
cabin. Sally was still staring at the monitor. He entered
their position, wind speed and direction, and the falling
barometer and temperature in the log. Then he crept up behind Sally and brushed his lips against the back of her
neck.

"I don't know if you are into the kinky stuff, but in some
navies failing to turn out for watch is a flogging offense."

"Can you cover for me? I've almost got it."

"Got what?"

"Could you make coffee?"

Hope turned on the gas, boiled water, and poured it over
finely ground beans. He placed a mug beside her and guided
her free hand to it. The other was clicking a mouse.

Without looking up, Sally said, "We know that dolphin
hearing is complex and acute. I'm wondering, could Ishmael
somehow be attracted to the sound of this boat?"

"As opposed to other boats?"

"Yes. Something unique about the sound that *Oona* and
only *Oona* makes cutting through the water. . . . Listen to
this. I'll toggle to the right-hand speaker."

Hope cocked his ear to the right-hand speaker. Underwater, *Oona* made a low-pitched grinding trill—a quivering
noise punctuated by occasional sharp clicks.

"Wait a minute. When did you record the boat?"

"We didn't do it on purpose. It was an accident. Remember? We forgot to pull the hydrophone out of the water after we recorded Ishmael. Later, you said something about we recorded the boat."

"Oh, yeah. Right. Right—what are those clicking noises? Him?"

"No. He's not in this. It's the bows slapping wavelets on the surface. Okay, now listen to what I toggle to the left . . ."

A low-pitched grinding sound emanated from the left-hand speaker.

"Similar?"

"Very."

"Listen to this: I'll play left and right simultaneously."

The two sounds merged like a chord.

"Almost identical, aren't they?"

Sally did not reply, saying only, "Okay, now look at the noise print. It drove me crazy all night. I didn't realize that it was from the boat."

"What did you think it was from?"

"I thought it was Ishmael's voice."

"I don't get it."

"Look!" Sally keyed Magnify Mode for Zoom Vertical and directed Hope's attention to the monitor. The noise print of a second audio track appeared below the first. "They're both enlarged. They represent just an instant of sound. The top print is Ishamel's voice. The bottom is the boat."

"They look the same."

"They are not exactly the same. There are all sorts of minute frequency differences—here, here, here, see? But you just heard: They sound almost interchangeable. And visually, even enlarged like this, the noise prints look remarkably similar." Sally yawned. "I'm so tired it took me forever to guess what it means."

"I'm not at all tired," said Hope, "and I still don't know what it means."

"Do you remember we speculated that Ishmael might have taught himself to spin-dance like a spinner dolphin?"

"Vaguely."

"Dolphins are great mimics. Well, look who he's mimicking."

"Us?"

"He's making noises similar to the noise of a catamaran wake." She looked up at Hope, her face shining, threw an arm around his neck, and tugged his face to hers. "He's taught himself to mimic the sound of this boat."

"Why?"

"Who knows? I just made the connection. It drove me nuts. I'm a sound person. I'm a pretty good one. I've done it for years. Probably a lot better at audio than as a shooter—though I'd never admit it to Greg."

She backed up her material on the VideoRaid, then jumped to her feet, paced an exhilarated circle around the saloon, and rushed to Hope and kissed him. "Do you see what this means? He's been following the boat since you first saw him jump."

"When the sub tried to kill me?"

"Absolutely. He followed you home. And he waited around outside Road Harbour until we came out. In fact, if we didn't come out, he probably would have swum right into the harbor."

"That would have woken up the natives."

"But like you say, why?"

Hope jumped down to the dive room and returned with the speaker he had waterproofed with plastic wrap. He plugged the cable into the stereo. "Let's stop, dip this over the side, and play the sound of the *boat*. Maybe he's too smart to fall for a recording of his own sound. But if he likes my boat enough to mimic it, maybe he'll fall for a recording of it when we're stopped."

"So I can get a clear, close-up shot of him."

"Close enough to find out who the hell he is." He considered adding, "Or whose he is," but decided instead to let Sally draw her own conclusions.

25

"WHY DO THEY KEEP STOPPING?" William Tree demanded.

Not one of the Killphin Project department heads summoned to the Captain Nemo Lounge had an answer. They stared in deep silence at the radar repeater, which emitted a cold blue-green glow from an aperture in the French-polished walnut paneling. Tree observed bleakly the poses they struck.

The long-range antenna high atop the *Star of Alabama*'s main-royal mast pinpointed David Hope's sailboat forty miles north of the windship, dead in the water. But not one of them—chin strokers, head scratchers, assiduous starers, belly rubbers—could explain what the deuce had stopped Hope this time.

Worse, not one single genius on his payroll could yet explain why the killphin was still swimming in company with the sailboat. Tree shifted uncomfortably in his vast chair to gaze up at the aquarium, seeking respite that not even a school of orange and white clownfish could provide this morning.

Everything was twisting out of control. What could go wrong was going wrong, and at this rate he wouldn't be half surprised to see the glass ceiling split wide open and flood his quarters with eighty thousand gallons of fish and water. He cast an even bleaker eye at the electronic North Atlantic chart, where satellite data filled out the picture beyond radar range.

His best hopes and worst fears were coming true simultaneously. Four nuclear submarines were depicted—courtesy of a high-ranking Tree cousin—converging for war games on the Denmark Strait. A fifth, the hapless *Vermont,* was headed that way, too, though far behind the others.

The single bit of good news was the colossal stretch of sea room that offered complete freedom of movement and absolute anonymity. With the exception of David Hope's stalled sailboat, the *Star of Alabama* had some 45,000 square miles of ocean to herself this morning. The nearest merchant vessel was two hundred miles north; the next, two hundred and fifty miles east. What happened out here was his business and his alone.

"Well, I have another question for you all. Has any genius aboard my ship arrived at a simple answer to the simple question of why the killphin likes that sailboat?"

Now, instead of staring at the radar repeater, they gaped at each other, each willing the boss man to choose another, anyone but me.

"This is not of merely academic interest, boys. You've got an out-of-control mammal out there that's your responsibility to herd back into our loop before he does any more damage."

Starc. Stare. Gape. Gape.

All the roads out of this fix were closing; every gate was slamming shut. He was darned near dead already; they just hadn't thrown the dirt on him. If he didn't fight back, he was a goner.

His father, who had served in the military training South American security forces, used to say: Folks can get used to pain and violence mighty quick, but until they do, it's a wonderful tool.

"Boys, you've all been living a charmed life up 'til now."

Heads swiveled his way, made uneasy by a tone in his voice none but Dr. Rod had heard before. As a mountain shed meadows in an avalanche, their benefactor had shrugged off an outer layer of civility and the base structure exposed was cold and raw.

"Scientists, engineers, technicians doing the work they love while enjoying recompense at double the going rate—triple when you count the perks." He nodded at the underwater port where four grinning researchers were gliding by in the ship's submersible.

The department heads gazed longingly at the port. With the ship drifting slowly on the North Atlantic Current, their biologists and chemists were happily sweeping the neuston layer with collection nets and hustling water samples back to their laboratories to measure oxygen, nutrients, and chlorophyll.

Tree's intercom beeped.

"Yes, Captain."

"Excuse me, Bill. They want to dip the Shipek grab."

"Tell them I said that I'm very sorry, Captain, but we can't sample bottom sediment just now. If that sailboat ever gets moving again, we can't be hanging around half the day while they reel in two miles of cable. Tell them you're concerned about a fast-moving front."

He turned back to his captive audience. "Well, I never object to paying for the best. But when I don't get the best for my investment, I feel like I've been robbed. Which is not good news for you all. I'm a man of the South—from the country, you understand—and we country Southerners have always taken stealing private property as a personal affront—which is to say, very, very seriously."

"What are you talking about, Bill?" Dr. Dan interrupted.

"I'm talking about discipline."

"Discipline?" Dr. Dan sneered. His Brooklyn accent turned harsher with contempt. "Bill, we're not a bunch of

Alabama slaves. You pay top dollar because we're tops in our fields. So can the cheap threats."

Considering the fragile state of Dr. Dan's mind, and his value to the Killphin Project, Tree hated to make an example of the neurosurgeon. But openly challenged, he felt he had no choice. Dr. Dan might as well have waved a sign reading "Do me."

"Wendell," Tree said, "go over there and hurt that man for me."

Wendell crossed the room in a bound. Dan Stern's eyes grew wide.

"Careful you don't injure his hands," Tree cautioned. "Just make him wish he had honored my simple request."

Wendell slapped Dr. Dan hard across his face, and when the surgeon's hands flew to the pain, the bodybuilder buried a big fist in his stomach.

Dr. Dan bent slowly at the waist, his mouth an incredulous, pain-filled O, his breath a frantic hiss. Wendell reared back and kicked his feet out from under him. Dan Stern crashed to the polished deck, doubled like a ball, holding his face and gasping for air.

The others were watching in horror and disbelief. Even Hughie Mick, who was no stranger to violence, looked awed. Though in fact the animal trainer was thinking back on the day they had escorted William Tree's father, a volatile man never up to Aunt Martha's standards, to the sanitarium.

"Starting right now," Tree said, "the *Star of Alabama* will go to a higher security level. Outside telephones are all switched off. The radio room is off limits to all but ship's officers. And soon as we finish this meeting, Wendell will collect your private satellite telephones—those you registered as Institute regulations required you to, and those you may have neglected to."

The frightened scientists stared hungrily at the Atlantic chart. But the icon that depicted the *Star of Alabama* stood all alone. The nearest ship was steaming away. It, and the empty chart, and the radar focused on the speck that was *Oona*, and the indigo water pressed against the porthole, and the writhing mass of the aquarium above their heads, all conspired to banish hope. They were trapped with a crazed Bill and his loyal crew on an empty stretch of sea considerably larger than the state of Maine.

"Answers, boys! What's the latest on my killphin?"

Rod tore his gaze from the chart to stare white-faced at the fallen surgeon. Tree could imagine the thoughts squirming in his brain. Dr. Dan would have held a chair at Duke or Harvard if it weren't for his emotional issues. Scientists of such caliber weren't supposed to suffer violence. That Dan was clutching his belly and moaning on the deck tore to pieces Rod's last hope that the garbage chute was a bluff.

"We'll start with you, Rod."

The killphin's co-creator looked away from Dr. Dan and said, "We're close, Bill. We're very close. We're almost done plotting new transmit commands through the damaged antenna. Same principle as NASA scientists retaking control of a lost space probe."

Tree glanced over at Ah Chi. The wire-thin Filipino answered just as quickly, "We're fine-tuning the tracking gear."

Rod added, "And it seems we got a break, Bill. The generator looks to be intact."

"How do you know?"

"The strength of the signals we are receiving indicates it's putting out plenty of juice."

Tree studied Rod with a grim eye. But he was secretly relieved to see the scientist regaining his composure. That meant that Rod felt he was close to restoring a complete linkup with the killphin and so might avoid his rendezvous with the garbage chute.

"Wendell."

Every man in the Captain Nemo Lounge braced.

"Meeting's over. Help Dr. Dan to his feet and bring me those satellite phones."

They shuffled off, shying away from Dr. Dan and avoiding one another's gazes.

Alone with the Mexican servants preparing his midmorning fried pies, Tree hailed the captain on his intercom.

"Retrieve the submersible. Then I want you to sail around to the west of *Oona*. When the sun's at our back, make a beeline straight at them and heave to nine miles off. If they move again, parallel their course at nine miles, but be sure to keep the sun directly behind us to blind them."

Twice in the past week, the maneuver to hover unseen within range of the eavesdropping device had worked.

"Am I to break away if they paint me with radar?"

Tree pondered that for a moment. Up until now, standard operating procedure had been to veer off in the unlikely event that Hope swept them with his radar. That had happened only once. But he only had to look at the chart to see that the submarines and the killphin were moving toward a final curtain and that it was time to block the exits.

"If they do, inform me immediately."

Twenty feet under the catamaran, about the only aspect of his Ishmael-luring scheme that Hope embraced with any enthusiasm was that the slow-moving North Atlantic Current carried with it the warm clear waters of the Gulf Stream. He could see a long, long way down before the indigo depths closed in.

Otherwise, everything felt crazy.

He could hear the sound of the boat sailing overhead, though it wasn't. *Oona* was drifting quietly. The boat noise tape was roaring from the plastic-wrapped speaker they had dangled in the water.

He could see Sally turning a slow circle beside him, panning her video camera like she was shooting reef fish. Except there was no reef. The chart showed bottom three miles away. And the "fish" she hoped to shoot soaring out of the sunlit depths was a monster dolphin with a history of ramming whatever annoyed it.

She was "protected" from three tons of angry mammal by a structure that resembled a shark cage, but which Hope knew was a Rube Goldberg contraption he had fashioned out of boat hooks, oars, a whisker pole, windsurfer spars, and the heavy cargo net he kept to drape over the side to give divers a handhold. Weighted down with two spare anchors, it hung between the hulls just below the sea surge.

She had with her in the cage support, if that was the proper word for a second diver blowing bubbles from a low-tech scuba outfit, a second shooter with a sixteen-millimeter film camera who on closer inspection—Hope guessed—must look more like a very nervous catamaran captain who was running the risk of breaking his neck by trying to look everywhere—up, down, and sideways—at once.

The musical line "What I Did for Love" kept running through his head. Though the truth, he knew, was complex. This sound-luring scheme was, after all, his idea. His plan to once and for all get the story on the the weird dolphin. So title the guy in the cage: Former Newspaperman Surfaces from Decade-Long Lack of Curiosity. More than a decade, he remembered. Which means I'm too old for this. He kept looking for the thick torpedo shape.

Sally tapped his shoulder urgently.

He had been looking the wrong way.

26

HOPE WAS ACCUSTOMED TO STOMACH-CLENCHING, brain-scrambling fear in his nightmares, but less so in waking life. At sea, at least, danger demanded immediate, often obvious action. Pointing a camera through the mesh of the cargo net offered none of the too-busy-to-think steadying effect of battling to reduce sail or zigzagging a survival course through murderous waves. This jolt was helpless, nightmare fear, and all the more immediate because he knew that he was wide awake.

The big animal approached aggressively, swimming straight at their flimsy cage. At close quarters underwater, the animal looked impossibly large—longer and thicker than a stretch limousine. It whipped through the bright water with powerful upflicks of a tail as broad as a bulldozer blade.

Sally signaled an exuberant *"Okay!"* with her thumb and index finger. Platinum for their boat recording. The animal heard some element in the soft roar noise from the speaker that attracted it like the noise of *Oona*'s wake. As it moved inexorably closer, Hope could feel the intense scrutiny of a fathomless dark eye, big as a soccer ball.

He felt a hard whack on his arm. Sally, gesturing with her camera. He switched his on and aimed at the creature filling the lens. Strange—just as Sally had told him when she rehearsed him with the camera—what he saw within the lens somehow seemed less dangerous.

When only a yard separated it from the cage, the big animal turned with an almost arrogant shrug and shot past, heaving them violently in a pressure wave of displaced water.

The killphin's sonar told it that the mesh was softer than steel bars or wire rope. It wheeled about and rushed back. The creatures within the cage were human, of the hard-soft-hard variety that indicated enemy.

It raced past again, probing with sound, surfaced to breathe, then hovered thirty feet under. The clarity of the blue water allowed it to watch their puzzling behavior from a distance. While the constant sound that it associated with the distinctive silhouette of the double-hulled boat bobbing overhead tranquilized its wary senses, the presence of the two divers provoked extreme vigilance. It echo-swept them again and again with a broad range of frequencies. That they were motionless did not fit the patterns that it knew.

For the moment, that puzzle was saving their lives.

Hope felt Sally's urgent grip. Even through her mask he could see her distress. She couldn't be out of air—unless the damned rebreather had malfunctioned. He gestured "surface?" with his thumb. She shook her head violently, pointed at her video camera's battery pack, and gestured frantically for him to give her the film camera. He did. Sally shoved the video camera at him and signaled "surface" with her thumb.

Hope signed, "Okay," indicating that he understood to take the camera up to the boat, remove the waterproof polycarbonate housing, change out the malfunctioning battery

pack, reseal its housing, and bring the camera back down—
preferably at the speed of light.

She turned her attention back to the dolphin, positioning
herself to shoot the animal's next swim-by. It lay still in the
sun-dappled water, presenting its long torpedo profile, and
watching them with one eye. Hope felt for the guideline they
had suspended from the dive steps, maneuvered his fins
under him, and kicked into motion.

He had just risen above the open top of the cage and was
looking up at the bottom of the boat when he sensed the
monster stiffen. Almost too fast for the eye, three tons of
aroused mammal spun around in the water and faced him
head-on.

He had a split second to consider fleeing up to the boat,
leaving Sally behind, or back down into the fragile cage.
Up, the animal could pick him off like a mackerel. Down,
he would block Sally's chances of getting out. He was
reaching for the dump valve on his buoyancy compensator when he realized it was too late. The animal was
charging.

It came so fast that it halved the distance before he registered motion. Fifty feet away it slowed and turned its head
slightly, toward the plastic-wrapped speaker, as if the sound
was confusing it. In that instant, Hope was suddenly enveloped in a shroud of air bubbles. Dense, they frothed the
water creamy white, turning it opaque as they exploded
around him in their rush to the surface.

Then Sally was alongside him, frantically kicking her fins
and stabbing at her low pressure inflation button. Hope realized that she had dumped a huge mass of air from her BCD
to confuse the animal and was now desperately fighting the
suddenly strong negative buoyancy of her weight belt and
the heavy rebreather.

The big dolphin turned from the speaker. Hope wedged
the arm holding the camera under Sally's backpack and, still
holding the guideline, kicked with all his strength toward

Oona and the shimmering surface, which looked to be a thousand miles away.

The line shook. Scissoring with his fins, he looked down. The cage had collapsed and an instant later, the monster tore into it again. Spars tumbled, his boat hook sailed off, bent in a U, and his spare anchors slipped into the deep. Only the net, tangled in the guideline, remained.

They burst into sunlight.

Hope shoved Sally onto the dive platform and pulled himself on as she scrambled up the steps. He was halfway up himself when *Oona* shook from a massive blow. Hope ran up all four steps before he looked back. Ishmael's dark gray head slid beneath the surface.

"Whoa!"

"Ohmigod!" Sally yelled. "That was incredible! Are you okay?"

"Fine, fine. You saved my ass."

"You saved mine. Oh wow. I was so scared. He is so huge!" She sank to the deck, laughing with relief and gasping for air. "Ohmigod, ohmigod. David, we did it. We've got tape, we've got film." She unbuckled her backpack, and flung off her mask and tugged at her fins. "You are a genius—oh, I can't wait to see the tape."

Hope took off his gear and knelt beside her. When their eyes met, she said, "What?"

"It is so wonderful to be alive."

"Better than dead, much better than dead." She reached for him, pulled him to her, hugged him hard. Before Hope could kiss her she was out from under and headed into the saloon, yanking open the video camera's housing. "Jesus, this stupid thing is stuck . . . Of all the—ah! There! David, come on, let's see what we got."

What they got, they learned from the monitor, were their clearest close-ups yet of the strange beast. They played them frame by frame. And in every frame that focused on the animal's back behind its dorsal fin, they saw a foot-long flexible wire.

"Not the sort of hardware it would grow on its own," said Hope. "I'm sorry, but that is definitely an antenna."

"Absolutely," Sally agreed. Beyond doubt, an instrument of some sort had been implanted in the big dolphin.

"Hey, wait a minute." Hope moved closer to the screen. "Pause the tape. Not there. Back, where he passed over us. . . . What is *that*?"

"What?"

"That scoop . . ."

"What scoop?"

"There. Like a depression in his belly?"

Sally studied the frame. "It looks like a shark or something took a bite out of him."

"If it did, he had plastic surgery. Look how smooth it is."

"They're fast healers."

"You told me, but that's like sculpture. Like an air scoop on a customized Corvette—Sally, can you zoom in with the AVID?"

While Sally digitized the tape into the editing system, Hope ran up on deck to retrieve the wreckage of the cage and put the boat back on course. He got the net and some lines aboard and made the happy discovery that he had lost only one of his anchors, the other having snared in the mesh. Reeling in the speaker wire, he found the speaker still attached. When everything was back on board—except for his oars, wind surfer spars, and an expensive whisker pole—he opened his sails to the wind, which had started gusting out of the west.

Before he had finished rinsing and stowing their diving gear, it began to feel dicey, as if it would soon start waltzing around the compass. Then he saw squalls marauding in the distance. Dark with rain, they marked the end, for sure, of the tropical fantasy they had enjoyed in the Gulf Stream and the North Atlantic Current. Beyond them stretched cold "north country." If they kept following Ishmael.

He put a reef in the main and cranked the jib in several rolls before he went below to see if Sally had been able to magnify the shot of the dolphin's belly. She was staring at the monitor, shaking her head.

"I think you were right," she said. "I pulled the clearest frame. What you're calling a 'scoop' looks hydrodynamic. Like it was sculpted by a plastic surgeon—it's really small, you know. It's only about two inches wide."

"What's that inside it?"

"You tell me," she replied. "I don't want to influence you. What do *you* see?"

The image was grainy, Sally having zoomed full magnification on the scooplike depression in the animal's belly. "I see a circle," he said, "and what looks like an infinity sign." He traced the double O in the air, like a figure eight.

"I'll give you a clue," Sally said. "Ishmael turned on his side as he swept past us, so the shot is straight down his belly from head to tail."

Hope studied it some more. "I am looking *into* that circle?"

"Yes."

"Through it, actually."

"Yes."

"It looks like a tunnel—the scoop is actually a tunnel, right? The water flows in the front end and out the back."

"Yes."

"And that infinity sign is *inside* the tunnel . . ."

"And?" said Sally, unable to contain her excitement. "And?"

27

"AND . . . JESUS H. IT'S AN impeller."

"Like a propeller blade?"

"Not a *propeller*. . . ." Hope answered slowly, trying to force his mind past the obvious. "No, that little thing isn't propelling Ishmael. It doesn't move the water. The water moves *it*. As the dolphin swims, water rushes through the tunnel and spins the impeller."

"Why?"

"Only one reason: to power a generator."

"For electricity?" Sally asked, still skeptical, until the possibilities dawned. "You're telling me that this animal is generating its own electricity? . . . But if I could generate electricity swimming, I'd never have to change camera batteries."

"Even better for a transmitter. Beats batteries by a mile. But why not? When you think about it, how else could you do long-range, long-term, offshore research relying on batteries? This guy can uplink data for years—as long as he lives."

Sally looked stricken by this final nail in the coffin of her hopes to film a new species. "To whom?"

"I think we both know to whom."

"Tree? We don't know that."

"What I don't know is why it's such a big secret. Why did he pussyfoot around?" Hope mimicked William Tree's buttery drawl: " 'Did you see anything unusual out here in the middle of the Atlantic Ocean, Miz Sally?' Why didn't he just come out and ask, 'Did you happen to see a monster-size dolphin with a sat phone on its back?' "

"Because Tree doesn't know anything about it."

Hope started to argue the point. But he noticed that Sally was blinking at the screen. "Wait a minute," he said, reaching out to comfort her. "I know what you're thinking."

She shrugged his hand away. "No you don't."

Hope put his hand back on her shoulder, moved behind her, and kissed her hair. Out the saloon's front windows he could see that several of the squalls were merging. It looked cold ahead and already the water seemed a little murky, as if, he imagined, the edge of the Gulf Stream "river" was eroding "sediment" from the "shoreline" formed by the cold North Atlantic.

"It's still an unknown species. No one's ever seen a dolphin like it."

Sally would not be moved. "Somebody has. Maybe Tree, maybe someone else. Their scientists must have computers full of data on it. Ishmael may be new, but he's theirs."

"I wonder where they found him," Hope replied.

He waited, but got no answer from Sally.

"And don't you wonder," he coaxed, "why they would risk invasive surgery on an animal that's so rare—one of a kind?"

No reply.

"It's a heck of a mystery, isn't it?"

Nothing.

He tried again. "Our mystery."

Sally looked up at last. "Our mystery?"

"We're here. We've got tape."

Her face lit like the sun. Her eyes were bright again, and

she flashed her teeth in a huge smile. She jumped up, hugged Hope, and kissed the monitor. "Yes! *Sixty Minutes* will kill for this. And every news network in the world. I mean, someone found a new kind of animal and fitted it with electronic gear and here we are on the scene shooting the . . . the . . ."

"Monstrosity," said Hope. "The sooner that we tell someone, the better."

"No!"

"No?"

"Not until we know what's really happening."

"I told you about the sub going haywire."

"What does that have to do with it?"

"Ishamel was there. That's where I first saw him. I saw him just before it happened."

"I know. You told me already. So it happened the same morning. It's a coincidence."

"Sighting a strange animal the same morning that the *Vermont* went berserk could be a coincidence. If he wasn't wired for electricity. . . . Besides, I have a sneaking suspicion that I spotted him on my sonar."

"When? You never told me that."

"Right before their emergency ballast blow. I was sonar-scoping for the sub and all of a sudden I saw a smallish target swim away. Next thing I saw, there was the sub. At the time I assumed it was a big shark, but now I'm wondering if—"

"So what if it was Ishmael?"

"I got the impression that their computers had been messed up by something *outside* the sub."

"What could a dolphin do to a submarine?"

"Two utterly bizarre events—this electronic mutant and an out-of-control submarine—at the same time and same place?"

"If it's Tree—and I find that hard to believe, too—then it's research. Very weird research, to be sure, but it's still some sort of marine biology research."

"It only looks like marine biology," said Hope.

"That's as silly as saying Woods Hole is a front for submarine warfare. You saw Tree's ship. He had forty marine biologists doing legitimate research."

Hope shook his head. "I would be willing to call a sub going suddenly berserk a 'mystery of the sea.' And no one can deny that Ishmael is a 'mystery of the sea.' In spades. But put them in the same patch of water at the same time and now we're talking about an impossible coincidence. They must be connected."

"So what if they are?"

"If they are, that animal is very dangerous. We should report it on the radio."

"We're not ready. We don't know enough."

"We know enough to be responsible. What you see in that viewfinder is part of a larger world."

"What I see is specific. Not some make-believe 'larger world.' "

"The people on the submarine were not make-believe."

Hope looked out again at the merging squalls. They had formed a column to prop an iron sky over a leaden sea. What had Commander Royce said to him? "We tried, sir. Believe me, we tried." Something had disrupted a seven-thousand-ton submarine's control of navigation, depth, and speed. The warship had acted as if the entire crew had been infected by a disabling disease.

Sally said, "Even if there is a connection, and I'm sure there is not, we don't know enough to tell anybody yet."

"How long do we risk waiting? A hundred men almost drowned on that sub. What happens next time?"

"Shouldn't we try to figure out what's going on first? Shoot more tape. Put together a package that really shows something. Information people can draw conclusions from. I mean, we're here, David. Who's going to shoot it if we don't?"

Hope had argued that line himself more than once in his newshound days: Observe or participate? Watch or warn?

Sally continued forcefully. "If we sail home to America with the videotape, where will Ishmael go? What will he do next? Wouldn't it be better to stick with Ishmael and keep on taping his behavior?"

Hope smiled.

"What?" she asked. "You agree, don't you? You know I'm right."

"When I was a kid reporter we learned from the lawyers to follow the money. I guess with this story you would follow the dolphin . . . There's only one problem."

He went to the chart table, checked the GPS, and entered their position and penciled their progress from the last reading. "He's still pointed at the Denmark Strait."

"Does that mean something?"

"The Navy kid who lost it said that the submarine was scheduled for war games in the Denmark Strait. Next month."

"What are you saying? Ishmael's joining the war games? Come on, David. You're making Tree into a monster."

"But today's May second. 'Next month.'"

Sally joined him at the chart. "The Denmark Strait is more than a thousand miles from here."

"He's already come three thousand. He's in the home-stretch. . . . But so are we."

"What do you mean?"

Hope took her hand and touched her index finger to the chart. "Here we are. We caught a heck of a ride on the Gulf Stream." He moved her finger north half an inch. Seventy-five miles. They might see the lights of a fishing boat, after dark. A boat that was a long, long way from home.

"Can you read those letters?"

"Yes." She smiled, teasing back, yet deadly serious. "They say 'steady as she goes.' "

"The boldface letters."

"They say stick to Ishmael like glue."

"They say, 'Flemish Cap.' They say, 'We made a deal.' They say, 'Time to go home.' "

"No," said Sally. "They say that it's time to accept my offer—be my partner. Share fifty-fifty. Do you have any idea what *Sixty Minutes* will pay for our tape? If we return with the full story in the can we can name our price. You deserve to gain from it just as much as I—*where are you going?*"

"On deck. To take in sail. That squall is getting close."

Sally followed him to the cockpit and stood by while he cranked a winch to roll the jib onto the headstay. "David, don't you ever want anything?"

Hope said, "I got out of real estate because I hated collecting rent. It felt like taking something for nothing."

"Even though you had fixed up the apartments?"

She followed him to the mast and waited while he reefed the main to napkin size.

"And I'll bet you quit your newspaper job because you didn't want a promotion."

He looked at her, surprised, lost his grip on the halyard, and had to lunge for the bitter end before it disappeared up the mast. "I didn't like the way the news business was getting silly. And the owner was using the paper to beat up on politicians who were better than she was. But yeah, maybe you're right. She tried to make me managing editor."

"*Another* superwoman? Were you sleeping with her, too?"

"That's not why I quit."

"Don't you ever hook up with normal women?"

"I've been trying to hook up with you."

"I'm not normal. I'm as driven as they were. You go looking for trouble."

"She was gutting the paper to pay for a trendy weekly she was starting up in New York. Laying off the older reporters, cutting benefits, and paying kids for attack journalism."

"Back to the moment."

"You asked."

"David, we've got a lot invested in Ishmael, whatever it is. Maybe I'm right and it's a pure research project. Maybe you're right and it's dangerous. But you and I are the only two people in the world who are situated close enough to him to find out how. Everything else aside, we've got a responsibility that goes beyond radioing a ridiculous-sounding warning that we can't back up with facts."

"Responsibility was my word," said Hope.

Sally said, "I will concede it is not coincidence, if you will concede that we don't know enough, yet, to report it."

". . . Let me look at the weather."

Sally followed him to the barometer on the saloon bulkhead above the nav station. Hope turned the indicator counterclockwise to line it up with the pointer. No surprise that the pressure was finally dropping. The broad-shouldered high was going off duty after putting in a lot of overtime. Depressions would pounce.

He pulled a seventy-two-hour forecast from the weather fax. Stacked-up low-pressure systems were starting to move. He showed her the big, bold Ls that crowded the western half of the Atlantic. "Depression. Depression. Depression."

Sally said, "One of your books says that the depressions track the Gulf Stream and the North Atlantic Current. If we follow Ishmael north, won't they pass south of us?"

"Some might."

But storms weren't their only problem. Warm southern winds, he explained, would travel up the west side of the retreating high. "Warm air over cold water makes fog."

He showed her the Sailing Directions paragraph that covered weather for late April and early May between forty-five and sixty degrees north and thirty-five to forty-five degrees west. South wind brought fog. "Walls of it this time of year. We'll have a tough time seeing the bow, much less Ishmael."

Even when moderate westerlies blew, they could expect to be plagued by low visibility, often less than half a mile. In between gales, the winds would be light and variable, tough sailing.

"And when the pressure really drops, we'll catch gales

from the southeast. Forty to fifty knots. Plus, it's going to get colder and colder. Guaranteed cold, overcast, and miserable."

"I get the picture. High discomfort factor."

"And when storm tracks merge, all this open water creates tremendously long fetches, which means waves like ski slopes. Don't think I don't want to keep following him. It's a great story. A great film. And some poor submarine crew might even thank us for saving their lives. So don't think I don't want to go. But boy, are we in the wrong boat."

"I know I'm asking you to risk your business and your home."

"No, it's not only that. *Oona* is not up to the job. We've been lucky so far. She's fine for cruising around the Caribbean, but she's overloaded. She's never had to deal with anything really rough."

"Is there any way we could improve her?"

"What do you mean?"

"Is there any way we could make her safer? More up to the job."

Hope had already been considering that. Ever since they had discovered Ishamel's generator, he had felt like a fish fighting a hook. But there was no twisting away from this one. Reluctantly, he answered, "Sure. Throw everything overboard."

Toward the end of lunch, when the servants had removed all but the dessert tray propped on the shelf of his belly, Tree summoned Ah Chi. The Filipino arrived jumpy and bright-eyed as a frog.

"Ah Chi, you do recall the front-door coupling virus you planted in Captain Hope's radios when we invited them to lunch?"

"Yes, Bill."

"Well, I want you to be ready to open that door."

"No prob, Bill."

The fat man watched his telemetry engineer bounce from foot to foot. When he buzzed for Wendell, Ah Chi bounced faster.

Tree addressed him matter-of-factly. "All of us sailing in the *Star of Alabama* are feeling the pressure, Ah Chi, even I. But that's no excuse to get high on pills when your shipmates are counting on you to perform your duties."

Wendell sprang into Tree's quarters in his workout clothes, dripping perspiration on the carpet and breathing hard. His broad face shone with effort and the physical pleasure of feeling pumped. "Hey there, Ah Chi. What's up, Bill?"

"Wendell, I want you to take Ah Chi down to the infirmary and help the doctors shove a tube down his throat and pump those pills out of his stomach."

"You got it, Bill—let's go, Ah Chi."

"Tell the doctor I want him back in the radio room—stone-cold sober—in three hours."

"Everything" was relative. Beer, wine, soda, and some of the drinking water could go. Diving gear could not. They deep-sixed much of the food, except for apples, peanut butter and cheese, and the rice, pasta, and beans they could cook in sea water. But not the cameras. Some furniture went over the side—not the TV. The cabin doors were looking pretty shabby, Hope told himself. Too many grubby hands slamming them over the years. Ditto for the head doors. And the doors to the storage lockers. Eight doors went over the side.

With the doors gone from the capacious lockers, there was no hiding the personal trash he'd been dragging around for years. He found old tanks, nonfunctioning; broken tools; books he would never read. The gear he had rescued from junk piles, intending to repair one day, included a two-hundred-pound generator. It was like cleaning out closets, attic, and garage for someone who had died.

As they humped the broken generator down the dive steps, Sally said, "I don't think that owning a catamaran is good for you. There's too much space. But I'm very touched. This is a brave thing you're doing, breaking up your home."

"I'm lightening the boat."

"But you're putting everything on the line."

"Big deal. You put your entire life on the line diving with that monster."

Sally grinned, triumphant. "I know why you're doing this. You know what I think? Now that you let yourself get tied up with me, you're desperate to 'unencumber.' "

"No more shrinking, please. I told you, I don't want golden handcuffs. I want a clear head."

"It's too late for a clear head. You're in this up to your eyeballs. With me. Welcome aboard."

Hope watched the detritus falling astern. It looked like some poor bastard's boat had sunk. He turned back. Sally was still standing there, holding out her hand. To his surprise, he felt a smile tug at his face. He took her hand and they shook. "I've been in worse situations."

He went below, gave the gutted saloon a rueful scowl, and switched on the radio, hoping to get some weather. Instead he heard William Tree broadcasting, *"Sailboat* Oona. *Sailboat* Oona. *This is the* Star of Alabama, *fixing to talk to the sailboat* Oona."

28

HOPE CALLED TO SALLY, WHOM he'd left in the cockpit, tracking the squalls.

"Tree on the radio. He's asking for you."

She jumped down into the saloon as Tree repeated,

"*Sailboat* Oona. *Sailboat* Oona. *This is the* Star of Alabama, *fixing to talk to the sailboat* Oona. *Miz Sally, is your radio on, Miz Sally? Captain Hope, if you're listening, could you please find out if Miz Sally has time for a visit?*"

Hope got up from the nav seat and motioned for Sally to answer the radio. She sat, keyed the mike, and said, "This is *Oona, Star of Alabama.* Switching to . . ." Hope pointed and she said, "Twenty-two hundred." She changed from the distress and paging channel to a talk channel and said, "Bill, is that you?"

"*Why, Miz Sally. How nice to hear your voice. I trust you and Captain Hope are well.*"

"Very well, thank you. Where are you calling from, Bill?"

"*Near the Gulf. Just thought I'd take a chance on a skip signal to say, Hey. Lonely here this afternoon. We put all the young 'uns off on a vessel I chartered to take them to the Azores—they're flying to a London conference. Just a handful of senior men left aboard and they're all holed up in their*

*labs. So I'm just sitting here under my fishies, all by my
lonesome."*

"Sitting in splendor, I recall," Sally replied, locking eyes
with Hope, who said, after she switched to RECEIVE and Tree
couldn't hear, "Fewer witnesses."

"Come on," said Sally. "That's really paranoid."

"We try, we try. And where are you?"

Hope shook his head. Sally keyed Transmit.

"Heading home."

"How's that wide boat treating you?"

"David says she smells the barn."

"And how's her captain treating you?"

Sally smiled at Hope, and before she keyed the mike to
reply said, "I'm going to shake Bill up a little."

"Careful," said Hope. "He's not stupid. He sounds to me
like he wants something and I don't believe for a minute he's
heading for the Gulf of Mexico."

Sally keyed the mike. "Captain Hope runs a full-service
charter."

Tree returned one of his deep chuckles. *"Ah told you you
two made a mighty attractive couple. Well, good for both of
you. . . . Tell me, Miz Sally, how'd you make out filming those
spinners?"*

Before Hope could stop her Sally said, "I took your advice."

"How's that?"

"I shot something unusual."

*"Well, good. That's what I said to do. What did you
shoot?"*

"I'm not ready to talk about it yet. Not until I put together
a demo tape."

*"Well, the Tree Institute often comes in early on projects.
Deserving projects."*

"Let me finish the demo, then we'll talk. I've got your
card. Can I call you when I get to Maine?"

"Are you sure you wouldn't rather want to tell me now?"

"Positive, Bill. One thing I learned from my ex-husband. He always said, 'They'll never see your film any better than their first look.' So just wait and before you know it I'll have a big, clear demo tape I can show around."

"Well, if you say so."

Hope signaled to Sally not to key the mike and said, "Do you think he's really heading for the Gulf?"

"He said he was going home for his birthday."

"Ask him how soon you could telephone him in Alabama."

"Bill, when can I call you in Alabama?"

"Anytime, anytime. Gotta go now. Good hearing your voice. Out."

"That was abrupt," said Hope. "Guess he didn't like the question."

"Should I call him back?"

Hope looked out the front windows, which were suddenly spattered with raindrops. From east to west, the sky was dark. "We don't have time. We're about to get hammered."

As they shrugged into foul weather gear and safety harnesses, Sally said, "I think I believe him."

"I think he was lying. And if he was, he knows we lied, too, about going home."

"Well," said William Tree, casting a wintery eye on the masthead radar repeater that pinpointed David Hope's catamaran forty miles to the north. "They were lying yesterday. They still haven't cut away to Maine. They are not sailing home. For the past twenty-four hours they've kept headed north-northeast . . . and I can think of only one reason why they'd be lying."

Wendell, who indulged an annoying habit of mistaking Tree's thinking out loud for conversation, piped up eagerly. "Because they've seen the killphin."

"No, Wendell. We know they've seen my killphin. They're lying because they've *filmed* my killphin . . . and very likely seen too much of him, in the process. What a darned mess."

"I told you we should run them over."

"And I will tell you again that they might still be an asset, being the only ones he'll let near him."

"But if they know—"

"Who are they going to tell without a radio, Wendell? They'll have to holler mighty loud."

Wendell's gaze fixed on the black box that Ah Chi had installed beside Bill's big red chair. A cable snaked out the back and into a conduit that led to the telemetry room. "Oh, yeah."

Tree fingered his intercom. "Philip. Tell Cook I would enjoy some fresh baloney sandwiches, right now. Slice 'em thick, like I showed him. No machine slicing. Big hunks by hand. And a pie. . . . Wendell."

"Yes, Bill."

"Round up Dr. Rod and Dr. Dan. Have them wait outside 'til I'm done eating."

Wendell said, "They'll be full of questions. Want me to tell 'em anything?"

"Yes. Tell them I want contact with that animal, now."

To William Tree's surprise, Dr. Rod and Dr. Dan entered his Captain Nemo Lounge almost jauntily.

"Well, you two have developed a spring in your step."

Rod appeared poised to jump close and clap him on the back, an intimacy that Tree arrested with a glance. Dan was more subdued, as befitted a man who'd had a brutal example made of himself recently. But even he looked like he was savoring some sort of a victory.

"We were heading your way when we ran into Wendell," Rod said excitedly. "Good news, Bill. We've regained partial communication through the damaged antenna."

"Wonderful," said Tree. "Are you getting any thalamus data?" he asked Dr. Dan.

Dan said, "He did a spy hop a minute ago. We got a still shot of a sailboat. A little grainy, but hey, compared to yesterday, even, who's complaining?"

That explained Dan's relative cheer.

"And that's not all," said Rod. "The computer model says that we can exert full control again, through the backup training radio."

"A short-range radio, Ah recall," said Tree.

"That's right, Bill."

"But we can't get close enough for short range."

"But if we do, we'll have total control, according to the computer model."

"Your 'good news,' " Tree complained, "comes with more qualifications than a sixty-day warranty on a used Chrysler. In other words, you can tell him to attack, but you still can't aim him precisely."

"Sure we can, but we just have to get closer."

"Actually, Bill," growled Dr. Dan, "the way I read it, the data suggest it may attack anyhow."

"On its own volition?"

"I disagree strongly," said Rod, running anxious fingers through his stringy hair. "There isn't one chance in fifty it would attack on its own."

Dr. Dan made a face. "Hey, I'm only a dumb surgeon. What do I know? Maybe that wasn't our killphin that attacked the *Vermont.* Maybe it was a killphin from Mars."

"How close?" Tree demanded, ignoring gloomy Dan's alarmist prediction for the moment. "How close must we get?"

"Close," said Rod. "It's Hughie's training radio."

"Is that the radio that Hughie used back in the pen?" Tree interrupted.

"Right, Bill. It's pretty much—"

"While walking the perimeter boardwalk where he could see the animal down in the water?"

"It's pretty much line of sight. But once there, we've got total—"

"Line of sight?" Tree roared in sudden exasperation. "He won't let us within line of sight. Contrary creature runs like a jackrabbit when it hears my ship—preferring the company of a couple of nobodies over the closest thing to a father it has."

Tree rolled back in his chair and stared up at his aquarium. The bull shark was circling aggressively. He stabbed at his intercom and snapped, "Jose! If you don't feed Señor Shark real soon he's gonna start munching on my butterfly fish."

He glared at the big chart. Three U.S. submarines were converging on the Denmark Strait. The British already had their boat in place, having been assigned the ambush by the game masters. The *Vermont* was late. She was steaming flank speed last he'd heard.

Tree could make only an educated guess at the *Vermont*'s position, the family's sources at the Pentagon being less informed than usual. The Navy had cloaked in extraordinary secrecy the *Vermont*'s travails and their bold fix-it-at-sea effort to scrub her computers. But it didn't take much guessing to imagine an atmosphere aboard the submarine as electric as a delta thunderstorm. Particularly when you took into account her commander's checkered past: the last time he had war-gamed with units of the British Navy—Operation Swift Friends in the Indian Ocean the summer of 2001, Tree had learned—the Brits had cleaned his clock, so thoroughly that the game masters had to alter "ground truths" in order to "reconstitute" his boat so that the games could continue. At which point the other British submarine—a diesel boat, no less—"sank" him a second time.

Tree erupted in a private chuckle that left Dan and Rod wondering. That captain must be pretty good—or darn well connected—if the Navy gave him the *Vermont* anyway, and Tree took some comfort in the certainty that the skipper driving his brand-new ship to these war games would be on his toes.

Overhead, fish scattered. Slabs of horsemeat splashed into the aquarium and drifted down, trailing blood like comet tails until the bull shark engulfed them.

"Rod. Would you excuse us, please?"

Rod looked stunned. What could Tree possibly have to say to a neurosurgeon that the killphin's co-creator couldn't hear? He hesitated, until at a glance from Tree, Wendell rose to his full height.

"Sure, Bill. I'll be right outside."

"Head on back to your lab. I'll call when I need you."

"Whatever you say, Bill. Catch you later, Dan."

Dr. Dan sat in mournful silence, anxiously tugging at his fingers.

Tree started to talk, thought better of it. The sentimental Wendell would not be able to handle what he was about to discuss with Dan. "Wendell, run up to the bridge. Tell Captain Grandzau to start catching up with the sailboat. And tell Philip to send down a pot of cocoa so me and Dr. Dan can have a little visit."

Philip, hovering ever near, marched in with a silver pot, poured two mugs from the Tree Marine Park gift shop steaming full, and withdrew. Tree raised his as if to toast Dan Stern and smiled, "Alone at last."

Dr. Dan had a bitter expression marring his face. "Am I supposed to feel grateful that your bully is gone? Is a cup of hot chocolate your way of indicating I won't be beaten up again?"

Tree dismissed the recent past with a ponderous wave of his massive forearm. "I'm willing to let bygones be bygones."

"Fucking generous of you. What's up, Bill?"

"You know what's up. There is one thing about that poor creature that only you and I know." He reached into the drawer where he kept his antique six-shooter and pulled out what appeared to be a Zippo lighter.

"The dead switch," said Dan. "I was wondering if you remembered."

"Well, I certainly do remember, Dan. I'm not a monster."

"Could have fooled me," Dan muttered.

"You're welcome to your opinion about that, wrong as it is. But we both know that I am not a madman."

"No, you're not," Dan agreed, expression darkening as he spiraled back among his demons. "You're so goddamned sane it makes me jealous. I sometimes think that fat as you are, you don't have an unhappy thought in your head."

"Life's too interesting to waste being unhappy—can I assume that the dead switch is still operative?"

"No reason why it wouldn't be. Whatever damage the animal suffered in his shark fight didn't go as deep as the brain or he wouldn't still be in action. I put the dead switch about as deep as I could go without coming out the other side. It's in there, primed to go boom."

"So I can still kill him if it becomes too risky to continue the experiment."

"You have the ability to kill your killphin. Anytime you think there are too many lives at risk, you can pull the plug, just as planned, and blow a hole in his head."

"Well, that's a relief. I do not like situations out of control."

"You'll destroy ten years of work."

"Better work than existence. I'm not entirely omnipotent. I have a family to answer to. You've got a wife and children, Dan, who love you very much."

Dan Stern shook his head, vehemently. "Nothing else ever worked for me except work."

"Well, I promise you it's not a step I'll take lightly. But wouldn't you agree that it's comforting to know I can kill the animal before it sets off a war?"

"Bill." Stern faltered. He stared down at his hands. His fingers were clasping and unclasping like demented spiders.

"Dan?" Tree replied gently. "I'm afraid we've all got to admit we've made a crucial miscalculation about our killphin. Cross-breeding *Stenella longirostris* with *Orcinus orca* got us the progeny of an agile spinner dolphin and a potent killer whale, which was wonderful. But we got so excited when we implanted electronic monitoring and control devices that we mistakenly assumed we had turned the creature into a machine. Ah suspect that Hughie Mick sort of understood, but Hughie's not the type to volunteer information to people who think they know better.

"Heck, I'm not blaming us. Fact is, the critter did appear to perform as advertised. He swam northeast because a GPS device wired to his brain's medial forebrain bundle—his pleasure center—makes him feel like he's in paradise when he swims where we tell him. He sought out submarines. And he obeyed instructions to change course. Or did, before telemetry went down.

"But even though he's riddled with implants, he's still a dolphin. There's no more highly evolved predator in the sea. They can outswim, outmaneuver, and outthink whatever they want to eat. But predators also possess what you might call a 'survivor's memory.' I'll bet you he's never forgotten a noise or a silhouette from his training years—which weren't always pleasant. There was plenty of necessary herding and poking and shocking and, face it, starving.

"So he's no machine. He's a capable predator with a heap of bad memories. And since we can't count on controlling him, we have to be ready to stop him."

"It's the most advanced artificial brain extension work on the planet," Dan pleaded hoarsely. "No one comes close to what we've done."

"I promise you, it's a last-ditch step that I'll take only in the extreme. You can have my word on it."

Dan jumped up.

Tree had a split second to think, My Lord, Dr. Dan is nuttier than I thought. Then hot cocoa was flying at his eyes and Dr. Dan was brushing past him and running out of the Captain Nemo Lounge.

"Wendell!" Tree howled, blinking through a burning haze

of pain and humiliation. No one had dared attack his person since he was a boy and a playmate had held him down and inked FATSO on his chest. A playmate who had never attained manhood. *"Wendellllll!"*

Only after Wendell had mopped his face and carefully rinsed his stinging eyes with cool water did Tree realize that Dr. Dan had snatched the kill switch.

29

AT FIRST LIGHT, HOPE FOUND a Dinah Washington track, and "What a difference a day makes" boomed from the stereo.

"Very funny," Sally groaned, staggering up from her cabin in a motley collection of fleece sweaters, pants, and long underwear that Hope had unearthed from *Oona*'s winter storage lockers.

It was little more than twenty-four hours since they had departed near-tropic conditions in the North Atlantic Current. After battling half the night through a welter of rain squalls, they found themselves sailing cold gray seas. Whitecaps were foaming, powered by an icy wet wind.

"I am freezing."

Hope tossed her a fleece watch cap.

"Soon as you go up on watch, I'm going to try and catch a nap."

Sally tugged the cap over her brow and peered out the spray-splashed windows. "Ishmael?"

"Just did a sun dance—minus the sun. He seems to like the cold. Did about eight spins. You know, sometimes he reminds me of Snoopy dancing."

Sally struggled into the damp foul-weather jacket hanging by the companionway. "Is it as awful out there as it looks?"

Hope said, "The wind's honking. I've got two reefs in the main and not a lot of jib out. Half-mile visibility. If it socks in any more, switch on the radar. Wake me for anything."

Before he stretched out on the mattress where the couch had been, he sat at the nav station to enter his watch relief in the log. "We did sixty miles in the last four hours. A hundred and sixty since we left the current." The remote Flemish Cap was history, far astern and fading fast.

Sally paused at the hatch to pull on gloves. "Do you really think Ishmael damaged that submarine?"

Hope shook his head. "I can't imagine how. All I know is that he was there when it went haywire. Next thing we know we're being followed by—or are following—an entirely new kind of dolphin. Then a marine researcher sails up in his own private hundred-million-dollar floating laboratory and tells you to film the unusual. Now we discover that our mystery dolphin is wired. And all along, he's on a course for the Denmark Strait, which has been the place to find nuclear submarines for the past forty years—being a choke point in and out of Russia."

"As if he were going to attack another?"

"But how? How does a twenty-foot fish-mammal attack a seven-thousand-ton submarine?"

"Not by force," said Sally.

Hope shrugged. "Stealth? Guile?"

"Did the crewmen you saw seem normal?"

"What do you mean 'normal'? They were mad as hell, but otherwise, nothing abnormal."

"I mean healthy?"

"One of the divers inspected both hulls on a single breath. Yeah, they were healthy. Why do you ask?"

"I don't know. Just a thought. You were talking about infecting the boat with a disease."

"From what I saw the crew was fine. It was the boat that was screwy. Where's your harness? The sea is making up."

"There he is!"

All night and all morning and into the afternoon, Tree's crewmen searched the *Star of Alabama,* hunting the deranged neurosurgeon from stem to stern, through the depths of her holds to every locker, life raft, and cabin and every conceivable hiding place on deck. Only when a shoe smacked onto the plastic weather top of the aquarium did anyone think of looking up. And there, high up the mainmast, the skinny little middle-aged man crouched like a frightened monkey on an upper topgallant yard two hundred feet above the main deck.

The effects of the long, cold night on his already fragile state of mind became apparent when Wendell headed up the ratlines after him. Dr. Daniel Stern started laughing.

"Wendell," Rod called. "Don't scare him."

"I ain't scaring no one. I'm just going to grab the son of a bitch and bring him to Bill."

The bodybuilder climbed as powerfully as a bear. He cleared the main top in less than a minute and was scrambling up the topgallant mast when Dr. Dan jumped to his feet and stood on the yardarm.

The ship was heeling hard, bowing before a strong west wind on the beam. Balanced precariously with one hand reaching into the concavity of the bulging sail, Dr. Dan pulled something from his pocket and threw it. It winked a dull silver against the overcast and fell in the sea some distance from the speeding ship.

Wendell swarmed over the yardarm and stood by the mast, holding tight. "Let's go, Dr. Dan," he called, straining to be heard above the wind. Thirty feet separated the two men. "Bill wants you."

"Tell Bill," Dan shrieked, "to go fuck himself."

"Now don't go talking like that, Dr. Dan."

"Tell him if wants to kill the killphin he'll have to find another way."

"He wouldn't do that, Dr. Dan."

"If you believe that, Wendell, you'll believe I can fly."

He stepped off the yard. The ship was still heeling and he fell past the hull into the sea with a small splash that was lost among the whitecaps.

"It's a sign," Tree said when informed that no trace of his Zippo lighter had been found. No doubt, he conceded grimly, it was the silvery object Dr. Dan had thrown before he fell. "It's a sign. I'm going to take it as a sign."

"What's a sign, Bill?"

Tree still saw no profit in explaining the kill switch to Wendell, even though it was now lost forever. So he said, "Dr. Dan taking leave of us. The man was saying, Go ahead, boys, I can't keep up anymore. Don't let me slow you down. Don't wait for me."

"You think so, Bill?"

"I know so, Wendell. Sure as I know my name. We must forge ahead."

"Where, Bill?"

"Wendell, I want you to run down to the galley and bring us back a mess of burgers. Can you do that for me?"

"Why don't I call Philip for you?"

"I don't want Philip fussing around me. This is man's work, now. We're going to hunker down and win this thing."

"Bill?"

"What, Wendell?" The bodybuilder was hanging at the door, leaning on the jamb, his face anxious. "What is it?"

"Dr. Dan said you were going to kill the killphin."

"Dr. Dan was a lunatic who killed himself jumping off an

upper topgallant yardarm. If you believe that, you'll believe anything, Wendell. Go get them burgers."

"You got it, Bill."

Alone, Tree pondered his future. Was Dr. Dan's nosedive really a good sign? So much hung on the killphin's success, so much was threatened by its failure. Whatever power he had over Aunt Martha was at stake. His magnificent ship was on the line. As was his ability to seize control of the family and fortune when the old lady finally up and died.

By the same token, nobody ever won a thing worthwhile not taking chances. Besides, what choice did he have? Sooner or later the Navy would learn that it was his killphin that nearly wrecked their sub in the Caribbean. They would not take it lightly. So maybe crazy Dan had saved him from having to make a tough call.

Better to forge ahead. Roll the dice for the big win.

"Could it be I'm getting used to the cold?" said Sally.

"That's because we're sailing so fast there's no wind over the deck."

They were in *Oona*'s cockpit, Hope attempting to adjust the self-steering wind vane, Sally holding the sixteen-millimeter camera on her shoulder, fitted with its longest lens. All morning she had watched the light struggle to increase from dark gray to marginally lighter gray as the cloud-hidden sun neared its noon arc.

It had been three days since they had actually seen the sun, and while she had captured many shots of Ishmael porpoising northward, she feared she was wasting film. It was way too dark for the video camera; even setting the slowest f-stop on the sixteen-millimeter camera, she was stretching the natural limits of film. And now it appeared that fog would soon obscure even their view of the clouds.

The wind—which had dropped off since yesterday and backed south—wasn't particularly strong, but the lightened

Oona was skimming the broadly spaced orderly seas so swiftly that twice Ishamel had sky-drilled out of the sea behind them, jumping in their wake, as if asking them to slow down to let him catch up.

"She hasn't sailed like this since I made her a dive boat," Hope boasted. "Hey, what are you grinning at?"

"Boys and toys," said Sally.

He went below to check the barometer and came back with a surprise. "Barometer's rising."

Within the hour the wind began veering west. It got colder, and soon a nasty cross-sea was building. But instead of the threatened fog, visibility began to improve. By two o'clock they could see two miles. When the light grew crisp, Sally unlimbered the video camera.

Hope checked the barometer again. "If it keeps clearing, I think I know how to find out if Ishmael is Bill Tree's doing."

"Other than asking him?"

"What would you think if you learned that Tree was nearby?"

"I'd think he lied about heading for the Gulf of Mexico."

"And what if you learned that Tree was following us?"

"I'd think that he was definitely connected to Ishmael."

She stood up with the binoculars and when *Oona* climbed a sea, she scoped the horizon astern. "I don't see any tall ships."

"The *Star of Alabama* has incredible radar. They can track us from forty miles back. Way out of sight. Come below. I'll show you something."

Hope checked their course and confirmed that the autohelm was doing its job. He sheeted in the sails a hair as the wind was continuing to veer. Then he led Sally down to the nav station and switched on the radar.

Sally stared at the screen, hugged herself, and shivered. "That is the emptiest, loneliest-looking monitor I have ever seen."

"We appear to be alone," said Hope. "Down in a trough between two big seas our radar can see maybe sixteen, eighteen miles. When we climb a crest, maybe twenty-four."

The boat was starting to rise as she overtook a fair-sized roller. The sea angled under the hulls from the starboard bow.

"Here we go up, up, up, and now we are seeing twenty-four miles."

"We're still alone."

"But what if Tree is lurking forty miles back?"

"He's out of range. The radar can't see him."

"See this button? It's the IR button. Interference rejection. IR lets the receiver reject signals from another radar unit so it doesn't interfere with what we're trying to see. Let's see what happens." He punched the IR button.

The empty monitor suddenly appeared to undulate. "Yes! Just what I thought!"

"What are all the swirly lines?"

"Somebody else's radar is sweeping us. Somebody who's farther away than we can see with our unit."

"But we don't know who."

"Not yet. But we can see him seeing us. And we know that they've got a powerful unit with their antenna high off the water. Like maybe up a two-hundred-foot mast."

"Or a really big freighter. Like a container ship."

Hope switched off the set. "Could be. But if this overcast will just keep lifting so we get some visibility . . ."

Daylight lingered in the high latitudes. At fifty-eight degrees north they were in line with Labrador and the Scottish Highlands. It was still bright at nineteen hundred, seven o'clock that evening. The wind veered northwest and the overcast lifted as suddenly as if giants had pulled the lid to look inside a pot.

"Here we go!" Hope seized the helm. "We'll pull a one-eighty, right back on our wake. Ready to jibe about. Grab that sheet, haul in when I tell you . . . now."

He handled the mainsheet.

The sails crashed across the cabin and filled with the wind that was now streaming over the stern quarter. Turned around, *Oona* took the wind over her starboard side instead of port.

Hope let out the sails and raised the daggerboard and she began to fly, hurling fine spray as she sliced the oncoming seas.

"What about Ishmael?"

"He'll wait."

"How long?"

"We're doing sixteen knots. If that's Tree sweeping us, the *Star of Alabama* is probably making another sixteen in this wind, so we're approaching each other at about thirty-five miles an hour. We should see Tree's topsails at twenty miles, maybe? Half-hour tops."

At seven-thirty, a white wedge nicked the horizon.

"Topsails," said Hope, scoping it through the binoculars. He checked the radar. Still nothing within twenty-four miles. "He's way below the horizon—what they used to call 'hull down' when only the sails showed. Thirty miles, maybe. That's him, all right."

"Why," asked Sally, "is Tree following us following Ishmael?"

"Why did Tree suddenly show up with a lunch invitation?"

"Because he knows about Ishmael."

"Knows? He's wired him with an antenna. To get data."

"Or control him."

They pondered that thought.

Hope asked, "I think we have to ask ourselves, Are we making a terrible mistake?"

Sally said, "What mistake?"

"Going it alone thousands of miles at sea. This has gone far beyond your original attempt to document a new species. Right?"

"Don't get confused about that, David. The antenna doesn't mean he isn't a new species. His size alone and—"

"Sally. Something is weirdly wrong."

"That's where *Sixty Minutes* comes in. We document this weird thing and they take it from there."

"The danger of waiting for our *Sixty Minutes* coup is we don't know the timing here."

"We don't know what he's doing."

"Worse, we don't know when."

She looked at him, hope and confusion warring on her face. "If we don't know what, why is that worse?"

"We know where he's swimming."

"We *think* we know where he's swimming."

"We also know that there are submarines waiting in the Denmark Strait."

"We assume . . ." Now she was the one struggling like a hooked fish, fighting for a way loose, fearing there was none.

"Sally, I'm sorry. If there is a surgically altered, electronically wired creature that might have attacked a sub already, then at the least, the lives of a hundred-man crew are at risk. But what I saw had an even worse potential than just sinking. I saw a nuclear submarine totally out of control. According to that kid on the *Vermont,* all its systems 'went wack.' All of them, computers, everything. He thought they were going to accidentally launch their Tomahawks. The *Vermont* is an 'attack boat.' What if the next time Ishmael tangles with a 'boomer'—a ballistic missile boat packed with nuclear warheads? It could wipe out cities. So I'm asking you, Isn't it time to 'call the cops'?"

"Okay. Okay. Okay—but not our film. Whatever is on the film is ours. There's plenty of evidence on the videotape. Maybe we can salvage something of it. Maybe CNN would buy it . . ."

"I'm sorry, Sally. It just seems too big a risk to wait any longer."

"I said, Okay. So who do we tell? How do we dial nine-one-one?"

That was the million-dollar question. Who with the power

to act quickly would believe their vague fears? What power would challenge a vessel at sea owned by one of the wealthiest men in America on the word of a charter skipper and an independent filmmaker?

"What about your CNN friend?"

"He's not that kind of connected," said Hope. "We'll tell Mother."

"Mother?"

"Old Mother *New York Times*. A buddy of mine is their Boston bureau chief now. I'll radio an e-mail, tell him about your video, see what he can round up on Tree, and get on the horn to the Navy."

He switched on the SSB radio. But before he had entered an e-mail address, they heard William Tree's big voice drawl, *"There you are. Now Captain Hope, Ah fear you might have gotten the wrong impression when you turned your boat around and came flying back at us like a barn owl."*

Hope looked at Sally and said, "Nothing to lose by talking to him, right?"

"Right. He can probably explain everything."

Hope keyed the mike. "Sally was just saying you could probably explain everything."

"Well, her faith touches me. Captain, why don't you just drop your sails and wait for us to catch up with our explanation?"

"I'd just as soon hear it on the radio. You did say you were in the Gulf of Mexico."

"The radio's not very private, Captain. Now I strongly urge you to just slow down and wait for us."

Hope looked at Sally.

"Why not?" she said.

"Because he's sailing a five-hundred-foot long, five-thousand-ton vessel with a steel hull. He's transferred most of his scientists to another ship and his crew looked like a bunch of pirates. He could cut through us like a meat cleaver."

Sally chewed her lip.

Hope said, "The way I see it, we have nothing to lose by keeping our distance."

"Miz Sally, are you there?"

Hope handed her the mike. "I'm here, Bill."

"Ah believe it's time you and I talked turkey. I've been doing a lot of thinking lately, and I'm inclined to allow the foundation to start offering a bit of carte blanche to qualified filmmakers."

"How would that work, Bill?"

"We'd write the check. You'd be the one to spend it as you saw fit. It strikes me that's how to inspire natural filmmakers to new and better work."

"That's very interesting." She looked at Hope, who was watching her intently. "But I'm kind of an old-fashioned girl. I'd still feel most comfortable showing you a demo tape before money changed hands."

Tree laughed. *"Old-fashioned? Saintly's more like it. Your colleagues hear of you turning down no-strings funding, they'll rescind your parking permit. Are you sure you wouldn't make an exception for the Tree Foundation? Show me what you have now?"*

"I'd have to have a postproduction house clean it up first."

"Ah've seen plenty of rushes in my day. I can see past the glitches."

"My former husband always said, 'They'll never see your film any better than their first look.' "

"You told me that last time we talked, Miz Sally. I am mighty disappointed. . . . Are you sure that there is no way I can persuade you and Captain Hope to slow down that little boat and wait for me to catch up?"

"Not this time, Bill. Let's get together back in the States. On dry land."

Sally handed Hope the mike and said, "If you are wrong about him I have just turned down the best deal any documentarian was ever offered."

"If I'm right you just saved our lives."

"Well," said William Tree. *"It's a comfort to know you won't be showing it to anybody else, either. Good-bye, Miz Sally. Good-bye, Captain Hope. Over and out."*

The radio went dead.

Hope jumped up and pulled on his foul-weather jacket.

"Aren't you going to send the e-mail?" Sally asked.

"Not before I remove my radar reflector."

"Why?"

"Make it a little harder for him to find us."

Darkness had fallen. He turned on the work lights, popped the hatch, hanked on his harness, and worked his way to the mast. He was mostly blind beyond the circle of light, but what he saw of the water around the boat and felt rolling underfoot spoke of a larger ocean than he had yet experienced on this voyage. The seas were big and getting bigger, and it didn't take any imagination at all to envision their unobstructed fetch over thousands of miles of open water.

He found the right halyard and lowered the reflector. Shades of Barbara's merry band, the kind of folks who kept their radar reflector ready to douse in seconds. He took it inside and stowed it as low as he could, in the bilge of the port hull.

"Does that make us invisible?" asked Sally.

"No. Depending on surface conditions and weather he might spot us occasionally, but at least we're not waving a neon sign."

He sat at the radio to send the e-mail to his friend in Boston. Sally leaned against him. "Oh, God, I hope I didn't make an awful mistake."

Hope reached around her, flipping channels. "Weird. . . ."

"What?"

"No radio . . . dead as a doornail."

"Can you fix it?"

"Sure. Probably fuse."

But an hour later he knew it wasn't a fuse. Nor had he found any broken connections he could solder, and it began to dawn on him that the fault was in the microprocessor.

"Jesus H. First radio I had you could fix with a hammer. Now it's all chips. Son of a bitch!"

"Now what?"

"We don't have a radio. I can't e-mail my buddy at the *Times*."

30

HOPE LOOKED AT SALLY. "WE are six hundred miles from anywhere and we are mute."

"But how did it happen? Right now, of all times? That is the worst luck in the world. I can't believe this. Isn't there anything you can do?"

Hope went up into the cockpit and stood in the cold, shaking his head. Sally joined him. "I can't believe this. Isn't there anything?"

Hope pointed at the white glow in the dark, a fiberglass tube fastened to the backstay. "I've got an old-style Class B EPIRB. Emergency Position Indicating Radio Beacon. It transmits a distress signal by satellite, coded to identify *Oona*. Problem is, it's only reliable near a coast. Fine in the Caribbean, but up here, we're in a satellite dead zone. With the new ones the satellites store the information and pass it on when they fly over a ground station. The other problem is, even if they did get our signal, the first thing Search and Rescue would do is canvass shipping in the area. And guess who would answer. 'We found some wreckage and an empty raft. We'll keep looking.' It could be weeks before we got spotted, if ever. And we don't have weeks. No, we are on our own."

"I still don't understand how it could break down just at this moment—when *Tree* was talking to you, no less."

Hope said, "I don't know. Maybe a power spike. But I've got surge protectors up the wazoo ever since my old radio got fried. To have the microprocessor just blow is definitely weird."

"William Tree radioed and our radio went down," said Sally. "I think he did it to us."

"How?"

Sally said, "What do they call it in the military, EW? Electronic warfare?"

"And ECM. Electronic countermeasures."

"Did he EW us somehow? Or ECM us?"

"Could be," said Hope. "Could be. And if it was military, my store-bought radio would have been a sitting duck."

"Like if Tree sent a power surge."

"I don't see how he could transmit electricity."

"But remember, his crewmen were on the boat when we had lunch. Could they have done something to it?"

Hope shook his head in bewilderment. "I didn't notice anything. The radio didn't look like it had been opened up or anything, but I wasn't looking for 'evidence.' Besides, we used it since then. For weather reports and talking to Tree. . . ."

"Then how did he do it?"

"I'm going to check it out again. Keep your eyes peeled for their lights."

Hope went below and checked every circuit on the radio that he could reach with his circuit tester. The weirdest thing was that electricity was entering and leaving the microprocessor. It wasn't burned out.

He brought Sally hot coffee mixed with cocoa.

"I checked the whole thing out with the circuit tester. Juice is reaching the microprocessor. And it seems to be passing through it. It's working, but it's not working. Like its brain got scrambled."

"Like a software breakdown?"

"Exactly. Jesus—" He looked at her. Sally's eyes got big in the red glow of the compass light. She grabbed his hand. "A virus!"

"He sent a virus."

"William Tree radioed and our radio went down," said Sally. "Can you do that? Can you radio a virus?"

"I guess. It's data. You couldn't do it to my old analog radio, but with digital, I guess you could. Data's data, right?"

"He did it to us."

It made perfect sense, thought Hope. But his euphoria evaporated quickly. "Knowing that doesn't change much."

"Yes it does! It tells us you're right about that animal. Tree is doing something terrible with that animal. I really thought you were wrong about the submarine, but why would Tree *attack* us like that? I mean that's what it is, it's an attack. He attacked us."

"Very successfully. He's still cut us off from the planet. How do we stop him? Flip on the EPIRB and hope we get lucky? Sail to Greenland? Does anybody even live there? Sail back to Newfoundland? Against the wind. A week. Two weeks?"

Sally said, "We've got to at least try the EPIRB."

Hope turned on the lights and went to get it. "I couldn't afford the fancy one that automatically releases if you sink. You have to switch this one on manually."

He unlatched it from the backstay, brought it back to the cockpit, and opened the protective casing. "Oh, Bill," he said softly. "You son of a bitch."

Sally crowded close to peer over his shoulder. "It's empty."

"His riding crew took it during lunch. . . . He was planning ahead. They knew we were watching Ishmael."

"We're on our own," said Sally.

"Man, is he a piece of work. EPIRB is your last-ditch mayday. Your only chance to get rescued. He gutted it. What was he thinking? What if we got in trouble?"

Sally said, "What do we do if we don't even know what he's going to do?"

"That animal disrupted a submarine."

"We've been down this road already. How? He's big, but he's not that big."

"No. They made him big so he could protect himself from guard dolphins. Like he wiped out those bottlenoses. But like you say, he's not big enough to physically damage a submarine. Or carry anything that heavy."

"Software isn't heavy."

"Their computers went wack."

"A virus."

"Like what they did to our radio."

"Ishamel delivers a virus."

"How? How do they penetrate into the computers?"

"The sub has various 'ports' to the outside. Fiber-optic cameras and sensors, sonar, radar, towed arrays for listening . . . very sensitive, very sophisticated . . . eyes and ears . . ."

"So they get through one of those ports somehow."

"It's only data. It's just streams of information—bad information."

"What if Ishamel has a little computer, along with his radio and his generator?"

"And the computer holds a software virus. What if they taught him to swim up to the nose cone or the towed array and hover there while the computer passes it through the port—through the sonar, I'll bet."

"I find that hard to believe."

"Even after you've met an oversized dolphin with its own radio and generator? You know, when you think about it, it's really very simple. Miniaturized electronics pack plenty of punch, but don't weigh much. If he weighs three tons, he wouldn't even know he was carrying a few pounds of gear if they put it in surgically, like pacemakers and artificial hips.

Simple stuff. The hard part must have been teaching him to swim alongside a sub."

"No," said Sally. "The hard part was controlling him."

"What do you mean?"

"He's sticking close to us and avoiding Tree."

"Smart."

"He's not so smart that you can say, 'Ishmael, give that enemy submarine a virus because it threatens the American way of life.' He's just a poor animal that they've tried to turn into a weapon."

"So how do we stop him?"

"Disarm him."

"How?"

Sally started to say, "I don't know—yes I do! He's wired up with electricity, right?"

"Generator, et cetera."

"Electricity is his Achilles' heel. All we've got to do is zap him."

"Zap him?" asked Hope. "With electricity?"

"I've got my portable light generator and two hundred feet of underwater cable. All we have to do is zap him in his generator and the surge will fry his computer and radio and everything. Like that surge fried your last radio."

"All?" said Hope. It meant going in the water with him.

"We'll coax him close again with the *Oona* sound and when he comes close we'll dive with the power cable and zap his generator."

"There's nothing left to make a cage."

"We'll be in and out as fast as can be."

The wind shifted southeast during the night. Dawn revealed a confused sea smeared with breaking crests. It was marginally warmer, but the barometer was dropping rapidly. Heavy clouds were banking in the southeast, and the wind started to whistle in the rigging.

"We better make this quick," said Hope. "We've got a full gale coming our way."

They had worked at it all night—spelling each other for short naps—while watching for the *Star of Alabama*'s lights and working the sails to match the shifting wind. The generator was in place, running quietly in the cockpit. They had cushioned it on blankets to minimize the vibrations. The cable was coiled on the dive steps, with one end plugged into the generator. Hope had fashioned the business end into a shock head with positive and negative electrodes that looked like an oversized plug. He attached a switch near the shock head so they could turn the power on at the moment it actually touched the big dolphin by jerking a cord.

Looking for a bright side, Hope decided that they would enjoy the advantage, in addition to getting in and out quickly, of not being burdened with cameras.

Suddenly Ishmael cleared the sea close ahead of the boat and spun six effortless turns before side-flopping back into the water with a huge splash.

"There he is," Sally cried. "Poor thing."

"We better wait for more light. We'll never see him underwater."

Hope, closely observing the "poor thing" execute its morning jumps, was struck by the fact that its relentless swim north seemed to have made it more powerful than ever, like a high school football player finishing the season bigger-muscled than he had started.

"Boy, they chose the right dolphin, didn't they? I'd like him on my side if I were in a war."

"They must have bred him," said Sally. "He's probably a hybrid."

"They mated huge with enormous."

They got into their diving gear, including their heavy dry suits for warmth. As the sun rose, the wind increased and the sea built. It was turning into a race between sufficient light to see underwater and sea conditions they could still dive in.

"Now or never."

Hope headed into the wind, furled the sails, and eased the plastic-wrapped speaker over the side. Sally turned on the sound and they went quickly down the dive steps. Hope had prepared lifelines, which he tied around their left arms in case the wind caused the boat to drift faster than they could swim. The risk of getting tangled in the lines beat watching the boat vanish over the horizon.

The gray water was a shocking change from the indigo depths of the Gulf Stream. The cold burned like ice where it touched his bare wrist between dry suit sleeve and glove. Visibility was nil. Hope could barely see the rudders and the daggerboard, which were spearing the water as the boat bounced.

Worse, the hull motion was frothing bubbles. If the animal did approach, it would be on top of them before they could see it. Or the bouncing boat would crush one of their skulls.

He tapped Sally's arm hard, and gestured, Up!

To his great relief, Sally didn't argue. She repeated the thumbs-up and followed her lifeline to the surface. Hope pulled himself onto the dive steps and helped Sally up. Then he reeled in the electric cable, feeling an abject sense of failure.

Sally looked just as chastened.

"It was a good idea," said Hope. "But not today. Maybe when this blows over."

In their brief time underwater, the stiff wind had started blowing spray and the surface of the North Atlantic had grown brilliant with whitecaps.

"Let's get the gear inside, right now, and the hatches shut."

While Sally cleared the dive steps, Hope double-secured the tightly furled mainsail and jib and raised his stormsail on the baby stay.

The barometer told him he'd be furling the stormsail very soon. And the latest weather fax guaranteed heavy seas thundering in. With luck he had an hour to prepare to fight a storm that he would have sailed around to avoid if he'd been concentrating on survival instead of trying to defang William Tree's monster dolphin.

He went below to check the steering cables. They were holding tight and seated well in the quadrant groove, which was fortunate, because this would be a hell of time to mess with them.

He put a pot of pea soup on to boil and made a quick pass through the cabins, securing stuff that would go flying when the boat started jumping around. "Sally, when that's hot, pour it into a Thermos. And could you make some coffee, too? And we should gnaw on something now."

He secured the fiberglass canister that held his canopied life raft to the bottom of the companionway. "Just in case," he told Sally.

"Why not keep it handy on deck?"

"Because it could get washed over. Also, capsizing is our likeliest worst case. She'll float upside down, so it would be nice to have the raft handy when we cut our way out."

"Cut?"

He started to explain that unlike a racing cat, *Oona* had no escape hatches in the bottom of her hulls. But he realized that he was being too matter-of-fact and that Sally looked a little frightened, so he grinned to put her at ease and said, "We'll go out your hull, that damaged bottom would be easier to cut."

Sally stared. Suddenly, she smiled with delight. "You made a joke."

"I always joke."

"Not about everything. . . . Maybe I should have been a shrink."

"We'd have lost a great filmmaker."

He pulled on sea boots and warm gloves and hauled his

cargo net up on deck. The sky was ribbed with long dark streaks pointing from the wind's source in the southeast to the northwest. The space between the ribs was getting smaller very quickly.

Working methodically in the cold wind, he attached an anchor and chain to the net to weight it. He brought up his longest spare anchor lines, tied them to either side of the net, and bundled it tight with sail ties. He hoisted the package onto the dinghy davits at the back of the cockpit, ready to be dropped in the water. He wrapped the bitter ends of the long anchor lines around the powerful jib-sheet winches and cleated them off.

"What's that?" Sally asked when she brought peanut-butter-and-jelly sandwiches and a Thermos of coffee.

"A drogue to slow us down, if things get hairy. I wish I hadn't thrown my old tanks overboard. I could have used them to weight it."

"Are you going to run or beat into the storm?"

Hope checked again that he had a razor-sharp bosun's knife in his foul-weather pants pocket to cut the line holding the weighted net.

"Run, for now. Maybe beat if we get in trouble."

"When do you use the drogue?"

"Only if we get in very big trouble."

31

"WELL, BOYS, MY KILLPHIN IS definitely swinging into action."

William Tree gripped the arms of his chair so hard they creaked. It took all of his strength to hold on against the *Star of Alabama*'s peculiar pitch and roll. The combined weight of the water in Tree's aquarium, which the naval architects had taken into account when it was going to be a swimming pool, and the sixty-thousand-gallon acute care tank, which they had not, made the great ship more top-heavy than originally intended. The result was that the few scientists remaining aboard were throwing up in their cabins.

The ship's seamen and engineers barely noticed the motion. Although when the wind topped sixty knots Captain Grandzau asked Tree's permission to bear off to the northwest to run more in line with the storm-driven rollers.

"No," said Tree. "Steady as she goes. Where my killphin goes, we go."

A full-blown North Atlantic gale was the least of his worries. The big question was, would the animal gently tweak the British submarine's systems as originally programmed? Would it deliver that all-attention-grabbing kick in the behind with some frightening but ultimately repairable mayhem? Or go haywire again and launch another total-systems attack instead of a partially disabling sales demonstration?

As the storm intensified, Wendell insisted on strapping him into his chair. Tree finally gave in. A ship-propelled fall to the deck could break bones, and with the weight he was carrying he had enough medical problems as it was.

Trapped in a body heaving against the straps, he thought how freely his killphin would surf the rollers in the early hours of the gale, riding the lift of following seas, long-jumping off their foamy crests. But if the huge, sinuous mammal appears to frolic, it was frolicking with intent.

Predators husband their strength, Tree knew well, to conserve it for the kill. The big waves offered a free ride—more speed for less energy—and the animal would take it until storm-whipped crosswinds plowed up colliding seas impossible to surf.

But still forced to surface regularly for air, the killphin would adopt a strategy of longer, deeper dives to avoid being battered. Steep dives to peaceful depths and lofty ascents to breathe would shorten its distance traveled over the bottom. What it had made up with speed in the early hours it would lose in the dives. Not that the animal gave a darn one way or another. Its reality was the storm. At least until it heard the threatening rumble of the *Star of Alabama*. Tree's marine acoustics expert claimed that the steel hull would boom warnings as far as fifty miles as the ship rolled and pitched violently. And when that happened, Tree thought bleakly, the animal would establish the direction from which the ship came, and run the other way.

Hughie Mick staggered into the Captain Nemo Lounge, stoically ignoring the seasickness that had turned him as green as an avocado. "Got something interesting for you, Bill."

Hughie had gotten creative.

"Going to show you two pictures, Bill. Waveforms from sound. The science boys call 'em noise prints. This here sound we got by making the computers improve it."

"Enhanced."

"Right, Bill—enhanced—now this here sound, we got back in the laboratory."

"Back at the Marine Park?"

"That's right, Bill."

"When?"

"Way back. See how the sounds look kind of the same?"

Tree inspected the printouts that Hughie held side by side.

"All right. I'll buy that. They look pretty much identical. What are they?"

"This here one—the enhanced one—is the noise that the sailboat makes in the water."

"And this one?"

"This is the laboratory."

"Our laboratory?"

"It's the background noise, Bill."

"It's called ambient noise, Hughie. What's causing it?"

"It's probably from a generator or something."

"Now hold on. Which lab are we talking about?" Tree asked, unable to conceal enormous excitement. Was he hearing what he thought he was hearing? "Are we talking about *the* lab?"

"The lab," said Hughie. "Where the critter was born."

Tree shook his head in amazement, enormous relief, and not a little irritation. "You could have saved us a lot of trouble if you'd thought of this earlier."

"I thought you'd say that," said Hughie. "And I can't say I blame you."

"Well, I don't blame you. I blame those high-priced animal behaviorists who should have known better."

"I suspect they're doing the best they can," Hughie smiled, as close to gloating as he would risk. "Remember, they had to spend a long time getting educated."

Dr. Rod chose that moment to burst in unannounced. He cast an angry look at Hughie. "Bill."

"What's up, Rod?"

"Well, I came to make my report. It looks like Hughie beat me to it."

"I would have preferred to get his report from either of you two weeks ago."

"Do you see what it means?"

"I see that it means we finally have a way to lure him back. If I understand properly, all you have to do is put a tape of this noise playing on the two-way hydrophones and he'll come home to Daddy."

"Not quite, Bill. I hope Hughie didn't mislead you into expecting immediate results."

Tree looked at Hughie, and the good ol' boy's expression faded so fast it looked like he had left the room.

"What is the problem, Rod? We need immediate results."

"We can't lure the killphin with a computer-enhanced soundtrack of that sailboat. Those noise prints Hughie's waving in your face show reconstructions of reconstructions of gobbledygook. The killphin won't buy it."

Tree stabbed at his intercom. "Captain Grandzau. Catch up with that sailboat now."

The captain's accent tended to thicken when he was perturbed, and Tree heard, "Ve don't know vere he is, Bill."

"Why not?"

"His radar signature has become minimal und now he is lost in sea clutter. There are vaves, Bill."

"Well, Ah know there are waves. I can hear 'em beating the side of the ship. You had no problem tracking him before when there were waves."

"Vell, these are bigger vaves. Und perhaps he lost radar reflector in high vind."

"Or hauled it down to make my life difficult," Tree growled to himself.

Captain Grandzau said, "Ven vaves go down, ve find him. Excellent radar. Ve find him, guaranteed."

"Go find him, *now!*"

"Is vind sixty-five knots, Bill."

Tree exploded, tugging at his chair straps like a netted polar bear and mimicking the German's accent with brutal accuracy. "Vas vind *eighty-five* knots off Cape Horn. We go where we please. Find him!"

Then Wendell piped up. "Sixty-five knots? Heck, Bill, they'll be drownded."

Tree nearly erupted again, but caught himself and corrected Wendell almost gently. "*Drowned,* Wendell. And no, I would not worry about that. Captain Hope did not strike me as the sort of sailor who drowns easily."

"That's too bad," said Wendell.

"No it's not. We need that man alive and sailing in order to make a loud and clear recording of that boat's wake. Don't we, Rod? Isn't that what you're leading up to?"

"Right, Bill. That's the only way we'll fool the killphin."

"Well, that makes sense. Otherwise, he'll go for the real boat and leave us in the ditch. But why not play the lab sound?"

"We tried that in the Caribbean."

"No one told me that."

"It was one of seventeen ideas we tried when the killphin got loose. It didn't work. It didn't seem worth bothering you."

"Next time, bother me," Tree said coldly. "Every time."

"Sorry, Bill."

"Why didn't it work?"

"For some reason he likes their sound better than the original. It's my thought that the killphin associates the earlier version—the home lab version—with some of the things Hughie did to him."

Hughie looked up, aggrieved. Tree motioned him to keep his trap shut, and said to Rod in a very dangerous tone, "If you played that noise in the Caribbean and it didn't work, why in the name of everything holy didn't you try playing the sailboat sound?"

"We didn't know about the sailboat then. It was just an idea that the animal would like the sound of home enough to come close enough to catch him, but it didn't work."

"Well, at least we've got the answer, if it's not too late."

Rod said, "Just so you know, Bill."

"Know what?"

"After we record their sound, we'll have to stop their boat before we play the sound so he comes to us, not them."

"Heck, stopping them's easy. Recording them is going to be the hard part. We can always stop 'em."

"The boat is stronger than we are," Hope yelled over the thunder of the white-frothed seas that were breaking on all sides. "You've got to get out of the wind and rest."

"I'm afraid to go below."

Her foul-weather hood covered her face like a burka. Through the thin slit between the low peak and high collar Hope could see only her eyes, which, he had noted, had begun filling with tears. He knew he had to somehow persuade her to rest in the relative peace of the cabin.

"In the old days—"

"I can't hear you," Sally shouted back.

He pressed his mouth to her hood and yelled louder. "In the old days, back in the sixties and seventies, catamarans broke up in seas like this. Now they're so strong, the only thing we have to worry about is pitchpoling, capsizing, or losing the rig."

"Are you trying to make me feel better?"

"I'm trying to stop you from zoning out," he shouted back. "I know you're scared, but half the fight is to keep your head on straight."

Sally ducked her head. "I want to zone out. I'm sorry. I'm

really, really scared. This isn't like diving, where I can control it."

Again he tried to tease her to life. "If I bash my skull you better be ready to save me."

Considering the forces that were throwing the boat around, the notion of smashing headfirst into a steel winch was not far-fetched. They had their harnesses tethered short as a precaution, and wore inflated life vests for cushioning. Already, Hope's left hand ached where he creamed it on the spokes when the helm spun wildly away from him, and Sally had banged her knee hard against the hatch. So far neither was bleeding, though Hope knew that they were getting too tired too soon.

He shouted, "Remember what I told you when this started? The good news is we've got plenty of sea room, plenty of room to run. So I can steer whatever course looks best."

Sally nodded stiffly.

He had long ago abandoned any hope of maintaining a specific course, much less trying to follow Ishmael. The seas were too large. Instead, he had been hand-steering for hours—picking safer routes for *Oona* among the erupting and increasingly chaotic crests—while trying to keep the wind blowing on a diagonal over the stern quarter and their speed just a little slower than the seas. Both the wind speed indicator and the barometer promised hours more of it.

Sally pressed her mouth to his hood. "Are you afraid?" she shouted.

"I've seen worse."

"Really?" She pulled back. Her brimming eyes locked on his and he knew that she did not want to hear a lie.

Hope worked up a smile instead and admitted, "But not that I remember."

"Are you afraid?" she demanded.

"Not yet. I'm just trying to hunker down and outlast it.

The boat's stronger than we are. The big problem is getting tired. Are you sure you won't go below?"

"No. I'm really afraid to be caught in the cabin."

"We need food. Could you go down and get the soup?"

"Couldn't I steer instead?"

"Sorry. Not today."

She ducked her head. He watched her take a full minute to gather her spirits. "Okay. I'll go."

"On the count . . ." He looked back, gauged the sea, and held up three gloved fingers. For an instant, he steered port, then hard starboard.

"Three! Two . . ."

Hard aport. *Oona* leapt onto a crest.

"Now!"

Sally shoved the hatch open, jumped the washboards, and slid it shut, seconds ahead of a sea that broke into the cockpit and grabbed Hope's legs like a marauding shark.

A second later the hatch opened and Sally started up. "I can't stay there. I can't do it. I'm terrified of being trapped if we capsize."

Hope knew he had to act fast before she spiraled from fear into panic. "Okay. Listen, we saved some apples, right? And some cheese? You know where they are?"

"I think so."

"I must eat. Just quickly race to the galley. Grab apples and water and a big hunk of cheese and the Thermos. Bring 'em in a sack."

She was shaking her head.

Telling her the truth—that she was the bravest woman he had ever seen, Barbara Carey included—wouldn't help. Nor would a plea to get hold of her fear for his sake. This was mind-boggling fear and it had to be derailed before she lost complete control.

He steered around a huge crest that broke behind the boat with a thunderous hiss, and a side sea that rocketed past them like a tandem tractor-trailer. Sally traced it with her eyes. It was, in its ferocious way, a very beautiful sight, glowing like cream under the dark sky. Hope was suddenly inspired.

"And bring your still camera," he shouted.

"What?"

"I want pictures. This is incredible."

She stared at him like he had lost his mind. Her gaze flew up at a mountain of salt water overtaking the boat.

"That's insane."

"No one's ever taken shots like this. Probably can't be done."

Crew Psych 101 finally worked. Through the burka slit he could see the "don't-tell-me-can't" glint burn the frightened tears from her eyes. She dropped down, shut the hatch firmly, and reappeared in a few minutes and swung a mesh bag filled with apples and cheese and a Thermos and water bottle over the washboards.

She secured the hatch and held a block of cheddar for him to chew while he steered with both hands, heading up to slow the boat to let a huge crest break. The cheese, and a bite of apple, tasted as rich and sweet as a hot pie. He steered around the crevasse behind the crest, but found himself with nowhere to go when the crest's kid brother ran under the port hull and tilted *Oona* forty degrees. He headed downwind to try to save her. Sixty-five was her absolute limit. Beyond sixty-five degrees only God could save her from capsizing, and God was clearly not in a giving mood today.

"Do you really want pictures?" Sally shouted.

"Yes! I've never seen photos of these conditions from boat level. If anybody can do it you can. It will be like underwater photography."

"You're humoring me."

"I could write a book on heavy-weather tactics," Hope bellowed back. "If I had pictures." And provided they got out of this alive.

The storm was in fact looking worse, not better. The wind

was still rising. Though the bigger problem was the hours the wind had already had to churn the endless sweep of open water.

Sally cast a speculative eye on the maelstrom. She pulled a light meter from her pocket and pointed it to port and starboard, back at the roller crowding after the boat, ahead at the crest that Hope was fighting to keep from catching up with, and up at the heavy clouds. "Will black and white do?"

Hope answered with an eager thumbs-up. Between the broken sea and the funereal sky the only color in sight was her blue eyes, anyway.

Sally went below. She was there awhile, and when she returned, she had exchanged her foul-weather hood for a snug dry-suit balaclava, in which black skull-molding garment she looked like a ripe and earnest novitiate.

She had her digital still camera shielded inside a flexible Ewa-marine watertight housing with finger holes that allowed her to adjust focus. She got out and hanked on just as sea broke over both sterns. Half of it plowed into the cockpit like a drunk's SUV jumping a curb. It smashed Hope into the wheel and Sally against the cabin bulkhead.

Hope headed downwind to take some speed off the boat, then up again to evade a breaking roller that was angling in from the side. When he could steal a look at Sally, he saw her framing shots of the seas astern. When next he looked, she was photographing the furled main and jib and the small stormsail, creating a visual record of Hope's response to the storm. She took a shot of the net and anchor ropes, then crouched low to shoot them framed by a breaking sea tumbling over the sterns.

It knocked her flat, and she slid to the end of her tether. She struggled to her feet, inspected her camera for damage, and pulled half an apple from her pocket. When she rubbed the apple on the camera housing's optical glass port to stop the spray from forming drops in front of the lens, Hope knew that if they ever did get out of this alive, she would be on his case forever until he wrote the book.

Sally dove below and came up with the camera reloaded. She shot three more rolls before she shouted to Hope, "Too dark."

Night was collapsing from the sky. Sally brought up hot soup.

"Thank you," said Hope. "That saved my life."

"Can you take a break, let me steer?"

"No. It's getting worse."

32

FIVE HUNDRED FEET BELOW THE storm the USS *Vermont* steamed in silence. The huge submarine's rock-steady attitude and the absence of mechanical vibration combined in a serenity unmoved by the forces exploding across the high latitudes of the North Atlantic. Were not valves, pipes, tubes, wires, ducts, pumps, gauges, and blowers exposed for instant access, the interior of the submerged ship could pass for a windowless office building, staffed by a hundred suburban gearheads working overtime.

Yet none aboard were fooled by the illusion of peace. The skipper was running them ragged with drills, drills, and more drills. He had popped a Tactical Weapons Proficiency exam at the Combat Systems Department and so many surprise torpedo drills that the weapons guys were practically sleepwalking. The crew was overworked, tired, and jumpy.

Suddenly the sonar operator on watch cried out, "Same noise! Same noise!"

Voices were never raised on the *Vermont*. The boat was so mechanically silent that a shout could give them away to a listener who had no idea they even existed. The captain set a standard of low-key cool that everyone emulated.

The SO looked around wild-eyed, saw Royce, who had stopped by the sonar room to check on a faintly heard mystery contact made earlier in the watch. "Commander! Commander! You gotta hear this."

By now senior sonarmen were running in to hunch over the operators seated at the hazy green video displays. On their heels marched the captain himself, who swept a hawk eye over eight pairs of tensed shoulders and demanded quietly, "What's up?"

"Nelson's got a contact, sir."

"It's the same noise I heard when the computers went down in the Caribbean." Nelson pointed at one of the screens on the stack of monitors in front of his stool. He jerked a joystick and a cursor arrowed toward a hair-thin white line on the green haze. "There, sir."

The sound guys all leaned close. Two disagreed in quick succession:

"Merchant ship at twenty thousand yards."

"It's only environment, sir."

A third supported the natural noise theory, with a derisive glance at Nelson. "It's *raining* up there."

"No," said Nelson, pressing his headseat to his ears. "It's a really quiet contact. The same—"

"Bearing rate?"

"Sir—it's gone, sir . . ." Nelson's colleagues traded smirks; they would ride his sorry ass for the rest of the patrol for this one. But the skipper was still concerned.

"Active? Somebody probing us? Somebody we don't hear?"

"Nothing, sir," answered the man on acoustic intercept.

"Could be a diesel?" Royce asked. No one wanted to answer that one.

Ultrasilent modern diesel-electric submarines were high on the skipper's nightmare list. For a twentieth of the cost of the *Vermont* you could build a handy little sub capable of launching deadly surprises. Had some war game master gotten proactively sadistic? Or was it warshot real, a hostile rogue?

"Towed Array?"

The petty officer listening to the hydrophones that were dragged a half mile behind the ship said, "Nothing, sir."

The captain telephoned the control center. "TMA, what do you have?"

But the lieutenant on Target Motion Analysis could only report that he had received far too little tracking data from sonar to estimate the contact's range or bearing—if it was a contact.

"A whale?" someone ventured.

"A whale?"

"It sounded a little like whale talk," Nelson said. ". . . I mean it was in that frequency. Except it was mechanical, too. Like a pump or a generator."

"It's a merchant ship at twenty thousand yards."

"It's not in the library." The computers had, in the moments since the sonar operator had recorded the sound, tried to match it in the vast file of friendly, foreign, and potentially hostile submarine and ship sounds.

"But it's the same as last time," whispered Sonarman Nelson.

The skipper said, "Manual drill." He ordered, "Take to manual all systems that can go to manual."

As he gave the order to remove the submarine from the grip of the thousands of computer programs monitoring, and running, its functions, the skipper glanced at Lt. Commander Royce. Both knew that few of the new ship's functions could go completely off-line.

Men scattered to execute the order. We all know it, thought Royce as he oversaw the throwing of switches and breakers. But you do what you can.

"Shouldn't you start your engines?" Sally yelled.

"Not when running."

The boat was going way too fast, but he was loath to head up. Attempting to turn a 180 in this mess could be fatal, putting her beam to the sea. And even if they survived the about-face, then what? The huge waves would bury her thin bows. But the problem was, if she went any faster that could be fatal, too.

He hated to risk the drogue. A passive defense—riding stern to the seas—meant surrendering any opportunity to counter threat with skill. It meant giving up the chance to steer away from a dangerous crest or sail around one of the gaping troughs behind the ever taller seas.

But he was exhausted. And with bone weariness came depression, and an awful feeling that he had done everything he could, but it still wasn't enough. The seas were the worst he had ever seen, worse than his one time around Cape Horn—a relatively easy passage, he thought now, in a tough little mono-hull.

Even as he wearied, the wind grew stronger and *Oona* kept threatening to overtake the seas. Hope kept bearing off to slow her down, but when a huge gust kicked them in the stern just as they were catching up with a tall crest, the cat accelerated.

Hope tried to bear off, but couldn't because it meant steering directly into the path of a breaking sea as tall as a two-story house. Steering around it allowed her to rocket ahead and before he knew it she was on top of the crest. She pitched forward. And suddenly he was staring down a long, steep slope that appeared to have no bottom.

Oona plunged.

He saw one chance to stop her from stuffing her bows, and one chance only, and took it. Like a surfer riding his board inside the leading edge of a wave instead of down the face, he turned the boat across the sea and prayed that exposing her beam wouldn't get her thrown on her side.

She took off down the slope at a shallow angle. The speed was startling, so fast that he could hear over the rumble of the seas the loud hiss of twin rooster tails that her sterns threw from the water. All he could do was try to steer. It was like skiing on ice, with not a clue how to stop.

She heeled steeply, tilting up on her port hull, passing forty, fifty degrees. He felt the wind shove the little storm-sail, levering her farther over as the face of the wave lifted her hull.

"This is it!" he shouted to Sally. "Hold on to my harness!"

At least, he thought, we're wearing dry suits. We'll stay alive a couple of hours longer.

The catamaran pierced the bottom of the slope, port hull first. Twenty feet of the bow vanished. She started to rotate. But before she turned upside down, the starboard hull dropped. Hope couldn't believe it. The hull had found a hole in the wave—a momentary void of air instead of water—and when it crashed down, the boat was still upright.

Hope released the stormsail sheets. Then he unclipped his lifeline, lunged over the back of the cockpit, and cut the rope holding the weighted net. Whirling forward, he leapt onto the cabin and started cranking the daggerboard up into its trunk. The thought flew through his mind that the guy who invented the single daggerboard was a genius. There was no way he had time or strength to raise two of them. At last it crept up out of the water and the shallow-draft, wide-stance catamaran was free to drift on the surface.

As he threw himself at the mast, to lower the wildly flog-ging stormsail, the boat came to an abrupt halt. He looked back. The drogue was a hundred feet astern—not far enough—holding her stern to the sea. The lines had fouled. But already it was slowing the boat, putting a counterdrag to the thrust of the wind against the bare mast. He tumbled back into the cockpit, locked the helm, and finally hanked on again.

"We've got to unfoul the drogue lines."

The forces on the lines were enormous, but as the boat climbed a sea and the drogue fell in a trough, there was slack for a moment. He and Sally worked at the winches until the lines whipped steel-hard out the water, threatening to part. When they slackened, they cranked again. It took half an hour and all the strength they had left in them, but eventually the drogue trailed a full three hundred feet behind the boat, where it rode in unison with *Oona,* crest to crest and trough to trough.

Hope signaled thumbs-down to Sally and bellowed, *"Inside!"*

They took a breaking sea through the hatch, right over the washboards and into the cabin. Hope slid it shut, dogged it down, and collapsed in the saloon, where six inches of water slowly drained away. It was quiet. And sheer luxury to be out of the wind.

Sally said, "I have never seen a person move that fast."

"I didn't think we could count on another miracle."

"Now what?"

"Food. Rest. Pray."

Hope awakened from a dead sleep in the middle of the night. It was cold. The roar outside the cabin sounded different and the nature of the boat's movement had changed. It was tugging at the drogue in a different way, less like a wild horse than a dog on a leash. He lay still, Sally in the crook of his arm. Neither had moved since they collapsed on the wet mattress.

He eased out from under her, opened the hatch, and climbed out into the cockpit.

A clearing wind had swung out of the northwest, peeling the clouds away to reveal enormous stars. The Milky Way lit a powerful sea, but one marginally less violent. He was too tired to retrieve the drogue, much less raise his sails. Let her drift for the rest of the night. Let the sea subside.

When he rose again at dawn, stiff and cold despite the dry

suit, the sea was still running, still wild. But the wind was steady on the compass and he saw that he would be able to raise a double-reefed main and good-sized sliver of jib by the time he had retrieved the drogue.

First he put water on to boil, brewed coffee, and brought a cup to Sally, who was watching him through steady eyes.

"Good morning."

She took the coffee. "Are we in heaven?"

"All I know is we're not dead. It just feels that way."

"What's it like up there?"

"We've seen a lot worse."

They took their coffee to the cockpit. Sally scanned the still-wild water for Ishamel. "There he is. Ohmigod, there he is. Ishmael! Come here."

The animal did a single spin-dance a quarter mile south of the boat. When they saw it again, it had covered a half mile and was far ahead, swimming north.

Then it vanished.

Fat white clouds tumbled across a bright blue sky. It was so clear that when Hope looked for Ishmael he thought he could see all the way to Greenland. And to the south, the warm Caribbean. Scoping the horizon with the binoculars, looking for Ishamel and trying to get the energy together to haul in the drogue, he fixed on an oddly shaped cloud that hardened, as he watched, into a pyramid of gleaming sails.

33

HOPE ZAPPED THEM WITH THE radar. "Seventeen knots close-hauled. That is some ship."

"It's Tree, isn't it?"

"Oh yes."

"Can we outrun them?" Sally asked.

"I don't know. But we're not running anywhere until we haul in the drogue."

Cleverly designed drogues, whether store-bought or jury-rigged, had a spill line you could haul that would relieve the water pressure to make it easier to retrieve, but Hope had had neither the time nor the material to be clever. He had, however, streamed it from the powerful jib-sheet winches and so, as the sails to the south stood taller and broader, he started cranking it in, fighting the force of the wind and waves pushing against *Oona*'s hull, cabin, mast, and the thick cylinder of the foresail rolled around the headstay.

"Why don't we just cut it?" asked Sally.

" 'Cause if we need it again, we'll really wish we still had it."

It was like trying to land a fish, cranking hard against the strain, then suddenly hauling in fast hand over hand when a shifting crest caused it to slacken, then cranking the winch again as the strain increased. By the time it was close enough to see the net breaking the surface, the *Star of Alabama*'s hull was visible, a dark wedge framed by spray.

Chains clanking on the deck, they finally got the net and anchor aboard. Hope hurriedly raised the main and some jib. "All right, we're outta here."

But which way?

The wind was clocking fifteen knots, gusting to twenty-five knots. But having shifted northwest, it was slamming new waves against the remains of the storm seas. The result was a short, steep chop.

The binoculars showed the ship hurling wings of spray. Backed by her enormous mass, her long steel hull was blasting the chop from her path.

Ordinarily, if Hope stuck to his north-northeast course he could do eighteen knots, easily, more than enough to stay ahead of the close-hauled *Star of Alabama*. But not in this chop. Poking along at ten and twelve knots, *Oona* was still banging her bridge deck. If he let out sail to try and speed up, she would bang them to pieces. And not make an extra knot in the process.

He bore east, off the wind, hoping to pick up an advantage on the swell, but the swell was barely getting started and it was the chop that ruled. He considered turning around and running, southeast, with the wind and the wind-driven seas, but the chop would rule for hours more in that direction, too. Besides, if he ran with the wind he stood an additional risk of stuffing her bows.

"I'm going to hold a northeast course," he told Sally. "I can't point any closer to the wind than he can. But this has got to be his slowest point of sail."

"But he's catching up."

"We don't have a choice until the sea settles."

"How long?"

"If this wind holds, a couple of hours."

Sally studied the windship in the binoculars. Then she

went down to the radar and moved the cursor to the only target on the screen, which displayed its distance, speed, and bearing.

She called to Hope at the helm, "He's catching up faster than that."

Hope gave the windship one more glance and turned his full attention to the broken water. Like yesterday in the storm, it was basically a steering job. But whereas in the storm he concentrated on dodging seas that would flip them on their back, in today's race with the *Star of Alabama* his goal was speed.

The clock was on his side. Every minute he kept ahead of William Tree's ship was another minute for the wind to return order to the sea. But when he put himself in Tree's big red chair he saw that time was on Tree's side, too. A long afternoon stretched before them. A long, long time before they could hide in the dark.

Oona slammed her bridge wing into a steep sea. She staggered, then blundered ahead. Most of the wave got trapped in the tunnel under the cabin and she sneezed, spewing spray that the wind whipped across the cockpit.

Then she was off, up above them, skimming the surface. From the corner of his eye Hope saw the knot meter jump to twenty. Then all of a sudden the water ahead looked like a rutted logging road, with two deep tracks for the hulls and a rough crown between them that bashed the bridge wing so hard the boat stopped dead. The impact threw him against the helm. He looked up, fearing the mast would fall.

But she was up again, flying like a gull, and this time he kept her on the high water until the knot meter flicked to nineteen. He held the number for so long that he almost believed that somehow she had learned to fly.

"We're holding our own," said Sally. "Tree's no closer."

A vicious cross-sea erupted ahead of the catamaran. Water spiked, rock hard. And when, despite Hope's best efforts, the bridge wing plowed into it, boat speed dropped to a bone-shattering twelve knots.

Hope got some good breaks. Wind shifts worked in his favor. So did a gradual reduction of wind speed. The sea settled considerably, though not enough for the catamaran to enjoy smooth sailing. Then, at four o'clock, while the huge windship tacked suddenly to take advantage of wind shift that would allow it to cut a corner and catch up, it suffered some damage to its rigging. To Hope's delight and amazement, the ship stopped. And as *Oona* forged ahead, he tried to scope out what had happened.

"Looks like they lost a yard on the middle mast—no, two of them. Jesus, they're flying all over the place. What a mess."

"How could that happen?"

"Stuff breaks. Use light aluminum to reduce weight aloft, you trade off strength. I doubt it will slow them much."

Even sooner than Hope feared, seamen were swarming over her rigging. The big ship recovered swiftly and came after them, unslowed by several gaps in her sails that looked like missing teeth.

By six in the evening, the race was over. The *Star of Alabama* was so close her crew could hit them with rifle fire. And Hope was somewhat surprised that they hadn't. He expected any moment a voice on the loud-hailer threatening just that. Instead, to his amazement, just when he thought that all was lost, the huge sailing ship backed her sails and stopped, turning until they could see her full splendor broadside.

"What are they doing?" Sally asked.

Hope shook his head in quiet dismay. "If they had cannon I'd think they were going to rake us."

There were, of course, no cannon and for a long moment the huge ship just sat stopped on the wrinkled brow of the sea, while *Oona* skittered away.

"I don't like this. Something's going on."

"What?"

"I don't know. Where's Ishmael?"

"I haven't seen him since Tree came."

"It's a trick. It's a trick. It's some kind of a trick."

Sally said, "David, do they have hydrophones?"

"Do they? They've got the best you can buy. The guy told me they got them from the Navy. Hydrophones, sonar, they've got it all."

Sally said, "Bill said they record 'cetacean conversation.' "

"Rod used that same phrase. I guess you learn to talk like the boss."

"Stop the boat. Stop!"

"Why? We're getting away."

"They've finally figured out what we figured out. They figured out that Ishamel stays with us for our sound."

Hope looked back at the huge ship. All five masts were set with every sail but the three she had lost. She had been after them, hell-bent. And had as good as caught them. Tree could have run them down and for some reason chose not to. Not, Hope suspected, out of kindness.

"They're recording us on their hydrophones," said Sally. "They had to stop their ship for the hydrophones to hear over the rush of water."

Hope steered into the wind. *Oona* dropped off her plane and wallowed, sails shivering.

"I know it sounds crazy," said Sally. "But it worked for us."

"We'll know in a minute," Hope said, scanning the *Star of Alabama*'s rigging for movement. High up on the ratlines of the mainmast, he saw a flash of sun on metal. Moments later, they felt a sharp explosion part the air inches above their heads. Hope and Sally threw themselves flat. Another explosion, like an enormous firecracker, inches from their ears.

"High-powered rifle," said Hope. "It's the slug passing the mast. They're trying to make us run."

He took the helm, let *Oona* fall off the wind, and filled the sails.

"They'll use it," said Sally. "They'll use it against Ishmael."

"Not this." Hope turned on both diesels and cranked their starters. "I don't know whose side Ishmael is on, but he's going to hate this noise, either way. Better get below before they start shooting again."

But there were no more shots.

Instead, Hope watched with a sinking heart as a pilot door opened in the side of the ship. "Oh, for Christ's sake, they're launching a boat."

"What for?"

"They're going to board us."

"What will they—"

"They'll sail *Oona* around the ship and record her wake. With their gear, they get every nuance, every vibration."

"What about us?"

34

WENDELL LED THE BOARDING PARTY, which consisted of himself, four tough little Filipino seamen, and a sullen Ah Chi, who had orders straight from Bill to round up the woman's videotapes.

The bodybuilder was unarmed, confident of his strength and speed, though he did wear a Kevlar vest, just to be on the safe side, which bulked him up like a linebacker. And the Filipino seamen crowded into the RIB with him were carrying plenty in the unlikely event that David Hope had a shotgun squirreled away. Those he had befriended had filled the long days with extreme tales of robbing ships at sea, looting and kidnapping, and if he hadn't fully believed the skinny little guys before, the deliberate way they had chosen weapons from the ship's armory convinced him their stories were real.

It was a wet, gut-wrenching ride crossing between the ship and the boat. What had looked like little waves from the *Star of Alabama*'s main deck were bouncing the RIB like a loose football. The outboard motors screamed when the propellers jumped out of the water.

The Filipinos hunkered down, shielding their weapons from the spray. Wendell stood tall beside the driver, hanging onto the handrails and soaked to the vest.

"Can't you make this thing go faster?"

"No, Wendell," said the driver.

"I'm freezing."

"Is wet," the driver agreed as the rubber bow tumbled over a steep sea and crashed into its trough.

One of the little guys tugged his leg. "Sit, Wendell."

"I'm not afraid of getting wet." He was trying to watch the sailboat, but every time they dropped behind a wave all he could see was the sails shuddering in the wind.

Ah Chi finally broke his silence. "What if they shoot, Wendell? The guys are worried about you. Give them a break."

Wendell hunkered down with them. "Okay—hey, what do you guys look so happy about?"

"Woman on sailboat."

"I don't know if Bill wants you messing with her."

"You ask Bill if it's okay?" another asked him earnestly.

Wendell looked at Ah Chi. The engineer said, "Leave me out of this."

"Well, wait'll we secure the boat, first, and get it sailing again. Then I'll call Bill on the radio. See what he says."

"Thank you, Wendell."

The RIB belly flopped over another wave, bashed seawater with her blunt bow, and raked them all with icy spray. Her engines screamed. "How much longer?" Wendell yelled.

"Almost, Wendell," said the driver. "Almost."

It was funny how from this little rubber boat even the sailboat looked big. He said, "Listen up, guys. Grab 'em, lock 'em in one of the cabins. You sail the boat." To the driver he added, "Soon as we get the sailboat sailing, you shut your motors. Okay?"

"Okay, Wendell."

"No noise."

"No noise, Wendell."

He was wearing a headset and now a radio crackled in his ears. *"Wendell, when are you fixing to board that sailboat?"*

"Any second now, Bill, any second, we're just pulling up to her now."

" 'Cause it's been a half hour since you left me."

"We had to load the boat and then the water is rough as hell, Bill, and—"

"I mean, it's not like I asked you to cross the whole ocean. I sailed you right next to their boat. Is there anything else I could do to expedite your arrival?"

"We're here, Bill. We're here right now. We're going on."

The driver rammed the soft bow against the dive steps in the back of the catamaran and the Filipinos swarmed aboard, brandishing knives and pistols and howling like folks headed for a riot.

"No unessential violence!" warned Tree.

"What if they fight?"

"We do not have time to waste."

"Yeah, Bill, but—

"Do I have to spell it out for you, Wendell?"

"So I guess I throw 'em overboard?"

"Get that boat sailing now!"

Wendell pounded across the cockpit and down the companion into the saloon. The big cabin with all the windows was empty. With Bill no longer chewing his ear, he realized that a deep silence had settled over the boat.

Ah Chi made a beeline for a laptop computer that was plugged into the TV.

"Where are they?" Wendell shouted, suspecting the little guys had gone ahead to do the woman without waiting for permission from Bill.

Ah Chi had drawn him a diagram of the layout of the boat before they set out. He stormed down steps into the port hull. Two of the heavily armed Filipinos were looking around, baffled.

He bellowed loudly for the others. They came trooping up from the other hull and down into the little cabin. "Not here."

"Not here? Where the hell did they go?"

That got him a lot of shrugs.

"Did you search all the cabins?"

"Yes, Wendell."

"How about the sail lockers?"

"Yes, Wendell."

He remembered that Ah Chi had said they had hidden their log under an engine. "Did you look in the engine room?"

"Engine box. No people room in engine box."

Wendell looked around, frantically, everywhere at once. It was a little bitty boat, hardly as big as a double-wide trailer. This was the dive room and storage lockers. There was a bunch of paint cans on the deck, as if someone had been pawing through them looking for something real quick.

"Get up there and start sailing this boat! Go, go, go."

When they had run up on deck, Wendell spoke into the voice-activated two-way radio.

"Bill?"

"What?"

"They're not here."

"Where are they?"

"I don't know where they went. Bill, it's creepy weird—"

"We don't have time for that now. Do what I told you. Get that boat sailing fast and furious."

"I'm doing it. I'm doing it. I feel it starting to move."

"And make sure Ah Chi doesn't forget Miz Sally's hard drive."

William Tree stabbed at his intercom, cutting off Wendell and hailing Dr. Rod down in the hydrophone room.

"Rod. Start recording."

"Tape's rolling, Bill."

Tree looked at the back-lit Atlantic chart. Three American submarines and the British boat were far ahead in the Denmark Strait. But the *Vermont*, if the best estimates of Tree's Pentagon sources and the minute calculations of the ship's computers were projecting correctly, would pass close by, under the ship, sometime between now and midnight.

Tree turned to Philip, who was pouring a refill from a silver pot. "Well, the gloves are off, Philip. You might as well strap on a firearm. Just to be on the safe side."

"Right you are, Bill."

Tree detected the change of Philip's accent—he would have to be deaf not to hear the English working-class echoes of the council housing slum Philip had escaped by joining the Royal Marines. He heard it whenever Philip traded his major-domo hat for his security chief beret, and it was reassuring.

In the hydrophone room, Rod stood by the audio tech listening through a second headset. "What's all that banging?"

The tech was watching the noise print on his monitor.

"Waves," Hughie Mick called from the door, where he anxiously fingered his short-range training radio. The five-thousand-ton *Star of Alabama* was pitching very slowly and gently on the Atlantic swell. But any fool could plainly see that little *Oona* was battling a much different ocean, the chop between the swells. "The boat's slapping waves."

"Can you edit it out?" Rod asked the tech.

"No prob."

Rod switched channels. "Bill? We're getting it. We'll need a few minutes to clean it up."

"Make them fast minutes, Rod—Hughie, are you there with Rod?"

"Right here, Bill."

"Do you suppose it might make sense to get yourself up on deck right now in the event my killphin appears, seeing as how the ship is stopped and that sailboat's sailing in circles?"

"On my way, Bill."

Tree watched *Oona*'s progress on the auxiliary masthead

cam, pressed into service after the mainmast cam was wrecked by falling yardarms. He could see Wendell standing in the cockpit, while four of the little guys dodged around him like mice to adjust the sails as she circled the ship. He touched the PAN switch and the camera swept an otherwise empty sea.

"Philip?"

"Right here, Bill." Philip had changed quite quickly into fatigues and combat boots. He wore a radio/telephone headset and an automatic pistol strapped low in a thigh rig.

"If swimmers wanted to board my ship, how would they do it?"

"If they knew the ship's configuration, they would dive under the hull and come up through one of the wells. But they'd need scuba gear. We draw twenty feet. That's a long ways down on a breath of air."

"Philip. Both the people on that boat are divers. They're not on the boat. Is it just possible they might have donned their diving gear and are swimming this way?"

Philip smiled at his boss, who was using a tone usually reserved for the thick-headed Wendell. "It is possible, Bill."

"Can we presume that someone is guarding those wells?"

"Not some*one*, Bill. Some*thing*. Or rather, I should say, two *things*." Philip's smile turned smug. He was looking forward to the apology he was clearly owed. Instead, Bill turned red in the face.

"You put the swimmer-nullification dolphins in the water?"

"Well, of course, Bill. The security of the ship is my—"

"Are those dolphins armed? Did you send them out wearing their needles?"

"Bloody well right, they're armed. If they're not wearing the needle all an intruder would have to do is tickle them under the chin thanks to the misguided affections of a certain animal trainer who will remain nameless."

"Recall them, for God's sake. Immediately!"

"Bill, I—"

"Now!" Tree roared. "Now. Recall them now. Get them inside the ship, now! Now! Now!" He gasped for air, sucking deep breaths as Philip issued orders through his headset.

"All right, Bill. We've sent the recall signal. But frankly—" He shut his mouth. Bill was interrupting again, in those tones reserved for Wendell.

"The ship is stopped, Philip. The sound of our wake scares the killphin. We're stopped. No wake. No scary sound. But the sailboat is sailing in circles around us while we record it. Making the sound he likes. What will happen if while we are recording the sailboat sound in hopes of luring the killphin within radio range, he just happens to swim close to see what's happening?"

"I see your point, Bill. I hadn't considered that the swimmer-nullification dolphins might attack him. But Bill, even if they did, the killphin would make short work of them."

"One slip, one mistake, one unlucky thrust and my killphin would be dead. Check and make sure they're back."

Philip obeyed immediately, snapping orders into the headset. But this time his expression darkened.

"What?" asked Tree.

It seemed that the normally obedient guard dolphins had not yet returned to their pen. "Something's caught their interest, apparently."

"Bill! Bill!"

It was Hughie Mick on the intercom, sounding frantic.

"What is it, Hughie? What's going on with the guards?"

"I don't know, Bill, I'm not down there. Alfredo's doing them."

"Well, Alfredo's doing an awful job. They won't come back."

"Something's probably caught their attention. I keep telling you they're not machines!"

"Well, get down there and get their attention."

"Goddammit to hell, Bill, will you shut your fat trap and listen to me, for God's sake!"

Tree, who had never heard Hughie raise his voice, much less curse him, said, "What is wrong, Hughie?"

"Nothing's wrong. I got him, goddammit. I got him, Bill. I got him!"

"Who have you got, Hughie?"

"Him! I got your killphin!"

35

A HASTY COMPASS BEARING ON the stationary ship, and a range guess of three hundred yards, had been helped by the scream of outboard engines twenty feet overhead. Hope and Sally had realigned their course and swum until they saw a lighted beacon in the murky water.

Altering course again, they homed in on what looked like the glowing ghost of a sunken liner and turned out to be the row of underwater ports that gave William Tree's Captain Nemo Lounge its views of the sea.

Swimming cautiously closer, staying clear of the light spill, Hope saw Tree himself—his face bright as the moon— seated in his big red chair with one hand stabbing buttons on his intercom. Philip the major-domo was standing beside him with a big pistol strapped to his leg. Then a skinny guy who looked like a sneak thief came rushing in and handed Tree what appeared to be a handheld radio.

Sally tapped his arm. They had to find their way into the ship. They backed away from the ports and descended the sloping side of the hull, down the keel. Two large wells loomed in the bottom of the *Star of Alabama*, as dark and mysterious as the open hatches through which Hope led divers into underwater wrecks. One, Hope knew from his wanderings about the ship, was a dolphin portal, the other a place to launch research submersibles protected from the surface waves.

One had light spilling from inside the ship. Fearing it was in use for the guard dolphins, he led Sally into the other, which was dark. But when they felt their way up past around a tethered submersible and surfaced in air, they discovered the top was sealed with a thick steel lid. It was impossible to climb out into the ship.

They clung to the submersible, whispering in the dark. God knew who could hear what on the other side of the bulkhead that formed the well.

"We've got to try the dolphin port."

They had two goals. One was the radio room. As many minutes as possible in the ship's communication center to send distress signals and place satellite telephone calls in hopes that a torrent of warnings could not be explained away as a hoax. Their other goal was to stay alive, which meant keeping ahead of the armed boarding party that had set out from the ship.

"I'll go first," whispered Sally, adding before Hope could protest, "No bubbles, I'm wearing the rebreather."

Hope said, "It will scope you with sonar. It doesn't care about bubbles."

"I'm the better diver."

That she could swim circles around him had become apparent within seconds of their escape from *Oona*. Even wearing the bulky rebreather, Sally was faster and—he discovered when he noticed how much air he was burning—in much better shape. Before he could answer, she led their descent, down the side of the dark well and out the bottom of the ship.

A big square of light a hundred feet along the hull marked the other well. They swam toward it, hugging the keel, peering around the murky water, guided by the light.

The attack came faster than either could see. Hope felt a

surge of water and heard a loud, metallic shriek of metal scraping metal and saw an explosion of bubbles and then a twisted silhouette of Sally sprawling like a puppet. He swam to help her, kicking his fins as hard as he could. Air was spewing from her mouthpiece.

He got his arm around her backpack and tried to push the regulator between her lips. Then he saw the guard dolphins, ten feet away. They were both wearing the needle harnesses. The needle had broken on the one that had attacked and Hope realized that it had hit one of Sally's metal tanks and hadn't pierced her body. He could feel her reaching for the mouthpiece. She cleared it and breathed.

The bottlenoses watched. Hope had never been so close to bottlenoses before, and was shocked by how big they were. And he had a powerful feeling of being closely observed by a creature that understood a little bit of Sally's predicament. Whether they were hesitating to attack an injured creature or simply regrouping to charge again, he could not know. It was like a standoff with a growling dog. Go at it? Or retreat? He could feel Sally trembling. He looked from one dolphin to the other, into their deep, dark eyes. He could not decide what to do and had the eeriest feeling that they couldn't either.

Suddenly, the guard dolphins peeled apart, to the left and to the right out from under the hull, and, as if shot from rubber slings, streaked toward the surface. Whether they had gone for air and would return, Hope couldn't know. He went the only way he could. He pulled Sally toward the lighted well, and fished from his belt a spray can of gray primer.

A tiny Mexican teenager, one of the busboys at the lunch, was leaning over the edge. He cried out at the sudden eruption of scuba masks and ran out the door.

Hope hauled himself out of the water, reached up, and sprayed the security camera lens with the paint. Then he reached for Sally, who was struggling over the edge of the well.

"Are you okay?"

Sally was gasping for breath. Hope helped her out of the heavy backpack, looking fearfully for any needle tears in her dry suit. Struggling to breathe and speak at the same time, she was able, finally, to gasp, "Knocked the wind out of me."

They opened lockers and found one with room to hide their fins and backpacks and headgear. Hope checked that the long corridor was empty, and led the way up the slight incline toward the distant bow, blinding cameras with gray paint.

"Where did you get that idea?"

"Barbara's eco-boys told me about it. Bank robber trick."

They heard shouts, dodged into a companionway, climbed the steps to the next deck. Hope sprayed another security camera. He shook the can. It felt empty. They passed an open door to a laboratory. "Wait."

There was no one in the lab, and no cameras overhead. Hope spotted a Bunsen burner on one of the work tables. "Grab those aprons." Sally pulled them from the wall. Hope gathered towels and notebooks and heaped them around the burner. Sally brought the aprons, which were rubberized.

"What are you doing?"

"Making smoke. Give them something else to worry about instead of us."

Their only advantage was that the *Star of Alabama* was a very large ship with a very small crew. Tree, a few senior scientists, some servants, and twenty ship's officers and crew, of whom several at least had pirated off to board *Oona*.

"Under the table," Sally said. "Put it under the table."

"Why?"

She pointed at the ceiling, which was studded with smoke detectors and sprinkler heads.

The Bunsen burner hose was too short. Hope shoved a chair under the table, put the burner on it. They swept every-

thing else under the shelter of the table, turned on the gas,
clicked a sparker, which ignited an intense conical flame,
heaped a tent of paper and cloth around it, and ran.

The smoke that billowed after them stank of burning rubber and before they dove into the nearest companionway, the
ship's fire bells started clanging, followed immediately by a
computer-generated voice intoning, *"Fire, fire, fire. Fire on
B deck. Fire B deck. B deck. Frame eighty-nine. Fire on B
deck Frame eighty-nine. Firefighters report to B deck. Frame
eighty-nine."*

Hope said, "Son of a bitch."

"What's frame eighty-nine?"

"The exact location of the fire. That's how you find your
way around a warship, by frame numbers, counting from the
bow. All right. They're going down to B deck. We'll go up
to the main deck."

The steps up the next companionway topped out in a
deckhouse that offered shelter from wind and spray. Hope
looked out to orient himself. They were just ahead of the
mainmast. The aquarium was aft, toward the stern. He could
see the crusted anchor cradled on the main deck and around
it a spiderweb of tangled lines. The damage to the mainmast
yardarms looked pretty bad. Several big spars were scattered
on the deck like the aftermath of a tornado on the forest
floor.

He looked up. All the sails had been furled and the yards
looked bone naked in the failing light. He saw three of the
crew silhouetted against the sky. They were rigging something high atop the mizzenmast. But instead of securing
damaged spars as he would have expected, they were erecting a whippy vertical shaft that looked like a radio antenna.
Funny time for routine maintenance, and he wondered what
it was. No clue from this distance.

He stole a look forward. The wheelhouse was a hundred
feet ahead and the radio room, which was behind and to one
side of the wheel, had a back door, as he remembered. But

Malcolm, the English ship's officer who had toured him around the ship, stood guarding it with a pistol in his hand.

"Son of a bitch."

Sally looked through the port. "Of course. That's what I'd protect if I were Tree."

"There must be sat phones in the cabins."

William Tree's Captain Nemo Lounge grew dark as the waning daylight ceased to percolate through his aquarium. Tree sat quietly, holding Hughie Mick's training radio. The long, arduous quest was over. His killphin was back in control.

Hughie himself stood with his hands in his pockets, ear cocked to the killphin's groans and clicks coursing through his headset. He was not entirely sure, yet, what was going on with the animal. The fire bells made it hard to hear, and lord knew what that racket reverberating through seawater did to the animal. But he had settled down some since Hughie had chased the guard dolphins off with a command signal that hurt bottlenose inner ears like a dental drill.

Rod was up on deck. His telemetry boys were trying to help with the line-of-sight problem by erecting an antenna on the mizzenmast to communicate with the killphin whenever it surfaced to breathe.

Philip, too, was wearing a headset and had positioned himself in the doorway to the next room, where he could remain attentive to William Tree, who was admirably unperturbed by fire bells, while studying the security monitors and issuing quiet orders to his deputies. They were closing in on David Hope and Sally Moffitt, who were leaving a messy trail of paint-sprayed cameras.

Suddenly the bells stopped.

In the silence, Philip relayed a report to Tree. "Fire's out."

"Well, it's about time."

Wendell broke in on the radio that linked them.

"Shouldn't I come back, Bill?"

"Just keep sailing around in circles. I will tell you when to come back."

"Getting dark."

"The sound of the sailboat is helping control him."

"You've got the record. Can't you play it on the hydrophone?"

Tree glanced at Hughie Mick, who shook his head.

"Hughie tells me that he seems to like the real thing better. Keep sailing that boat in circles." He stabbed the intercom. "Captain, don't move the ship. Don't spook him."

"We sit as long as you like, Bill. Did you catch them yet?"

"Soon."

"Bill?"

"What, Wendell?"

"I'm worried about you there. They're nuts, lighting fires."

"Philip's got things in hand. Just keep sailing. Over and out."

"Bill!" The *Star of Alabama*'s captain, again, calling urgently.

"Yes, Captain."

"We might have picked up maybe a submarine on the passive sonar."

The privileges of performing the occasional classified research for the Navy included the opportunity to obtain very special sonar for your marine biologists. As Tree had assuaged skeptics, if his researchers were listening for giant squid and happened to overhear a submarine, it wasn't like they were a bunch of hostile Muslims.

"Very faint," Captain Grandzau went on. "Maybe not there. But Lieutenant Starskowitz thinks yes, and he is good."

"Well," Tree asked the captain, "how close does Lieutenant Starskowitz think it is?"

"Certainly within twenty miles."

Which pretty much jibed with what Tree's cousins at

the Pentagon had reported about the course of the *Vermont*. Things did seem to be falling into place. Or out of place, depending on who you were, Tree thought, musing on the hapless luck of the *Vermont*'s captain. A naval officer needed luck in his career; there were too many brilliant officers to surpass without luck. At sea you needed even more luck to even up the odds against you, it being unnatural to cross water, and downright perverse to travel under it.

"Vat should I do?"

"Do nothing," said Tree, adding with a chuckle, whose inappropriateness chilled the captain's marrow, "Particularly do not make any noises that could be misinterpreted by that submarine as unneighborly."

"You are joking, Bill. *Ja?*"

"*Ja,* Captain—Hughie? Just how much control do we have over this animal?"

Before Hughie could answer, Dr. Rod swaggered into the Captain Nemo Lounge and silenced him with a superior look.

"Well," said Tree, "you look pleased as a man who's just figured out the unified theory."

"How much control, Bill? I'll show you how much control. How would you like to see a Las Vegas show?"

"I'd rather see my killphin."

"Give me ten minutes to wrap up the telemetry tests and he'll dance for you in a spotlight."

"Spotlight?" Hughie snickered. "The animal's not trained to surface to a light. He obeys sound."

"And radio," Rod shot back. "We've got him nailed on radio again. And we've worked up a little trick to remind everybody of the limits of animal training and the advantages of a radio link drilled into his goddammed brain."

"Trick? What kind of trick?"

Rod turned his back on Hughie and explained to Tree, "It's simple, Bill. We've wired a motorized searchlight to track the killphin's radio signal. When he comes up to breathe, bingo, he's in the light."

"This is a heck of a time to waste time with tricks."

Dr. Rod answered him in serious tones. "It's getting dark, Bill. I want a damned good look at him before we send him to work."

William Tree's vast body swelled in a mountainous nod of approval. "Ah am glad to see that someone else is doing some thinking around here, at last. I am pleased, Rod. I am mighty pleased."

36

EVERY PRIVATE CABIN HOPE AND Sally entered was equipped with a computer, game joysticks and headsets, a DVD television, a short-wave radio receiver, and an intercom with buttons for room service, but not one single satellite telephone. After a fruitless search of the sixth cabin, they hid with the lights out, in whispered discussion of their dwindling options.

Out the picture window port they could see *Oona*'s lights circling the ship a quarter-mile off.

"They'll find us sooner or later," said Hope. He had run out of spray paint on B deck. If the private cabins had security cameras they would be caught already.

"If they get off, we can try to swim back to the boat."

"Then what?"

"There's no phones, there's no radio. There's no way to warn anybody."

"What if we swim back to the boat and hang on in the water until they leave?"

Hope lost sight of *Oona*. "What am I saying? We can't catch up while they're sailing her."

"They'll catch us soon, here."

"They should have a recording by now. Why don't they just get off and come to the ship?"

Sally said, "Maybe the recording didn't work. Maybe they're sailing to attract Ishmael."

"Maybe we are really screwed."

"I hate this. I hate that we can't do anything."

Hope said, "Tree is just doing what he wants and we're standing around watching with our thumbs in our mouths. If I had a gun I think I'd run into his room and shoot the bastard."

"They have the guns."

"There must be an armory on ship. Where they keep weapons."

"David, they know we're aboard. The armory will be locked and guarded."

A beam of light speared the dark.

"Wait. Wait! What was that? What's happening?"

The light darted across the wave tops and slid out of the view of their port

"What are they doing?"

Again the powerful beam swept the dark. This time it caught movement—*Oona* sailing through it, bright as a three-D animation. The light did not linger on the catamaran, but swept past, like a busy clerk rushing to help a waiting customer, and raced across the water. Suddenly it stopped on something that sliced a steely gray line through a wave.

"Oh my God," whispered Sally.

Hope was accustomed by now to the quickness of a filmmaker's eye. Sally observed in a glance what he could not. She pressed her face to the port, tracing the light's erratic path.

"Watch!" she said. "Here he comes."

"He?"

Then Hope saw the steely gray flicker again. "Is that Ishmael?"

"Breaking surface to breathe."

"Are you sure?"

"I'm not—look! Oh my God, there he is."

The beam of light froze on a single patch of the ocean as Ishamel erupted, spinning, dancing on his tail, fell backward and immediately leapt again.

"What's wrong with him?" asked Sally.

"I don't know."

"He's frantic."

The big dolphin reminded Hope of a swordfish desperately trying to cast a hook out of its mouth. "He's fighting. Like he's trying to get away."

Ishmael climbed into the light again. It started to spin, but instead of drilling the sky, it managed only two turns before flopping on its side.

"There's nothing holding him."

"He's acting like he thinks there is."

"That poor animal," said Sally. "Something terrible happened to him."

"Not happened," said Hope. "Happening. It's happening right now, as we watch—where is he?"

The beam shot down from the main deck and lit a patch of water like a theater stage. The dolphin jumped.

Sally cried, "How do they do that? How can anybody be so quick with the light?"

"He's drawing it," said Hope. "They've keyed it to his radio signal. And that's how they're doing him."

"How do you know?"

"He's got an antenna. Right? I just saw them rigging an antenna on the mast. And when we saw Tree through the port, one of his people gave him what I thought was a handheld. But Tree doesn't need a handheld radio. His intercom console hooks him everywhere."

"Then what was it?"

"They've got the animal under radio control. Probably like they used to. Look at it. It's going crazy out there."

"That poor thing."

"That 'poor thing' is Tree's weapon."

"How can we stop him?" Sally asked.

"I'm not a fighter," said Hope. "I'm a seaman—ah!" He pictured the main deck, a tangle of wrecked rigging. He *was* a seaman.

"Okay," he said. "We'll start with another fire."

"They'll find it and put it out."

"I don't care. I just want them off the main deck."

The last interruption William Tree expected at this moment was the distinctive trill of his secure satellite phone. And just in case it was who he thought it was, he switched on the digital recorder he had had Rod's technicians build into the phone.

"Hello?"

"Where *are* you?" she asked in her high, thin voice.

"Not in the jailhouse, ma'am."

"Do you have any idea why I'm calling, William?"

"No, ma'am," he lied. She was calling to cut him off, which meant he was going to have to make one awful decision all on his own. End the experiment forever. Or push ahead and win.

"Well," she said, the high quaver growing shrill, "you know we're a big family."

"Yes, ma'am." Tree tweaked a switch on the training radio and on the mast cam monitor he saw his killphin leap as if electrified.

The animal shone like silver in the searchlight and he was struck by how any creature without scales could be so smooth and sinuous. He'd expect such seamless grace from a jumping marlin or a slithering snake, but not from a mammal. He tweaked it again and up the killphin flew.

Rod stirred. "If we're going to use him now, let's not wear him out."

On the satellite phone Aunt Martha was rattling on about

the family, leading up to the ax. There would be no delaying if he decided to stick with the killphin. Right now or never, the instant she cut him off he had to move or give up.

". . . and a big family has many irons in the fire."

"Yes ma'am, I imagine we do. 'Course, I've been at sea some time and haven't kept up with all of them."

"Well, you're not expected to, William. That's my job."

Strange, he thought, not her way to beat so much around the bush. Ordinarily, by now she'd have cut him off at the knees and would pause only to watch him hobble off on stumps. Getting old.

"More irons than you would imagine, William. When a young man goes in one direction, he doesn't necessarily know what his cousins are doing in another."

"Well, therein lays our strength, Aint Martha. Many irons in many fires. Concentrate on the Trees and the forest will take care of itself."

Aunt Martha said, "Well put, William," and Tree sat up, startled by her sudden and wholly unexpected warmth. "I apologize for beating around the bush, but not every iron attains the shape we hope for. And sometimes the fires start burning trees—William, we need your help."

"What's gone wrong, Aint Martha?"

"You don't want to know," she answered in a grim voice that had Tree instantly guessing which of his cousins had dropped the ball.

"Oh, but I do want to know, Aint Martha. I most assuredly do."

"By comparison, it will make the Enron scandal look like a little fat boy got caught stealing a ham."

Tree looked up and cast his bull shark a smile. "That could only be Cousin Rupert," he said gravely.

An angry snort told him he was right.

"And I'll bet he's not alone."

"They got so greedy," said Aunt Martha. "They put their names on things."

Tree played the innocent wandering sailor, saying, "Well, ma'am, I imagine it must be hard seeing all the big flashy money around and not want a piece of it."

"I've got some scapegoats lined up, but they won't be enough if the lid comes off. Unless we rally all our friends and throw a whole lot of dust in our enemy's eyes, we'll be facing congressional committees and federal prosecutors—not to mention a self-serving denunciation from that hypocrite in the White House."

"They ain't gonna send a little white-haired old lady to the jailhouse."

"I would gladly go if it would save the family."

"Well, that's not gonna happen."

"Never underestimate the power of an indignant populace. We could end up the Court TV sinners of the month."

"How can I help, Aint Martha?"

"You would serve this family well if we were able to command the sudden and full attention of our friends and enemies."

"Is that a green light, Aint Martha? Are you telling me to go ahead with the demonstration?"

"Now."

"Just so you know, ma'am, the professors say there's a chance the demonstration will go haywire."

"That's a chance we'll have to take, William. We have a lot to lose."

"Yes, ma'am. Of course, if the sub sinks her crew will drown."

"They're warriors. They knew the risk when they signed up. And I believe that their families get pensions."

"Before it sinks, it could launch a cruise missile or two."

"The very thought makes me sick, though I doubt they're aimed at Alabama. Enough 'coulds,' 'ifs,' and 'strong chances,' William. Nothing's going to go wrong, anyhow. You've been working on this ten years. Get to it."

"I just want you to know the risks."

"For God's sake, your people are in desperate straits. Do it now," she said, and hung up.

"Well, I'll be," said Tree.

"What happened?" asked Rod.

"I'm gonna be a hero."

He plucked the training radio off the shelf of his belly, and a jack-o'-lantern smile was just starting to travel up his face when the fire bells started ringing again.

Philip ran to his security monitors.

"Fire, fire, fire. Fire on E deck. Fire on E deck. E deck. Frame 147. Fire on E deck, Frame 147. Firefighters report to E deck, Frame 147."

Frame 147 was in the engine room. Every hand on the ship would respond. Tree radioed the crew on *Oona*. "Wendell, you better get back here right now."

37

I'M NOT A FIGHTER, I'M a seaman. It was running through Hope's head now, like rap without a rhyme—or a mead hall chant to build courage and drive off doubt.

With all hands running below to fight the fire, they had maybe five minutes, with luck, before someone spotted them in the dark. This time, at least, they had gotten the fire right: thick smoke generated by mops soaked in light diesel oil. They had ignited the mops under the protective overhang of a day tank, which exploded with a hollow *boom* just as they climbed up out of the hull onto the after end of the main deck. They ran forward to the middlemast.

His plan was to jury-rig a whip to lift the immensely heavy Civil War ship's anchor that Tree had displayed behind the aquarium. But as he feared, to hold it in place in rough weather one of the flukes had been welded to a steel plate.

"There's a fire station inside that companionway," he told Sally. "Get the biggest steel pry bar you can carry. Or an ax if there's no bar. I'll meet you at the anchor."

In the tangle of the fallen spars and rigging, Hope located a yardarm brace, and sawed the heavy Dacron line loose with his sheath knife. Unraveling it from the wreckage, he pulled the brace to the side of the ship and onto the ratlines and climbed with it thirty feet to where the ratlines joined the mast.

As he hunted for a block on the mast, movement below caught his eye. He looked down and saw, through the distorting lens of the plastic top of the aquarium and the water, William Tree in the lighted room below, still in his red chair, attended by three of his people.

He couldn't find a block, so he reeved the brace through a smooth shackle instead. He dragged it back down to the main deck and tied it to the old anchor's shank ring.

Sally was waiting with an immensely strong and heavy steel bar. Hope guided one end under the anchor's fluke that was welded to the deck. They got their shoulders under the bar. "One. Two. Three!" They shoved up together. "Again! . . . Again!" The leverage did it. The weld snapped. The anchor was free.

He ran to the sail control pod, confirmed it was identical to the one Malcolm had let him play on, set the selector to YARD, and moved the toggle.

The brace drooped from the anchor. "Wrong way."

He toggled the other way.

His line grew taut. The anchor ring clanked. The shank stood straight, and the two heavy flukes rose off the deck.

"What's that noise?"

A sharp buzzing coming from the sea. Sally ran to look over the side. "They're back. Their boat just drove into the pilot hatch."

"Where's *Oona*?"

"Just sitting there."

The anchor was three feet off the deck, slowly rising. Hope could hear the brace rubbing through the shackle, fighting friction. "Did they furl her sails?"

"Yes. They probably figured they might need her again."

"She won't sit long, even under bare poles. All right, here we go."

The anchor was about to clear the steel rim of the aquarium. But it was swaying with the motion of the ship and it suddenly bashed the rim with a loud boom.

Sally peered into the aquarium. "They're looking up."

"Tell them to smile—*look out for that!* It's starting to swing. Don't let it hit you."

He jumped to the anchor and tried to shove it away from the rim. But the two thousand pounds of iron dangling from the brace felt as solid and heavy as a truck and it pushed toward the rim of the aquarium bulkhead. He couldn't stop it and had to jump out of its way before it crushed him.

Instead of crashing into the side of the aquarium, it cleared the rim and swung out over the center. Hope lunged for the control pod. He got there too late to drop it. The vast, unwieldy weight had already reversed course, like a pendulum, and was swinging back over the deck.

Hope toggled the brace to stop lifting. "Next sweep," he said, reaching for the red-backlit quick-release control labeled LET FLY.

Then a voice from the dark, inches from his ear, asked, "What are you doing to Bill?"

38

BEFORE HOPE HEARD SALLY SCREAM, "David!" he was flying across the deck with an explosive pain in his shoulder and a sense that the big man was looming large. He hit the teak, trying to roll away before he stood. But Wendell was on him like a cat, scooping him up, seizing the collar of his dry suit in one huge hand and drawing back the other in a cinderblock fist.

Hope caught a blurry glimpse of it receding into the dark behind Wendell's head and he knew he wouldn't survive the blow. The punch to his shoulder had practically torn his bones out. He heard a heavy thud, like the earlier explosion of the day tank, and felt a deep impact and thought, I never even saw it coming.

But it was Wendell who staggered, releasing Hope's collar and swaying as if the ship had suddenly rolled. He expelled a sudden rush of air, and then whirled from Hope and lunged at Sally.

She dropped the heavy pry bar, which clanged to the deck, her face a mask of surprise and dismay. She had hit him with the steel bar, hard enough to make him let go of Hope, but the bodybuilder was still standing and, having absorbed the blow, now gathered his forces in a galactic rush.

Hope dived at his legs. He caught a boot in the face that made him see stars, but hung on as the giant's momentum caused him to fall. Wendell landed on the bar, grunted with pain, then roared to his feet, clutching the length of steel like a baseball bat. He swung so hard it whizzed through the air, missed Hope's head by inches, and went for Sally again, stepping into the swing, pausing only to be sure he didn't miss again.

Sally backed away, one eye on Wendell, the other on the anchor, which was swinging back over the aquarium.

"Now!" she yelled. "Get Bill."

Hope lunged for the control pod.

Wendell started after him, saw the anchor swinging toward the aquarium, and in a flash leaped onto the rim and braced to stop it. To Hope's astonishment, Wendell blocked the two-thousand-pound weight with both hands. Muscles swelled in his neck, veins stood like cables. He leaned into the anchor, growled deep in his chest, and pushed.

Hope banged down on the LET FLY button.

"Well," William Tree said, waving the training radio at Dr. Rod, Hughie Mick, and a cold, wet Ah Chi, who had just delivered Sally Moffitt's videotapes and hard drive. "It's a funny world where ten years of hope and dreams and hard work all come together by pushing one little button. Let's hope Mr. Killphin is up to it."

Hughie, who was habitually more alert to danger than his privileged bosses, looked up first as Wendell fell backward onto the thin plastic winter cover of the aquarium. But it was Tree—savoring the moment when he would signal the killphin to attack the *Vermont*—who saw the anchor drive Wendell through the plastic, scattering fish and crashing into the reinforced glass ceiling.

Tree had an awful sense of knowing too much all at once. He knew that Hughie was running toward the door and that

Rod and Ah Chi were turning after him and that there was no way on God's planet that he could ever lever his body out of his chair, much less sprint to the door. The glass held for what seemed like eons—though it could not have been more than half a second because he could not lift his finger to the button soon enough. He actually saw Wendell pinned under one of the anchor's flukes, staring down at him bug-eyed through the glass. Then the ceiling split and a thousand fish and eighty thousand gallons of water roared into the Captain Nemo Lounge like a tidal wave.

The water slammed him from his chair and pounded him to the deck. Then, as it filled the room, it lifted him and it looked like it might sluice him out the door if he could hold his breath long enough.

He managed to stand, get his chin above the water, and gasp a breath. A jagged slab of broken glass sliced his arm and in trying to fend it off he slashed his hand. The pain was startling, burning from salt. Raw light was suddenly pouring down on him from the exposed aquarium lamps and he saw the door only thirty feet away. His heart pounded with the effort as he plowed toward it, spreading the red stain of his own blood.

Drown, bleed to death, or make it out that door were the options he saw as he gathered his spirit to survive. The water rose over his head. But he proved buoyant and rose with it. Fish brushed by, hundreds, frantic, flapping, swimming, and he had a close call with a stingray's black needle tail. But he kept heaving his legs step by step, pushing toward the door, going with the flow. Well, he thought, I'm going to get out of this fix after all. Then a portcullis of triangular teeth flashed in the light and Tree saw his bull shark swimming at his face.

First the song of *Oona* stopped, disorienting the killphin. Next the fire bells stopped vibrating the water. Then it heard

a loud crack and a thunderous roar. The caustic tingling inside its head stopped.

With powerful upsweeps of its tail it dove deep—suddenly aggressive, sweeping the water below with the frequencies it employed to hunt shark, the boneless pelagic
wanderers on which it had learned to feed.

In the course of three fifteen-minute dives it found nothing to eat. But moments into its fourth dive, the killphin suddenly encountered at three hundred feet sound waves that
were not shark echoes but an active probing that pumped its
survival senses to high alert. Something large and still lay
below, looking for it.

The killphin swam toward it, spraying sound, the echoes
of which quickly established the familiar shape and size of
a nuclear submarine—a hard shell, a hundred soft shapes
moving within. It aimed for the nose cone, the source of the
sonar noise.

From overhead and far away it heard the song of *Oona*.

Like most submariners, the men of the *Vermont* got through
the long, demanding patrols with knife-edged humor. The
mysterious sound associated with the near-fatal computer
crash, which had briefly terrified them yesterday, had already been dubbed "The Thing," while their shipmate who
had recognized The Thing had been nicknamed, outside the
hearing of their officers, "Same Noise Nelson."

But when Same Noise suddenly announced, "It's back,"
every man in the sonar room snapped to attention.

"Wait, there's something else—"

"Yeah, I got it."

"No, no, no, on the surface."

"The ship."

"No, not the ship."

"Run it through the file. . . ."

"Sounds like a sailboat."

"What sailboat?" snapped the captain. He knew in his heart that the contact was coming for him.

Another called, "I'm tracking maybe a big fish, maybe a whale."

"It's the same noise, sir," said Nelson.

"It's closing on the bow," reported TMA.

Before the captain could stop it, a prayer rocketed through his mind—a blood-promise to God that would split his life into an irretrievable past and a dreamless future: If the men of the *Vermont* got out of this alive, he would re-sign his commission. He felt heartsick, wrenched by a physical pain at what he was giving up. Yet upon the deep sadness came a liberating feeling of relief. If, as he sus-pected, whatever was cruising around out there had his name on it again, he would need every bit of "higher influ-ence" to help save his ship.

"I'm losing it, sir."

"TMA?" the captain snapped.

Target Motion Analysis said, "Breaking off, sir."

". . . No, I'm losing him now. He's leaving."

"I've got him too, sir. He's going away."

They listened to ever-deepening quiet until the monitor noise prints had all flatlined.

The *Vermont*'s skipper whispered, "Thank you."

"What did you say, sir?"

The captain looked around, trying to absorb into his memory every familiar image and every shining face. Hanging beside the high-tech monitors, or spread open beside them, were loose-leaf operating manuals and books of procedure. They survived by the book. They excelled by the book. There was no more precisely run place in the world than this well-lit space, and he would miss it heart and soul. "I said, the boat is yours, Mr. Royce. I'm going to bed."

*　　　*　　　*

In the morning, the wind was still out of the northwest, presenting a clear sky, which Hope knew couldn't last, and a blessedly empty horizon.

"There are two things I don't want to see today," he said, "or ever again: that ship behind us or that dolphin ahead."

Oona was reaching southwest.

He looked back into the white ball of the rising sun. No red dawn; maybe he was too pessimistic. The decent weather might hold another day. Thank God for small favors. And big ones—the eastern horizon was empty. Just to be sure, he switched on the radar. No ships for twenty-four miles. Still, he swept their wake once again with the binoculars, just to be on the safe side.

Sally said, "I think we're clear ahead, too."

Hope turned around slowly and painfully. The ache where Wendell had smashed his shoulder now extended from his elbow to his hip, and his other shoulder and both knees throbbed from tumbling across the deck. Sally, too, looked worse for wear, but mainly from exhaustion, having stood watch for what remained of the night once they got back on board and Hope had raised the sails.

She smiled back at him. "What are you staring at?"

"Let's just say I'm feeling even more affection for you than ever."

"Because I shared my air with you on the way home?"

Hope had run out on the swim back—a long swim to catch up with the windblown boat. He said, "That, too. You look wiped out. Why don't you catch some sleep? I'm okay up here."

She was back in a flash, her face ashen. "David, they took my tapes. They took the AVID hard drive. They took everything I shot. All my footage."

Hope said, "Your VideoRaid is in my BCD."

Sally stared in disbelief. "You . . ."

"Since you made me a partner I figured I'd better do something to pull my weight."

She ran below to the dive room and returned clutching the backup unit, which Hope had sealed in three layers of Ziploc freezer bags.

"I grabbed it on the way out, just to be on the safe side."

"I love you, Captain Cautious. I was so scared I didn't even think. Oh, thank you, David. Thank you." She hugged him with fierce strength.

"Ow! That hurts."

"Sorry, sorry. Let me kiss it . . . thank you, David. Thank you so much."

As he drew back to kiss her, he saw, a hundred yards behind the boat, Ishmael drilling holes in the sky.

"He's back."

They watched him cavort for several minutes. "He seems better," said Sally. "Back to normal."

Hope agreed he was not the frantic creature they had seen leaping in the searchlight. "Maybe he knows they can't run him anymore."

"Watch him," said Sally. "Let me get my gear on."

"What for? You can't shoot underwater in this sea."

"Not the camera. But this is our chance to fry his generator. God knows what stuff they put in him. God knows what he'll do."

Hope started to argue.

Sally said, "All that stuff needs electricity. If we ruin it maybe he can just swim away. David, he could live thirty years. What if he bumps into another submarine?"

Hope knew she was right. But he hated the idea of tangling with the monster again.

39

HOPE GOT THE PORTABLE GENERATOR running quietly in the cockpit, cushioned on blankets as they had the first time to minimize the vibrations. He led the shock head back to the dive steps. When he pulled the cord to test the switch and touched the head to the stainless steel backstay, a fat yellow spark jumped with a loud *crack*.

Sally came out suited up and dragging the rebreather and he thought, What if I lose her?

"I really don't feel like going back to Maine alone," he said. "Let me do it."

"No."

"Let's flip a coin."

"No."

"Why?"

"I'm a better diver than you. The only reason you ran out of air is you were sucking it up like an amateur with a resort card."

"At least let me go with you."

"Alone with no bubbles I have a better chance of not spooking him." She took his hand. "You have to trust me to do what I can do. I'm not Barbara. I'm not going to get killed. And if I do, it's not your job to stop me."

She buckled into her backpack and put on her fins and reached for the shock head. Hope would not let it go.

Sally said, "You were the hero last night. Today's my turn."

Hope handed it over. "You're right. I won't even tell you to be careful."

Sally bit down on her mouthpiece and jumped into the sea. He grabbed a face mask and snorkel, stretched painfully down the steps and onto the dive platform, put his head in the water, and traced the electrical cable down ten feet to where Sally was holding the long shock head close to her body.

The big dolphin rose swiftly into the light and rushed past her. Sally turned with it like a matador. It passed closer. Hope saw a flash.

The animal thrashed to the surface.

Sally dragged herself up the wire, kicking with her fins. Suddenly the dolphin dove. Sally reached for Hope, who pulled her onto the dive platform as the dolphin barreled up and smashed into the hull so hard it shook the boat.

They hauled in the shock head, unfurled the sails, and headed west. Ishmael trailed them, swimming hard to keep up when the wind strengthened, slowing when the wind slowed.

"I can't tell if he wants revenge or if he still likes us."

"Let me get my camera." She came back in a second, white-faced. "David, there's water."

Hope grabbed a flashlight and jumped down to Sally's cabin. Seawater was floating the floorboards. He shoved one aside, lay down, and probed with the light. "Son of a bitch, he broke through the weak spot."

"We're going to sink."

Hope reached into the cold water and felt the flow hard against his fingers. "Oh, wow. He's really done us."

"David, answer me. Are we sinking?"

Hope looked at her. "You're going to have to sleep on my side."

"Are you joking?"

"We're not sinking. But we're not sailing at fifteen knots anymore, either. The other hull and the crash boxes on this side will keep her afloat, but we're in no shape for the next storm, that's for damned sure. Not even a gale, unless we can pump her out and plug this, somehow . . ." He felt around some more. "Except it's way too big to plug."

They slung a sail under the weakened hull, and pulled it as taut as they could. Hope felt the leak again. "Not so bad." He started the pumps and pitched in with the hand pump, and when they had pumped out enough water so the boat was not listing more than five degrees, he raised the sails and headed west.

"We'll be lucky to do five knots. But we're sailing."

"Look at Ishamel."

The big dolphin was doing a spy hop in their wake, watching them sail away. "We're not making the same sound," said Hope. "The sail has changed our wake. We're just another boat."

Sally zoomed in with the video camera. "He's just standing there. Like a child hoping we'll come back."

Adrift on the fire- and flood-damaged *Star of Alabama,* Rod sat cold and alone in front of a monitor watching a fading image of the killphin's last sight of *Oona.* Something had blown out the animal's electrical systems, and this thalamus image transmission that was shrinking smaller and darker even as he watched was surely the last.

Captain Grandzau walked into the lab. The man had aged twenty years in a day. Rod assumed that he himself looked much the same.

"That's him?"

"What's left of him."

"There's a naval vessel alongside, offering assistance. A

submarine. You might want to get rid of anything you would not like to explain."

"David, are we going to make it?"

Hope had not spoken much in the past several days, but she knew him well enough by now to know that he was simply hunkering down for the long haul. "Not to Maine."

"Where?"

"I make it about fifteen hundred miles to St. John's, Newfoundland. It's the closest harbor." He scanned the sky, as he did relentlessly, and took his third look in an hour at the barometer. "Neat little town, St. John's. Good place to haul the boat. Enjoy a comfortable hotel room for a few days, while I get the hull patched."

"What are you going to do for money?"

"My insurance should cover some of it. Once I get her out of the water I can do most of the work myself. Plus you owe me three grand."

"To Maine, I owe you three grand."

He returned her sidelong smile. "Can we work something out?"

"Just kidding. Of course. You don't really have insurance, do you? You're just saying that to make me feel better."

"Of course I have insurance. The boat's all I own."

"You mean when you risked the boat back in the BVI the insurance would have covered it."

"No. I can't afford full insurance. It's an 'agreed value' policy. I'd never get enough to replace her."

"So you did take a chance helping me?"

"I told you, I took a stupid chance of us getting hurt—but I'm glad the way it worked out for us."

Sally said, "David, I've got to tell you something."

To her astonishment, he flinched. Did he really think she wouldn't try to do something to make things work with them?

"What?" he asked, guarded.

Sally said, "Nothing bad. I just want you to know that I'm having a really nice time."

"Fifteen hundred miles at five knots might change your mind." The distancing joke.

"I'm saying that I enjoy being with you."

"Well, good. I'm enjoying being with you, too. But?"

"No but. I was just wondering, would this St. John's hotel have a hot shower?"

"You better believe it. It's a sailor's town."

"And a huge bed?"

"Only one per room and we can't afford two rooms."

"How much longer to get there?"

"Two weeks if we're lucky. Provided we don't get beat up again. More likely three."

"David, you realize when we get there I can't stay more than a night. I have to get to New York to try to sell our footage. Though I'm not too sure to whom or how. But I'll try."

"I could call my buddy in Boston. Maybe he could help."

"I'll have to get time on someone's machine and reconstitute them first. Polish a demo."

"Then what?"

"If we get lucky—if I can sell it—I could bring a bottle of champagne to Maine."

"You'd be welcome to come to Maine without champagne, too."

How could she say it without sounding like a brushoff? "I couldn't stay. If I don't get lucky I'll have to find work right away."

He took her hands and looked her in the eye. But she could see him hunkering down, just as he would for rough weather, preparing for the worst. He said, "Even if you got lucky, you would still look for a new project. You're not the kind to sit around counting money. Where will you go?"

"Last resort, I'll probably go back to Belize. There's a

dive shop that keeps asking me to teach underwater video. . . . Do you ever get down to Belize?"

"It's a great place to sail a catamaran."

"And?"

"And what?"

"What else would you do besides sailing a catamaran to Belize? David, I'm asking, what will you do with your life? Will you write your book on heavy-weather sailing?"

"Sometime."

"What will you do in the meantime?"

"I'll sail to Cuba."

"Cuba?" That came out of nowhere, she thought. "What's in Cuba?"

"Paradise not yet lost . . ."

"What are you talking about?"

David said, "I've been thinking." And then he launched into a straight-faced rap that reminded her of him flashing a hopeful smile the day they met and gassing on about what some charter client had told him about rum and the Caribbean. A smart woman—with a big heart. Noticed things most people didn't. A woman alert to need—who of course had been Barbara.

"In the sea around Cuba," he said, "the reef fish are still enormous. There are fish people haven't seen elsewhere in fifty years. Groupers as big as SUVs, clouds of yellowtails, squids, crabs, crocodiles, and so many angelfish you'd think you're in heaven. It's because Castro's dictatorship kept the tourists out and stifled development, which kept a lid on pollution and overfishing.

"But now there's a battle taking shape in Cuba to protect the reefs. Many Cubans are primed for eco-tourism. They've protected amazing sanctuaries already. They may be poor, but they're not stupid. They see the destruction in rest of the Third World and they know they're sitting on an amazing treasure. But it's touch-and-go. They want to protect the reefs for tourism, but the big-money crowd, the greedy corporate types and the rich exiles, want to build a million hotels for the tourists and catch all the fish to sell to the restaurants."

"Could it be that you're picking up Barbara's cudgels?"

He looked surprised. "I hadn't thought about that. Could be. They're honorable cudgels."

"Would you write newspaper stories about this?"

Hope shook his head. "The reefs are too beautiful. I couldn't do them justice in print. But they would make a magnificent documentary film."

Sally felt her mouth drop open. He was still telling it with a straight face. She asked, "You want to make a documentary?"

"A film with a goal: flat-out slick propaganda to establish sanctuaries to preserve Cuba's coral reefs forever."

He meant every word, Sally realized. He was not kidding. She said, "That's a tall order."

"I'd have to hook up with a top-notch underwater nature filmmaker. I'd just drive the boat, help with the script, do the shopping."

He still wasn't quite smiling, but he didn't look quite so hunkered down, either. "How," she asked, "would you choose your filmmaker?"

"She will have to be very experienced, with at least a half-dozen films under her belt, hard-working, committed—an all-or-nothing person. Brave, a brilliant diver, and excellent company. She'll need solid still-photography skills. And she should be an audio whiz, too. Did I mention ambitious? And it wouldn't be a disqualification if she looked cool in a skin suit, was unattached, and looking to rectify that situation."

"Unless you're looking for a girl-child, she's going to have a past, and maybe some unresolved issues. Maybe she was hurt or thinks she screwed up her marriage."

"To get the job, she should understand that the husband made a stupid mistake giving up such a woman."

Now Hope was smiling the hopeful smile he'd come on to

her with in the bar in Road Harbour. It lit his eyes and softened the weary lines scoring his face.

Sally asked, "How would you fund this project?"

"I'll start with whatever money I earn from our footage.
I'll keep expenses down by fitting the boat out as a live-
aboard studio. I wouldn't need to draw any salary—just food
and boat expenses. But this filmmaker I find will have to be
good at applying for grant money."

"Are you qualified to judge that skill?"

"Oh, that's easy."

"Really? How do you tell?"

"I'll look deep inside her sea bag. Somewhere down in the
bottom, rolled up in plastic, will be a tight white dress and a
conservative black jacket and a pair of interesting earrings
cleverly chosen to assure wealthy investors that they're talking to a woman who's made her own name."

If you liked *Sea Hunter,* you'll love

The Ripple Effect
by Paul Garrison,

the stunning new thriller, available in hardcover
from William Morrow.
For a sneak preview,
turn the page!

BOOK I
The Swan Pond
March–April 2002

1—

THE "SWAN POND" at Anse Marcel on the northwest coast of St. Martin, a popular Caribbean tourist island between Anguilla and St. Barts, was a lousy place to disappear if you'd ever devoted body and soul to getting rich in New York. Hidden up a narrow, twisty creek and ringed by dense vegetation, the natural cove might have sheltered pirates or escaped slaves in simpler times. But in the month of March, 2002, it was a marina for blue-water charter yachts. While tucked ashore among the bougainvillea, a five-star health club resort—the ritzy type the French called a *privilege spa*—offered a clear view of million-dollar hulls, flawless teak decks, lofty masts, and polished chrome. Sooner or later a Wall Street guy would run into somebody he knew at the Swan Pond.

So Aiden Page kept his head down while he scrubbed diesel soot off the transom of a Swan 44 he had just delivered from Martinique. When he did look up, it was to whisper Hail Marys that on this off day, between last week's clients flying home and next week's en route, the only people to recognize him—the boats' deck hands and cooks, and the shore-based mechanics, riggers and varnishers—would know him as "Chuck," a quiet loner from some landlocked place like Kansas or Iowa where Chuck must have learned to sail on lakes.

He appeared, at first glance, similar to the other paid crew cleaning the boats this brilliant winter morning in the high season—a seafaring man in cutoffs and a faded polo shirt, face tanned, hair and beard bleached yellow by the sun. Squint lines radiating from his eyes suggested he had left his twenties far behind; his perpetually bowed head hinted at disappointments or remorse; but a restless vitality and a handsome face offered the possibility that the best years stretched promisingly before him, if only he could get out of this current mess.

He had a sailor's broad hands, and arms hard with muscle. But his legs betrayed the camouflage of the working seaman: unlike most professional crew, whose lower limbs were spindly from years confined to small decks, Aiden Page's were still muscled from daily workouts at the Downtown Athletic Club. If anyone noticed, he hoped they would take him for a pumped-up race boat gorilla from the "Heine," the annual Heineken Regatta that the Island had just hosted. Though at an athletic five-ten and one-seventy, Aiden Page was built more like a bowman than a winch grinder—and he had the scars to prove it: an "O" branded on his left cheek by an errant jib's stainless steel clew ring; and a pale crescent on his chin, which never took the sun, courtesy of a foredeck face plant in a club race back on the Sound.

Thank God the fierce tropical light made everybody wear sunglasses. If there was one aspect of his appearance that would give him away to anyone who had ever met him, it was a distinctive feature shared by several of that arm of the Page family that emigrated from Kiltimagh in County Mayo—one eye bright blue, the other bottle green. Blue for dreaming, green for money, his father used to laugh. And look where that had got them.

When the transom was gleaming, he got busy Windexing the ports.

A pretty crew girl in a bikini bottom and loose shirt, who had already made several attempts to get friendly, leaned down from the high-sided Halberg-Rassey ketch moored beside the Swan. "Newsprint works better than paper towels," she said. "The ink makes the glass shine." She handed him a section of the *New York Times,* which was stained with coffee cup circles and crinkled like parchment by salt spray.

Aiden shut his mind to a generous flash of bra-less brown breasts. He couldn't risk hooking up with anyone who would ask questions. So getting laid would have to wait until he worked himself a lot farther away than the Caribbean. He was dreading the arrival of tomorrow's charter clients; he didn't recognize their names on the manifest, but he couldn't breathe easy until he had scoped them out at binocular's distance to make sure they had never met.

The newsprint worked as advertised, until the paper got wet. He reached to wad a fresh sheet and suddenly felt the breath knocked out of him. Like the boom had whipped across the coach roof and smashed him square in the chest.

"Hey." The pretty girl was back, peering down from her side deck, looking a little puzzled by the stricken expression of Aiden's face even as she said, "We're taking our van into town. Want to come for lunch?"

Aiden crumpled the paper and ran below.

The Swan's owner was seated at the nav station, reading bills from the charter company. He looked up at Aiden stumbling down the companionway. "Chuck, can you explain—"

Aiden hurried past the nav station, around the saloon table, and locked himself in the forward head. Heart pounding, breath storming through his lungs, he spread the sheet and tried to focus on the print.

Headlined "Portraits of Grief," the page was laid out like

a high school yearbook, with head-shot photos and six-inch biographies. Aiden, who had deliberately not looked at a newspaper in six months, surmised that the *Times* had committed to posting an obituary for every single person who died in the September 11 terrorist attacks.

Smiling up at him was a photograph he remembered well. He'd kept a copy on his desk, right next to Morgan's. The publicist's photographer had shot him and Charlie at a company party, arms over each other's shoulders. They were grinning happily at the camera, back in '99 when you could do no wrong and the money would flow forever.

CHARLES PAGE and AIDEN PAGE
Brothers Inseparable
in Life and Death

Charlie and Aiden. Aiden and Charlie. While in no way two peas in a pod, recalled friends and family, the "boys" as they were also known, were a team to be reckoned with. Charlie was older, steadier, and more worldly. Aiden flamboyant, the cutup. When they raced sailing dinghies as kids, Charlie was always helmsman, while daredevil Aiden leaned so far in the hiking strap he occasionally fell overboard.

On a memorable Christmas several years ago, Charlie chartered a jet to take employees of HHH Investment Bank and their families to the remote Tonga Islands in the South Pacific. Aiden organized sailing canoe races across the Polynesian lagoon and acted as bookmaker for the high-stakes betting. He and Charlie were the odds-on favorites, but lost to a long-shot dark horse: Aiden's teenage daughter Morgan. "It turned into a very expensive race," one banker recalled, ruefully. "The mail room clerk who bet on the kid went home a lot richer."

Charlie was HHH's CEO, Aiden his CFO. Aiden also served as HHH's fire warden, a job he appeared to take much more seriously than most things in life. When last seen the brothers were shooing traders, bankers, accountants, lawyers and secretaries into the stairwell that led out of the North Tower.

Aiden could not help but notice that Brothers Inseparable in Life and Death was bracketed by better people. A fireman, last seen going *up* the stairs, and a nurse who had stayed to tend to a burn victim in the lobby. Community volunteers. Churchgoers. Perfect parents, who would forever be missed by their children, which was the part that really killed him. Even worse than leaving Charlie to dic.

2—

Morgan Page was afraid of the subway.

She had loved the trains before 9/11. They had been her magic carpet. It was the first thing she learned when they made her move to the city. You ran down the steps and in five minutes you were a million miles from your mother's apartment. Summon the courage to change to the IND or the BMT and you got another million.

But now she rode her bike. You'd have to be too dumb to live to let yourself get trapped underground when the next attack came. Fortunately, all winter long it hardly snowed so she could ride everywhere she had to go. She rode to school, which they moved temporarily to Brooklyn after the attack. After school she would ride all the way up to Central Park. Outdoors, away from crowds. Later, it got easier to skip school and ride straight to the park.

She could bike to Chelsea Piers to swim, but didn't often. It was scary when you thought about a bomb exploding in a truck in the parking garage under the pool and getting sucked down a funnel of water to the jagged wreckage. She could bike to her piano lessons in her teacher's snug little brownstone studio, which seemed pretty safe because it was so small; except even there you could feel through the walls the thumping of a helicopter as if they were attacking again. And she could bike to her shrink, who had an office in "Shrink Land," a tree-lined section of the West Village where a lot of her friends went before 9/11. Her turn, now. Twice a week.

This was Tuesday. It had been a long weekend. Even weirder than usual.

"Osama came to my room last night."

She slumped in the chair, staring at the grease stains the bicycle chain left on her sneakers. The shrink, Dr. Melton, looked even older than her grandfather. He had been headmaster of a private school—except it was a progressive school so they called him principal, like they did at her special public school. When he retired from school, he kept the kids for patients. And their parents for couples therapy trying to save their marriages. Which was how her mother knew him. Which made Morgan wonder why she was here: Dr. Melton hadn't done squat to save her parents so what was he going to do for her? He was small, with round cheeks and little glasses that reflected the light so you couldn't really see his eyes. Like what was he thinking? Forget it. You'd never know.

"He's even taller than people say," said Morgan.

"Who is taller?"

"Osama . . . He's really, really tall."

Dr. Melton gave a little nod and his glasses flashed. "You say, Osama. Are you referring to . . . ?"

He had this way of asking, without asking, that was really hard not to answer. Morgan said, "Yes. Osama Bin Laden." Anger she had never known before seemed to be always bubbling under her skin. She could hear it in her voice, a mean sound like a box cutter slitting cardboard. "Who do you think I'm talking about?"

"And what did he do this time?"

"Like last time. And the time before. Like I told you, already. He just stood there, looking down at me."

"Where were you?"

"In bed."

"Asleep?"

"Until he woke me."

"How did he wake you?"

"By standing there."

"Were you afraid?"

"What do you think?"

"I wasn't there, Morgan. I only know what you tell me."

She looked back at her sneakers. "Yes."

"Yes what?"

"Yes, I was afraid." She touched the jade dragon she wore on a chain around her neck. She had bought it in Chinatown. They told her it meant good luck. She had been holding it in her sleep, tight in her hand when the terrorist came back to her room. Unbelievably tall. Thin as a rope.

"What did he do when you awakened?"

"He reached up and starting unwinding his turban. He just kept unwinding. Yards and yards of white cloth just 'un' and 'un' and 'un.' When he got down to his skin, it unwound too, and he kept unwinding it, stripping it from his head and his face. I could see bones. His whole skull. All bones. But he kept unwinding and stripping the bones away and inside . . . there was his brain. Like in a cup."

She looked up right into the glare of his glasses and asked in a small voice, "What is happening to me?"

"Let's talk about that, Morgan."

"I mean, before—until Christmas—it was just school blowing up and the tunnels caving in and water rushing . . . This is much worse. It won't stop. It's on my mind all the time. I can't stop obsessing."

"Did he touch you?"

"What do you mean?"

"In your dream, did Osama Bin Laden come onto you sexually?"

"Yeeuch. God you're weird."

Dr. Melton watched her shrivel up in the chair, trying to disappear inside her own arms. She was a short, stocky little fifteen year old, solid as a fireplug. She had a turned-up nose that made her look younger than her years, and a firm jaw that made her look stronger than she was. A pretty face—though hardly the beauty her ice-queen mother was. Nor had she inherited the raffish elegance her tall, handsome father had possessed in such abundance—though she had also been gifted, if that was the proper term, with his strangely compelling blue and green eyes.

In ordinary times, before 9/11, she was the type of girl mothers hauled into his office seeking solace for not having dates and fitting in with the hot crowd at school. While guiding her to an understanding that her parents' divorce wasn't her fault, he would have searched for ways to assure Morgan that she might spend high school and college with fewer boyfriends than the hottest girls in her class, but would have many deep friendships, while concentrating on the things she was good at—her science projects, her music, her sailboat racing. He also knew, but couldn't say, that around the time she turned thirty some smart, decent guy ten or fifteen years older would see her for the treasure she was. Happy days awaited. But it was a long wait until then. She would be waiting half her life. Still, it would have worked out. She was, at heart, an optimistic kid—or had been before 9/11. She had even had a boyfriend of sorts before 9/11. A boy pal.

"How's Toby?"

"I don't know."

"Don't you talk?"

"Naw. I feel so stupid, like I'm too scared to get on a train to visit my best friend. I really let him down. I used to take the train out all the time, after we moved."

"Can't Toby take the train into town?"

"His mother won't let him."

Melton sighed. Psychiatry careers would be made, country homes refurbished, and trust funds established with the profits from undoing the damage wreaked by over-protective suburban parents.

Before 9/11 he could have handled her problems by rote. At worst, she'd have grown up with awful taste in men. Now, he didn't know. Though he did suspect that she was in deep trouble and he was feeling increasingly inadequate to help her. At least she was still talking, but wouldn't be much longer, he feared. With spring upon them and summer prom-ised, most New York kids were getting over the attack. Left behind would be those too embarrassed to admit their fear, their isolation, and their misery. And he knew that when a kid went underground, a kid was lost.

"What about your friend in Tonga? What's his name?"

"Paea."

"Do you write?"

"No."

"Didn't you tell me he wrote you?"

"He's like ten thousand miles away."

Melton nodded. Person by person, friend by friend, she had stripped herself of connections.

"How's school?"

"Okay."

"Your mother called me."

He liked how she could not lie. A blue eye and a green eye focused hard on his and she said, "The school told her I skipped some classes."

"Where'd you go?"

"Riding my bike."

He waited. She wouldn't lie, but she could omit—a trait she shared with her father, who had been a world class omit-ter of pertinent specifics. Finally, Dr. Melton asked, "Where?"

"Up to the park. . . . Up the river. . . ."

"What do you do there?"

"I look at the boats."

"Are there boats in the winter?"

"A couple. . . . They're for sale. . . . Sometimes I just want to get on a boat and check out."

"What does 'check out' mean?"

"Disappear."

"Where?"

"Thin air."

Melton smiled. "Your mother expressed another worry . . . And I must admit I've never heard this one from any parent ever before."

"What?"

"She says you don't use your cell phone enough."

"I check in."

"She means that you're not running up minutes talking with friends like you used to."

"Oh."

"Is that true?"

"I don't have anything to say to them. . . . And they sure don't have anything to say to me—How can I be into flossing?"

"You mean dressing up?"

"They're all excited buying 'poodle skirts' at the Goodwill? Like nothing ever happened?"

"Is it lonely?"

"I don't know."

They talked about her grades, which were going down, and the science competition she had decided not to enter. "I just don't care anymore. . . . Mom's trying to make me go to Oxnard."

"What is Oxnard?"

"California? Like a retirement place? It's near L.A. She wants me to stay with Grandpa."

"Would you like the change?"

"He's so sad. I can't do it."

"Your grandfather lost both his sons. . . . Maybe he could use some help. Why not try it over spring break? Your mother could be right. The change might do you good. A different view out the window for a week."

"She just wants me out of the house so she can bring her boyfriend home." And with that Morgan went back to inspecting her sneakers.

"Well," Melton said after an unproductive silence, "if you had the power, what would you most like to see happen?"

She straightened up, though still staring at her shoes. "I would like to be in an airplane flying over Saudi Arabia while a mega-tsunami washes it away."

"A mega-tsunami? I presume you mean a particularly enormous tidal wave."

Still looking at her sneakers, though considerably more animated, Morgan Page said, "It would start with a landslide in India. On the coast of the Western Ghats. One of the mountains would fall into the sea. And the wave would race across the Indian Ocean. It would only take a few hours. There'd be no warning. No one would notice it because even a mega-tsunami isn't very high until it reaches shallow water on the coast. Then it would get very tall. It would drown the desert and flood the Persian Gulf and the Red Sea all the way to the Suez Canal."

"That would be some wave," Dr. Melton said lightly.

"Half a kilometer high, at least."

"I'm too old for metric," said Dr. Melton, looking for her reaction, hoping she would smile, or at least give a teenage sneer. "What is that in feet?"

"Sixteen-hundred-and-forty, point four-one." No smile. No sneer. Cold as ice.

"And some big landslide to start it."

"One happened 4,000 years ago on the Island of Reunion. And they say it could happen on La Palma in the Canaries—any day. Their volcano almost fell into the Atlantic Ocean in 1949. One more little nudge and good-bye Boston, New York, and Washington."

"Are you studying this in school?"

"They did tsunamis in Geology."

"Did you do a science project for this?"

"Kind of," she answered vaguely. "I did a 'What I did on Christmas Vacation' paper a couple of years ago for Physics. Wave phenomena?"

"Still, isn't it hard to imagine an entire mountain falling into the Indian Ocean?"

She looked at him, eyes bright as emerald and sapphire. "God could do it."

"God. . . . Yes. . . ." Not an eminence in most of his patients' reveries. "Do you think God would do something so horrifying to all the innocent people in Saudi Arabia?"

"Why not? He did it to all the innocent people here."

Why not, indeed, although as revenge fantasies went, Morgan's was pure Godzilla. Which was something of a relief. Too many of the children who came to him since 9/11 harbored fantasies far less grandiose and therefore more dangerous. Landslides and mega-tsunamis might reek of mass murder and genocide, but it was much easier for a child to get a gun. Angry as she was, this child wouldn't hurt anyone. She was more a danger to herself.

"Would you call this one of the things you're 'obsessing' on?"

"Yes—No! . . . Yeah, maybe. . . ."

"Morgan, would it be fair to say you are bitter?"

"Would it be fair to say I'd be whack if I weren't?"

"Would it be *accurate* to say you feel bitter?"

Her eyes filled and she said nothing, even when he coaxed her with the thought that bitterness stemmed from anger and that anger was a necessary stage in the healing process. At last, mercifully, her fifty minutes ended. Although he hated finishing on such an empty note. What had he given the child to take with her?

"I'll see you Thursday. If you get that dream again and it's too much, remember you can always call me. The service will find me in an emergency and I'll get right back to you."

Morgan slung her book pack over her shoulder and fished her bike-lock key from her jeans.

"Daddy telephoned last night."

Dr. Melton looked at his watch to hide his dismay. Adult patients pulled every stunt in the book to prolong a session, hustling extra time for their money. Teens, whose parents paid the bills, bolted out the door. That this child was standing stock-still, earnestly awaiting his reaction cut to the heart of his fears. He was suddenly overwhelmed by a stark vision. He'd been getting it often since 9/11. He had been chased by soldiers in some war-torn place like Kosovo and he was hiding in the bottom of a well. If he looked up at the bright circle of sky overhead, he knew that he would see Morgan Page holding a hand grenade.

Perhaps she hadn't understood the ins and outs of the dot com financial debacle; who did? But the child had been unusually close to her father and she had understood his suffering, and had acted—acing every admission test and interview so he could send her to public school instead of expensive private school. Unable to help him through the divorce, she blamed herself as even the healthiest children did. Nor could she understand why he had been the one to die instead of her. Overwhelmed, she was counteracting survivor guilt with denial. And when that failed, Dr. Melton feared, her next attempt to right the wrong might well be self-destruction.

"Your father is dead, Morgan. He and your uncle were killed when the terrorists flew hijacked airplanes into the World Trade Center."

"He telephoned."

"Where did he call from?"

"Some island."

"How do you know?"

Her expression shifted, as if she had changed her mind about confiding something very important. "I can't believe he could just vanish, like you blew out a candle."

"How do you know he telephoned from an island?" Melton repeated, but he saw that he was too late. Her face was closing up, layer upon layer and when she finally answered him, her thoughts were hidden like a wall safe behind a painting. "He and Uncle Charlie always kidded about running away to an island."

"Any island in particular?"

Morgan shrugged.

"To retire?"

Morgan shrugged, again. "I don't know."

"Did you dream about the telephone call after Osama or before?"

Her chin came up and her strange eyes bored into his. "It wasn't a dream. I didn't dream it."

"What did he say?"

Morgan held his gaze for a frighteningly long moment. He was back in the well, waiting for her to release the grenade. Abruptly, she hung her head, the picture of dashed hopes and rejection. "Nothing. He hung up on me."

"How do you know it was him?"

"He was drunk."

"How do you know he was drunk if he hung up so quickly?"

"He called me Kitten."

". . . And? . . ." Melton looked again at his watch. Now where was this going? "What does 'Kitten' mean to you?"

"He only called me 'Kitten' when he was drunk."